Chambers

SARAH GERDES

Copyright © 2012 Sarah Gerdes

All rights reserved.

ISBN: 0692594124
ISBN-13: 978-0692594124

Printed in the United States of America

First American Print Edition 2016
Reprints 2018, 2020, 2022, 2023

Cover design by Lyuben Valevski
http://lv-designs.eu

Inside illustration by David Majors

ALL RIGHTS RESERVED. NO PART OF THIS BOOK MAY BE REPRODUCED OR TRANSMITTED IN ANY FORM OR BY ANY MEANS, ELECTRONIC OR MECHANICAL, INCLUDING PHOTOCOPYING, RECORDING, OR BY ANY INFORMATION STORAGE AND RETRIEVAL SYSTEM, WITHOUT WRITTEN PERMISSION FROM THE PUBLISHER. ADDRESS PO BOX 841, Coeur d'Alene 83816

DEDICATION

For Conor, the inspiration

CHAPTER 1

"Cage, over here," called Mia.

What could she possibly want now? The girl already had my attention. She'd kicked a rock that ricocheted off the tree, hitting the metal rim of the barrier next to my shoulder, nicking my cheek.

"Take a better aim next time, would you?"

She laughed at me. Her giggle was infectious, the kind that gurgled up from her chest, letting you know she was really happy.

I hated that. For once, I wanted to let the anger that had seeped into my soul swoosh around and come back out again so it could erupt in an explosive, volcanic plume.

"He'll be out soon," she chimed, her brilliant voice bouncing around the edges of the tunnel opening before rising through the air.

"Unlikely," I muttered. The guttural sound rumbled down the shaft and into the darkness.

Dad had been gone for over an hour, three times as long as he'd promised. I had enough time to go back home, meet the delivery guy for my nunchucks, and return, and wait. I felt for them now, a specialized set of foam over wood, perfect for practicing on anything. Or anyone. I removed the set from my back pocket as I looked down below. Dad's obsession was the tunnels before my feet. The entryway to another world, he said. His world was one of dark caves and bats. Icicles and frozen lakes. Winding catacomb tunnels, stretching for miles underground like the tentacles of an octopus.

"You read his latest paper?" Mia asked.

I didn't bother to answer. The singular benefit of being a twin was the ability to know someone else's thoughts, intimately.

She laughed again, drawing out a sigh. Before she could speak, I held up a hand. I didn't need any more reminders about how great our volcanologist father was, or his revolutionary thinking that was changing the world of geology, nor the prestige of his articles. None of it changed the reality that we'd been banished to a no-nothing, small town in Washington state with an unpronounceable name: Enumclaw. Or that this move was inflicted upon me at the worst possible time in my life, my senior year of high school.

"Let me guess. At this point, you're on the school part right?" She laughed at me again.

If Mia had been a friend, I'd have hit her.

This time her rock nailed the tip of my shoulder, stinging.

"That's for wanting to punch me."

That girl. I really had to work on keeping my back straight. My instinctive defense posture was to curve my shoulders, preparatory for a crouch and assault.

She was relentless.

"One more time," I threatened. She laughed again, and I knew what was coming.

I whipped out the nunchucks just as I heard the crack of her foot hitting a rock. With a flip of my wrist, I grabbed the metal chains. I lifted one end high, spinning them just in front of my shoulder, deflecting the rock designed to hit my chest, which instead careened off a tree near her, rattling the leaves. One fell on her head and she started clapping, giving me a hoot. I rolled my eyes.

"I'm sick of it, Mia," I finally said, replacing my weapon, turning towards the mountains. "We wait on him until he decides to pop his head out, forgetting every commitment he's made, and then expects us to be a happy family. It's crap."

Mia smacked another rock around—ting, chuck. From the sound of the kick, it was a heavier rock, and heard it coming towards my head. She never would have bothered if she weren't sure I'd repel it. I sliced my right hand up flat against the side of my head, the rock gliding off the back of my hand.

She giggled. "Knew you'd get that," she said smugly.

I turned to face her, ignoring her comment. The girl was trying to kill me.

"Don't you get it?" I asked, facing the temporary object of my anger. "He doesn't care about us. And you defending him no matter what infuriates me."

Mia sat down with her legs crossed, flexing her feet and stretching the back of her thighs. Just looking at her was another reason for irritation. She was long and lean, gifted with the body of a high jumper and an equally calibrated metabolism. The girl ate as much as a sumo wrestler yet never gained a pound. Yet she hid her body underneath baggy sweats, the kind with decals across the butt and long hoodies with the logos of brands I wouldn't wear. Her thin, blond hair bounced back and forth in her ponytail. Her only flaw was the smattering of freckles across her nose and cheeks. I grimaced. Most freckles look like spots of dirt that couldn't be washed off. On Mia, they looked cute.

She gave me one of those "don't-hate-me-because-I'm-beautiful-looks" and I turned away from her.

Suddenly, the hairs on the back of my neck rose, and a prickling sensation rolled to the crest of my scalp. I dropped my right knee and spun and watched Mia fly overhead. In an attempt to tackle me, she had flipped over my knee and was dangling at the edge of the tunnel.

I thrust my left hand out, under her stomach, gripping the back of her legs with my right. The forward momentum threatened to throw her into the depths of the black hole.

"Push with your arms," I whispered, leaning down on her back to prevent her fall.

Her jostling body stopped as her long arms attacked the rim.

"Got it," she said. Adjusting my grip on her upper body, I told her to push back with her shoulders. As she did so, I pressed down on her legs and moved her away from the opening.

"Wait," she whispered as she stood up. "I think I heard something."

"Come on, Mia," I said, unwilling to pander to her fantasy. Saving her life demanded a bit more respect than she was showing.

She commanded me to be quiet. She was serious: she never told me to be quiet. Then, we leaned toward the tunnel in silence.

"You come with me or I'll kill you." I recognized the man's voice, but I couldn't place it.

"Then you'll have to kill me," my father responded calmly. A scuffling preceded a gunshot and a scream. Without a thought, I released Mia, who beat me to the metal ladder our father had attached to the inside of the hole.

"Go!" I whispered, although I knew Mia needed no encouragement. She slid down the ladder with fireman-like precision. I heard the thud of her feet hitting the dirt and dropped down myself. She gripped my arm and pointed, directing my attention to the far wall. In the middle, it looked like a large hole was closing, the perimeter reducing by inches, sucking out the light on the other side. Our father was on the other side of the opening.

"Get back," commanded my father, before a hand covered his mouth. I ran towards him, sticking my hand through.

"No!" screamed Mia, who grabbed my arm out of the hole. Seconds later, the gap had become a sheet of impenetrable, volcanic rock, separating us from the only family we had.

CHAPTER 2

Inside the tunnel, the surface of the rock was smooth and cool to the touch. Bumps jutted out in spots, feeling like small marbles eternally caught mid-roll. I knew they were air pockets, captured within the melting lava when it streamed underground. The catacombs themselves were the product of huge tunnels of air that formed within the lava run. A glint of light captured my attention. The fading sun had hit the dangling mirror on my father's backpack, which was nearly invisible in the shadows of the tunnel.

That was strange: the precious bag never left my father's side. Dad claimed it had the most important material possessions in his life. I could never understand what he meant since he never shared the contents with us. Still, I'd never seen Dad without it. That it was here, in a dark corner, meant something.

I pushed my hand inside and felt around. A large flashlight, pen and a ball were pushed together, along with a notepad of sorts with leather on the outside. I gripped the handle of the flashlight, pulled it out and unceremoniously dropped the bag on the floor.

"Find anything?" Mia asked, standing close beside me.

CHAMBERS

I clicked the flashlight on and off but it didn't work. Something inside rattled. Not a good sign.

"Doesn't work," I said, trying to keep the disgust out of my voice. At least he could have replaced the batteries. Mia suggested Dad might have tried to hit his attacker over the head with the light and damaged it. The idea made me scoff. Dad had never been in a fight in his life. He didn't even have the nerve to ask for a raise from his boss after his last paper won some award.

I stood and walked back to the wall, placing my hand on the cool surface. The texture of the rock changed from flat to rippled, as though the lava had dropped from top to bottom, forming horizontal layers of noodles.

I sat down, thinking about what we just witnessed. Was it a trick, like a slight of hand? How did the rock wall close? I checked my watch. Just fifteen minutes had gone by, and it was nearly six at night. I remembered my date with Alexandria Smith, the cutest — albeit shortest — of the cheerleaders, who had asked me to a movie and Mexican food. Moving hadn't really been all bad. I had the advantage of being the new guy at a small high school where all the kids had known each other since first grade. Dad was even letting me take the car, a used Toyota Forerunner.

"Now's not the time to be thinking about your date," Mia said sarcastically. "She's nothing more than eye candy anyway," she said. "And too short at that."

"Not a lot of Mia's running around," I retorted. I could practically hear her preen in the dark. It wasn't flattery. It was true. The best-looking girl in school was my sister, even if most of the other boys found her too aggressive because she didn't take their crap. As her brother, I was happy she was blind to guys, thinking most were idiots. However, even I knew that one day, when she least expected it, some guy would come in and sweep her off her feet.

"Shouldn't we go get the police?" Mia asked.

"What are we going to tell them? 'Hi guys, our dad was kidnapped and disappeared through a block of rock? Oh, and the last time we saw him was right before the wall closed in front of our eyes. And before that it was yesterday, because he spends more time at work that he does at home. Mom? Sorry. She's dead. But thanks for asking.'"

Mia grabbed my arm. "But what if he can't come back?"

That would mean he's dead too, a notion that caused me a twinge of guilt. Ever since Mom's death, I'd held a Mount-Rainier-sized grudge against my father. No matter what Dad said or how many times he apologized, it did no good. Dead was dead. Let Dad suffer under the weight of my hate. He'd earned it. Now that I faced the possibility Mia and I would be left alone, I was even angrier with him.

"Mom wasn't all perfect you know," Mia said roughly, a tinge of sadness coloring her voice.

A lightening rod of anger swept through me, but I bit my tongue. It wasn't her fault, I told myself.

"She was to me."

"Well, you want to be separated and live with a foster family?"

Point well taken: we weren't close to eighteen. The moment our dad would be declared missing, the state would confiscate our home and everything in it. We had no aunts or uncles. The grandparents were dead. We'd be separated, put into foster homes, becoming wards of the state.

"There has to be something else here," I said, dumping the contents of the backpack on the ground, directly under the fading light above. It would be dark soon. Mia dropped to her knees beside me, and we spread the items on the hard floor.

The notebook was unconventional: the leather was wrapped around two metal plates on the inside, like a thin computer. It was bound by three very small ancient looking rings, the two sides held together with a leather strap on one side, wound around a small metal knob on the other. A metal pen, a silver star at one end, and the tip missing. Other items included the small, cracked mirror hanging outside the pack with pink plastic that looked like it was from Mia's old Barbie collection, and a compass that didn't work. The pack should have included a GPS device, a working light, and at least a topographical map or two.

"No food, no light, nothing," I said, replacing the items. If this was the way he worked all the time, Dad was either really smart or just plain lucky. Mia turned the pack inside out and upside down, shaking it several times. The look of surprise and disappointment spiked my blood again. He could hurt me. That I could handle. Not Mia. She trusted him more. Loved him more. The emptiness left her without words.

Why would Dad carry such worthless trinkets around—for years? "Maybe his notebook will tell us something," I said abruptly.

I unwrapped the leather from its metal hook and flipped it open. The first page felt more like an ancient wooden pulp than the paper we were used to. The weight felt coarse and odd under my fingertips. I cursed under my breath. Even this was useless. Not a single word, drawing or scribble.

What was he doing down here? And why had someone come after him? I threw the notebook down. It slid and clanged, hitting something in the dark. Mia moved from me.

"Cage," she called, picking up the item. "Check this out." She held it up, and in the fading light, showed me a round, metal object the size of a grapefruit.

She handed it to me. It was divided in the center. With a twist, it unscrewed, releasing two parts. Inside were five empty spaces resembling the divots in an egg basket. She bent again, placing the notebook in the sack without comment.

I refocused on the empty container. No breath mints. No exotic jewels. Once again, nothing.

I twisted it back and forth absently. Darkness was descending upon us. In moments, it would be pitch black. The ladder was nearby, and Mia had one hand on the rail.

What were you thinking? I wondered rhetorically, as if my dad were in the room. Getting yourself abducted, leaving your pack in the dark, and never breathing a word that you may be in danger.

A breeze traveled through the tunnel and spread over me before hitting Mia in the face. Her hair danced to one side as she inhaled.

"Where did that come from?" she asked, her blue eyes wide.

I shrugged. If only the walls could talk to me and tell me what they saw and what I could do to replicate my father's disappearance. I rolled the ball back and forth in my hands, wishing for the impossible.

"Wait," a voice whispered in my head. The sound startled me. I was unsure if it was real or imagined. I looked around as evenly as I could. Mia was staring up at the last of the light. She hadn't heard anything. And I know she would have recognized the soft, female voice.

"I'm here with you." The voice was accompanied by another soft breeze. This time, I didn't look over my shoulder. I looked down at the object between my hands. It had started to glow.

I didn't believe in life after death, or answers to dreams. I'd never been to church. There was no such thing as heaven or purgatory, or in between. Death was final. Now, in the dark, an orb was glowing brighter by the moment and a voice I knew and missed and loved was talking to me. It came again, urging me to wait. I inhaled, quietly. My heart beat and ached at the same time. It had been years since I had heard that voice, and I wanted to savor it. So I waited.

Behind me, I heard the soft sound of pebbles falling on the ground. Part of me wanted to turn around, but I didn't want to risk it.

"Go," encouraged the voice.

For a second, my legs remained in place. My high school—would I ever see it again? The martial arts awards that lined one shelf above the bed. Alexandria and her lean, tan legs...

I glanced at Mia. I stood and held out my hand to her. She pressed her lips together, nodding, putting her hand in mine. I slung the pack over my shoulder, holding the orb in front of me.

Together we turned around and saw that the sound of falling rocks was coming from a hole that was growing at the center of the wall, extending taller and wider. I waited until it was high enough for us to walk through, then led my sister forward.

I'm coming for him, Mom, I thought, and passed through a threshold into darkness.

CHAPTER 3

The journey through the wall was short. I'd half-expected to see Mom standing on the other side waiting to greet me; the kind of experience that I've heard happens to the dead.

The orb in my hand was warm. It had lit the way for the few steps we'd taken in the dark. Now that it had done its job, the heat was receding.

The sun blazed down from above, this time through a small, triangular hole.

"A man hole?" Mia asked, releasing her hand. She was so independent. She wasn't afraid to jump up, open the lid and attack Dad's assailant.

"Wait," I cautioned. We'd come through rock, but where were we now? I held the orb higher, the light hitting its dull exterior. Pulling my sleeve down around the palm of my hand, I brushed the metal. A film came off easily, revealing a glinting, gold object.

"Is it gold?" Mia whispered.

"Perhaps, but we know it's not solid," I answered. Pure gold would be a lot heavier. It was also hollowed out inside with different compartments. But it certainly could be gold plated. Then I remembered the other voice we heard talking with Dad, who said 'give me what I want.'

"This must have been what he was after," said Mia, her eyes wide with wonder. She'd arrived at the same conclusion. I nodded.

Above our heads we heard the sound of many feet—hundreds—along with the exhales and pounding of horse hoofs. The entire cave vibrated with a low, uneven thudding.

"Sounds like a procession or event," Mia whispered.

I shook my head. "I didn't know anything was happening in Enumclaw."

As the glow of the orb dimmed, I searched for a way up the wall. A crude ladder was carved on the side, leading up to a metal plate. Mia looked at me expectantly. *What do we do now?* I thought, waiting for my mother to answer. But all I heard was silence.

Mom, are you here? I turned around, expecting a wind to come, bringing with it the still small voice I'd heard before. None came.

The vibrations above ceased. I waited for a few moments, Mia watching me. I removed the pack, put the orb back inside then put my arms through the leather straps. The pack itself was thin and flat, nearly hidden under the hood of my thick sweatshirt, which I then pulled over my pant pockets, hiding the nunchucks.

Using both hands, I scrambled up the ladder and pushed against the metal plate. It wasn't nearly as heavy as I expected, and it easily moved to one side. Mia quickly hopped up and out. I lifted myself up beside her, standing up.

"Get down," she whispered, an urgent tone in her voice, touching my shoulder before I could take in my surroundings. "On your knees, head to the ground."

"What?" I questioned as she dropped down herself. Ignoring her request, I looked around. The skyline bowed like the underbelly of a boat, a frozen smile comprised of reddish, copper tiles. The soldiers surrounded us, a hundred dark eyes glaring. They were dressed head to toe in black, carrying six-foot-long wooden weapons with razor edged knives slicing through the air at either end. I had seen those blades on walls and in the martial arts books, and knew that they could slice a sheet of paper in two from three feet away, or lop off a head just as easily. The ones we practiced with were shorter, the edge thicker, but just as deadly.

I wasn't going to wait until they got closer to see if the soldiers were skilled. I dropped to my knees, bowing my head so low my nose touched the cobblestone we were standing on.

"Where are we?" I whispered, the beat of the soft soled feet closing in. I didn't dare glance in her direction. My forte was math and science, hers was history.

"China, it has to be," she whispered back, so low I could barely hear. "A long time ago." My heart raced. Another continent. Different country. Years ago.

"What year do you think?"

"Fifteen hundreds," she replied.

"Do you know where?"

"This looks a little like the Forbidden City in Beijing, but that place looks different," she continued, her voice hushed. "This looks more like the ruins in the books, the city Beijing was designed after the original. That means this place is Nanjing." The girl was a walking encyclopedia of facts.

A rush pushed through me. *This* is what the guy was willing to kill Dad for.

Time travel.

At least we could speak the language. Learning Mandarin and martial arts were the only good things I got out of the few years we lived in Beijing during Dad's last job. They were skills I'd easily acquired, each adding to the already exotic nature of a foreigner at a new school.

The men skidded to a stop around us, spears pointed at our heads. My peripheral vision told me there were dozens, which seemed like overkill for apprehending two teenagers. With my nose still on the cool stones, I peeked up to see men carrying an ornamental box, the first in a line of similar boxes, though the ones following weren't nearly as ornate.

A cry halted the procession. Another command moved the box twenty paces away. All I could make out was a gold platform that flipped down from the box. From it, a pair of embroidered slippers emerged. An autumn leaf flipped and turned in front of my face, partially hiding the feet that moved in our direction. Whoever it was knew how to walk silently. The shoes stopped inches from my face.

"You have trespassed on forbidden ground. You are spies and will be imprisoned."

"No!" I heard my father yell. I hadn't seen Dad when we'd come out of the ground, and I felt instantly better knowing that he made it through alive.

"Shut up, Fleener." It was the same gruff voice I heard back in the tunnel. I knew better than to respond or lift my head. What little I remembered of Chinese protocol was enough to know that challenging authority didn't go over well with most adults, past or present. A guttural expulsion of air let me know Dad had been hit in the stomach. He was probably puking blood right now. His coughing and spitting confirmed my suspicion.

I glanced sideways at Mia to see how she was handling it. She nodded her head so imperceptibly I barely saw it. She was okay, and telling me to relax. I waited a few seconds to see what they wanted.

"If you are found guilty, you will be killed."

CHAPTER 4

I turned slightly to my left, enough to see blood trickle from a crack on the left corner of my father's face, his cheek pressed to the ground beside me. A foot was on his back, the point of a spear pushing into his puffy flesh. He faced me, though his eyes were closed. I wondered if he'd crapped himself.

"Rise," commanded the speaker. The man's voice was to my left, not in front of me. Whoever wore the shoes was silent. He was the one with the power.

To my right, I saw Mia begin to lift up and I followed.

"Him only," he said, pointing in my direction. Mia grunted and sank down again. Being on her knees in front of a bunch of men chapped her. I rose, towering above a slight, narrow man clothed in dour grey. He squinted at me, assessing the level of threat I posed. His arms hung stiffly at his side, a sure sign he didn't have any fighting skills. Those standing behind him were a different story. The armed guards were ready to drop, jump or fight on command.

"You are allies," accused the little man in front of me, pointing his finger at Dad and another Caucasian man. Now that I was able to see, I recognized the face that matched the gruff voice. It was Dad's boss, Draben Long. The person who had attacked him was a...friend.

I shook my head no. "This man had kidnapped my father and we came here to get him back," I responded, pointing to Dad.

"They were trying to steal the Emperor's carriage," shouted someone from behind me. "I saw it!"

"I saw it as well," cried another.

My mind processed the scene before me in a heartbeat. Suspending disbelief was my only hope for sanity. It was now confirmed. This wasn't present day because there were no more Chinese Emperors: that had faded out in the early twentieth century. If only I could ask Mia, but I couldn't. The swords were real, which meant that intruders were indeed killed without a trial, without notice.

"That man," I began, and was cut off by a chop to the neck that dropped me back to my knees. I felt the familiar pain endured during practice, knowing the skin and muscle between my neck and shoulder would soon be paralyzed. The condition would last only a few seconds, but it was infuriating. I'd get a headache afterward.

"The Emperor hasn't asked you to speak," shouted the man.

I looked up. Was the small man standing to my right the Emperor? I swayed slightly, considering him with the same level of interest and skepticism he had for me.

The Emperor was standing apart from the crowd. He looked much younger than me; he could only be about 14 years old. He was shorter, narrower in the shoulders, and wore a gold, square hat and a lavishly embroidered cloak with matching shoes, silver and gold threading glinting in the light. On his waist hung a long sword with a jeweled handle, encrusted with rubies, diamonds, sapphires, and emeralds. His face showed traces of acne along the edges of his smooth skin, his round cheeks framed by straight, black hair stopped just below his ears, a few longer strands streamed down to his shoulders. Beyond him was the sedan, the ornately carved box with square windows sitting atop four wooden poles. Eight servants held the poles hip height.

"Leave him alone!" yelled Mia, still on her knees. I glanced at her. She didn't see me, but I knew she would have ignored me in any case.

The same man who had been talking ordered his men to silence Mia, gesturing to the nearest guard.

The guard moved quickly towards Mia, raising a long, wooden stick to beat my sister over the head. As the guard crossed in front of me, I kicked out my foot, brushing an inch off the ground, hitting the guard's ankles. The guard stumbled two steps and then twirled, his stick ready to strike. Before he could swing it, I leaned down, extending my right leg up at a forty-five degree angle chest-high. My heel connected with the guard's ribs, crunching the bones. As the man dropped to the ground beside me, I depressed an elbow into his back. The guard arched in the opposite direction before he groaned and fell.

The man in grey screamed an order for three more guards to attack.

I crouched, gearing for the battle. My fingertips tingled as they always did as the adrenaline pumped through my veins.

This was going to be interesting. My black belt test had involved fighting two assailants at once, though they didn't have the desire to kill. Afterward, I'd been bruised, my left hip so sore from a well-placed heel kick I could barely walk, and a hand so swollen it was useless for a week. Now I had three assailants and a sore shoulder. The odds of coming out of this unharmed were less than great.

I jumped to my knees, sidestepped the first guard who lunged at my chest, using my left hand to chop his neck, my right to flip up his pole and crack his back. The movement knocked the guard's pole up and into the air. I grabbed it, twisted it above my head for velocity then smashed it down above his ear. The man staggered, and then fell backwards, stunned. The second guard whirled his short wooden stick within arm's length of my back. He then thrust the weapon downward at my head, expecting to have a clean attack. I used both hands to raise my pole to block the blow, which hit the center of the wooden pole, directly above my eyes. With my opponent's hands still raised in the air, I kicked him in his groin. The man's knees collapsed inward, and he dropped to the ground, I spun the weapon like the blade of a helicopter, connecting with his head. The crack reverberated throughout the courtyard.

The two encounters happened within seconds; I hadn't thought before my limbs acted. My body had never responded this way in class. The tingling sensation sped through my entire body, brightening my senses like my best fighting fantasies. The charge of a real fight was better than I'd ever experienced.

The last guard leapt toward me with a guttural cry, his pole twirling and whooshing with the sound of a giant fan. With a new surge of confidence, I stepped directly into his path, thrusting my pole like a spear into his chest. The force of the blow threw the guard into a somersault. The man landed with a thump and a clang as his long, wooden pole smacked the ground beside him. He lay inert for a second until he arched his back, kicking his legs off the ground before he pushed off his hands. In a moment he was on his feet again, running towards me. A foot away, he jumped high, a leg outstretched, heading towards my face. It was a stupid move, executed with the assumption I'd recoil from fear.

I didn't. I dropped forward into a handstand, attaching my feet to either side of his leg. I drew my feet down, pulling his entire body with it. The crash of his tailbone shattering made the soldier scream in pain. He writhed on the ground, unable to sit, move or walk.

I stood, touching the pole on the tip of my foot. With a flip of my toe, I lifted it in the air, and grabbed it with my left hand, flipped it vertical by my side. I had no time to assimilate my perfected skills. The instant the end of the pole stopped near the base of my foot, three more dark-clothed warriors set to descend on me. After annihilating the three, I was looking forward to another round.

"Qi Tai, please," The Emperor said with the voice of authority. "I think that's enough." The guards stopped dead, and the man in grey, Qi Tai, pursed his lips and bowed his head. The fingers on his left hand extended out straight, a single point of defiance to the young Emperor's command, before they slowly retracted, a sign of reluctant obedience.

The Emperor turned to me, his eyelids lowered.

"What were you going to tell us about that man?" the Emperor inquired, his teenage voice cracked as he spoke, though his words carried the arrogance and command of a ruler.

Just at that moment, I heard the narrow, whooshing sounds of arrows flying through the air.

"Duck!" I shouted in Mandarin. "Get down!" Before anyone could stop me, I shot forward, knocking down the man in grey and dove to cover the Emperor. One of the guards tried to stop me but failed, flying right over me. I heard Mia gasp, then scream. Shouts of murder arose and I suddenly had hands all over my body, ripping me off the ground. The Emperor's eyes were wild and shocked, as though I'd committed a far worse crime than getting his clothes dirty.

"You…will…die…" the Emperor said, furious as he stood up, standing motionless as servants rushed to brush off the dirt from his garments and fix his hat.

"Look" yelled Mia. "The arrows got Draben instead of the Emperor."

The boy glared at me, unwilling to turn until he was forced to do so by the silence in the area. All eyes were on the body on the ground, riddled with arrows.

"It's the exact angle where he should have been standing," continued Mia, unabated. She was correct. The right side of Draben's chest and stomach were pierced with multiple metal shafts. He was directly in the line of sight, where the Emperor stood.

The Emperor stepped back from me, the guard jumping up himself, placing his body between me and the ruler. "To your place," the Emperor said to him. The guard said nothing, falling to the Emperor's right. He didn't have to say a word. I could tell by his heaving chest, he was reeling from the fact I'd saved his boss, not him, and his adrenaline was racing through his body like a horse unable to stop after reaching the finish line.

I respectfully bowed low from the waist before speaking, taking my own deep breath.

"He took our father from our home and we followed," jerking my head towards Draben's motionless body. "I didn't know if our father was alive or dead. We came to help him. She is my sister," pointing at Mia. "We were unaware we were trespassing." I looked up at the angle where the spears had come from. "If I were you, I'd send someone to chase down the assailant. The direction of the spears mean it was—that one, over there," pointing to a tall building with a large dragon statue placed in front.

I looked at my father who was ignoring the building altogether. He was glaring hard at the backpack that was still resting on my shoulders. Could the man even acknowledge that I'd just saved someone's life? And not just anyone, but the freakin' ruler of China?!

"I've already sent men, Emperor," the man in grey coolly responded. The Emperor nodded in satisfaction and continued talking to me.

"What reason did he have to take him away?"

I bowed again. "My father is a volcanologist. Someone who studies volcanoes. I don't know why he did it, and unless we ask him, we'll never know. Look at him. He's a peaceful academic. Harmless." Even on the ground, Dad's bone thin body was evident. His clothes sagged, his shoulder blades practically bounded out of his shirt, his exposed wrists had veins protruding, making him appear older than he was. His singular attractive feature was his eyes, bright, bluish green, and the same hue as my own. Unfortunately, they were usually hidden below the sagging eyelids threatening to close.

The Emperor looked between Dad and me several times, making his own assessment. It was a humiliating experience, one that I had lived through many times before whenever my friends met my father. I had to convince more than a fair share I wasn't adopted, using the eyes as proof.

Today, Dad looked worse than usual. His hair was a mess and his shirt was ripped under one arm where Draben had likely taken hold. He had a bruise coloring a part of his cheekbone. It would swell nicely, I thought, suppressing satisfaction. For all the fights I've had to contend with over the years, he deserved to get a taste of his own.

The Emperor turned to my father. "Who is he?" asked the Emperor, pointing to Draben.

"My boss," Dad replied, and then clarified when the Emperor looked confused at the term. "The person I work for."

Dad didn't bother to tell him the story of how Draben came to know my dad. It would have raised more questions and maybe problems.

Draben was a legend in the scientific community. The son of a physicist, Draben had discovered a new star at fourteen and had gone on to observe a new galaxy before he could legally drive a car. By the time he received his doctorate at the young age of twenty, Draben had authored two books on volcanoes, which vaulted him to the top of his profession. It wasn't until he put forth theories about alternative life forms inhabiting the earth that his career took a turn for the worse. Draben's mental health was questioned, his research grants were revoked, and he was out of a job. That is, until he became director of research at the Washington Volcanic Studies Center and recruited the famed volcanologist George Fleener from his prestigious post in Beijing to join his efforts.

The teenage Emperor stroked the stringy hair on his chin. It was not a full beard, though longer than a meager soul patch below his lip. He seemed less interested in listening and more curious about me. Perhaps it was because I was closer to his age. Or, I had just saved his life. That had to count for something.

I could barely comprehend that a man I knew was lying dead before me, his hardening body a dozen feet from where I stood. The Emperor glanced over at one of the carriages, as though searching for something he could not see, then returned his attention to me.

"Do you travel alone, or like Marco Polo did years ago, with many others?" The Emperor looked around, as did Qi Tai. The soldiers standing around us stared straight ahead, though the Emperor's words caused a subtle posture change.

Mia was right. That was well before the Forbidden City in Beijing had been created by Emperor Yongle. This was Nanjing, the original city of the Ming Emperor's. "Just my sister. Mia and myself. My name is Cage."

The Emperor motioned to a guard, who hastily removed the metal cover and descended into the hole we were still standing around. As we waited, I overheard the man in grey talking with the Emperor.

"Zheng He is due in days, Emperor," he whispered. "We must prepare the welcoming celebrations. Meet in council to discuss the next naval strategy. This…we don't have time for."

The Emperor's gaze slid to Mia. He looked inquisitive, his eyes unmoved from her hair, as though the strange color was as odd as us appearing out of the ground. Mia's hands were spread on the ground, fingers out wide, exposing her nails bitten to the quick. She had a scrape on the top of her fourth finger of her left hand, itself black and blue, no doubt caused by her crunching an opponent on the soccer field.

"Emperor…" the man said again. In a snap, the Emperor's face turned from Mia, then towards the hole.

"Go find out what is taking him so long," commanded the Emperor, gesturing to a nearby guard. He was impatient, like someone who was not used to waiting more than seconds for satisfaction. At once, the man leapt forward, descending feet first down into the darkness.

"Your counsel," he said to the man in grey, his request spoken like a command.

The man answered rapidly, his eyes darting between the Emperor and the hole in the ground, evidently in a rush to get it all out before the two emerged. He spoke of a feast for two thousand in the main hall followed by fireworks with a dragon procession through the Imperial Palace. "The people want to see him," he said, "to celebrate his accomplishments."

The talking abruptly stopped when the Emperor shook his head.

"Not enough. More."

The man sputtered. "But Emperor. What more can be done? That is all we have prepared."

"Create an entrance for the arrival of his ship. Line the waterways with boats full of red lights to show his glory. One hundred on either side. Place lanterns on the hillside in the pattern of the dragon, white for the outline, blue for the eyes and red for the flames coming out of the tongue, for he is the naval force of the Empire, dominating all."

The man nodded his head obediently, mentally taking notes.

"Where does he enter from?"

"I had thought his normal path; the back entrance to the Forbidden City then to the Palace."

The Emperor frowned, his eyes moving from the hole, up, over our heads. "He is the Admiral of the people, not just the country. Let the people see the symbol of our greatest achievements.

"From the dock to the Forbidden city, light the way—"

"But…Emperor. That will be thousands…"

"No, millions. Do it. And light the pillars on at each guard station and open the main doors to the Forbidden City, candles lighting the way. Have children—girls—throwing red rose pedals on the street before he comes through the streets." The boy-ruler eyed the hole.

"Give the boys one green candle and order them lit while he proceeds to the Imperial Palace. There I will wait to greet him at the entrance."

The man's eyes were wide with consternation. Based on the look the man gave his commander, he didn't have a few hundred thousand candles or truckloads of rose petals stored away in some bin.

"It will take thousands of workers—" He cut off when the Emperor raised his hand. He bowed low. "It will be done."

Satisfied, the boy met my gaze and I looked down. The minutes felt like hours, the silence dragging time forward. For a fleeting moment, the excitement of entering another time left me and I wanted to pretend this wasn't real, the entire scene before me a charade of the most elaborate kind. A trick created by my sister, a genius when it came to acting out at home, not opposed to donning a hat and broomstick, singing *The Sun will Come out Tomorrow* from Annie, her ever-optimistic attitude towards the lack of sunshine in the gray state of Washington. Here, the sun glimpsed through the spotty cloud cover, glancing off the mountains in the distance. Sets could be erected and actors dressed in costumes. Moving of mountains? Unlikely. I pressed my hands hard on the ground, causing pain in my wrist. It wasn't a dream that I could wake from. We were here, and our lives were hanging in the balance, depending on what the guards found down below.

The scratching sounds of climbing drifted up from the entry to the catacombs moments before the guards appeared. The first guard who had descended ran directly to the Emperor, waiting until he was given permission to speak. The tunnel was empty, he said, his voice cracked as he spoke, ranging from lower to upper ranges. The two men had gone in every direction, following the passages of the tunnels until reaching the end.

Silence.

I risked a glance up at the Emperor and Minister, who exchanged glances.

"Intruder. Look up."

Mia raised her head at the same time I did. The Emperor raised his hand, pointing it at me.

"My Minister of War, Qi Tai, believes the Forbidden City is infiltrated with spies. Somehow, you have come through tunnels few use, and few know about. No entrance. No exit. Yet you are here. It could be magic, but you don't appear to have special gifts or magical powers. You look strange, yet talk our language. How do I know you aren't spies, here to collect information for those who would overthrow my government?"

"As I said, my father is a collector of information. Arriving in this area must have been Draben's doing, not his. With Draben dead, we only want to return to our home."

Of course, we can't have anyone see us return through a rock wall, I thought. I'd have to gain our freedom then find a way to return the three of us back down in the hole, in the middle of a busy town square.

The Emperor gestured curtly for Qi Tai to follow him. My head was down, though I looked to the right, giving me a direct view of the two walking away.

Qi Tai followed a pace behind the Emperor, who made his way directly and swiftly to a box. To his right, a bodyguard clad completely in red walked a pace behind; his manner wary, like a caged animal ready to strike, always watching for the next move.

He stopped instinctively just before the Emperor halted in front of a yellow box. I couldn't help stare at the guard, who kept his face turned from me, searching the area for hidden attackers. Until then, I hadn't noticed other figures dressed in red, the shapes noiselessly positioned in quarters of the yard. He waited, a silent protector, as the Emperor remained by the golden colored sedan, holding court with Qi Tai.

To the right of the sedan was another, this one light pink. It too, was held off the ground by four men, as were two other sedans that followed. No movement came from within the first or second box, until a spot of brown caught my attention. I quickly made out a pair of brown eyes, large and round. Each was outlined in thick, black liner with eyelashes long enough to be visible through a sheer curtain. I blinked, unsure the brown eyes were looking at me, until I felt the intense stare.

The eyes blinked back.

I smiled, unaware I had done so.

"Cage," whispered Mia. "What's so funny?"

I tore my eyes away, looking over at my sister. Her nose was still touching the pebbles, her face red with contained fury. She understood Mandarin as well as I did, and was insulted that she wasn't allowed to participate in the conversation. If it had been any other circumstance than saving her life, she'd be talking up a storm. "Nothing," I responded, glancing up again, sure to keep my head still. The eyes were gone from behind the veil.

Qi Tai moved away from the Emperor and his bodyguard, stopping several feet from me.

"Foreigner, look up," said Qi Tai, waiting until I had done so before he spoke. "The Emperor will make sure you pose no threat. You and the others will be locked up until such time as we feel it is safe to let you leave." He twitched his fingers, reminding me of a western movie where a cowboy was about to draw his gun. "In a…Cage," he finished, giving me a jagged smile.

Like I hadn't heard that one before, I thought, nodding my head, unwilling to give him the satisfaction of getting angry. It was better than prison, unless I was going to be placed with a band of tigers.

Guards moved forward, two placing their hands on Mia's arms. Bad move. She kicked one and shrugged off the other. A guard prepared to slap her when the Emperor commanded the guard to stop.

He strode beside Qi Tai, his hands raised, his eyes betraying his shock and surprise.

She stared defiantly at the ruler, just like she did so often to me. Now she righted herself to her knees, her back straight and arched. She was not much shorter than the ruler who stood in front of her.

"You seem capable enough to walk yourself," he remarked, fingers once again stroking his chin, just enough of a lilt in his voice to give her the opening of a response. "I've seen what your brother can do. What do you offer?"

Mia's eyes practically glinted with anticipation. The invitation was all she needed to show off. She glanced at the ground. I saw what she was looking for her, but the Emperor misinterpreted her action.

He motioned for her to stand, his eyes opening slightly wider as she reached her full height. She was taller than he was, by half a hand.

"Do you like that carriage?" she asked, pointing to the yellow one he had stood in front of.

His eyes dimmed, wariness making the corners of his mouth droop in a grimace. It was unlikely he'd been talked to by any female, not to mention a strange girl with blond hair.

He nodded.

"Pick a spot on it," she suggested, her voice too firm for Qi Tai's liking, as he started to make a comment but was cut off by the Emperor's hand. The young ruler assessed Mia's question for a few moments, then pointed to the front corner. The carriage was embellished with gold threaded tassels that swayed in the soft wind. Each hung six inches or so from the top, the bottom of the braided ropes ending with a red colored ball.

"Watch the end of the first tassel, then the sixth one."

She bent down, scooping up a handful of pebbles. I knew she was good, yet my heart pounded in anticipation.

The moment she bent down and picked up the rocks, a flash of red moved in front of the Emperor. The Emperor's bodyguard had positioned himself in front of the boy, his body offering complete protection. I didn't blame him. It was his job and his life if the Emperor's was lost.

Mia clucked her tongue, shaking her head, the message clear.

The bodyguard clenched his fist but didn't move.

"Xing, step aside," the Emperor requested. "She aims not for me," looking at my sister for affirmation. Once Mia nodded her head and bowed, the guard did so, though reluctantly.

He'd not finished moving before Mia volleyed a rock in the air, hitting it on her knee, bouncing it to the inside of her foot then cracking it forward. It projected out, a rocketing missile heading directly for the corner of carriage. Before the Emperor could utter word, the small rock hit the red tassel, knocking it against the carriage with the clarity of a ping. Mia casually let the other rocks drop with the ease of pennies going into a wishing well, lifting her knees up with the precision of a prancing horse. One rock she hit with the back of her foot, its surface hitting the red tassel, six down from the original. Every ping was six down from the previous, just like Mia intended.

The Emperor kept the composure on his face, though he couldn't keep the respect out of his still-wide eyes. He'd probably never seen a female do anything of the sort.

When the final tassel hit the back of the carriage, and Mia was done with her exhibition, she turned to the Emperor. The Emperor watched her thoughtfully, giving no indication of pleasure. Next to him, the bodyguard Xing's hands were now loose by his side, the warrior stance returned, ready for what may come next.

"Take them," said the Emperor.

Five guards in black surrounded me and Mia, though the men held their arms straight. I spread my hands out, palm up, unthreatening, conveying I'd follow willingly. With a nod of my head to the guard in the front, a short, stocky guard with a slight scar on his chin, indicating I was ready to go. Mia moved behind me, and she did so quickly, eliminating the option of being handled by the men. Dad wasn't as smart. He remained where he was, and as a consequence, was jerked up and told to follow behind Mia and me. After the Emperor ascended into his sedan, we waited until it moved out.

The sedan with the intriguing passenger passed before me.

Qi Tai yelled at me, telling me to avert my eyes, then took the option away. From behind, a thick piece of cloth was roughly strapped around my eyes and pulled tight. My mouth was gagged with a large, wooden ball affixed with rope on either side. A rope was then placed around my neck. I thought it was overkill in a masochistic kind of way, wondering what other ancient torture I was going to endure during this short venture through time.

"Your bound tongue cannot tell what your eyes cannot see," said Qi Tai. "To the back," he directed his guard, who spun me around.

About an hour later, the shackles, gag and eye covering were removed and I was pushed into a mass of stinking, heaving bodies. Instinctively I stepped backward, causing a squeal underfoot. It appeared to be a large rat of some sort, but I had no time to verify. At that moment, a group of men descended upon me.

CHAPTER 5

"White man!" cried a voice.

"He doesn't belong here!"

"Bad luck!" shouted another.

Fingers and hands teamed on every part of me, pulling and ripping. My body reacted when my mind didn't. I'd trained for hours in the practice of fending off just such a crowd.

Dropping to the floor, my left hand on the ground, my right leg swooped left, an inch off the floor, crushing ankles with a force great enough to lift the bodies up before falling to the feces covered floor. I lifted my right leg chest high to give lift to my left leg, which lashed out at a dark presence before me. It landed with precision, emitting a cry from the recipient. All I felt was a grind of bone and skin on the bottom of my foot.

"My nose! My teeth! They're gone!" cried the man. "Kill him!"

Before the others had the chance, I turned left, crouched, then unwound my lower legs first, then upper body like a snake uncoiling bottom to top. When my arms struck out at the same time, the palms were flat, hitting bodies with a force of an airplane propeller, crushing chests and inflicting internal injuries. The move cleared a space around me that wasn't immediately refilled with bodies.

"Ja!" I screamed, knocking back the hands around my face. "Get back or I'll kill you!"

"Get back!" screamed one, his voice angry and fearful.

"He has bad spirits with him!" cried another in terror.

"Or good spirits," said another voice, more somber than the others.

"Don't come near me," I growled. "You won't live to see the morning."

In my fourth section belt, I'd learned how to explode the internal organs of an opponent, and in my fifth section, how to break a neck. I'd practiced both enough in slow motion for the movements to feel like second skin, and now had no compunction in using what I'd learned. We'd just begun training on pushing out energy into our movements, channeling the force of the human energy to set an opponent off balance. It was a sliver of unseen power, used in ancient times to give a warrior the margin of time necessary to kill the adversary.

My master advised against practicing outside the dojo until we were fully trained unless absolutely necessary. If I ever saw him again, I'd tell him this counted as one of those times. I wasn't going to die in some dank prison and leave my sister to servitude or death.

The excitement over, the crowd moved away, preserving several feet on every side of me. The thrill of using years of practice was a complete rush. My moves were better than I had ever hoped. The other prisoners retreated to their dark quarters, the low murmuring of complaints absent of comments about me.

For hours, I considered the grim situation. I realized that the last time I saw my father, his face didn't share his surprise; fear and concern yes, but not surprise. I had no doubt he'd been traveling around the world, using the orb. Nothing else explained his lack of reaction. In fact, it explained his many disappearances.

"Work is taking me away," he'd say, and I'd naturally assumed he was in an office somewhere. I never had the desire to go visit him. When he had 'out of town trips,' I never looked at his tickets, or for that matter, saw a ticket. "Just a day trip," he'd say, telling me and Mia he'd be home before dark.

Even on the weekends, Dad went fishing once in a while, usually when Mia or I had other sports activities already planned. Come to think of it, he never brought home any fish. While I attributed his comical failure to his lack of skills, I now understood he went back to his most recently discovered catacombs to explore some more.

Had he been gone days or weeks on the other side, leaving and returning without a difference of time on our side?

The sound of snoring was overtaken with a fit of coughing, the hacking of a person's lungs getting ripped out, full of phlegm, followed by the worst possible noise and an eruption, violent and putrid. Angry shouts came, each a form of a curse, telling the sick man to find another place to sleep. The entire area was momentarily disrupted as bodies moved away from the stench that permeated the air. After the commotion died down, the bodies were once again motionless, save for the snoring and occasional shuffling of a person turning positions.

My being in the square had probably done little or nothing to change the course of the Emperor's life. He was on his way to the Palace. On route, he met strangers, interrogated us, took us hostage and now I sit in a cell. Though I had no idea where Mia or Dad were being held, I felt confident it was away from others, isolated, without consequence to the future.

One person who did have a life changing experience was Draben. Did death here mean death in another time? It had to. He couldn't be raised from the dead in order *to* return home.

But what had caused Draben to take Dad through the portal in the first place? Maybe Dad had been going to find havens of gold, and Draben discovered the truth. The thought of a stash of money and jewels somewhere was appealing, though I doubted Dad was up for the task. We had very few material possessions. Dad drove an old car, we lived in a rental in the woods on the outskirts of town. Not much extra money. Fortunately, Mia and I had become expert shoppers, hitting consignment stores as a choice of first resort, peppered with pilgrimages to the outlet shops that dotted the Washington State freeways as routinely as truck stops. The fashions were always six months out of date or the wrong season, though hoodies eliminated the need for spring and winter jackets.

Whatever Dad had been doing during his treks to the other side, I'd get to him, discover the truth and get back. I held out hope we'd return before school started tomorrow.

I glanced through the small slat in the upper right hand corner of the cell. The moon peered through, the only source of light available. It was a full one, high in the sky. Getting home before sunrise was a pipe dream. Maybe before Monday.

One thing was sure. I'd have to coach Dad to say nothing about Draben when we returned home. It wasn't his fault Draben got himself killed. This relied on the assumption no one saw Draben descend into the hole with Dad before Mia and I arrived to wait for him. Even if questions were asked and a motive suspected, murder was hard to prove without a body.

I waited until the moon sunk lower, the light barely a sliver now. It was enough for me to verify the eyes around me were closed. The undistinguishable mass of bodies was huddled close to one another for warmth. A few inches still separated me from the others, enough to lie down and sleep, had I the inclination. I didn't. Though the cold had crystallized the mud, straw and crud concoction on the floor and reduced the smell, I'd determined that only the soles of my feet were going to touch the ground. It meant I used my squatting meditation pose, then a standing position designed to reduce the swelling from leg to leg. It was not the first time today I thanked my instructors for the grueling hour-long sessions where we did nothing but hold our arms out, our legs locked in a uniform position. "But why?" I'd asked after my first session with holding a pose, years ago.

"The mind overcomes pain," he had said cryptically. "Set your mind."

Quietly, I took the pack off my shoulder and removed the orb. Small glints of light bounced off the metal. I hadn't noticed the engravings on the outside before. A small lip was on the top of the orb. I pressed it, and a band of thin metal rose upward. It resembled a sail on a ship, though only an inch high. I wondered what other secrets the orb held, and gently turned it clockwise. It opened up in two parts. Looking around the room one last time, I made sure that no one was observing my actions.

One half of the orb had several holes. Placing my index finger in the first hole, I traced the surface, which was rough. A second indentation was smooth, with stripes of some sort. Three other holes were equally unique; each one had a different texture that reminded me of the surfaces of different balls: a football, a soccer ball, and golf balls. I lifted half of the orb to my face and noticed a thin, round point in the center. It was slight, like a grey toothpick.

It didn't appear long enough to fit into the other side. Remembering the wind in the tunnel, I couldn't help myself. I thought of my mother, asking her for help and guidance.

No response came.

"Whatever," I muttered, regretting my outreach into the dark. Mom hadn't spoken to me before I went in the tunnel, why would she come back around now?

I touched the top of the point and felt a jolt in my hand. The shock was enough to make me drop the orb on my lap and look around the room.

Still no movement.

Holding the orb cautiously, I lifted it up slowly and watched the metal needle in the center spin. Light started to spray from all sides, engulfing the entire room in radiant beams. When the sphere was full bright, my mother entered the room, walking across it, as an actor on a stage. Her thick, auburn hair brushed her shoulders, a curl catching the corner of her mouth. She playfully brushed it aside, her smile wide and happy. She was as tall and lean, flawlessly wrinkle free, her green eyes stinging with the joy of life she had up to the day she died.

My gut ached with loss. She was so beautiful. I'd forgotten. Three years of purposeful avoidance had wiped away good memories.

She raised her hand to say something, her eyes suddenly betraying fear. She cried out, but I couldn't hear her words.

"Are you well?" asked another voice in the dark. It wasn't threatening. It was the voice of someone old.

The light collapsed back into the needle, and was gone.

"Fine," I replied. He'd not seen the light or my vision.

I dropped the orb to my lap, quietly screwing the two lids back together. I slipped it back in to the pack and had half-slung it over my shoulder when I thought better of it. Whipping off my hoodie and shirt, I put the pack on first, then the shirt, then hoodie. It was uncomfortable and no doubt looked like a pregnant woman walking backwards. Nonetheless, it accomplished my goal. I moved it side to side, testing the shake. The ball barely moved.

The voice chuckled softly.

"I'll let you be then," though he clearly didn't want to leave me alone. He remained by my side, hovering expectantly.

"Wait," I said, feeling safe and curious. "Where am I?"

The man shuffled closer. He was not afraid of me.

"In a prison," he told me. The snoring of the other men covered our words. No kidding.

"I mean, underground but in the city?"

"Yes, underground in the dungeon, but outside the Palace." Still within the confines of the largest blocks of rock in the world. If it was anything like its successor, this City was a massive fortress, housing hundreds of thousands of people who served the Palace. Within the City was the Imperial Palace, the domain of the Emperor and Empress, and their closest advisors and servants. Somewhere, under the city was this dungeon, safe from outsiders. Theoretically, in the safest place in China.

"Do you know what year it is?"

"Ahh. It is true then." The man reached for my face. I intercepted the action. He seemed harmless enough, but no telling where his hands had been during his time down here.

"What is true?"

The man made movements in the dark. It looked like a sign against evil spirits, but I wasn't sure. I told him I didn't mean anyone harm, but I'd defend myself should it be necessary.

"Fists don't defend against wisdom," folding one arm over the other, stroking the long, grey hair on the side of his face. The room was full of men with dark hair, some braided, others not. I noticed those with braids were bald, shaved it seemed, with a mass of hair sprouting near the crown in the back, the braid falling down the back or the side. This man's clothing bore evidence of being clean and elegant at one time. The dark, grimy silk had spots of cleanliness, where the gold threading shone off the moonlight. The man's hands were not rough, stained with grease or torn or bruised from manual labor. His nails, slightly dirty underneath, were manicured and glossy on the top. Even his language was unique, the inflections well above the station of a common field worker.

After moving his hand, he brought it back up again to my face and I recoiled. He saw my hesitancy and told me he needed to prove I was real. His hand was so light it felt like a springtime breeze, and he moved it along the base of my arm to my elbow, resting his hand on my shoulder.

"It was foretold that a white man would emerge out of the dark, into our lands," he said. "I knew the signs. Only one person listened, and I shouldn't have told him."

The man was speaking cryptically, an odd mixture of emotions coming through the words he spoke. At first it was excitement, like waiting for the tipoff of a tournament basketball game. Then regret, missing the winning shot with all the disappointment and sadness that goes along with letting the town down.

"Who are you?" I asked him.

He told me he was the Imperial archivist, personally responsible for keeping the royal records.

"My family has been keeping the Imperial records for generations," he explained. For centuries, the archives had been maintained, he continued, rubbing his hands over my arm as though it was going to suddenly disappear. I thought of the beautiful brown eyes behind the carriage curtain that had vanished just as quickly. I dismissed the thought. They were only eyes, a set I'd surely never see again.

"What year is this?" I asked again.

"1403: you have met the second Ming Emperor, young Jianwen. Two years ago, when he was placed in power, the Minister of War asked me when I thought the next cycle would begin."

Qi Tai was the Minister of War. The man in grey who I was sure put it in the Emperor's head to throw us in prison.

"He put you down here?"

The man shook his head, pointing to the moonlight. "I doubt the Emperor even knows."

I sighed, impatient with his riddles. *What does he mean by cycle?* He drew closer, resting his hand on my arm. The touch was oddly comforting, like a grandfather preparing to tell a story.

"We didn't know exactly when you would come. It was not foretold in the records. Only the event itself, and the signs to watch for. I was doing my Imperial duty, telling the Minister to watch for foreign visitors.

"When the other foreigners came, it was believed they were the ones spoken of in the records. They were imprisoned until Qi Tai was assured the men wanted only trade, not fighting or glory." He was referring to Marco Polo, whom the Emperor also mentioned. Of course.

"You were imprisoned because you predicted incorrectly?"

He shook his head, his face so close to mine I could smell his breath. "The priests don't want the people to know what is recorded. It's bad luck. Qi Tai was afraid I would tell someone else."

The man looked me up and down. He placed his thumb and forefinger on my triceps, as if the size were going to help solve this riddle in any meaningful way. He'd obviously been expecting something, or someone, of significance. Instead, he got me, a high-school senior wearing a blue hoodie.

"Does the Emperor have an Empress?" trying a different line of questioning.

The man chuckled at the tone in my voice.

"Yes," he answered, his eyes twinkling in the moonlight. "But you must have seen the Empress's attendant, or cousin, not her."

My face flushed red. Even in the dark I was sure he'd tell the difference. He laughed, and I winced. Different centuries, same desires.

"How…?" he wasn't in the square. He had no idea who I saw or what occurred up above.

"Outside the Palace walls, no one sees the Empress but her servants, and the Emperor. Had you seen the Empress herself, you would have been relieved of the manhood between your legs. She rarely ventures out of the Palace walls unless the two are going to another palace outside the Forbidden City."

That was comforting. I didn't relish the thought of becoming a eunuch before I could vote. He tapped my hand, like an old man knowing a young man's desires. "I do have some friends who remain loyal to me and keep me informed on what happens above."

He removed his hand, straightening his shoulders up, extending his small form to its limits, inspecting me.

"Now, are you ready for your task?"

"As soon as I can find my father and sister, I'm gone." He hadn't even told me the difference between the priests and the ministers or what the cycle thing was all about. Not that it mattered. It would be hours now until we were set free.

The old man blinked. My answer was not what he expected. I started to explain the word 'gone,' my teenage slang not liable to translate well back a few centuries. His brows released wide and high in surprise. He moved closer again, this time, his nose an inch from my face.

"You don't *know*, do you?" he whispered, a bit of awe and perhaps fear in his voice.

I withdrew from him slightly. "Know *what*?"

"I never thought I'd see it in my lifetime. It's been fifty-two years and I've lived long enough to witness the end of one cycle, and the beginning of another." He backed away from me, placing a hand on the top of his hat, the other covering his mouth. When he removed his hand, opened and shut his mouth several times, as he struggled to find the right words to convey his feelings.

"You don't even know it's *time* do you?"

"*Time for what?*" I asked in frustration. He'd told me the year. I figured it was night. What more did the man want? So he guessed correctly that a white man came out of the ground. The Italians, now me. "You keep saying things I don't understand. Words without any context. I have no clue—no *idea*—what you are talking about!" A chill in the air caught the underside of my top, drafting up to the point on my back held flat by the satchel. I shivered, crossing my arms to keep warm.

The sound of a door opening at the far end of the hall stopped our conversation.

Before the man answered, guards entered, yelling at the prisoners to stand. The moon had vanished, the morning sun had crept through a small opening at the top of the cell.

"What are they doing now?" I asked.

"Picking prisoners," the old man replied, inching towards me. His hesitant manner was gone. "You will be chosen," he predicted, worry deep in his voice.

"Why?"

"Information, then death. You are not here to find your father. You are here…" The noise roused other captives. A toothless man wandered to the bars, standing beside a teenager. One ready to end his life, the other, prepared to defend it.

The shouts of prisoners commenced at the far end of the hall, as the lead guard moved between the corridors of cells. Five more guards followed, ignoring the taunts. Some prisoners threw pieces of straw and dirt at the passing group, hitting one guard in the face. The man didn't turn or blink. He followed his superior wordlessly.

The archivist held my arm, leaned close and whispered under his breath, the words coming fast. "We are not all like Qi Tai. He is not us…he is…something else. Our people are good. Honorable. We are…" he searched my eyes as though they would tell him what I needed to know.

"What am I here for?" I asked urgently.

"To learn. You must learn, but the knowledge will only come bit by bit." The assembly stopped in front of my holding cell.

"You!" pointed the guard, the finger at my chest. The other prisoners moved back and away, as though the invisible hand of death could extend to their own lives.

The elder gripped my arm, preventing me from moving. Now his mouth was so close to my ear it tickled.

"You don't have much time," he whispered, his voice strained. Fearful. He put emphasis on the last word, pressing my bicep with his brittle fingers.

"I still don't know what you're talking about!" I retorted. The guard barked at me, a Mandarin curse word. He thrust his keys in to the lock, swearing profusely when the key broke off.

"Find the tapestry in the hall, outside the Empress's room. Do it quickly. Now that you have crossed time, you only have a year."

"A year before what?" I shouted over my shoulder as the guards descended. I gave a last glance into the holding area, but the old man had faded into the shadows.

CHAPTER 6

My escort ignored my inquiries about our destination. The dark hallways seemed shorter without the blindfold on, the route out of the dungeon easily mapped. I saw we were headed towards an immense courtyard, the size of two football fields that looked like it served one purpose: to torture and kill. A stretch of gravel, about fifty yards, was covered with knives, swords, balls with spikes and other machines I didn't recognize.

The center of the courtyard expanded to a wide, stone-lined quad. The flat, rectangular space was filled with hundreds of males of all ages. In one section, lines of boys, barely eight years old, punched in uniform sequence, counting each numbers out loud. Other boys, pre-teens from the look of it, practiced different fighting styles, ranging from hand-to-hand combat to weapons sparring, and knife practice. The opponents were life size canvas dummies stuffed with straw. The advanced fighters used human opponents to perfect their skills. Yet unlike my own practice sessions, where we aimed for accuracy, these teens hit with full impact. On cue, a flat-handed punch to the back sent a student flying towards me. I dodged as he rolled on the corner of his shoulder, properly rounding his lower back to form a ball, then bounded on his feet. He turned, arms up then attacked the one who had thrown the punch.

My heart raced to join the fight, wondering how my modern skills would fair against the ancient, pure forms practiced here. They had masters on every corner, if belt and stance was an indicator of rank, each continually stopping the students, adjusting a pose or providing context for a move that was improperly executed.

We continued through the fighting, sparing and throwing, to the stretch of weapons. Dozens of men held wooden staffs, the long Jong bongs that I'd used yesterday, as well as the short dong bongs, half the size and twice as deadly. At least in this area, students had protection against unintentional death. Full body suits, thick with padding covered the men neck to foot, their heads enclosed by full metal armor. The eyes were shielded with a fine mesh, tight enough to keep out a blade while allowing the fighter to see. The metal blades on their weapons were covered with brown canvas, lashed over the razor sharp edge. We continued walking to the furthest side of the field where males my age sparred in complex formations, one against many. I counted twenty men attacking a single fighter. The student blocked a hip kick, warded off a leg thrust to his chest, spun to deflect a spin-kick from behind, but was undone by another student who spun low, knocking his ankles out from under him.

"Should've jumped up," I muttered under my breath. Easy mistake to avoid. Never, ever, keep your feet on the ground, in one place for very long. I learned that before I even had my first degree.

I realized that we were walking towards Qi Tai, still wearing grey and standing with another man. The soldier left my side to join Qi Tai. The man observed me with keen interest. He kept glancing over the guard's head at me, as though trying to match what was being said to how I looked. At least I'd caused no problem on the way, and I was hoping that I was racking up points for good behavior.

The guard gave a stiff bow, returning to his station beside me.

"General Li" said Qi Tai, turning to the man beside him. "As our captive is eager for a fight, I turn him over to you…for now."

General Li stepped forward, his stocky, barrel figure at odds with the thin, wiry figure of Qi Tai. His face was a patchwork of straggly, black hair, reaching a thin black line of hair circling his upper and lower lips. A dark tuft in the shape of a V was right above his chin, his eyes were fierce and cold. One hand was firmly attached to the hilt of sword on his belt, the other gripping a metal sling on his shoulder.

"That's fortunate. The Emperor wants you to fight one of my guards," he informed me. "If you win, you assume the duty of your opponent. If you lose, you will spend your time with us guarding the servants who clean the dung out from the Emperor's Palace."

His face didn't betray enjoyment, and I was beginning to get the impression he felt this challenge was wasting his time. A forefinger lifted from his sword, waiting for a comment. I had no intention of staying long enough to take on the role of a guard in the Forbidden City.

"This is your trial," he said curtly.

"When do I get to visit with the Emperor and be cleared of charges?" I pressed, his attitude annoying me. "And where are my father and my sister?"

Something flickered across the General's face, a slight hesitation when I mentioned my sister. Kindness? Compassion?

"The faster you choose your opponent, the sooner a reunion will take place."

My shoulders automatically relaxed, the posture loose as I spread my right foot slightly further away from my left. His finger immediately rested back down on his sword. He'd recognized the change in my stance, eyeing me warily. My fingertips tingled in anticipation and as I watched for the General's next move, I slowly, methodically, crossed the fingers over one another, an exercise to limber the joints. The exercise, taught in the very first belt section, increased the blood flow through the joints, lubricating the connective tissues that reduced the possibility of tears and fractures.

"To the death?" I asked the General.

He nodded back. "If warranted."

That was vague. Death was never warranted, except in self-defense. Rule number one for a true martial artist. Only the blasphemers used skill to egregiously harm, using talents and weapons to hurt.

The consequences of actually killing someone here in the Forbidden City reached far beyond the idea of just taking someone's life. Assuming this was real, I could actually change history by ending an entire family line—a family that could have continued to produce great warriors or skilled artists. I calculated the math: from this time to mine. Approximately four generations per one hundred years, six hundred years...I'd wipe out hundreds of generations with just one fatality. Hundreds of faces flashed through my head, all unborn, unable to live because I killed a person in front of me.

"I'm ready," I said stiffly, bowing slightly after I did so.

General Li gestured to a group of men who had lined up behind him. All five were garbed in black Imperial Army uniforms, the buttons flowing down the front on the left hand side, a strap at the waist, the emblem of the dragon on the shoulder. Each wore head covers with a dragon emblazoned on the forehead to prevent me from knowing the age of my adversary. Short, tall, thin, stocky, the figures differed in build and height. I'd have to make my decision based on the expression in the eyes.

It was always the eyes. Intelligence. Wit. Fear.

Two looked at me with small, dark pupils, peering out from between narrow lids. The brows were knotted together, seething anger. Angry opponents made stupid mistakes fueled by emotion. As long as I was going to be fighting I'd at least like a challenge. The third looked at me once, then down at the ground. I flattered myself thinking he'd heard of my first fight, and the man knew he wasn't up to the task. The fourth flitted his eyelashes nervously. Though either might have had the skills to be a potential challenge, I discarded both as unworthy opponents. The last thing I wanted was a timid fighter or one lacking confidence. The last set of eyes didn't look away, nor did they appear angry. These eyes met my own equally.

I pointed to the man at the end. In that moment, I realized I was still wearing the backpack. There was no time to focus on it now. I had a fight to win. And no ability to land on my back and crush the means for us to return to our time.

The General smiled.

"You. Step forward."

The guard wasted no time. A second after his bow to the General, he ran at me and unleashed a jumping front kick, which I ducked by twisting to the ground in a low floor sweep. He shot past, which opened up a hole for my cocked elbow. As I rose from my crouched position, I spun and drove my elbow into his ribs.

The guard didn't collapse like the guard from yesterday. He put his hands over his shoulders and sprung off the stone ground, landing on his feet in a frontal attack position. From his belt, he took a metal star that he threw at me. The blade sliced my cheek before I could duck. The warm trickle of blood ran down my face as he leapt, his left leg extended towards my face, his right leg bent, and both arms headed for my eyes, finger tips extended.

It was a bad decision. I swung my right leg up in a counter-clockwise circle, deflecting his flying body. The outside of my foot swept him across the face, the force rippling through his chest, pushing his legs off balance. He hit the ground on his shoulder and rolled in a somersault to an upright position.

This fighter was agile and quick. Once he was on his feet, he came at me with a four-kick sequence—a front kick to the chest, then a reverse swing kick, followed by a floor sweep, spinning his foot an inch off the ground with a rotating spin kick. As I blocked each move, my other hand punched, pounded, or cut into his body until he pressed up against the weapons wall. Ancient training had been improved over the last few hundred years.

"Do you surrender?" I asked. I didn't want to hurt the guard, just hold him off until the end of the fight. The man responded by turning toward the wall and grabbing the closest weapon. He gripped a short, metal sword with both hands, slicing the air in diagonal, downward strokes and nearly cutting off my hand.

Instantly I bounded backwards and glimpsed a single wooden pole on the ground. I lifted it in time to block the second downward thrust of his sword. My head was still attached to my shoulders, thanks to the block, but the metal sliced cleanly through the wood. Instead of one piece of wood in my hands, I now had two short sticks. I unconsciously adjusted my grip and thrust one stick into his belly as I swiped his head with the other.

It took the wind out of my opponent. As he caught his breath, I sprinted to the weapons wall, dropped my sticks and selected a short blade ideal for hand-to-hand combat. His body language told me he wanted payback for throwing him on the ground. A close fight with blades in hand was more impressive than a ground throw. I knew how I wanted to end the fight.

All I heard was a blade slicing the air and I instinctively ducked. A five-pointed Chinese star whirled past where my neck had just been. It went clean through the wooden weapons pole. Over my shoulder, I sensed him coming toward me, his sword raised for another assault. Waiting until the last minute, I bent slightly, then with a tremendous push off my legs, did a backwards somersault in the air, up and over as he screamed in anger. Landing behind him, I slid my left hand around his neck and gripped his chin to turn his head toward him. With his right hand, I placed the knife at his throat and whispered in his ear:

"Do you surrender?" I asked, tone low, pressing the blade against his neck.

"I'd rather die," the man answered. He body was tense, ready for the point to be inserted, the blood to drop down his shirt. This guy was a fighter to the end.

I pulled his head back farther, pressing the knife deeper into his flesh. I would either break his neck or slice his throat until I got an answer. Fighting in this time was for life and death. No going back, for him, or I.

"End it," commanded Qi Tai.

"I can still fight," said the guard through gritted teeth.

"Kill him and be done with it," repeated Qi Tai. One more press of the knife, and his existence was over. I tilted the knife on its edge and waited for the man's reaction.

He didn't flinch.

"Enough!" said the familiar voice of the Emperor. He must have come to the square sometime after the start of the fight, and I'd been far too busy to notice. His face was controlled fury. I wondered if he had been informed ahead of time, and was angry at not witnessing the combat, or angrier I hadn't killed a guard. "You take Xing, my personal guard, for this...*test?*" he hissed, low enough for only me and the men to hear.

After a short pause, Qi Tai soothingly told him how he thought it was important to test the guard's fighting skills against the potential adversary. "We want to learn all we can about their skills to see if we can defeat them," Qi Tai explained. The Emperor angrily responded it was the General's army that would be defeated if this were the outcome.

This was the man who stood beside the Emperor at the square, his *personal* bodyguard? Maintaining the pressure of the knife against the guard's I couldn't help but feel a surge of adrenaline push my ego up a few notches. Nice.

Still gripping the back of the guard's uniform, I slowly tilted the edge of the knife on its flat side to prevent him from retaliating. With the Emperor looking on, I doubted the guard would attempt to start up again.

When I was convinced he didn't intend to continue the fight, I removed it entirely and released my hold, shoving him away from me, towards the General. With one long arm, the General tore the hood off the guard's hood then spat on the ground. Xing was a teenager, no more than a year older than myself. How was that possible? Knowing his age reduced the glory of my victory somewhat. I was hoping the guy was a twenty-nine year old prize fighter, the grand champion of the country. That's what it *should* have been. But a teenager…?

Xing went before the Emperor in humiliation, disappointment and perhaps a bit of fear in his eyes. The Emperor was none too happy with the outcome either. He gave a quick nod, dismissing the guard.

As Xing moved in front of Qi Tai and the General, I heard the General hiss. "Stay out of my sight."

Xing was forced to walk in front of me. As he did so, he gave me a side glance full of hatred. Xing's head was bowed low, a sign of disgrace, though his body language said otherwise. No one spoke until the defeated guard left the square. Even the other students practicing had stopped all commotion, on their knees once the Emperor had set foot on the premises. They'd probably watched the entire battle, entranced with the foreigner fighting the guard.

"You were told to kill him," the Emperor said to me. "You ignored a direct command. Why?"

I bowed before speaking.

"The fight was for life," I responded. "Not death."

"Who are you to be the judge?" he asked, tilting his head. He wasn't being belligerent. His eyes betrayed genuine interest in the philosophy behind my statement. Once again I felt this curious stare, the kind reserved for looking at a person who emerges from a car wreck without a scratch, or that comes running from a house full of flame without a burn or smudge of dirt. When I spoke, it was as though I were a ghost, and the Emperor still couldn't quite determine if I should be locked up or released from the chains that bound me.

"My master taught me a warrior must decide if the taking of a life is justified. In this situation, it wasn't."

"Will you take a life…when justified?"

Something about the way he said it let me know death was a daily occurrence, as I'd witnessed with Draben. No judge or trial. No waiting period. When in doubt, kill. Everything I'd been taught about fairness and being innocent until proven guilty didn't apply in the China of 1403.

"As your guard, I'll protect you. And yes, I will kill, when necessary."

Qi Tai grunted, dismissing my answer. He leaned over to the Emperor, whispering. The Emperor nodded, in evident agreement.

"Your last name," the Emperor demanded.

"Fleener," I said, thinking how hard the name had been to pronounce for my friends in China.

"Cage Fleener," the Emperor said, trying out the foreign word, though it came out more like a yaw sound. "I'm confident you will protect me." The corner of the Emperor's lips curled in a slight smile. "If you don't, your father will be killed."

That sufficed. I nodded. Then, I did something on instinct.

"Emperor," I began, bowing low, so as not to show disrespect by speaking out of turn. I raised my eyes, receiving his permission to speak. "What of my sister?"

Qi Tai turned to the Emperor, as though he wanted to speak, flushing when he received a raised hand from his ruler.

"She has been placed inside the palace, near the Empress, where her skills will be put to use." A bodyguard to the Empress? It wouldn't surprise me. Her kicking prowess made an impression, no doubt of that. I didn't see her in any other role, since she certainly wasn't going to be forced to serve anyone food or clean toilets. She was the lead taskmaster at home, making sure me and Dad kept the house in some type of order, the toilet seats down and crumbs off the counter. I raised my right eyebrow, willing him to continue, but he wasn't going to indulge me. He nodded his head to Qi Tai and the General, dismissing me with a nod.

Guards briskly flanked me, my escorts back through the Forbidden City, into the Imperial Palace, and towards the chambers reserved for those who protected the Emperor.

Within an hour, my ear-length hair was cut short, barely an inch long, to fit under the hood.

A man bearing a load of neatly pressed clothes walked in, bowing, extending his arms. His head was down as he waited for me to accept his offering. The silence told me the significance of being the Emperor's personal guard. Men bowed, unable to meet my eye, for they were not worthy. It wasn't what I believed—it was what they were told, and how they were taught to behave.

Uncomfortable with the deferential treatment, I lifted the garments and placed them on the wooden table. The man then asked my permission to wait.

"Why?"

The man answered without looking up. "The clothes must fit perfectly or you cannot serve." As he spoke, those who had adjusted my hair left and two others entered, each holding an item I assumed was intended for my use. One thing at a time.

I nodded at the tailor, assuming that's what he was, and he lifted a hood. He corrected me, telling me the mask was to only to be worn outside the Imperial Palace, on the grounds of the Forbidden City and outside the walls. It was designed to prevent others from knowing those who protected the Emperor. I was glad. Wearing the confining hood would get claustrophobic. The back of the mask rubbed my neck, irritating my skin.

The man asked me to remove my hands, lifting the back of the hood up and over my head. He efficiently sewed a softer piece of cloth over the area, slipped it back over my head and asked me how it felt.

I nodded. The irritation was gone.

He glanced at my top. I still wore the hoodie and shirt, the backpack as yet undiscovered underneath. I removed both in a fluid movement, the act drawing a respectful comment from the tailor. My dojo masters railed against building muscle, forever telling us the repetitive movements restricted blood flow to the joints, overdeveloped certain muscles and reduced flexibility. I listened, to a degree. I still had a need to look good in swim trunks, and a defined chest was my beach body prerequisite.

Balling the clothing around the backpack, I noticed a wooden dresser, near the mat that served as a bed. I asked the man if he knew if this was to be my bedroom. Seeing I was unwilling to set down my personal belongings, he assured me they would be quite safe here.

"It is the Imperial Palace and we follow a code of honor." He said it stiffly, though with respect, for my position as the Emperor's guard was well above his station as a tailor.

Even with his assurance, I opened the dresser and placed it inside rather than on top. The look of confusion was plain on his face.

"Sentimental value," I said, my voice even.

He measured my shoulders, his palms up, stretching his arms out wide. He lifted the fabric to see if it would fit without alterations. It didn't. My broad shoulders were evidently much larger than Xing's, requiring the tailor to remove the sleeves and extend the length several inches. The pants were drawstring with bound ankles, useful for fighting. Although modern day outfits were long and loose, we'd been told it was more style than function. Winning a kicking battle was at risk if a cuff was caught on a blade. This was far more functional, the tight binding stopped at the top of my shoe. These were interesting, as much like a wrestlers shoe as anything I'd ever seen. The flexible materials had the give of a slipper but the strength of leather, the top extending up, over my ankle, the bottom covered with a dark, rubbery substance. Even so, the tailor needed to adjust for my height and size.

As the tailor made his alterations, sitting on the floor, quietly attending to my new wardrobe, I went to window, interested in anything and everything. In a few hours' time, I'd transitioned from trespassing infiltrator to protector of the Emperor.

I pushed open the window covering, a thin mesh-like material placed within wood that slid back at a light touch. Outside, a path of dark marble ran in either direction, a parallel white marble path next to it. Both continued around the corner. I was sure the yin and yang were significant but had no idea what it meant.

With nothing more to look at, I started to close the window when the sound of a woman's voice singing softly below caught my attention. It was very quiet…so low it could have been mistaken for the whistle of a flute.

"How's it coming?" I asked the tailor in Mandarin.

"Soon," he said, his eyes concentrating on this task. "Normally I make four sets for bodyguards, but was told to only make you two," he muttered to himself, shaking his head in unquestioning confusion. "Why I'm bothering is a wonder, since…" He broke off talking to himself as though he said something out of turn.

The singing was still soft but sounded distinctly closer. The voice seemed to round the corner near my room. I stood straight as an arrow, unmoving, even my eyes. She walked like an angel, stepping lightly and rather fast along the black marble even in her high-heeled slippers. The girl's dark brown hair was removed from her face, wearing the barest of make-up. The singing continued as she made her way closer to me, still oblivious to my existence. Of course, I *was* up above her, looking down, and not in her line of sight.

She drew close, an updraft of wind caught her scent. It was a perfumed cocktail, mixing lilies and cinnamon. The sheen on her pale blue dress matched a jewel pinned to just below her shoulder blade. The buttons ran from the brooch up her neck, ending where a dangling earring of green and blue stones hung from her small, perfectly formed ear. Somewhere, in the back of my mind it registered I was inspecting every centimeter of this girl. That same part told me I didn't want to stop.

The music continued, even when the wind blew a wisp from her expertly set hair in her face. Now that she was closer, I noticed lighter brown streaks in her hair, auburn highlights that were unheard of in China. And her face, it was long and oval yes, but it had a different quality, high cheekbones with a somewhat angular chin line. Even her lips were at odds with the Chinese girls I knew. They were wider and fuller, a thicker upper lip with rounded points in the center instead of abrupt, pointed lines. It lifted and fell on a plump lower lip that was downright...juicy looking.

With a long, narrow finger, she took the strand back from her parted lips, placing it in its rightful position. She was nearly in front of me now and I drew a breath, encouraging her scent to come my direction.

"Bodyguard, I am ready," called the tailor.

Bad luck! I cursed. The singing stopped as did the girl, who looked up, shocked to see me.

The eyes! It was her. The person from the carriage. The one who was surely the attendant or cousin, if the archivist was correct.

She blinked, a crimson color moving up her face before she recovered herself.

"In a moment," I told him, my eyes not leaving hers. I frantically tried to recall any folk tales about guards making eye contact with servants and remembered none. She looked down, but I saw a smile on the corner of her lip.

"That was a beautiful song," I said, hoping she'd look up again with those large, brown orbs. I'd recognize those anywhere. The girl had to be an attendant or relative. I wasn't sure, but figured the Empress would never be left out of her chambers alone. A servant yes. Royalty no.

She rewarded me with a glance, one similar to the Emperor who was trying to make up his mind if I was friend or foe.

"I saw you in the square when we…arrived…" I began, hoping to stall her a bit, but knowing it had to be short. I had a job, at least for now and didn't want to push it. "Now I'm the Emperor's bodyguard."

For some reason, this erased the modest smile from her face. Her lips flattened, and her eyes became dark from her eyelids lowering slightly. Her posture somehow removed herself from me, the entire effect one that placed miles of distance between us instead of an arm length.

"I know."

The tailor called for me again, giving her the chance to formally bow before she continued on her way, her pace, as it was before, though now she was silent. I didn't wait for her to round the next corner. I knew she wasn't going to look at me. My stare continued long enough to appreciate her well-formed backside, hugged by her form-fitting silk outfit.

The tailor was looking at me when I turned, standing nearby with the jacket in one hand and the pants in the other. His eyes betraying none of the inquisitiveness I knew he felt.

Both jacket and pants fit exactly, as I knew they would. This was the Imperial Palace: the lowliest of tailors was a master craftsman. The man told me he'd create several more outfits in black for excursions outside the Imperial Palace, now that he knew my size. Soon after he left, another servant arrived and placed a square, gold pin was placed on my shoulder, inscribed with the outline of a dragon.

"What's this for?" I asked, noting none of the other guards wore the same piece of jewelry.

"This designates you as the lead guard in the Emperor's unit."

The man tried unsuccessfully to keep the unease from his voice. I was a white foreigner. A person not to be trusted, now put in place to protect their leader, their most valuable possession.

CHAPTER 7

I replayed my brief conversation from the morning with the Emperor again and again in my mind. Telling anyone I could kill someone else and be okay with it hadn't been untruthful. I had the knife to Xing's neck, I had gripped the handle so hard the slightest movement from him would have slit his neck. Even now, a pulsing sensation in my fingers confirmed my desire to cut just a little, creating enough fear to put a stop to his actions. I shied away from the next emotion I felt.

Before today, the only serious injury I'd inflicted on an opponent was a broken arm, and I'd been severely reprimanded by my instructor for using excessive force. A change had come over me in a matter of hours. What concerned me wasn't that we were in a foreign place or that the lives of my father and sister depended on my ability to fight. It was my easy acceptance of death, killing, and its role in my life as I now knew it that bothered me.

But I didn't have much time to worry. It was nearing lunchtime and I heard noises come from the courtyard. Soft, low whisperings, in keeping with the aura of the place. With the exception of the guards' quarters, much of what I'd seen so far gave me the impression that I was now part of a rarified world. There was no fighting or yelling. The air was free from the noise of the street. What should have been an eerie silence was instead peaceful, like one of those strange, sci-fi movies where the world had been cleansed.

The famous Chinese warrior Sun-Tzu, said to keep your friends close and enemies closer. This had to be a trap.

The hair on the back of my head confirmed my inner warning. Something was not right. My fingers ached, and I looked down, seeing I'd unconsciously crossed the fingers one over another, in preparation for fighting. My body knew…even when I didn't.

A knock at the door was followed by the entry of a guard. He was dressed in black, a pin above his left breast. It was not identical to my own, as it was green instead of blue, both lucky colors. Yet the insignia of the dragon was the same. I supposed he was one of the Emperor's unit.

"It is time," he said, bowing stiffly. "Follow me."

I did as I was told, keeping pace as we moved swiftly through the guard's station, walking on the black path then through a series of short paths towards a white, marble palace. He led me through an immense doorway that opened to a small antechamber that connected to a main hallway.

"Wait here." He left, returning a few moments later. I wanted to ask him what we were doing and what to expect, but figured he'd keep his mouth closed. He didn't have the authority to speak to me, I was sure. In silence, I followed him to a room the size of a gym, where the Emperor sat alone, guards on one side, a tall, white haired man on the other.

Waiting at the corner of the room, the Emperor lowered his head slightly, indicating I proceed. Guards stood every few feet around the perimeter of the room, with the Emperor himself seated near a silver-haired man. In the corner were several musicians, one sitting with a large drum with a golden band around it, placed between his legs. Another sat at on a stool with a string instrument while a third lightly tapped round, silver symbols of several sizes. The three played soft, background music.

My path was clear. A narrow, red carpet led the way to his throne. As I walked towards him, it was a challenge to keep my focus. On either side of me was the most incredible display of swords I'd ever seen. Unable to help myself, I slowed, walking in awe alongside many of the weapons I'd only heard about, or seen drawings or replica pictures of, that were now in front of me, within touching distance.

"Blade royalty," I said to myself without thinking.

The Chinese sword, the Sanmei, more than deserved to be hung on the wall. It was a work of art. Two soft layers of steel surrounded the inner, central layer. My master had spent hours reverently educating us on the beautiful simplicity of the ancient weapon. The softer steel gave flexibility and resilience, leaving the harder, brittle core a wickedly sharp edge. This was only the basic element of the sword. The master swordsman, who had learned from his master and his master before him, handed the sword through the generations along with intricately inscribed instructions in the fine metal. To the uninformed observer, the words would appear to be nothing more than ornamental sayings. I knew better. They were the secrets of cutting, deflecting, footwork and guarding, unique to that sword, and the person who had made it. The sword itself could kill, but the wisdom of the battles kept the bearer of the sword alive.

"What do you mean?" called the man by the Emperor. The voice, cold and sharp, rang through the empty hall. It was directed at me obviously, and I stopped, bowing, then spoke.

"It's magnificent," I said, gesturing to the entire collection on the wall. I continued my walk, looking up and down, soaking in the beautiful sight. Even if these were still in existence, six hundred years in my time, I'd never be allowed to see these weapons this close. No one would. Locked away, preserved in some deep vault, only the wealthy or royal would have the chance. One after another, I took in the weapons of war. It occurred to me the arrangement wasn't in order of age or significance, or even historical usage.

"Stop," commanded someone from the front of the room. Unsure who spoke to me, I bowed without making eye contact to anyone. "The Emperor wants to know if you can use that one." I looked up at the hand, pointing to a series of swords in front of me. Of course, I could use any one of the differing swords, and the guy was an idiot if he thought he was going to trick me with the phrasing of the question.

"You have several types of Dao swords here," I said. "I can use all of them."

My words had the intended effect, dizzying their thoughts about my understanding of their land battles and weapons. The Minister spoke in undertones to the Emperor, who didn't take his eyes off me. The swords to my right were influenced by the invasion of the Mongols, a warring neighbor, forever invading and destroying Chinese lands and murdering their people. The Mongols fought differently than the Chinese, less sophisticated, rougher, with slashing and cutting movements rather than the elegant, almost artistic way of the Chinese. To better defend themselves, or rather, to kill their enemy faster and more efficiently, the Chinese created four versions of the Dao, each one molded and shaped for offensive and defensive situations, but all deadly weapons of war.

Were I to know too much about the history, I might be a Mongol sympathizer, one who wanted to topple the Chinese rule. On the other hand, an ignorant body guard was a useless bodyguard, unable to fight against a known threat.

The white haired man conferred with the Emperor, then asked me if I had trained with the Mongols, though the skepticism was clear. I wasn't short, dark haired or burly.

"Of course not," I answered, a slight arrogance to my statement. "If I were on their side, do you think I would have entered China, alone, without a weapon?" A flick of the Minister's eyes, and the guards in the corner adjusted their position, drawing closer to the Emperor, standing at the ready. He didn't trust me. That was going to pose a slight challenge when it came to protecting the ruler.

"When would you use…that one?" asked the Minister, pointing out the modest curve along the length of the weapon.

"I would only use the liuye Dao if I were riding a horse," explaining it was perfect for the cavalry, its nature by design.

"On the ground?" he continued, raising his hand, seeing I was about to speak.

I withheld a smile. "With or without a shield?"

"With," he answered without hesitation.

Higher up on the wall was a deeply curved blade, perfect for slashing a person in two. It had been designed exclusively for shield play. "The pain Dao."

The Minister raised the brow above one eye, neither pleased nor unhappy with my knowledge. "Show me the sword that includes a bird feather as a part of its name."

Please. I knew this in our second belt, long before touching a weapon was allowed. It was a part of gaining an appreciation of weapons, learning the lineage, understanding the beauty. In my time, guys walked in off the street, signed up and paid lots of money, mistakenly thinking they were going to learn how to flatten someone day two. Most dropped out after they were required to spend an hour throwing a single, front punch, hundreds upon hundreds of times, followed by the other arm. It was 'weeding' as my master said. Removing those that wouldn't practice true martial arts. The months of learning about weapons was time enough for the masters to see who embodied respect for a weapon. Those few were then chosen to learn.

"This, right here. The full name is quill saber sword," I answered, tracing the lines of the beautiful piece above the blade, about a hand length from it. The one I stared at was golden, a magnificent piece with etchings starting at the tip of the blade and continuing up to the handle. The flat, circular edge was a quarter inch thick, also in a gold tone. The grip was entwined with a flat, metallic cloth, broad enough to be gripped with both hands when need be. "Incredible," I uttered. The masters had talked of pieces such as this with such an aura of awe and respect. Here it was.

When the man remained silent, I began walking again, my eyes scrolling up and down the impressive wall. Next on the wall was a yanmao Dao, which was largely straight with a curve at the center of the percussion, near the blade's tip. It blended the thrusting attacks and handling of the jian, but kept the Dao's strength for cutting and slashing.

I nodded, glancing at the Minister. "This is a good one for defending against multiple attackers," I offered, not waiting for him to ask. If I was going to have a test, why didn't he just give me a pen and paper? Better yet someone to fight against. The guards around the room looked as eager as I felt.

Then I came upon a single sword, one that was unsheathed, within a glass box that was mounted to the wall. The hilt was black matted metal with gold etching, the carving of dragons and tigers, symbols of the Emperor, wealth and success. Inlaid gold was on the end, the spirals dropping to points on either end, curling back towards the center of the hilt. At the opposite end, nearest the blade, the handle bore the golden molds of the revered animals, the layers of etching on the gold exquisite.

"The royal blade," I said, in awe. This was made by a master, for the Emperor.

"How..." started the Minister, his eyes flashing warily. A flush contrasted against his face, and his lips moved as he struggled to collect himself. "No one outside the Palace has ever seen that blade."

Crap! History versus present. It was going to get me sliced up if I didn't watch my mouth.

"Is it not the Emperor's and isn't he royal?" I said, trying to sound logical, not defensive. The Emperor remained silent, stroking his wispy hair in a motion reminiscent of a forty-year old businessman, not teenage ruler. He lifted a finger, beckoning the Minister. With a nod of his head, the Minister agreed.

"Can you use what you can identify?" The man asked me. That was asking a lot of any person, musician, basketball player or martial artist. Describing a free throw wasn't the same as making the shot.

Then another idea stopped me short.

"Yes, I can use this," I replied, purposefully talking slowly, keeping my eye focused on his. "But I would not."

The words hung in the air with the expectation I was going to finish my statement. The Emperor's brows creased, and I bet he was thinking about the promise I made only yesterday to defend him, and kill when necessary. My statement had nothing to do with killing.

The Minister could take it no more. "Why?" he asked, the muscles on his cheek protruding as he eked out the word. His single word question carried the overtone of an insult, a personal attack on him.

I looked him up and down again, trying to confirm my suspicion. Worst case, I'd be wrong and look a fool. Best case, I'd guess right and lock in my good impression. I searched his top for a pattern, an insignia, anything that denoted his rank or position. He was expecting my answer and I had to give him one. Just before I opened my mouth, the Minister turned to the Emperor, making a remark.

Then I saw it. A crouching tiger embroidered on this sleeve. The animal, ready to pounce on its prey, was surrounded by the other symbols of the Shaolin, the truest form of Martial Arts; Zen, health and combat. This was he. The Minister of Weapons. It had to be.

"Master?" I bowed low, lowering my voice, almost whispering the word. For if he oversaw all the weapons, then he himself was a master of swords. He was still bent when he turned his head to me, his look of shock clear. I had no idea it was his before I spoke. The man rose to full height, waiting for me to proceed. "I didn't say I *can't*. I said I *won't*. This," pointing to the weapon, "is meant for a master. Not a…" I hesitated, searching for the right word, "… warrior…like me."

Something about my statement, the recognition of unworthiness, affected him. His eyes darted above and around me. My vanity made me hope he was wondering how I would look, wielding the sword. It made me bold.

"Of course, someday, it would be my privilege to use one of the others." I sighed then, an audible exhale of longing. For the second time today, I felt the hesitation of returning to my time a bit…too quickly.

I closed the distance between the end of the carpet and where he stood, glancing to the left side of me several times. That opposing wall was adorned with the battle gear. The helmets on the walls, the body armor, chest plates, full upper body guards and lower body coverings, some mounted on metal dummies, others on hooks hanging from the walls. I bowed again, this time for two reasons. Protocol to the Emperor demanded it. Respect for the Master of Weapons I gave on my own.

"Perhaps you would like to demonstrate your skills now?" the Master asked, the wariness in his expressing changing to anticipation, as though he had wrongly assessed me and now wanted confirmation.

My eyes slid to the wall. "Can I choose my weapon?"

He nodded. "Except *that* one," gesturing to the glass case.

I couldn't believe it. A dream come true. Holding an ancient blade, the edges so sharp the slightest touch would cut the skin, wielding it at the angles of a down or up cut, finding its mark. Even more, I was going to do so under the watchful eye of a true master. Not to take anything away from the teachers of my time, but this was…unreal. He made the weapons, he was endowed with the knowledge of use. I could learn more for a single technique adjustment from this man than I may gain in year of training from another, less knowledgeable person.

CHAMBERS

Of course, using the weapons in a form would be less exciting than practicing on a person. Perhaps he'd let me demonstrate on the armor. With no body underneath, less chance of death.

I pointed to the armor, hopeful the Master agreed.

He crossed his arms, shaking his head. Bummer. Oh well. Even touching the things would be good enough. Thinking he expected me to choose my weapon, he gave a sudden shout.

"Training guards! Now!"

Doors slammed open and shut. The drummer banged on his instrument, slowly at first, then faster and faster, picking up speed as the other players joined with the clanging of symbols and strings. I didn't need to hear the running of feet. The energy of the room had changed, the guards around the room altered their stance. The Emperor leaned forward, eagerly. He and the Minister of Weapons had planned on this—testing me. The questions were the warm up. This was the event.

The thrill of the unknown blended with a sick feeling that dropped to my belly as I centered.

"If I pass this demonstration, will we be released to go home?" I quickly asked, looking from the Minister and Emperor. The thrumming of the feet grew louder with the pounding of the drums. "And see my sister?" It was close. Seconds now.

For once, the Emperor answered. "See her?' He nodded his head solemnly. "Yes. Released...?" He left the question without an answer. One who is dead has no need to be released.

All at once, men in full warrior garb entered the room, ants swarming the hive from all side. They descended upon me.

CHAPTER 8

Without thinking, I lifted a Dao and Jain from the wall and sprang away from the Emperor, to the middle of the room.

From the left I felt a whir of a baton and crouched, arching the blade from my elbow, blocking the down thrust with an up angle, deflecting it then curving it in a C, hitting the man's ankle.

"Wai tou!" cried the Master, Mandarin for *out*. Had the man not worn full body armor from head to ankle, his foot would have been severed, a writhing, one legged fighter, and he would be out of battle. Another attacker had his blade skimming the floor, curving up to slice my crotch in two. Using the Jain in front of me I knocked the blade to the floor, the cross-cut both his thighs with the weapon in my other hand in one direction, then up to his chest in the other, a reverse Zorro. The metal clanged over the Master's shout, the mental image of the guard's thighs splitting open and the guts pouring out his chest already gone when the next adversary made his move.

Then one after another, the attackers came out at me, from above, slashing down with a short blade, from below, crouching with a long blade, hoping to lop off my feet. My hands and feet worked as tightly as a choreographed dancer, moving and turning to block, cut, and slash my opponents to their defeat. Time and again the Master yelled, ending the fight for me against those who would have died. Periodically, blades connected with my shirt sleeve or pant leg but didn't penetrate the skin.

The tailor…he knew this was coming as well. I'd get ripped up, torn to shreds, dead. Why make more than two sets indeed?

Pride that I was holding my own suddenly turned to fury. Aggression tipped the balance in my favor. The handful of remaining attackers got creative, one pushing off the wall before he twisted his upper body, rotating the blade in a downward circular motion. Instead of fighting the blade, I attacked the legs, thrusting the tips of my own weapons between his, upending his balance, throwing him to the ground. Before he had the chance to spring up, I took both blades and scissored his neck, cutting the material in two. Had he been unprotected, his head would have rolled off.

A whoosh from above caught me off guard and I instinctively dropped to the ground, blades extended in either direction, one knee bent in the traditional tai chi stability pose, my back thigh resting above the ball of my foot. The milliseconds felt like an eternity as I waited for the guard to swoop down. Only then would I know where to position my weapons.

Then the figure dropped on me, a blade centered directly above my spine, ready to penetrate the length of my body like a skewer. Injury was going to be unavoidable on this one as I slid to my left and the blade hit the front of my bicep. I felt the blood trickle on my shirt but grinned with the imminent victory. The man left the rest of his body wide open, placing his entire bet on killing me, not on an additional defense. With both hands free, I adjusted my grip, and slid both blades on either side of his ribcage, a standing crucifixion.

"Wai tou!" yelled the Master and I was vaguely aware of applause at the gesture.

That left one more person somewhere behind me, moving from side to side. Instead of turning, it was time to display a bit of Chinese acrobatics injected with a few modern day moves. Without changing the position of the blades, I dropped and rolled back, tucking my knees to my head then shoving off with my arms, rotating a back flip in the air then landing on my feet, facing not one but two opponents. They were momentarily stunned, collecting themselves with a glance to the other, trying to figure out how to end this battle. The banging of the drums and symbols were ringing in my ears, the crescendo indicating a desire for a climactic end. I'd give it to them.

Defying my teachings to wait and defend, I moved towards them, feet turned in slightly and bent at the knee, the warrior's fighting stance. The swords twisted and cut through the air in rotating, circular motions as I neared the remaining fighters. They separated, attempting to circle me in a two on one combat formation. In response, I stopped, drawing the attack. It came first by the guard on my left who jumped up, foot out for a kick, then spun, reversing his angle in an attempt to distract me from the point of the blade. At the same time, the other guard went low, his short weapon ready to slice my ankles. Above and below, the effect lopping off my head and feet at once.

As the blades rotated I coiled, bent at the waist, using the motion of tucking the blades against my chest to rotate from the chest to legs, spinning horizontally right through their weapons like a pavement roller compressing the air. When my opponents were directly above and below, I thrust out both weapons, hitting the crotch of one man, his organs gone in a flash had he not been wearing protective mesh. The other guard's head would have had a blade poke through the skull to the neck had he not had a helmet on.

I was still spinning when my right shoulder landed on the edge of the carpet. I turned the edge of the weapons flat against my chest, points over my shoulder as I rolled once more then came upright using my stomach muscles. In a single motion I was on my feet, surveying the bodies around me. The men were on their feet or lying on the ground in the same positions where they had fallen. That was the code of the warrior: Lie where you die. There were twelve. Not quite the twenty I'd been hoping for.

The pounding stopped as I stood, the silence broken only by jagged breathing from those that had fought.

"You did well," complimented the Emperor.

The Minister of Weapons clapped twice and my opponents leapt to their feet, lining up along the carpet by the other guards. As a group, they followed a signal I didn't see, turning to me and bowing, then left the space as quickly as they entered it. The entire event had taken less than five minutes.

"Closer," said the Emperor, beckoning me to the front of the room. On my way, I replaced the weapons I'd used during the fight. Making my way to the ruler, I worried slightly about how my body was going to withstand fighting once or twice a day. The fear left me almost as fast as it came. When I stopped in front of the two, my arms felt like new, as though I'd never fought. This wasn't like being immortal. It was natural steroids at work. Superman without the cape.

"Wi Cheng," introduced the Emperor, raising his hand to the Minister beside him. He did so with much greater respect than his hand-lifting to Qi Tai. Wi Cheng, Minister of Weapons and master swordsman bowed to me. It nearly took my breath away.

"On the way to meeting the men in your guard unit you will be taken to see your sister," the Emperor granted me. "Then you will return to me for duty."

I bowed, still charged from the exhilaration of winning. I hoped Mia's time had been spent uneventfully sipping tea with other servants as I'd been fending for my life. Dad on the other hand, he could be in a dungeon like the one I'd been in for all I cared.

A stab of guilt hurt me more than the single slice of the sword that marked my bicep. We had come to find him, to save him. Was it wrong to want him to hurt in some damp, rotting hole? To feel damage and pain like the kind he'd inflicted on us? Mia would say yes, it was wrong. She'd advocate forgiving. I frowned. That's what mom would say as well.

"A healer will see about that wound on your way there," Wi Cheng said, gesturing to a servant who was hovering in the corner. His gaze had turned from surprise to thoughtfulness. "You are using skills unknown to me," he remarked seriously, an undercurrent of disbelief. He'd lived decades, taught by his own masters and had seen it all. He knew every technique known to his people. He was wondering how I'd defeated the men. Europeans didn't know martial arts. Only the Chinese.

"I learned from a M...teacher...in my home country." Then it hit me I'd have to lie if he asked which country—mine had yet to be discovered, and I couldn't have the Chinese write about it in the Imperial history books. "We do things differently."

His lips pursed up, the skin on his chin stretching from the lower part of his jowls towards his long nose. He clasped his hands in front of him, under his robe, hiding his wrists. A respectful, easy stance that indicated he no longer felt threatened.

"So I see," his statement given with a lilt of inquisitiveness. I wanted him to give me advice on what to do better, to get him aside in a room and talk. He gave the impression he'd like to do the same thing. His eyes bore in to mine. Wi Cheng knew I meant to say Master, and substituted teacher for the word, a lame attempt to avoid disrespecting a true master. He could have called me out in front of the Emperor, but didn't. Since he kept his mouth shut, I owed him one. And he and I both knew it.

The Emperor gestured for Wi Cheng to lean down, and he did so, looking at the floor, not me. When he rose back up, a black dart caught the corner of my eye.

A spear sliced through the air, coming directly towards the Minister. Wi Cheng didn't have time to turn before I rolled. I dove forward on the floor, pulled out the Jain from the Master's belt and lifted the blade directly up in the air, deflecting the point of the spear just as the tip touched his cheek.

The long weapon clattered to the floor as guards swept out of the room in the direction of the spear, the others rushing to form a circle around the Emperor who had sat still during the brief attack. It was only seconds for the area to be cleared of the men, but sounds of angry reprisal was outside the marble barrier.

The immediate threat gone, I stood, lowering my arms, staring through the window, ready for another attack, but it was once again empty.

"Master," I said, bowing, my heart racing. I should have stopped the blade before it met its mark. I dropped the Jain in my hands, the flat side of the blade on my left hand, blade towards me, holding the handle lightly. I extended his piece, keeping my eyes low. His cheek bore a nick of blood.

He received it with a look of disbelief and silent thanks, touching the blood on his face. Wi Cheng gazed in the direction the spear had come, then at the windows around the room. His expression wasn't one of worry or fear. It was…acceptance. And all the peace that came with knowing finality was near. It was going to be years until I accepted my fate that way. Right now, I was going to live, and fight to the death if I had to.

I walked backwards, on my way to my former place on the red carpet.

"Stop," said the Emperor, his voice oddly forceful and surprisingly deep. "You have twice earned the right to guard me." He extended his arm forward, to his right. "This is your place now," pointing to a location about a foot to his right.

It took me a moment to assimilate the real change in status. Though I didn't hear an audible sound of surprise from those left in the room, I might as well have. Only the most privileged within the Palace came within feet of the Emperor. Here I was, a seventeen year-old foreigner standing near the most powerful person in the world.

I'd just taken my place when Qi Tai entered the hall. He rapidly made his way to the front, looking at the open spaces where guards had been previously. Approaching the Emperor, he bowed to Wi Cheng, his eye attracted to the cheek, red with blood. It was then he saw me. Whatever he was going to say at first, he changed his mind. I wasn't given the position. As the Emperor said, I'd earned it.

"We are hunting down the intruder now. How he got through our defenses, I can only guess," he said, staring at me coldly.

"The Emperor's guard saved my life," Wi Cheng informed Qi Tai, calmly returning the look of disbelief on Minister's face. "Using this," lifting the weapon. "That was after he defeated a dozen of the Imperial guards. All who would have been dead had it not been for the body armor they wore. He sustained minimal damage."

Whatever Qi Tai had expected to encounter upon entering the room did not match what he heard.

"It is a privilege to serve the Imperial family," the Minister of War said, the tenor of his voice implying what he didn't say directly. Whatever he wanted me for, this wasn't the time or place to pick the fight.

"His sister," said the Emperor. "Where is she now?"

"She is supporting the kitchen staff that serves the Empress," said Qi Tai, a corner of his whip thin lips curling in a way meant to put me at ease. It failed. The way he said "serves" bordered on a slur. "She won't be disciplined unless she errs." I got the distinct impression it was exactly what he expected would happen, in spite of my heroic display.

"Qi Tai, let us speak in private," said Wi Cheng. He walked to the far end of the room, past the instrumentalists who had left sometime during our conversation. They began speaking in low voices. The older man pointed to the window, no doubt retelling the arrow incident. If I were him, I'd be seriously questioning the Minister of War about the spy network he supposedly had set up. It had failed today, that was for sure.

"You do not ask to see your father?" the Emperor inquired quietly, turning to me. His voice was informal, youthful even. It cracked on the last word. The question itself shouldn't have surprised me. His own dad must be long dead or else he wouldn't be on the stand. It was easy to envy the Emperor's ability to make decisions on his own, without oversight, his authority and control unrivaled.

"You told me he will be well treated," I responded. A week sleeping in crap wouldn't go half the way to making up for the mess he made of our childhood. "I expect he will be."

The Emperor nodded once, eyeing me inscrutably. Had he wanted another answer?

The Emperor pulled back when the older men returned.

"I understand that your protection skills are worthy enough to extend their lives for another day." Qi Tai said as he spun a large ruby ring around his bony finger. Yeah, and with the added benefit of an unnamed, invisible assassin suddenly roaming the Palace.

The Emperor requested I be shown the guards unit, using his former tone of voice. "On the return, let him see his sister."

"Emperor, may I request that our guest come visit me during his...stay?" asked Qi Tai.

The Emperor nodded his agreement, implicitly dismissing me. Before I was going to leave, I asked who would protect the Emperor in my absence.

"They will," Qi Tai answered, motioning forth five of the men who had returned from the chase. Qi Tai didn't mention catching an intruder, and I wondered what had become of the invisible assassin. Another fight down, and the day was young.

"I'm ready," I told Qi Tai, bowing to tell him to lead the way. With a show of irritation, he turned and I followed.

CHAPTER 9

The five guards on the Emperor's day unit all looked within a year or two of my age. At the front of the line stood a guard nearly as tall as me, but not as stocky. His eyes were wary, his body distrustfully distant. He bowed, not as low as perhaps he should have, given my superior role in the group. The others followed, each with moderate bows.

Qi Tai grunted and left, his duty over. I felt his antagonism as he walked away, guessing his thoughts. He'd love nothing more than this group of fighters to destroy me. Once he left, I took over.

"What is your name?" I asked the first guard.

"Wu," he replied stiffly.

His manner didn't come as a complete surprise. I'd ousted his leader. He probably heard of my display in front of the Emperor. I was sure news traveled as fast as an arrow around this group of tight-knit warriors. If Wu was second in command, I expected he was itching to have it out with me to take my place as I took Xing's, the opportunity to be next to the Emperor an enticing possibility.

"Let us begin," I said formally, asking him to tell me the routine. He did so grudgingly, with plenty of stalls and silences. It was disrespectful and set bad precedence for the others.

I asked him about the process of switching our unit to the night shift. The moment he started speaking, I lashed out at him. With my hand palm up, fingers close together, I dove them into his throat. The hours of practicing punching with herb bags had given the block of bone and skin the power to penetrate wood. Done with enough force, the move could shatter the Adams apple, cutting off his sound forever. A little harder, the connective tissue and bone from the spine to the skull would sever, reducing him to a quadriplegic.

The act dropped him to his knees, his hands flying to his neck. He choked, unable to break, his body writhing in pain. The four other guards instinctively charged, then stopped. Insubordination meant death.

Wu writhed on the floor, hands at his throat. His eyes were wide with terror and fury. He knew.

I towered above him, no emotion in my voice.

"I could have taken your voice. Broken your body. I have not, as you are well aware. The sound will return. When it does, use it to answer my questions with respect. The next time, you won't have the option."

I turned to the other guards, my distaste for them equaling theirs for me. Together, we waited as Wu regained his composure, massaging his neck. He propped himself on one arm, choking out a cough. He stood before me, inching down a bow, every centimeter more humiliating and degrading than the next. When our eyes met again, I asked him if this incident needed to be mentioned to the Emperor.

A brief jerk of his head was his reply. I cocked an eyebrow.

"No," he said, bowing low again. Every part of his body wanted to fight me. I could feel his hate and repulsion emanating like a force of heat from a stove. Further conversation was forestalled. The door to the Emperor's rooms opened and a servant entered, requesting me.

Wu moved to his station, watching me for the command. I turned to the others, who subsequently bent low.

"I'm leaving you to return to my place by the side of the Emperor," unsure if they were going to follow me or not. The Emperor had told me I could visit my sister and I wanted to have some alone time with her. "On the Emperor's instructions, I'm to visit the servants' area where the food is made for the Empress." I disliked informing Wu of my movements, but it couldn't be helped. I'd get lost if I attempted to wander around on my own. "Where is it? The straightest route," I reminded him.

He grimaced, but told me what I wanted to know. "Three rights and a left on the black path," he told me quickly and without emotion. "Behind the yellow building with a pink tiled roof. It is female only. You will not be allowed inside. Stop at the doorway or you will be reported."

The servant left me and I took off, wondering why he included that last part. I'd have expected him to tell me the opposite so I'd screw up and get thrown out.

The answer was the Warrior's Code. Warriors don't lie. He wasn't going to break his honor for me, a lowly nothing. Still, I couldn't quite accept the fact he was being an upright guy.

I ran down the black path, wanting to arrive and have time to talk. I slowed my pace as I came upon the doorway to the yellow building with a pink tiled roof. The theme with the Empress seemed to be pink. This too, hadn't changed in a thousand years.

The door was shut, and I was unsure what to do. If I couldn't go in, how was I going to see her? The windows were covered with a silken mesh, too soft for rice paper. I touched it lightly, feeling the soft material. I imagined the breeze drifting in while leaving the chill outside. It was also nearly sheer. I pressed my nose against it, attempting to see through. A bird started chirping from somewhere inside the room, and I ignored it, leaning in.

As I did, my nose met with a warm body on the other side, pressing with equal strength against me, searching, wondering what was on the outside. Before I could register surprise, our noses had touched, my lips feeling the warm air of a woman's breath from the inside.

"Oh!" she said, pulling back, her own surprise catching her off guard. The pumping of my heart had nothing to do with the quick sprint from the guard house. I'd had an encounter with the brown-eyed girl.

The commotion of unintelligible twitters from within the room told me I was the unexpected stranger, and the door would surely be locked.

"On the Emperor's orders, I'm here to see my sister. Mia." The sounds within quieted as they listened. Death would fall upon a person who used the Emperor's name in vain.

The door opened a crack, and the face of a short, wizened old woman appeared.

"She is not here," she told me. "She is…occupied," telling me it will be some time before she returns. The look of confusion on my face registered with the woman. "She is not used to the…ah…clothing and shoes," offered the old woman.

She lifted the skirt of her dress, revealing high-heeled sandals, the type that cut the toes in the wrong places. I grimaced. "And this," she explained further, running her hands along her own dress. It looked more like a straitjacket than an outfit. The contraption was the complete opposite of my comfortable, loose-fitting uniform. On second thought, probably better I not see her now. A few hours in that and she'd be a miserable human being.

I asked the woman to tell her I stopped by, and she agreed. "Is she being treated well?" I asked quietly. I looked over her head, seeing the other women moving about the room.

Her lined faced cracked like a prune as her eyes creased in a humored smile. "She doesn't like it," she said confidentially. "But she's trying." That was Mia. I nodded, understanding completely. I glanced over the elderly woman's head, hoping to catch a glance of the incredible body that went along with the lips I'd nearly touched.

"Be gone with you," she said curtly, knowing exactly what I was doing. She shut the door in my face. I heard a low, laughing sound behind me. It was Wi Cheng. My face warmed at the observation.

"I'm going to the Emperor's court," he informed me. He bowed his head slightly to the right. "Let us go together."

CHAPTER 10

In the mornings, the Emperor settled disputes among Imperial Ministers, picked new advisors for the dozens of ministries that comprised the governmental structure, and dealt with other, unexpected situations.

"Like yours," Wi Cheng said, the sound of a smile in his voice. I cast a sideways glance at him. His eyes were vividly aware of the surroundings, constantly sweeping in front of us and from side to side. A learned attribute of a warrior that over time becomes second nature.

"You didn't expect me?" I asked, remembering what the archivist told me in prison. Qi Tai could have told others about the white man coming. The question caused Wi Cheng to observe me as we walked, his grey eyes seeing far more than they should.

"Our teachings tell us that others exist all around us, in this world and in the next." His right eyebrow rose in an inquisitive arch, interested in my reaction. I gave none. "I expect you know that."

His gait matched my long stride, his joints showing none of the age evident on his face. Another trait of a master. His joints were limber, the skin on his arms and face tight, the long hours with bags of herbs banging against his body parts keeping him strong and toned. A muscle rippled under his top, the V-neck of the shirt unable to hide his pectorals. It occurred to me he was more than capable of dodging the spear in the hall, had he seen it.

"Was the spear staged? Another test to see what I would do?"

Wi Cheng nodded his approval at the question. "What good is it for me to defend myself, when it was not I who the spear wanted?" He was talking about fate, like he would have let it nail him in the side of the head if his time was up. But since I was there, his fate wasn't to die that morning. Instead of enthusiastically jumping up and down about living another hour in this life, he walked on, as though nothing out of the ordinary had happened.

"And if I were to have died saving your life?" I'd never saved another's life before, and I was feeling rather like a hero. His nonchalant attitude took away some of the pride from my victory. I hoped he wasn't going to tell me that was my fate and all. I'd like to think I had had some control in my destiny.

"He who lays down his life for another is rewarded. In this life or another." That was encouraging.

He said nothing more about the earlier incident, and I knew a major display of appreciation wasn't forthcoming. It was a part of my job now.

Wi Cheng told me that today lunch was light, nothing more than tea and rice cakes in private quarters. He'd been informed the Emperor was finished and we were to join him in the Ministry of Justice, where the Emperor meets with occupants of the palace and the Forbidden City. The commoners came with complaints, and the Emperor handed out punishments, including sentencing servants to jail for minor misdeeds.

Wi Cheng left me at the steps of the building, stepping inside long enough to bow to the Emperor and Qi Tai, who stood to his left. I said goodbye, promising to see him when I was off duty.

I unobtrusively greeted the two men, taking my place to the right of the Emperor. In some ways, it was as gratifying as being the Emperor myself. The ministers acted like defenders and prosecutors, representing commoners in their complaints. When a third party opinion was required, the Emperor sent for a Minister who had experience in a particular area, like the Minister of Agriculture when a farmer wanted to change his crops and needed permission. The poor guy had traveled days to get the Palace and waited a month for admission. He'd not had the benefit of a shower before seeing the Emperor, and cast a smell so strong in the large room I was sure the area would need fumigation.

The Emperor gave no notice to the toxic effect of the man, though I had to practice a form of deep breathing to keep from hurling. The man's hat was down low on his face, then removed as he bowed before the Emperor and made his request. Emperor Jianwen listened politely and sincerely to every word. I was impressed. My inclination would have been to dismiss the guy with a simple yes or no and let him get back to his field.

The man's eyes were dark, evidence of no sleep and probably little food. His arms were bone thin but strong looking. He had the weary countenance of oppression, a person who worked hard but with little hope of change. I wondered why he had come this long way if he had such little hope. I overheard Qi Tai advise the Emperor to reject the man and hear the next case; words the farmer also overhead. He shook his head, though he kept his eyes down. I could nearly see the lifeblood go out of him and on to the floor. It was not his place to plead or influence the Emperor.

The Emperor didn't see the farmer, for he was looking up at the roofline of the hall, thinking. I noticed this was what he did when he was making a decision. He looked up and side to side, as though searching for guidance from the spirits.

"Call for the Minister of Agriculture," the Emperor said, the command sending a courier scurrying. It wasn't long before the Minister appeared, and proceeded to grill the farmer about his land, the type of soil, the weather patterns and what he intended to do with the crop once it was harvested. The farmer answered every question, and even offered that if he were to produce his expected yield, he would give the Emperor's storehouse fifty percent.

The Minister looked at the Emperor for approval, and to the farmer's extreme disappointment, Emperor Jianwen shook his head no.

"Emperor..." began the Minister of Agriculture, but the teen raised his hand.

"Fifty percent is not the right amount." The farmer's eyes lowered with sadness. His journey had been in vain. "You must keep more to feed your family in case of a flood or draught. You shall be allowed to farm the crop you desire, but instead of tithing fifty percent, you may keep eighty and tithe ten to your community store house and ten to the Imperial storehouse. All China will benefit from your good work. Go in peace."

From the look of exhilaration on the dirty farmer's face, I thought he was going to erupt with joy. Instead, he started bowing over and over in gratitude, nearly weeping his thanks. Qi Tai looked like he was going to vomit, while the Minister of Agriculture nodded his head, agreeing with the wisdom of the young ruler. This kid was smart. The farmer would return, loyal to the Emperor, telling all of what happened.

Qi Tai was livid. "Do you realize what this will mean?" he said in an undertone only I could hear as the farmer left the room. "You will have hundreds of others coming to ask for changes."

Emperor Jianwen was unmoved. "Let them. The Minister of Agriculture can attend to their requests. It is good for the farmer. Good for the country. Next."

The incident was forgotten when the next man was brought forth in chains. He was accused of stealing, the evidence, a piece of metal from the Forbidden City given, and three merchants providing different accounts of the thefts. The man admitted his guilt, his countenance different from the criminals I'd seen offer a guilty plea. This man didn't claim he committed the act out of a necessity, such as feeding his children, nor did he deny stealing. He just said a simple "yes," when asked if he stole.

Qi Tai recommended death, and once again, the Emperor disagreed.

"His right hand only," Emperor Jianwen said, leading forward, pointing to the man's hands. "Use better judgment with the one that will remain."

It was late afternoon when the doors were closed on those still desiring to see the ruler. They were returned to the Forbidden City, the process starting all over again tomorrow. As the sun began to set, the ministers departed, including Qi Tai and the Emperor, all preparing for dinner.

I followed the Emperor back to his own Palace, an enormous building of white marble with a yellow tile roof, a color I now associated with the Emperor only. Inspecting the massive hall helped me pass the time. The three-story building had stone carvings on the floors and walls that were so intricate, I had to squint to see the pattern below my feet. White was the dominant color, the clear, nearly translucent walls were symbols of heavenly purity, so said the inscriptions. Emperors were considered gods, directly descended from above.

Inside the Emperor's Palace, paintings of the Emperor fighting, winning battles, slaying dragons, riding beasts, all attested to his prowess. Gods apparently had no issue with killing man and immortal beings alike. There were other murals capturing the benevolent side of the ruler, extending his hand to peasant children, offering an apple to a girl in black, and her long black hair poking out from under a hat. The tips of the rice in the field glistened with gold, shying away from the Emperor's presence, the very grass subservient to his greatness.

The last image was pure fantasy. Commoners weren't allowed to even look at that Emperor without his approval. All had to bow, on their knees, as Mia and I had done. There were only three eunuchs who could look directly at the Emperor within his quarters, and could only do so in order to wait on him. They were chosen at birth, separated from other children, and blessed with an anointing ceremony that allowed each to touch the Emperor without soiling his revered presence. The maids in the Palace were considered one step below heavenly beings. Like angels in waiting, I heard the sounds of movement, floating in and out, but saw no one. I asked Wu about it, and he flatly told me a visible servant was a dead servant.

As I shuffled from foot to foot outside the Emperor's private rooms, tea was served to myself and the guards. It was a dark, thick liquid, crammed with sweet and bitter flavors. It was the strongest caffeinated drink I'd ever had, for my senses went on overload and I got a headache. Falling asleep from boredom was impossible. I'd be lucky if I got to bed before three in the morning.

It made me think of Mia. I wondered in what capacity she served the Empress, herself enshrined in her own grand palace of pink marble. Mia was fantastic, but an angel she was not.

I heard movements from within the gold and silver inlaid doors, a commotion of rustling, the commands and whispers of servants given to one another, distinct, but not clear enough for me to make out the words. A chime alerted me to the Emperor's imminent presence, and I stood straight, making eye contact with my team, interspersed down the hall. Fans from above whirled slowly, causing the sheer silk stretched above us to sway slightly. When Emperor Jianwen emerged, a ringing of bells announced his arrival, causing a momentary lull in activity outside. His very presence was an honor from above, a living deity walking this earth with his small, pointy-toed, golden-threaded slippers.

Shoes aside, his outfit was remarkable. His jacket stretched two sizes larger than his own shoulders, creating a block figure for someone I knew to be smaller. Silver and gold threading created patterns of dragons, the contrast on the off-white robe more vibrant than a high definition screen. The high collar was fastened with gems, the rubies and emeralds large, the size of dimes. The colors matched his hat, a round, flat-topped design with jewels attached with more golden thread. From his side, a short sword hung, the detailed inscriptions on the blade so fine, it looked like it had been crafted from needlepoint.

He didn't look at me as he walked past. I followed behind, two paces, as custom dictated. The other guards preceded us to the dining area, ensuring the safety of the Emperor. He walked on the white marble path, I on the gravel, to the right. Marble was for the earthly God, pebbles and gravel served us, the mere mortals.

The paths of the Empress and Emperor met, the white and pink paths lining up, parallel. Whereas the Emperor was by himself, the Empress had one female behind and beside her. *The* girl. She stared straight ahead, two steps behind the Empress, walking on the gravel to the left of Empress. A glimpse captured her brilliant blue silk outfit, covering her from neck to ankle. I had no opportunity to look further, as the four of us walked silently towards a building I'd not yet been in.

I kept my eyes steady as I passed through the entrance to the largest room I'd ever seen. The ceilings were three stories high, but instead of an upper section for spectators, this room featured balconies with drapes. The front of the rectangular room held two long tables set on a gold platform. At one table sat the Emperor, at the other, his Empress. Down from each were a chosen few, Qi Tai and the General were to the Emperor's left, though spaced down from him, far enough to distinguish rank, but close enough for him to talk to if he so desired. The Empress and attendant were joined by the old woman who I had spoken with at the building where I'd expected to find Mia. While the older lady looked at no one other than the Empress, the beautiful girl in blue looked up once in a while, though her eyes flicked from mine without the slightest bit of recognition. She was pretending to look through me, not at me. Fair enough. I liked a girl who was hard to get.

The room was set for a banquet, laden with enough food to feed hundreds. Below the raised pedestal were the Ministers if I interpreted the robes and sashes correctly, then other members of the Imperial family, or special individuals that rated high enough to eat in the presence of the Emperor. The commotion of the room accelerated as the final participants in the meal sat down.

Ice carvings were brought in, unicorns, dragons and Buddhas with symbols of love and prosperity. Servants, dressed in pale green, carried the massive structures, and I took no notice of the dozens of men until I saw small blades hanging from their belts.

It couldn't be. Carvers? *All* of them?

More carvings were placed in the center of each table, several dozen by the count. When placing the ice blocks down, great care was taken setting flowers, fruits and nuts in and around the centerpieces.

Eunuchs dressed in white glided in the room, a single line separating into three, moving effortlessly down the aisles, pouring the cups for those seated.

The room was in a constant state of commotion. Watching those coming to and from the room to serve the Emperor was fascinating, though draining. Any one of these individuals could access the Emperor, sending a shot through the air, a dart, throw a knife, pull a bow back and let an arrow fly, or poison the food.

I began looking at each dish that was presented to the Emperor. He would taste it, nod his head if he approved, and it would be served to the Empress. Dishes he didn't like were immediately removed. Those in the general assembly didn't eat the dishes served to the rulers. Neither their food nor their lives mattered to me. The Emperor's did.

Wu drew near, but I ignored his approach. He assured me that the spears wouldn't get through today.

"It's not the spears I'm worried about right now," I told him.

"The food tasters will die first," Wu said, standing beside me.

"Poison?" I guessed.

He nodded, suggesting the Palace had more than its share of servants willing to eat the food even if dying was the consequence. "One goes straight to heaven, dying in the place of the Emperor." He paused, then jerked his head to an area behind the Emperor and Empress, implying the food tasters were around the corner. "That's what your sister is doing now."

"Qi Tai said she was serving the Empress, not put in the line to eat poison," I muttered, unhappy with the news. Wu evidently expected me to become upset with the notion she was at risk but I kept in check. Partially because whatever Mia put her mind to doing, she mastered. And it came to food, she had one up on the world. She could even tell the difference between types of bottled water in a blind taste test, always selected the most expensive water kind saying it was 'the purest tasting.' More importantly, I wasn't going to let his comments get to me.

I affected disinterest when he gave me details about checking for the right herbs, flavors and the easiest of offenses, dirt in the food. When this failed to get a rise, he told me what would happen for minor infractions. Dirt on the shoes: twelve lashings with a bamboo stick. Walking on the marble reserved for the Emperor: pounding rocks for a week. It was more than I needed to know.

My lack of response disappointed him, for he bowed, and ignored me the rest of the evening. When the Emperor finished his meal, a final round of tea was served and the Emperor and his Empress rose from their seats, preparing to leave. I'd been so concerned with the Emperor, I'd focused on him exclusively, not his counterpart.

As she and her attendants walked in front of me, I had my first real opportunity to regard the Empress. Even though she was diminutive, her profile was regal. She walked stiffly, her tall, wedged shoes requiring slow, methodical motions, her hands clasped together at the waist. Like the Emperor, she was draped in precious jewels, large, ruby earrings hanging from her ears, a matching row across her forehead, affixed to the crown she wore that was mounted on a small, delicate hat. Her eyes were deep-set, though small, matching her petite frame. Her lips were painted red and set in a flat line. She had little color on her cheeks, though her eyes were heavily made-up, like an actress getting ready for the stage. The Empress's dress was covered with dark pearls. She was flat chested, which was no surprise, since she looked younger than the Emperor.

The girl in blue, the one who's lips had almost touched mine, who smelled like flowers and had the hypnotic voice, kept her eyes fixed on the back of the Empress's head. She was taller than the Empress, but shorter than Mia. For me, she was the perfect height.

I wanted to keep looking as she passed by, but didn't. I felt another set of eyes on me.

To my right, I caught Wu's look. It was black and deadly.

"Don't," he mouthed. Not much had changed in hundreds of years, I mused. So, he had eyes for the girl? Or something more? May the best fighter win.

The Emperor retired to his own room, the sound of his personal hand servants scuttling about within. Behind the golden doors, inlaid with silver, gold and adorned with precious stones, I imagined the layers upon layers of clothing being removed.

Silence came upon the inner room and I stood at the ready. The door cracked open and the Emperor's voice was within, low and confidential.

"Cage. Closer."

I neared the crack in the door, and Wu steeled his eyes away by turning his back.

"Well done." It was all the Emperor said before the door shut from the other side. I never saw his face, nor that of the servant. Even so, the comment gratified me. It had been a good day. A good first day. With a bit of guilt, I realized I'd not even talked to the Emperor of leaving, or finding my Dad. I'd have to rectify that tomorrow.

The nighttime bodyguard came and replaced me, his name was not offered and I didn't ask. Something about the process made me think the Palace guards believed it was safer, more secure, for us not to know one another. So be it.

Wu and I walked to the guard station, to the room I'd been in with the tailor. Now I took another look around, first checking the dresser. The backpack and orb remained in the chest, along with my clothes, as I knew they would be. Stealing was against the code of honor. It meant disgrace, and like nearly everything else, death.

I was put in one corner of a large, shared sleeping area where nearly sheer curtains separated individual sleeping mats. A wash basin, and chest press for clothes were the only luxuries used for personal items. The communal bathing area was down the hall, featuring running water from tanks perched overhead and underground sewage.

"Dinner is served in the next room," Wu said, gesturing through the open door, across the hallway. "Follow me," he suggested, without elaboration. Getting information from this guy was getting on my nerves. I'll figure it out soon enough, I thought, sitting on the chair. If that's all I had to deal with, a few days of this was going to be a piece of cake. I got to roam with the Emperor, eat great food, and experience the benefits of being close to power.

The Ministers eyed me with concern, as though they couldn't quite understand how a foreigner had been given a position of such importance. They remained silent as we walked by, bowing respectively whenever I was near. Authority wasn't questioned in this time period. It was nice to have adult men defer to me, the position of authority outweighing the age difference.

It also made me realize just how much I missed out on life not having a powerful or illustrious father. I would never be like the other kids at school, whose dads worked as bank vice presidents or as the chairmen of the board, drove nice cars to school and went to Mexico during the winter and Lake Tahoe during the summer. My Dad was a low-paid, highly respected intellectual academic. I'd suggested he consider giving consulting a try, knowing one of my friend's dads worked in finance at a software company during the day and free-lanced on the side. "You'd make money," I'd told him, hoping to get a new car by the time prom came around.

"Unethical," he'd replied, without giving my suggestion the simple courtesy of consideration. It wasn't unethical if he didn't have a non-compete agreement, my friend's dad had told me, shaking his head. He didn't have to say what I was thinking. My dad was a mealy-mouthed academic with no backbone or ambition.

Once again, my thoughts toward him turned spiteful.

"He's never going to change," I muttered to myself out loud, my back to the entrance of the room.

"What's that?" said Qi Tai in a half-whisper. He'd slipped back in the room as I'd been looking at the ground. It caught me off guard. The sudden, silent appearance could have been deadly.

I rose to my feet and bowed. "May I provide you assistance, Minister?"

"After you eat, come to the Ministry of History," he said, the lips of his mouth set in a straight line. His black eyes gave away nothing. "We'll be waiting for you."

I had no idea where it was, but would figure it out. I bowed low, accepting the request. When I looked up, he was gone.

CHAPTER 11

I crossed into the small, rectangular room where Wu and the others sat on the floor. In the center, a low, wooden table held bowls of soup and cups of dark, green tea. A large black pot was in the corner of the room, kept warm over red coals held in a metal basin.

Wu rose, and the others followed in unison. He gestured for me to take a seat at the end of the table. "You are the leader," said Wu. "You drink first."

This may be true, that I was to have the first drink, although from my experience in modern day China, that wasn't the case. The leader raised his glass, and everyone drank at once.

Something in his tone and his look made my stomach roil. Wu's face was wide and thick, his eyes penetrating, the wary glint still present, and his cheeks were slightly flushed. I noticed that everyone's cups were steaming from the hot liquid. Except mine.

"Since we are to be as one, we shall drink as one," I said.

Wu nodded approvingly. He was the spokesperson for the others, who in turn, bowed in acceptance.

When I stood up, Wu's head movement stopped, the others were frozen.

I retrieved the pot of tea and set the lid on the table. I poured my entire cup back into the pot, then took the remaining cups on the table and repeated the act. When I was done, I replaced the lid, swung the pot a few times, and then watched the faces of each man as I served the tea.

Each one stared, motionless. It was as I thought.

Then I raised my cup, gesturing the group to do the same. Eyes glanced around the room, uncertain. Slowly, hands gripped the squat mugs, their burden of truth pushing against the desire to lift the cup to their lips.

At that moment, a female servant teetered in the room. Her presence broke the tension as several guards looked up.

I was furious. What timing. Nothing could be done until she'd gone. I put my cup back down on the table and waited, the others following my lead.

The girl walked painfully slowly, making her way awkwardly to the other end of the table, her back towards me. I was at knee level, and I wasn't going to be caught staring at her, though she struck me as uncommonly tall. As she bent down to place a bowl of food on the table, one of the men poked her in the leg.

She retracted just enough to throw off her balance. The bowl went forward, straight towards Wu. He launched backwards off his feet, not quite achieving a back flip. He landed on one leg, the full weight of his body careening towards the fire pit, face first.

I hurled my ceramic teacup toward the rim of the coal pit. The hit instantly tilted the edge of the basin away from Wu's face and back into the wall behind it, breaking straight through the divider.

The action saved Wu's face, but it lit the room on fire. In a moment, the white, rice paper walls took flame. I didn't wait for Wu to ask for help. I grabbed his hand and jerked him up, American style. I yelled at the men to move the table, lift the mat and douse out the fire.

"Use the tea," shouted the servant girl, her voice distinctly non-oriental.

"No!" yelled Wu, shoving her with enough force to knock her through another wall of rice paper, which landed her in the hallway with a thud. When I heard her yelp of anger, I realized that only one girl I knew could yell like that. Under the white and grey kimono, on top of the three-inch sandals, hidden behind a huge, black wig and thick, ornamental make-up, was my sister.

"The cloth," I yelled at the men. "Get it now!"

Three guards darted in to the sleeping quarters as Wu and another guard did their best to drape the floor mat over the enormous wall of fire. Knowing it would spread to the entire building, I crashed my foot into the adjoining walls. Without a point for the fire to jump, it would stop spreading.

When Wu saw what I was doing, he worked on the other wall, and we were able to dismantle the room in seconds. Flames were still licking the ceiling when the three guards returned with wet cloth, which they draped over the floor and what was left of the structures.

"If that idiot hadn't tried to grab me, none of this would have happened," said Mia, glaring at the guard who had pricked her knee.

The guard avoided her gaze, as well as Wu's and mine.

Mia saw the others bowing to me, in a line, and knew immediately what it meant. "Nice," she said, her flattery pronounced, until she grimaced as she looked down at her dress which was covered with stains and torn in several spots.

"Well?" she said, placing her hands on her hips. "What are you going to do to him?"

The guard bowed towards her, mumbling an apology. She glared. It didn't satisfy her.

"I can't," I said in English, assuming none of the others spoke the language. "It's not appropriate."

"Are you kidding me?" she yelled. "After what he did?"

"He was only making a pass at you," I said. "Could you blame him?"

I knew that her anger wasn't about to be tamed by a little flattery. I reminded her she was a servant and these were men, let alone Imperial Guards. She had no rights or reason for recourse.

"I can't believe this. You're taking their side." She'd never been this angry with me. Now, more than ever, I needed her support, but lacked the time or patience to tell her exactly why.

"You don't understand," I said, exasperated. "If I do one thing wrong, you and Dad are dead."

I could say no more. The sound of hurried footsteps cut short our dialogue.

"What is going on here?" demanded Qi Tai, standing at the doorway. "I've been waiting at the Ministry of History and now…this?" A dozen men stood behind him, ready to do his bidding. He assessed the pot on the floor, the cups, and the fire. "What have you done?" he said to me.

"He saved the compound from burning," interjected Wu, before I could speak. He'd silently come beside me, now bowing before the Minister of War. Qi Tai looked at him with disbelief.

"Was she at fault?" Qi Tai demanded, pointing to Mia. Wu glanced at my sister. "Well?" Qi Tai said, looking directly at Wu.

"No, she did nothing."

"Then tell me what happened," Qi Tai demanded.

"The pot of coals fell over, igniting the walls," Wu said. "Cage acted quickly, putting out the flames."

As he spoke, the other guards lined beside him, two on each side, creating a physical barrier between the Minister of War and me and Mia. The message was clear. Qi Tai would have to go through them to get to us. The guard knew I had saved his life, and the lives of the others, and I had not betrayed their secret.

Qi Tai's face was flush with rage. He was at an impasse. "Wu, you understand what this means?"

Wu somberly nodded. "We follow Cage Fleenaah," he said.

Qi Tai cursed profusely under his breath. He looked at me. "Do not come to the Ministry tonight. Another time...perhaps." Then he shot me another look of loathing, and turned on his heels. The contingent obediently departed, leaving us alone.

As a unit, the five turned and faced me. Wu bowed low, and said, "You have earned the privilege to be our leader. We follow you now."

I searched the faces of the five. They were like me. Grown men on the inside, teenagers on the outside, put in the precarious position of guarding the most important person alive.

"Let's clean this up," I suggested.

Wu bowed slightly. Deferentially. "I'll get the servants," he said, turning away.

While he was gone, I drew Mia to one side, urgently asking her questions about her safety.

"I'm a servant, a taster for the Empress," she said quietly, ripping her arm from my grip. "Forced to wear these heels and do whatever I'm told. I live in a cramped room with a hundred other girls my age. The first night I had to share a bed with a stinking, snoring girl who cleans toilets. What's going to happen next? When are we going to get out of here?"

Quickly, I recapped the Emperor's decision. "I have to serve the Emperor until he determines we're safe to leave." Before I could tell her about the prophecy from the archivist, Wu returned.

"Get going," I encouraged Mia. Wu's eyes followed my sister out of the room, then reverted to meet my own.

"We can eat with the other Palace guards," said Wu, motioning to follow him. Another guard groaned. Wu laughed. "It's not as good as our food though."

The six of us walked through the main armory, across the open training ground and into the guard station. Dinner had already been served, though Wu directed a woman to bring what was left. Plain noodles, rice and broth, and a sweet, round deep fried fruit for dessert.

Dinner conversation was easy now that the group accepted me. I marveled at their age range, all between fifteen and eighteen, though most were big for their age.

"Does the Emperor like guards that are close to his own age?" I asked the group, directing the question to no one in particular.

"There is no one else," shrugged one guard who was second in line after Wu. His eyes were focused on his noodles, avoiding an unspoken truth.

I looked at Wu for understanding. "Safety," he said simply, as if that explained it all. When I didn't respond, he continued. "It's standard when a new Emperor comes in. Everyone else is put to death."

"What do you mean, everyone?"

"Everyone over a certain age. The brothers, sisters, aunts, uncles. Everyone. Especially the old guards. Those left behind can't be trusted. Only the Ministers stay. That's why they are old and grey. The rest of us are young."

"Even the children?"

Wu shook his head no. "No young ones related to the old Emperor remain in the Palace. Within the Forbidden City, yes. They are the children of those that work in the Palace itself."

I was confused. Why were Wu and these other boys were alive, if Jianwen had been in power only two years? The entire place should be filled with pre-pubescent girls and boys.

Wu explained that this last transition was unique, since it was within the same family, Grandfather to Grandson. Those within the Palace agreed with the decision. "It meant their lives." At that moment, he leaned forward, preventing anyone not at the table from hearing his words.

"But it's worse now. Jianwen's uncle wants to rule. He'll do anything to get inside the castle."

"Is this common knowledge?"

Wu looked at his second in command, made sure his eyes and ears were preoccupied with his companion, then uttered I needed to be cautious around General Li and Xing.

Wu might have thought the others weren't paying attention, but they were. This information about Xing had overstepped their comfort level, for all four at the table stopped talking and looked at their plates.

"Xing is General Li's son," the second in command offered, breaking the silence. Now everything was beginning to make sense. I had displaced the assassin.

Sleep didn't come easy, despite the cleanliness of the mat. I feared if I continued to do my job, the Emperor would never let me go.

"Wake up," I whispered to Wu, unconcerned it was the middle of the night. "What will happen after I've proved my innocence to the Emperor?"

Wu coughed softly. He remained quiet for a very long time, waiting, it seemed, to confirm others were asleep.

"Marco Polo was well treated," he said, avoiding my question.

"He came with something to trade. It was the reason he was let go." The only thing I had of value was the orb: time travel must be worth something. But if I gave it up, we could never get home. I also had modern fighting skills I could teach Wi Cheng. The idea had merit, but it also had risk. Only a master had the right to enhance a traditional form for his students. My knowledge could permanently influence martial arts, changing what I would have learned hundreds of years from now.

"I have nothing really," I acknowledged, frustrated.

"Yes, you do," Wu countered. My heart skipped a beat. Had he broken the honor code and looked in my chest? I concentrated on keeping my voice even when I asked him what he had in mind. "It's obvious to everyone. Your sister. She is already desired by several men, and has been requested as a wife. By whom, I do not know."

Mia, a bride? Concubine? At seventeen? Was her destiny to bear children, clean the laundry or work in the fields? The best case, she'd live in the Palace or the Forbidden City, the wife of a merchant, selling chicken eggs or clothes. She'd rather die.

CHAPTER 12

The following day we returned to the Imperial Courtroom for the affairs of the government. We arrived first, as was customary, the Emperor taking his time getting situated prior to signaling the great doors to open, admitting those who sought his counsel.

"How do you like your post?" he asked me, his voice low and monotone. He reached for a bowl made of pure gold, resting on the top of a golden pedestal. A servant darted forward to conduct the task, holding the lid as the Emperor took a handful of darkened, dead animals. Nodding to the servant, the lid was replaced and he extended his hand as he waited for my response. The treats looked like dead bugs, and I undiplomatically shook my head.

"Chocolate covered crickets," he said, popping two in his mouth. When he spoke, his head was bent, his back turned to the others, as though he were mumbling to himself. I took the hint, adjusting my own body as though I were assisting and protecting his back.

"It's interesting," I said in a half-whisper, answering his question.

His doubt showed on his face: his thin brows raised, one dropping, leaving the other in an inquisitive arch.

"In this country, the punishment for lying is death," he reminded me.

I looked at him, knowing he could have said it louder, initiating swift action. Clearly, it wasn't his intent. "Parts of it *are* interesting," I said, thinking of the swords, the fighting. The girl. "Others are quite dull," unable to refrain myself from glancing around.

"Dull is better than dead," he said flatly, without the slightest bit of humor. He had turned to me, his lips barely moving as he pronounced the words. He was taking a long time straightening out his sleeves in preparation for the session in front of him, gesturing to a servant in the far corner for tea. "You agree?"

I cleared my throat. "Definitely."

"Xing and the guards made it safe for me," the Emperor added. Did the Emperor really not suspect his former bodyguard? "It is unfortunate he is gone. The men respected his leadership."

"What becomes of Xing now?" I said, thinking death would be an easier route for the former Imperial Guard. I glanced around nervously, realizing I'd spoken out of turn. The Emperor didn't seem to care when none of the others looked on.

"He must prove himself worthy to serve me again."

Qi Tai now approached us, stopping two steps down and to the left of the ruler. He hovered over the ruler; a grey-garbed ghost, always in the Emperor's shadow.

Qi Tai escorted the Emperor as he attended official meetings, presiding over the endless stream of complaints. It had taken less than twenty-four hours to convince me that being the ruler of the largest, most impressive country in the world during the fifteenth century would suck.

When I had to use the bathroom, Wu took my place, moving back when I returned. Relief from boredom came during the noon break. We were led to a smaller food court. I assumed this meant an Imperial version of soup and sandwiches. Once again, I was wrong. Lunch meant a lavish meal followed by entertainment.

This time, the Empress joined her husband. The notion that two middle school kids were married struck me as just…wrong. I tried not to stare but couldn't help myself. Yet they were serious, stately, even glamorous, sitting in front of the room, observing the performance.

I subtly looked for the Empress' attendant, but was met with disappointment. On one side of the room were fifty or so ministers. Though their ornate outfits set the group apart, it was their haughty manner of talking and acting that concerned me. Eyebrows were permanently arched in an ever-present state of surprise and delight at themselves was combined with a sneer of disgust as they looked down their noses, usually at their food. When a servant came to offer more food or refill a cup of tea, the minister would quickly remove his hand, retreating from possibly touching the help. The servants looked as though they were being cursed at, scolded or dismissed, and not politely.

From within the group, a pecking order seemed to dictate who spoke when, and if the food was actually eaten. Those with long sashes did most of the speaking, and others with high hats spoke only when addressed. The entire scene reminded me of bedtime stories from the royal courts.

CHAMBERS

Qi Tai and the General were seated at the first table with the Emperor. Servants stood on top of the tables motionless, acting as living statues to replace the carvings from last night. Two people, dressed in reds and green, formed a tight circle, hands and feet joining so closely they formed the shape of an apple. Seven others were bent in different fruit shapes, complete with exotic plumes on their heads and feet. I couldn't tell if the performers were male or female; the costumes hid the evidence. Regardless, the Emperor and Empress ignored them: they'd seen it before.

I was still mesmerized and looking to notice even the slightest movement of eyes or a hand when a large dart from the upper right corner of the room swept down towards the Emperor. My heart jumped until I saw it was a trapeze artist, flying through the air above the tables. The acrobat held two wands, yellow and blue, that dipped and arched, moving in synchronized time. A second acrobat joined, and then a third: one with flames, another with sparklers.

My heart raced with stress from the possibilities of disaster. Four tapestries rotated off the walls, turning wide to allow jesters to tumble, bound and flip down the aisles. There was music everywhere, but I couldn't tell where it came from. I looked up and around, my eyelashes touching the tops of my eyelids. Yet throughout the entire extravaganza, the two teenage rulers sat as dead fish, eating their food, glancing periodically at one another. Neither ate very much, and the table was void of conversation. A servant approached the Empress, who leaned, whispering. Not long afterward, the attendant with the beautiful eyes appeared.

She came to the side of the Empress, bowing, listening. She remained standing off to the right. As far as I could tell, no other female was in the room.

As I observed the area, I discreetly observed her when I thought no one else was watching. The few times our glances met one another, she looked down, or straight through me. Her head never moved an inch, and I couldn't tell what she was thinking. She was so different from the Alexandria's of the modern world, where the eyelashes fluttered, the head tilted, or the body fidgeted. Those represented the body language I had learned that signaled the earliest ideas of sexual interest.

Suddenly, a magician mistakenly set the tail feathers of a parrot on fire. The Empress looked stricken as did her attendant. The Ministers kept talking, amused that the bird was aflame. No one bothered to douse it with tea or water before the bird attempted to take flight. If it reached the silk above, the entire ceiling could catch fire, falling on the group below. The bird careened in to the air, lurching this way and that, trying to flap the fire out.

Not again. I immediately yelled for Wu to take my place while I ran towards the nearest table and leapt…high into the air. The bird squawked as I neared it, veering right. With a one-handed cartwheel thrust, my body arched over a man in a skintight, yellow costume, bent in the shape of a banana. The bird dodged left then swooped low, avoiding me as it prepared to go straight up, reaching the safety of the upper rafters. I had one chance to get it before the first silk lit in flames.

"Push me!" I told the banana. I hoped his leg muscles were as strong as his stomach. He understood, bringing his hands and feet together, forming a tabletop. I jumped on the mostly flat surface, crouched then pushed at the same time as the acrobat. Our combined effort launched me up and into the path of the flaming bird. In its rage and fear, it swerved, trying to avoid capture. I arched back, reached my left hand as far out as it could go, grabbing the burning tail. Firm in my grasp, I clutched it to my chest, smothering the flames with my shirt.

The sound of shocked silence turned to scuffling as I heard Wu order the men to get out, as he and the other guards rushed in. I locked my elbows around the animal, bracing for the fall.

On the way down, my right shoulder connected with the edge of the tabletop, forcing it into my chest. Instead of resisting, I buckled my chest, forming a U around the bird, pulling my knees tight to my chest. I instantly remembered my fifth section training, when the masters had taken our group to the woods outside Beijing. We'd hiked to the top of a forest full of logs and boulders. We were told to roll down, using our jujitsu skills to avoid every obstacle.

"Go with the energy of the forest, not against it," one master told us, reminding us to be flexible, pliable and subtle. "One cannot win a direct hit with a tree."

No kidding. Though my legs were close to my body, I released the taut muscles at once, a split second before I hit the floor. Instead of rebounding against the stone, my side absorbed it, as I visualized water seeping on the ground.

The room was silent as I lay on the floor. Wu and the other guards ran towards me with a bucket of water, ready to throw it on me.

"It's out," I said, carefully easing myself up from the floor. The flying gymnasts, magicians and jesters were open-mouthed as I regained my posture. The bird was now calm in my arms, its beak closed, and its wings firm and mostly undamaged. I spotted the magician and walked towards him.

"This is yours," I said, outstretching my arms. The bird let out a terrified chirp, and I heard the laughter of a woman. I looked up. It was the Empress's attendant. She schooled her look immediately, though the merriment didn't leave her eyes. Even the Empress smiled, as she glanced at the Emperor.

Qi Tai had moved from his seat to the Emperor, leaning close to his ear. The Emperor's face turned stone cold. He nodded once at whatever Qi Tai had said.

"Twenty days in prison," Qi Tai announced, pointing at the magician.

The man with the bird looked crestfallen, but I heard an exhale of relief escape his lips. Had his trick set the room like an inferno…well, I was sure what that would have meant. Death, like everything else.

I walked back towards my place beside the Emperor, catching a quick look pass between him and the Empress. The Empress blinked once, returned to her tea and took a sip. Moments later, the Emperor stood up, ending the meal for all.

The rulers walked on their paths until they diverged, the attendant never turning my way as she followed silently behind her mistress. I started to turn right, towards the Ministry of Justice, then noticed the Emperor was not going in the same direction. He'd turned back to his Palace. I hurried to his side, and he said nothing. As I wasn't allowed to speak first, I couldn't ask about the change in schedule. It wasn't my place to know. I glanced behind me at Wu. He shook his head, though I suspected he knew and didn't want to tell me. When we arrived at the Emperor's door, he turned to me.

"I'm not feeling well," he said. "Find Qi Tai and tell him to cancel the afternoon session. I will be present at dinner. Afterwards you may visit Wi Cheng if you wish. Have Wu stand guard." He didn't wait for a response before he entered the door that was held open by a servant.

CHAMBERS

Wu had overhead the request, bowing to me when I turned around. The Emperor had given me a direct order, and I was bound to carry it out myself. I asked my second in command where the man might be found.

"He will most likely be in the back rooms of the Ministry of Defense," said Wu. "Beyond the Ministry of Justice." Did he know something I didn't? The more I observed, the less I believed things were as they appeared.

It didn't take me long to reach the bronze building with square pillars in the front, framing the doors with an arch, also of bronze. Guards stood on either side, and seeing my red uniform, I anticipated a bow. I took the steps two at a time, pausing for their acknowledgement. They barely moved their heads.

"Wait," one said, knocking on the door, announcing my presence. Receiving a curt acceptance, he stepped back and I moved in to Qi Tai's domain.

It was dark, the walls a deep red, the corners nearly black, the hanging lights giving the room a gothic feel. If the Emperor's room symbolized purity, this was the embodiment of evil.

"Qi Tai?" I called.

"Come," he said, his voice echoing from the darkness.

From out of the shadows, a servant walked to my left. His head was shaved, his hallowed cheeks pale and drawn. He peered up at me, his narrow shoulders bent and warped, making me wonder if his back had been lashed by a whip and had never truly healed. His voice rasped from heavy breathing, as he lifted his arm to show me the way.

I followed him through the room, thankful that he moved slowly so I could take in the surroundings. To my left was a large, flat, rectangular table, three times the size as the one we had at home for Ping-Pong. It was covered with a miniature landscape of a city, complete with the ridges and valleys, ponds, lakes, and the running river that coursed through town. In one corner was the Forbidden City. The Imperial Palace was perfectly replicated, right down to the calligraphy on the walls of the Ministry of Justice. I caught the sound of water, and noticed a trickle coming from the stream as it passed through the moats.

As I passed by the edge of the table, the servant put up a hand, gesturing me to wait. He slid open a panel door, then stepped aside for me to pass through.

"Go," Qi Tai said to him. I waited until I heard the door slide shut behind me, then walked towards the Minister of War. In my peripheral vision, I could see maps on three of the walls, highlighted with red dots and lines, interspersed with other colored figures. Rows of folded papers were kept on dark, wooden shelves that reached up to the ceiling. Qi Tai stood beside another large table, writing tools and ink littering the top.

I bowed stiffly, and gave him the Emperor's message. He tilted his head, rolling two balls around in his hand, studying me. Unable to leave without his dismissal, I waited. The seconds seemed like an eternity, as he reveled in making me wait on him. I tempered my rising anger, which was just the reaction he wanted. I forced a placid, bored look on my face.

"An impressive display of abilities today," he said, rolling the balls faster. A friend of mine had a set of Chinese rolling balls but could only move them around in circles, one direction then the other. Qi Tai's long, pale fingers seemed to barely touch the metal objects they moved effortlessly into figure eights.

I bowed.

"Your sister is proving herself a fast learner as well." The right side of his face twitched, and a wrinkle of his otherwise taut skin moving up his temple, a fissure of emotion across a rock face. Today he wore a black hat, silk and square, and a red sash tied on the side. His long braid hung to the right, draping down past his chest. "She memorizes quickly. Uncommonly so."

Mia was blessed with near perfect recall. Her Mandarin had always been better than mine and if she read anything once, it was stuck in her head forever. The only time she didn't get A's on her tests was when she got lazy and skipped over paragraphs.

"She is talented," I acknowledged. Anything I said to the man was dangerous.

"Hmmm…" Qi Tai moved the balls to his other hand, then back and forth, up and over his hands. "I wonder what else she could learn," tilting his head. An oppressive feeling came over my chest, his words a lasso, constricting me. His slur of the word *learn* could mean anything.

"If you have nothing more for me…" I began, purposefully not asking for his permission.

"Not quite," he said softly. "See there," he pointed towards the open area in the prison yard, the one used for punishments. "Your father has been moved. He was causing unusual issues with the other prisoners."

He must be boring prisoners to death with his incessant talking of volcanoes and their impact on society, I thought. Or, he was infuriating the prisoners by asking a question and then ignoring the answer. If the response didn't meet his expectations, he ceased to pay attention.

"He does have a difficult way with people," I replied, thinking of how Dad treated one of my math teachers. It wasn't as though Mrs. Sanchez was stupid. Her knowledge of algebra just tapped out at the eighth grade level, and she was angry and confused when I was using advanced equations Dad had taught me. When Dad saw she couldn't follow him, he pulled out his phone and started working. She was so angry she got up and stomped out of the room. I was transferred to another class, got an A, and had never been bothered by a math teacher again.

Qi Tai turned back to me. The perfectly shaped objects were spinning clockwise in his open left hand so fast that the dim light of the room was glancing off the sides.

"What do you think moves these objects? Force? Energy?" He raised two fingers on his right hand, his eyes locked with mine across the tops of the spheres. The balls slowed and stopped, then each started spinning again, this time, in the opposite direction of one another.

"Power is not always seen. It's experienced," I responded.

On the last word, he flung the balls at me and I ducked right, the palm of my hand crossing over my face, shielding and pushing the balls left. The moment I touched the metal, the spheres cracked in two, landing on the floor with a thud. The sliding door opened, the servant entered, picking up the four halves. Inside were small, clear, diamonds.

"Authority has its rewards…don't you think?" The servant held the four halves open to me, two in each palm, the glittering stones brilliant, even in the darkness of the room.

The center of my palm itched with suppressed desire. Each diamond was the size of my thumbnail. Just a few of these could buy a house, pay for college, or cover the cost of a great vacation around the world.

I felt his eyes on me, watching my emotions.

"I'm giving it to you," he said. The old man nudged closer to me, lifting his palms higher. I looked to his eyes, but they were lowered, avoiding mine. I had the uncomfortable feeling the man had been put in this position before. He knew the outcome. What happened after the gift had been taken.

I stepped back from the outstretched hands, bowing to Qi Tai, thanking him for his offer.

"I only want to return to my own land, Qi Tai, with my family. Until then, I serve the Emperor."

A thin, low laughter erupted from his lips. It was an empty sound, like a vapor pulling the life out of a room as it poisoned the air. "Yes, Cage. Remember that. You serve the Emperor."

I asked him where I'd find Wi Cheng and he told me. By the time I arrived at the doorway, my back was drenched with sweat, and it wasn't from the short run.

CHAPTER 13

Before I entered the Ministry of Weapons I took a deep breath to compose myself. I thought about Qi Tai's other comments about Mia. Was he inferring that he wanted her for himself, one of the men Wu had in mind that had asked for Mia's hand? The thought repulsed me.

I straightened my uniform and knocked, waiting until the door was opened. A little man wore a grey cap, his head bowed low. Realizing I wasn't the Emperor or a senior Minister, he cautiously raised his eyes, moving over my body an inch at a time until he reached my face. His eyes popped and his mouth dropped, the slight tan fading to a greenish white. Not a welcoming sign.

"Hou," he said, asking me to wait as he hurried off, leaving the door open just a crack. I stood, folding my hands, glancing around the austere building. The threshold lacked the golden lettering of other buildings, but was decorated with ornamental steel on the doorway that snaked down in the patterns associated with success, wealth, spirit, soul, strength, and cunning.

"Welcome," said Wi Cheng, opening the door wide. I glanced up from my observation, bowing stiffly.

"I've just been to see Qi Tai," I volunteered, also informing the Master I had the Emperor's permission to visit him this afternoon. "Wu is in my place," I added, just in case he thought it strange I'd left the Emperor's side.

"Wu is competent," he said, the remark neither a compliment nor criticism.

Wi Cheng offered no comment about Qi Tai. I assumed that this meant he was tolerated. Why didn't the Emperor get rid of him, I wondered, as I followed Wi Cheng through the entry way, arriving at the answer before my thought was finished. He'd been given to him, the legacy of his Grandfather. As one of the old guards, like Wi Cheng, Qi Tai was here to stay.

I'd expected to smell burning steel and hear the banging of hammers against metal, but the building was quiet. As we walked down the carpeted hallway, many of the doors were open, revealing men in white uniforms and white hats working on blades resting on their laps.

"We smelt the steel elsewhere," he explained, noticing my inquisitive stare. "The delicate work is done here." Wi Cheng stopped, putting his hand in the air for silence. We watched the slow etching process as an ancient man scratched away on the metal with a needle so tiny it looked invisible, thinner than a single human hair.

"Did you notice the bed behind the man?" he asked. I shook my head. I'd looked nowhere but at his hands, moving slowly across the steel. "They never leave," he said, explaining that the men were more valuable than the guards. "These men hold the secrets of a thousand years of fighting, keeping the knowledge of all the battles, all the swords from hundreds of years. They are the very masters who allow our armies to be victorious."

"The Emperor doesn't ever let them leave?" I asked, wondering if I was mistaken about Emperor Jianwen's intentions for my family. Wi Cheng reproved me for my judgmental comment.

"They were born into this life. It is all they have ever known." He drew his hands to his chest, a meaningful gesture of togetherness. "We are their family."

"How many people know where the swords are made?"

Wi Cheng didn't answer until we walked through a set of wooden doors opened by other servants who gave me the same blood-draining look of shock that I'd received upon arriving at the building.

"Sit," he said, retrieving a steaming cup of tea from a simmering kettle. The room was gracious, though not large and dark like Qi Tai's. Light shone from slats in the roof.

"Natural light is better for practicing," he said, watching me intently.

I accepted his cup of tea, resting my left hand on my left knee, the pose one used for meditation. It was possible he was asking me to describe the tie between light and knowledge, though I hardly expected to educate him on the basic philosophy of his art form.

"Of course," I said. "Knowledge is required for a lightness of being, practicing can be done anywhere, even in the darkness of night."

He nodded in agreement, the comment accepted. "If knowledge is light, young Cage, then tell me. What knowledge comes out of the dark, that is not dark itself?"

I took a sip of the tea. It was sweet, with a tang at the end, like a cayenne spice. "Someone who is seeking. A blind person lives in darkness but can still see."

CHAMBERS

The Minister nodded again. Did he know what the archivist told me? Did the archivist lie when he said he told the Minister of War, when in fact it was the Minister of Weapons? I distinctly remembered him saying he told no one except Qi Tai who threw him in jail, likely for the rest of his life.

I glanced around the room searching for an answer to my own question.

Then I saw it. The answer was all around me. The swords had more information than one could ever want. Sword making and Chinese culture went hand in hand, the precious metal inscribed with the most important records, the sacred words of the civilization. Just as the master sword makers took care to detail how to best use a sword for a circumstance, swords that remained intact through battles, leadership changes, or any major events received the information, just like a diary. Nanjing was one of the oldest cities in China, around for five thousand years, and Wi Cheng, the Master over this form of record keeping, and though on metal instead of parchment, would have information just as accurate, and just as telling, as the archivist.

A slow smile spread across Wi Cheng's face as he sat across from me. With both hands, he removed his hat and placed it on the ground beside me. Pressing his hands together, he used the traditional martial arts symbol a Master used to greet a Master. My mouth wanted to drop open and fall on the floor. Instead, it clamped shut. He was doing something I'd never seen before…and yet…seemed so…familiar. It was like waking from a dream that didn't make sense, then experiencing the same events in real life.

"It is good to see you again, Master. I barely recognized you this time."

The cup slipped out of my hand as I lost my grip.

"It is not for me to explain," he said, his voice conciliatory but firm. "The cycle has begun, and once again, you must be victorious." More cryptic talk from an older man, a wiser man, who knew more about my life…or rather, past lives…than a mystic looking in a crystal ball. "You need the secrets written on the swords," he continued, glancing up at the weapons around him, placing his hands on his knees. He took a deep breath, the air rolling from his belly to his chest, filling him with vigor, his eyes lighting with a challenge.

He stood then, moving to a chest. From the clicks and tangs, it was secured from the world by multiple locks that Wi Cheng released. When he turned, he reverently held a long broad sword in the palms of his hands. As he drew nearer, I saw it was covered with the tiniest of writing from tip to handle, the calligraphy beautiful, yet strange, as though the writing itself had a pattern to it.

"Start with this. It is the oldest of our weapons, and carries with it all that I know. Refresh your memory as fast as you can. You do not have much time before you will be called away."

CHAPTER 14

I jogged back to the Emperor's domain, unaware of the time that had passed with Wi Cheng. My mind was whirling so fast I could barely concentrate on putting one foot in front of the other. He knew me, and assured me it didn't matter if I ever remembered him. I had to retain what I'd just learned, solving the riddles of the sword before it was too late. Would I be able to do it, as he assured me I would? Wu stepped aside as I walked towards the door.

"Any sound?" I asked. Wu shook his head.

I didn't see the Emperor for the rest of the evening and I was glad.

A servant came out, informing me the Emperor cancelled evening meal. The servant left to tell the kitchen. I thought about the hundreds of others now preparing for their evening meal.

"What do we eat now?" I asked him.

Wu smirked. "Tea," he said, then left me alone in the hallway. I heard him pad down around the corner, walking up and down the area, meeting up with the other guards that circled the perimeter of the Emperor's palace.

Once the nighttime unit relieved us of our duties, we sat at the table for evening tea. The Imperial craftsman had replaced the burned, disheveled room within a day of the fire. The builders and woodworkers recreated the dining area with perfection. Not a splinter was out of place, nor could you smell any of the remnants of the fire.

We sat, quietly waiting. Once again, Mia entered and brought us our food. This time, she walked like she'd been born in high-heeled sandals, moving swiftly through the room, efficiently dishing the soup before handing out the cups. I glared at Wu's second in command, though it was unnecessary. All the eyes in the room were watching him, and he wisely refrained from stretching out his hand.

I didn't look at Mia's face, since a person in my position would never stoop to acknowledge a servant pouring tea.

Mia poured the hot liquid and placed a cup before me. When she did, her pinky finger slid under the mug, so subtly and quickly, only I noticed. Once she'd gone, I casually rested the mug in my lap, listening and talking with the others, feeling the bottom. It was a note, attached with a gummy substance. Long after we all went to sleep, I read the note by moonlight.

You would not believe the food I have to eat, her note began, and I feared she was going to detail each plate. *I have to taste it, spit it out, and after each time, an old woman named Gee grills me like I'm taking the SAT. The minute I give her the right answer, she's giving me kisses to the cheek like a grandma. Now, I know more than twenty types of tea that is served. Guess what else? When I passed the test with the guards (no, they don't know what happened), I was promoted to serve the Empress's tea for the morning and evening meals. It's great fun, and not so bad in the high heeled sandals now. I'm up to learning the salads and soups, which means I'll be able to be at the afternoon meals pretty soon. It's only a matter of time before I'll know hundreds of foods and can be with the Empress full time.*

Her smug tone came through loud and clear. She had a right to be proud. I couldn't taste the difference of one tea from another. It all tasted like warm dirt, and looked as black as mud.

Mia was the one to be consuming mass amounts of food, not me. She was the one who had the metabolism of a rat, her senses just as keen. I wondered if her own natural gifts had been enhanced from the time travel. Her talent for memorizing hadn't included foods. It was the only explanation for her ability to comprehend so many foreign, complex tastes in forty-eight hours. I continued reading her note.

The downside is Qi Tai shows up at odd times, always watching me from the corner, sometimes he gives me his own tests, which I ace of course. I think he just likes to make me nervous, as though I'll break down and tell him what's happened. I smile extra big when I pass the tea if he's in the room. Besides Qi Tai, this isn't so bad now that I'm used to it. Have you heard anything from Dad, or do you know where he is? I've given up trying to get the others to tell me, though I'm sure they know. Hope to see you soon, love you, Mia.

Mia was in a better place than I'd imagined. At least she was far away from the cesspool where Dad was being kept. The following morning, Wu and I were standing with the Emperor in the general assembly hall as he oversaw Palace business. The morning had been busy with a farmer requesting more land for growing rice, a Minister requesting a larger hall for his students, and two merchants who needed the Emperor to resolve a dispute. One had accused the other of lowering prices to lure customers to his store. The other vigorously defended himself, saying the complaining merchant's prices were too high. The peasants had to have a choice of the best products for a reasonable price.

I realized how people in my time still argued over the same, mundane subjects, rarely able to resolve their own issues. Instead, they chose to appeal to a higher authority, no matter their age or level of wisdom.

The Emperor looked thoroughly bored as he listened to the men's tirades, ending the argument by ordering one merchant to sell only cloth and shoes, the other to sell ready-made clothing and fruit. No competing products; no dispute. Both men left agreeable to the decision, already debating among themselves who got the better products.

The door at the end of the hall opened with a clang. General Li bowed low before entering, then walked to the Emperor's side.

"A letter has arrived from Zheng He," General Li said in a soft voice before handing a small sheet of paper to the sitting Emperor.

"When?" the Emperor asked.

"Just now, my Emperor."

To my satisfaction, the General glanced my way, just as I anticipated. I resolutely stared past the General, focused on the doorway that led into the great marble-floored hall.

The Emperor read the letter, refolding it to the original size.

"Wu, take this to Qi Tai," requested the Emperor.

The General put forth a hand.

"Emperor," he bowed, to soften the impact of his interruption. "I suggest Cage run the errand to the Minister of War, who is by the Imperial Food Court at this time of day. He will learn the grounds better if he does so."

The Emperor nodded, and Wu passed it to me.

"Wu will give you directions," said General Li. His eyes were dark and malicious, then turned to Wu. "He should take the direct route, by the canals."

Wu nodded once. He turned his back to the General, detailing the route I was to take as the General listened, nodding. In the background, I heard the General and Emperor talking about the preparations for the Admiral's anticipated arrival. I was actually looking forward to being a part of it.

"Remember what I told you," said Wu, his eyes intense.

Wu bowed to the General, who took my place by the Emperor's side. I walked past the General, note in hand.

"Return quickly," General Li ordered, his eyes suspicious as always.

What was I going to do? I wanted to ask him. Run off down the lane, have a cup of tea and consort with the enemy? Once out of the meeting room, I broke into a sprint and ran smack into a mob of scholars who were on their way to the dining hall. The crowd irritated me, and I looked for a way around them. I cut to the right, past a brook that lined the outer rim of the courtyard, and found the gravel path that was approved for commoners to walk upon. My thick-soled, red slippers made barely a sound on the finely crushed rock. I had to watch my step. If someone were to report seeing a single toe land on the white marble reserved for the Emperor and his consort, Wu said I'd receive lashes with a bamboo staff.

However, running after so many hours of standing still felt exhilarating.

I ran up and over a tall bridge the color of green jade. The canals were full with junks ferrying cargo around the Imperial Palace from the city itself. I'd overheard the guards talking about the complex network of slipways that had taken each one days to memorize. I tried to memorize them as quickly as possible, all the while watching the placement of my feet.

I watched the progress of a junk as it passed underneath me. The long, wooden boat with an open bow and stern and a sloping roof in the middle held baskets of green fruit in the front. The back was piled waist-high with multicolored sacks. The skipper shifted his oar diagonally in the water to make way for a larger junk. Farther down was a dock full of men unloading crates, flowers, and dry goods. After the goods were counted and loaded into straw baskets, shirtless men attached the baskets to the ends of long poles that they loaded on their shoulders. The strength of the men impressed me. The ends of the poles bent from the weight as the servants began their slow walk up the long lane toward the Palace.

I turned right and ran up and over a white, stone bridge where sculpted tigers silently growled from their protective perches on both sides of the bridge. At the bottom of the bridge I turned left past the canal office, where officials catalogued the inventory of supplies. A man ran from the office, directly into my path. I jumped up out of the way onto the office porch, missing the man by a finger's length.

Wu told me to watch for a set of locks controlling the water level of the canal network. I ran by those used for moving barges, others for the midsize junks, and the smallest for skiffs carrying officials to and from their quarters, each one with different levels, bars and pulleys, forcing the water up and down with precision. At each point, a lockkeeper managed the flow of boats coming and going and entered them in his logbook. No one went unnoticed in the Emperor's domain, but each lock was a possible entry point for would-be assassins.

Just past the next dip was a beautiful park set in front of the Empress' compound. This was clearly the long way to her palace, since the paths directly behind the Emperor's own home were not nearly as far.

As I passed through the golden gates that marked the entrance to the Empress' home, I slowed to a respectful walk. It made no sense why the Empress lived so far from the Emperor. If I were in the same position, I'd have an underground tunnel with a direct route to her bedroom.

"Pardon me," I said, cutting in front of two palace officials. I ran through a small orchard of pear trees, now dry and brittle from the cold. Fall had turned to early winter during the last few days. Snow felt imminent.

Two buildings beyond the Empress's pink, marble home was a large garden and behind it, the Ministry of Food. I found Qi Tai within, huddled with grey-bearded men, talking in low tones.

The talking stopped as I drew near. When I was within an arm's length, I stopped, bowed and addressed myself to Qi Tai, announcing the letter from Zheng He.

"Once again I see," said Qi Tai, as though he expected someone else. "Getting to know the grounds?" He cast a glance to his companion, then back at me. "Our newest intruder is now a delivery boy, who also protects the Emperor," laughing dryly.

I ignored his barb. "The Emperor requested I deliver this to you, Qi Tai," my hand outstretched.

Qi Tai took the dispatch with more force than necessary. He turned and continued to speak with the older men without further acknowledgment.

I waited, unmoving. While Qi Tai was speaking, the others remained quiet, pointedly staring at me. The Minister of War slowly turned to me, a red tinge of anger crowding up his neck.

I bowed again, this time ever so slowly, accentuating my show of respect. All the while, my eyes never left his.

Qi Tai forced himself to bow his head ever so slightly. The moment he'd done so, I turned, smiling with satisfaction. He'd hate me more now than he ever did, but it wouldn't matter. There was nothing he could do to me until I screwed up.

Out and down the path I flew until I came to the Empress's domain. Quickly, I rounded a corner, knocking over a girl servant. She cursed in at me in English, and I threw my arms around her.

"Mia!" I half-yelled, quickly lifting her off the ground, brushing the dirt from her pale, yellow robe.

"I barely recognized you—again!"

"I got promoted," she said, giving me a little bow. It had only been a day, but she'd changed. Her lean face had filled out slightly, though her high cheekbones and strong jaw were as smooth and tight as ever. The white powder had masked her freckles. Fake, black eyelashes had extended her own, the effect positively mesmerizing.

She raised a corner of her mouth, an irrepressible giggle bubbling up. She scanned me top to bottom.

"Nice ninja outfit," she said, her mood dramatically lighter than it had been just two days before.

"Ninjas are Japanese, Mia," I reminded her, and she hit my shoulder. She queried me urgently about what had happened since I received her note.

"I'm sort of liking this job now," she admitted, asking me if I'd read her letter without allowing me to talk, "but still want to leave. How long do you think it will be?"

I told her it was going to take a few more days, if we avoided accidents and trouble. For the time being, I kept the comments from the archivist to myself, along with my suspicions about Qi Tai.

"Can you last another few days?"

She nodded as she twisted her ankles around, working out the kinks. "I hope Dad can. The Empress's handmaid, Bao, told me he's in prison." Mia didn't mention the vile circumstances one encountered in the dungeon and I wasn't going to tell her. She'd expect me to do something, or worse, she'd try to fix the problem herself. For a moment, I was tempted to share the experience I had with Mom back in the tunnel, which felt like a lifetime ago. Still, it felt more wrong to keep something so personal from my twin.

As she lifted a leg behind her back to stretch her thigh muscle, I decided against it: she still wasn't ready to deal with what I had been going through. Everything about our situation was confusing enough without trying to comprehend operating the orb, or possible visions or the latest information from Wi Cheng's sword.

Instead I congratulated her on her promotion, changing the subject away from Dad. She excitedly elaborated on how Bao had recommended she be trained by Gee. When Qi Tai elevated her standing from food server of the guards to one of the Empress's own, she knew it was because of her demonstration for the Emperor in the courtyard the first day.

"Qi Tai told me I was a valuable guard of the Empress as well, and threw an apple at me." She couldn't stop her giggle as she told me how she'd caught the apple with her foot, hit it to her knee, lopped it to her other foot and kicked it back to his other hand. "He was impressed," she concluded, raising her eyebrow as she nodded in satisfaction.

"Mia, I don't have much time. A man—a prisoner—said something strange to me, as if he knew us." Not telling her about the archivist didn't mean I wasn't going to follow his advice. "He said we 'don't have much time.' Has anyone else said something like that to you—I mean, here in the Palace? Do you remember anything from history classes that might help us out?"

She stared at me with the same scolding look I was so used to receiving from her. Her superior, obstinate streak needed to be tackled out of her, but not now.

"Skip over the lecture on how I should have listened in history and tell me what you know. A fourteen year-old Emperor. The year is 1403."

"Hold on a minute," she cautioned, recognizing the intensity on my face, the call signal I was serious. "The third Ming Emperor overthrew his nephew. The City burns to the ground, and then the new Emperor moves his palace to Beijing. That becomes the Forbidden City that still exists as a tourist attraction in our time. What has—"

"Do you remember exactly what occurred?"

Mia's faced registered shock. She'd been so focused on learning how to properly serve teas and soups and walking in platform heels that she'd never thought about the bigger picture.

She glanced around before she moved closer. "The Emperor was betrayed. The history books never acknowledged who did it: I guess it's a mystery. But historians do know that someone from the inside let in the prince's armies. It was treason."

"Do you remember when, Mia?" I asked, grabbing her arm. "Spring. Summer—what?"

She shook her head. "Winter," she whispered, fear halting whatever she was going to say next. We had lived in Washington State long enough to know that snow was quickly approaching. She touched my arm. "Cage, it was never proven how, or if the Emperor died—or if he and the Empress escaped."

A cold chill ran down my spine, and it had nothing to do with the weather. We had to get out of here, and fast, before we changed the course of history.

CHAPTER 15

A wave of panic flowed through my body as I ran towards the Emperor's Palace. I had been foolish for not confronting the archivist head on. And I still didn't fully believe the words I'd read on the sword. I'd been here before. My family had fought a battle in this place before, when Wi Cheng was a student, studying under his own master. More unbelievable than that was the sword said the boy who came *from the darkness* had saved the life of a healer, removing an evil demon from his body. It didn't say *how* I did it, just that it happened. As strange as it sounded, the facts sounded...familiar, almost comfortable, like an old pair of jeans that fit right after years of wear.

I ran faster, imagining General Li standing by the Emperor, ticking the time off on his fingers, each second representing another verbal whiplashing I would receive for being late. I ran up past the carved, marble lions that stood baring their teeth, keeping out dangerous souls. As I was crossing the bridge, I heard a rushing sound just before I saw a flash of a long, black rod. Before I could jump, dive or dodge, it crossed in front of my right ribcage, making full impact in the center of my stomach.

Whoever held the weapon was strong: it held fast as the full weight of my body arched over, flipping me towards the ground. I bent my head to the left and down, protecting my skull, allowing my right shoulder to take the brunt of the impact. My stomach was reeling in pain as I rolled across the ground. I felt the metallic taste of blood in my mouth mixed with an acid that seeped up my throat.

I knew I was in trouble. My masters had taught me that if you can recognize the taste of bile it meant an internal organ had been punctured. Then I saw a man dressed in dark clothing closing in on me.

I had to decide: get up and fight, or run. My injuries put my skills at a disadvantage. Yet an attack in broad daylight meant that my enemy didn't fear the repercussions of getting caught. Or, he was beyond scrutiny.

I had no choice. I began rolling, now inches from the water.

"Ayahh!" screamed my attacker, seeing his prey escape. Once again, I heard a whirling sound just before it connected with my head, and suddenly I was deep into the water.

The cool liquid enveloped my body, disbursing the flashing lights and explosions in my head. It didn't help with the pain I felt in my torso, a paralysis that now stretched to my legs. When I came up for air, the current was taking me under the wide bridge, away from where I needed to go.

I took a deep breath and dove back down into the freezing cold water, paddling as hard as I could. The water was nearly black in the shade, making looking above me for any sign of my pursuer impossible. I placed my hands along the sides of the canal, searching for a wall, an escape route.

A hard board thumped the top of my head, driving me lower. My lungs screamed as I pushed up for air. A boat had passed over me, and now I could see another one following close behind. I hid in the dark shadows as I held the wall with one hand, my nose just above the surface. When the boat moved in front of me, I felt the side of the hull for a notch thick enough to grasp.

My attacker must have seen me. He had moved to my side of the channel, and was yelling at the captain in the waterway. Meanwhile, the second boat captain scolded my pursuer to be respectful within the Palace Grounds and lower his voice.

"Don't bother us with your petty fights. You don't belong in the Palace grounds. Get out," he said, threatening to report the attacker.

The distraction gave me time to take a breath and duck below the water. Slivers of wood pierced my fingertips as I clawed for a strong hold under the surface of the boat. Finally, a metal panel on the side of the boat provided just enough lip for my nails to cling to.

My arms strained against the current as I fought to keep the bulk of my body within the shadow of the boat. I tried to remember the height of the barrier on the embankment, or where the canal led. My legs were frozen and useless, dead weight dragging after my body. Blood and bile continued to fill my mouth, threatening to cut off the air in my throat. A buzzing within my brain was growing louder from the hit on the head.

I lost my grip just as I heard muffled shouting from above, the noise ricocheting off the sides of the canal. The boat slowed, and turned down another lane.

I rode the boats' current as long as I could, then floated to the surface. I let my hands graze either side of the canal, hoping that I could find a pipe or bar extending far enough for me to grip. I craned my head back looking for another boat, but saw none. I had no idea where I was or how to get out of the water.

I hovered along the wall as long as I could, gathering the strength I'd need to lift myself up and over the edge.

Though my eyesight was hazy, I made out a large tree trunk several boat lengths from my position. I couldn't entirely see what lay beyond the tree other than red branches covered with golden yellow leaves.

Taking a breath, I centered my strength in my core and visualized lifting my body up, then gripped the wall as best I could. Clumsily, I heaved my body up and over the bank. I crawled to the far side of the tree trunk, crouching at its base. It was blind luck no one was around. The stillness was serene. I closed my eyes, thinking that I would rest for just a moment. The Emperor wouldn't mind.

All of a sudden, I felt a warmth spreading over me. In my haze I saw Mom's arms wrapped around me, holding me tight. In the safety of her love, she welcomed me, wiping the water from my face, kissing my forehead as she did when I was a kid.

You can stay with me forever.

It was what I wanted to hear—to be back with her. To have her be by my side, smile at me when I came home, to applaud my successes.

She pressed me tighter towards her. I understood that being with my mother meant leaving this cold world for one of warmth and light. The flash of the heavens shining down through the glass in Wi Cheng's room fluttered into my mind, drawing me purposefully towards it. The idea disappeared just as quickly as I realized that joining my mother meant leaving my twin.

The thought of Mia alone, or in the grasp of a Qi Tai shocked me out of my seductive comfort.

Reluctantly, I gently pulled back from my mother's embrace. She knew the reason and smiled. The choice had made her proud. Mom kissed my forehead one last time, her lips lingering before she was gone.

"You made it further than I thought," said another quiet voice.

I looked up, unable to process what I was seeing. Was I having another vision or a visit from an angel? In a moment, I knew it wasn't either.

It was the Empress's attendant.

CHAPTER 16

Her brown eyes stared at me, sure and unwavering. She glanced at my hands, examining my face and arms.

"Someone hit me," I mumbled incoherently, attempting to push myself off the ground. It was a stupid move. My right leg buckled underneath the pain. She instinctively reached out to steady me, her face close to mine. The tip of her forefinger lifted my chin up for her examination. In my haze of pain, I began to make out her face more clearly.

"Stay still," she cautioned, her warm breath flowing across my chilled face.

She ran her fingertips across my chest and down my abdomen. I was beyond pain now, the sensation of the examination was soothing over my deteriorating body. A wave of concern washed over her face, pushing down her eyebrows and creasing her beautiful mouth into a frown.

"You are wounded inside as well." Her voice betrayed urgency. "Can you walk?"

I struggled to stand. She leaned in to me, placing her shoulder under my armpit.

"Lean on me, I know how to carry injured men." Her shoulders were thin, but her body was strong, able to hold me up. When she looked up to me, our lips nearly met for the second time.

"Someone wants me dead," I murmured, a chill running up my back causing my upper body to shiver. She slid her arm around my back, not quite making it to the front of me. She pressed and I gasped.

"I know," she said, quickening her pace. Her tone told me that we were both in danger. She led me through a maze of narrow alleyways and I began to recognize the buildings near the armory. As we struggled to walk side by side, her scent of lilies and cinnamon encouraged me onward. Ever since I'd first seen the girl, I'd wanted to get a closer look at her, then listen to her voice and touch her. Yet this was hardly the romantic interlude I dreamt of.

"Why are you helping me like this?" I choked out, shaking so hard that my words were barely intelligible. Her grip tightened, making me gasp again. She pushed and pulled me along until I could move no more.

"Stop," I pleaded. She ducked beneath the overhang of a large, Cyprus tree and into a garden where I threw up blood in clots. She placed her hands on my abdominal section and whistled.

"We don't have much time," she said, urgently. I understood all too well. Soon enough I wasn't going to be able to breath.

"What is your name?" I whispered. If I were going to die, I was at least going to know this angel's name and put in a good word for her at the pearly gates.

"They call me Bao." She was the one who had helped Mia. "Come, let's go this way. It is not far now."

I staggered back to my feet and in a few moments, we were near the pink marble building where I'd nearly kissed her through the silk. She leaned me against the side, telling me to wait quietly.

Sweat had rolled down my forehead, stinging my eyes. I'd heard other students talk about the signs of shock, but had never experienced it until now.

When Bao returned, she held a soaking wet rag in one hand and a large mug in the other. She nimbly untied my jacket. Her inhale made me try to cover up. She impatiently batted my hands away, pressing the compress against my skin, but not before I saw an ugly discoloration stretching from my sternum down to my hip.

The first sensation was cold before the rag's healing properties began heating my skin. It turned into a burning that was almost as painful as the spikes of pain in my gut.

"This should stop the internal bleeding," she promised me as she glanced over my shoulder. The slightest movements were painful, but I did what she said. She placed a hand on my back.

"Fingertip acupuncture?" I joked, wincing through gasps of pain.

She nodded, explaining that certain points on the back connected to stomach organs. Her lovely hair came undone from her bun, passing between our faces and caressing my skin with the delicacy of a feather.

Bao continued moving her hands, unaware of my inner musings. She was trying to determine if other organs were damaged.

"Help me," Bao whispered, guiding my body down to the ground. I lay on my back, and she turned me over to my side.

"Now, drink this," she said as she handed me the mug. I involuntarily gagged as I drank: it was a bitter, black substance that had a tar-like texture. "It will dull the pain, but only for a short time."

"Breathe," she said softly, pressing her forefingers down between my shoulder blades and back. The jags of pain made black dots appear in front of my eyes. As I tried to maintain focus, she continued encouraging me.

"Another breath," she said, having placed her fingers on my inner shoulder blade. She repeated the exercise, all the while continually scouring the alleyway.

"Whoever did this to you knew what they were doing. You must see the Emperor's doctor."

I shook my head no. I'd be put in some hospital, left to recuperate for a week or more, right when we should be getting out of here. I leaned away from her, spewing. Her strong hands held my waist, the humiliation of needing her help was overpowered by the gratitude I felt knowing that she was there. She bent down, oblivious to the stench I most surely gave off. She took a sash from her waist, wiping off my forehead and then my mouth, rolling up the cloth when she finished. When she was done, she asked if my legs were feeling better.

It was the last words I heard her say. My mouth had ceased to work, the lips felt frozen in place. I willed my eyes to open, but they remained clamped shut. As the effects from the drink she'd had me drink took effect, blackness closed in.

***

I floated in and out of consciousness, experiencing moments of peace and intense sensations of pain. I dreamt that I saw my mother again. This time she ran to me, then stopped beyond an impassible wall of haze. When I tried to pass through, I stepped in a gooey, dark stream, the liquid moving up my foot and leg, pulling me down into a dark crevice.

"Fall forward," she yelled. I lurched forward with all the strength I had, trying to push towards her through the haze. She was within an arm's length of my grasp. I stretched my hand out, stretching the skin on my fingers. A touch was all I wanted. A physical feeling of what I had—before.

"Help me, Mom. Grab my hand!" I screamed out loud, waking me from my dream.

I choked, the gag reflex hurting my throat. My mom was gone.

"Drink this." It was Bao again, pressing a cup to my lips. I felt her hand behind the back of my neck, lifting. This time the drink was sweet, but it was equally disgusting.

I turned my head away, angry. She grabbed my chin, this time roughly. "You must," she said, forcing me to empty the mug. With her hand still at the base of my neck, she searched my eyes. "My mother died three years ago, after the Emperor came to rule," she said, inspecting my face again. I waited, trying to clear the fog that dulled my senses.

"Was she...did the Emperor have her killed?"

She shook her head no. "She said the decision was hers to make. Father agreed."

She pressed a compress around my face, covering my eyes. The pressure of her hand sent a shiver down my neck. She pulled my wet shirt down over my stomach, adjusting the fabric, the backs of her fingers moving along my waist, sliding down to my navel. When she was just above my pants she lifted her hand, pulled down the outer uniform jacket and refastened the straps.

"Now you are ready," she said, confidently. But ready for what? Between the visions of my mother and the strange conversations I was having with men who knew more about me than I did, and threats of death, I wasn't ready for anything.

"I don't think I can move," I confided. My legs were barely functional before, my insides bursting.

She tapped my shoulder. "You must go. We cannot prevent fate."

In that moment Bao reminded me of Mia. She didn't take no for an answer, nor was she giving me the opportunity. When my sister acted this way, it was irritating. But to have an attractive girl tell me what to do was invigorating.

I reached for the back of my head. A large bump of matted hair and half-dried blood testified of the oar making contact.

"The Emperor will be at the end of the dining hall as usual," she said, pushing down my hand. "That's where we must go."

"How long have I been sleeping?"

"The sun has set a quarter since I found you."

I guessed that meant a few hours. The place should be crawling with guards looking for me. The Emperor must think that he was right all along: I was an escaped spy, roaming through the Imperial Palace.

"Mia," I said, suddenly eager to move. My disappearance could trigger her arrest.

Bao put her hand to my chest, restraining me. I noticed her skin was a gentle brown, not typical for even Chinese who spent time in the sun.

"Your skin…" I said, holding her hand up, intentionally intertwining her fingers with mine. Her long fingertips touched the ends of my own, a deathly pale of grey in stark contrast against her flesh. "Your mother. Was she a foreigner?"

Bao paused, holding my hand, letting the urgency of the situation transpire, the silence a confirmation. We had something in common.

"Was she Italian?" It was the only possibility to the closed world of the Palace. I wondered who her father could be, and if she would tell me. What if it were the General, or worse, Qi Tai? It had to be someone powerful or she would have been put to death when Jianwen came to power.

I drew her hand towards my lips, kissing her skin as she let her then fingers slip through my own.

"Your sister is safe," she said softly. "She knows nothing of what has happened. Come; let's not keep the Emperor waiting." She slid her hands around my back again.

We made our way through the back alleys of the Palace, towards the dining hall. When we were near the massive structure, she told me I needed to walk the remainder of the way alone while she went to find the Empress.

"The Emperor must see you walking towards him on your own." I understood. She could be implicated as a spy or helping a spy. I nodded.

She removed her arm from me, pointing to the door. I paused, gratitude mixed with desire to know more of her life. She was exotic, learned, close to my own age, yet she had the countenance of a woman far older.

"Do you blame your father for your mother's death?" I asked.

"He could not have saved her," she said, her words tinged with acceptance and compassion where I expected bitterness.

"I must accompany the Empress now," she said, moving from my side.

My legs buckled.

She immediately kneeled in front of me, her fingers gripping my chin. She forced me to look into her dark eyes.

"He must see you like this," she said, sympathy in her eyes. "It is the only way the Emperor will believe you've been attacked." She'd healed me only enough to walk, but not so much to hide my bruises. She was smart…and knew more than she was revealing.

I nodded, lacking the time to question her further. She still held my chin in her hand, examining my resolve to walk alone. I looked at her full lips, willing her to lean into me.

"Bao—you are like your name." A beautiful treasure, though I couldn't bring myself to utter the words.

Her eyes didn't leave mine as she released my chin. The help was more mental than physical. She waited until I struggled to my feet before releasing her hand.

This is for Mia, I thought to myself, forcing my legs to move forward.

I waited until Bao had disappeared through the doorway then stood as tall as I could and walked over to the threshold of the hall.

CHAPTER 17

The moment I entered the hallway the Emperor saw me, clanging his tea cup to the table, causing a ripple of silence to overtake the room. With a flip of his fingertips, the guards swarmed me.

Qi Tai sat at the far side of the Emperor's table though General Li rose, hand on his sword. To his right, Wi Cheng sat at a table with others in clothing that resembled his own. He gazed at me, accepting my disheveled look without surprise. Those closest to him looked less like officials and more like swordsman, their elderly faces taut, their strong arms defined from constant fighting. The group was also a sharp contrast to the softness of the others in the room who spent more time eating, living a life of ease and luxury.

Five from my own squad were prepared to block me. Two had long, Jong bong poles, two had short dong bong swords, and Wu held a set of nunchucks. As custom dictated, I bowed low, waiting for the direction to proceed. I held out my hands, showing that I had no weapons. It should have been obvious to all. I was barely capable of walking.

"Come forward," the Emperor commanded, his eyes wary, unsure of what he was seeing. I moved slowly towards his table, grimacing in pain with each step as the Emperor sat back in his gilded, oversized chair. He took a sip of hot tea, brushing his mouth with the back of his hand.

"Speak," he commanded, looking me over from top to bottom. My hair disheveled, my face, swollen and sore. My fingertips were bloody.

"I delivered the message to Qi Tai. On my return, I was attacked at the jade bridge."

The Emperor looked at Qi Tai for confirmation.

"It is true that he delivered the letter hours ago," sneered Qi Tai. "What he has been doing since I do not know."

I put my hands on my shirt to lift it when two swords were at my ribs. It was Wu and his first in command. I stared at the Emperor waiting. He nodded for me to proceed and the others removed their weapons.

My skin told a better story than I did. The Emperor leaned forward, inspecting the blackened skin. The internal wound had spread even further, giving my pale skin the color of a mottled plum. "The attacker used a Jong bong, and I escaped, but not without other injuries." I then turned around, pointing to the back of my head.

"Wi Cheng," called the Emperor, and the Minister went directly to his side. After a moment, Wi Cheng came to me, touching me lightly. His thumb was placed on one bruise, his forefinger on another, measuring the distance between the two marks. He proceeded to do this, the movements resembling a choreographed display. The pattern he made showed the sequence of hits I'd taken. I bet he knew exactly who did this, or at least the type of warrior. When he returned to the Emperor, he placed himself with his back towards the other Ministers, his face dropping so close to the Emperor the wisps of the Emperor's hair hid Wi Cheng's mouth. No one saw what he said. Emperor Jianwen's brows creased in anger. His eyes were steeled at me. When Wi Cheng stopped talking, Emperor Jianwen called for an Imperial page. The boy leaned down, the Emperor spoke and the page ran out of the hall.

"Sit down, Cage," the Emperor said with a bit more kindness in his voice, directing me to a gold bench near the corner of room. He took a bite of food, dismissing Wi Cheng. I concentrated on breathing in the least painful way.

As the Emperor ate in silence, I noticed he picked at his food, going through the motions, as though he wanted the rest of the room to believe all was well. But I could tell that something else was wrong. I suspected that the Emperor was wary of someone in this room. My attacker had to be an insider: how else would he have access to the Palace grounds? Wi Cheng must have realized that he had probably trained him, and informed the Emperor.

I scanned the crowd. The typical lunchtime activity had resumed, a low-level of noise coming from the reverent discussions in the hall. One of the Ministers spoke of the upcoming feast for the Admiral and it caught the Emperor's attention.

"Are you preparing a dinner fit for the Admiral?" asked Wi Cheng, his voice good humored, though his eyes were distant. Had he known I was going to be attacked, the onslaught beginning so soon?

The man who he addressed excitedly talked about the food preparations, punctuating his words with little spikes of excitement conveyed by his hands up and down. Wi Cheng politely nodded his head as he listened to the hundreds of dishes to be served, and the ice carvings that would honor the Admiral and decorate the tables. On and on the man droned, talking faster than the average Minister, barely stopping for a breath, and only then when a servant came up and refilled his tea. Then the chattering paused slightly as he gave thanks, then started up another sentence.

My squad stood at attention, an arm's length away from where I sat. A cup of tea was brought forth and placed in front of me by a servant, who bowed then retreated. I raised the cup to my lips, the action hurting my rib cage. The revolting smell of the tea made me sneeze, catching the attention of Wi Cheng.

Soon enough, a middle-aged man appeared at the doorway. He was dressed in dark blue silk, the color of the ocean, its high collar accented with gold embroidery that extended down the lapel in diagonal, maze-like shapes. He was bald, with a crown of black hair perched at the top of his head, a long, black braid hanging to the side of his ear. His eyes were muted, observant yet guarded.

The Emperor motioned him towards me.

"Doctor, tell me if he was attacked as he said," the Emperor asked. I pointed at my head and began to tell him what happened when he cut me off with a wave of his hand. His examination told me my words were unnecessary. He'd diagnose all he needed himself.

His fingers were as light as air as they touched the hair on the back of my head, lifting the hardening mass up and aside. I barely felt the tips of his fingers around my neck as he touched both sides from behind, pressing against the lymph nodes on my throat.

He moved my head, pressing on the back of my skull, causing me to flinch. "Keep still," he said politely. "Let me see your back."

I struggled to remove the sticky, wet clothing that had pasted itself to my body. With another touch, he pressed my hand down, just as Bao had done, lifting the material himself. He silently examined my back then stood in front of me, probing my abdomen as Bao had done.

The assessment didn't take long.

The doctor turned and bowed before the Emperor, who had stopped pretending to eat.

"He has internal bleeding that appears to have stopped. The injury on the back of his head has caused damage, though I don't think permanently."

"Bingwen," the Emperor addressed the man, "could he have done this to himself?"

"No, Emperor. Impossible."

I caught the eye contact between Wi Cheng and the doctor Bingwen at the conclusion of his examination, and another glance from the Emperor to both General Li and Qi Tai.

"Test him," said the Emperor, taking some unspoken cue from his advisors. At this, Wi Cheng took a sip of tea, his look one of calm. The Emperor had to know I wasn't going to torture myself. This test had to be for the benefit of the elders in the room.

Bingwen bowed. Turning to me, he told me to extend my arms out, shoulder height. He placed his hand on my right wrist and pressed down.

"Resist me," he said. When he pressed down, I did so. My arm stayed shoulder height. "Repeat after me my exact words. I am a boy."

I smirked and said the words. As I did so, he pressed down. The arm held as strong as it had before. His eyes on me, he nodded ever so slightly, rewarding my answer.

"I am a girl," he said.

I paused. Had I heard him correctly?

He raised his eyebrow in response.

"I am a girl." When he pressed this time, my arm dropped down. He awarded me the slightest of smiles.

"The body cannot deceive when the spirit knows the truth," he said softly, words only I could hear. "Now we will ask harder questions. Answer simply," he advised, his eyes bearing down on me. The dark brown arches of his eyebrows pulled at the side, the conservative, guarded look returning. He turned to the Emperor for direction.

"Did you go directly to deliver the letter to Qi Tai?"

"Yes," I said, nodding. My arm stayed high.

"Did you try to return immediately?"

Again, I answered I did, and my arm remained in place. The doctor grunted to show the others he was pressing down hard on my arm.

The Emperor glanced at the General for further suggestions.

"Do you know your attacker?" The General asked. The Emperor nodded his agreement that I answer the question.

"No, I don't." The arm remained motionless. "I saw neither face nor hands. All I saw was his black outfit."

The Emperor pondered this information and the General scowled. The doctor asked permission to ask a few questions of his own. The Emperor nodded, and the doctor turned to me.

"Did you heal yourself?"

I paused. My body knew the truth. From the corner of my eye, I had seen the Empress and her attendants enter the dining hall and take their positions at the Empress's table.

"No," I said, maintaining eye contact with the Emperor.

A slight rustle behind me told me this information wasn't well received.

"A girl, no, a woman found me by a tree. She put a compress of some type of my stomach."

"Had you known her before?" asked Bingwen. Before I could answer, the Emperor raised his hand.

"Leave us," he commanded to the Ministers in the room, asking Wi Cheng, General Li, Qi Tai and the doctor to stay. I dropped my arm as the hallway emptied.

General Li directed Wu's second in command to close the doors. When the clang of the heavy metal protectors shut, the Emperor contemplatively pulled on his thin beard.

"Do you have knowledge of others trying to penetrate the city?" Bingwen asked. General Li raised his hand as if to intervene, but the Emperor silenced him with a wave of a finger.

I hesitated. Mia told me that someday, sometime, others would try to take the stronghold. Did this count as knowledge, and if it did, how in the world was I going to tell him I knew this because I'm from the future?

"I've heard rumors that there is a man who wants to be Emperor, but have no specific knowledge of who that is or why."

The Emperor motioned to Bingwen, who in turn tapped my arm. I raised it, and repeated my last sentence. The sound of my heart rang in my ears, the thumping was so loud. The doctor rested his hand on my wrist and pushed. I waited another heartbeat, holding it as firm as I could.

It held.

Bingwen was apparently satisfied I told the truth, and gave me permission to drop my arm. It was a relief he didn't ask more about Bao, or my recovery. The doctor turned to me, his back to the Emperor as though he were examining my face.

"You did well," he muttered under his breath. Bingwen then turned to face his ruler. "Emperor, we have a conspirator in our midst," said the doctor, his tone foreboding.

Bingwen seemed to know me, even though I didn't remember him. I wondered then, if this was a part of a bigger strategy. The glances between him and Wi Cheng, his leading questions, and his mutterings to me. This doctor definitely had an agenda. I only hoped it wasn't going to hurt me when I discovered what it was.

"A conspirator is not someone who has twice put himself on the line in order to protect the Imperial family, under circumstances he could not have planned, nor knew of," interjected Wi Cheng thoughtfully.

"He is of value only when capable of defending you," offered General Li. "We need healthy guards. Not cripples."

"Then heal him so he can continue to offer his protection," countered Wi Cheng.

Qi Tai responded, twirling the ring on his finger, "He could heal in jail."

The Emperor was in a precarious situation. Three advisors, each powerful in their own way, giving him contradictory advice. I wondered how he managed to keep them happy and avoid open rebellion.

The doctor broke the rising tension.

"Emperor, he has given you no cause to be placed in jail, at this juncture. May I escort him to the hospital for more treatment? I agree that he must be made well enough to protect you."

The Emperor looked relieved, and nodded, placing Wu in charge during my absence. Wu bowed, moving himself behind the Emperor. The role clearly made him happy.

"Come," requested the doctor, motioning me to follow him.

Once we were out of the Emperor's presence, he slowed his pace to match mine. He explained his building was not far from the dining hall. The elaborately furnished building identified the minister of health as someone of importance. He was not young, and certainly had survived the last Imperial transition. That was a risky decision: one who could heal also knew how to take life away.

"If Bao hadn't found you in time, your kidney would have exploded," he said as we passed the Empress's pink, marble home.

I glanced at him sideways and nodded. No point in lying when he knew how to verify all that came from my mouth.

"Did she know that?"

"We suspected an attack, though we didn't know when or how. When you didn't return, Wu told her to go look for you."

Wu? Sure, I saved his life, but I imagined he'd like to go back to the way it was before, with Xing leading the group. Now he and I were even. Crap. I liked being one up.

"Wait here," said the doctor. He walked slowly toward the Empress's home, announcing himself and entering through the side door. I heard the voice of another man, or at least I thought it was, but it was higher.

A eunuch. Of course. The only type of man safe inside the Empress's home.

Bingwen came out in a hurry.

"Quickly, quickly," he said, pulling me through the doorway.

He prevented my questions by raising his fingers to his mouth as I followed him through a short corridor. Against the wall were ornate credenzas, inlaid with jade and other precious stones. Resting on the surface, vases, short and small, sat amidst carved statues of gold and bronze. Intermixed were hand-painted plates, the details so small it made a computer's work look simple. On the walls paintings hung between swords, the gilded coloring of the frames bouncing from the hilts.

We passed an open cabinet containing hundreds of jeweled eggs, which I presumed could only be worth a fortune in my time. I thought briefly of Qi Tai's offer, along with the servitude that would come with it.

"Faster," he said, irritated. Bingwen led me to a vestibule where a tapestry hung from the top of the ceiling to the floor.

"Here," he said, before I could utter a word.

It was massive hanging, covering the entire side of the room. Fifteen-feet tall by twenty-feet wide. I could spend an entire day analyzing the detail of the artwork and the story it depicted.

A battle between a soldier on a white horse alongside a dragon against an army on the ground was the theme of the top corner. The fallen men appeared paralyzed in fear or pain. Their hands were stretched halfway up, protecting themselves from what was descending upon them. It was a scene of a victorious conqueror in his moment of triumph.

I slowly made my way down the length of the hanging, tentatively reaching out to touch the cloth. The rough threading prickled my skin. The next scene featured women in luxurious circumstances, playing instruments, and singing, or sitting with hands folded, the raging battle of no concern.

"There," Bingwen interrupted, directing my attention to the lower right hand section. "We don't have much time. Look at it. *Quickly*."

I followed his gaze. Thousands of golden threads had created a large, golden orb, identical to the one in the chest in my room. It was nearly the same size as the real thing, an exact replica, down to the inscriptions on one side.

"How did you know?" I asked in wonder.

"Look closely and remember," he whispered, anxiously, but calmly, keeping his eyes on the hallway.

A thin line of golden thread connected the orb to another man. I could feel the urgency from the doctor, and tried to understand the significance of the person.

This particular man was a giant compared to the small men beside him. He held a staff in one hand and a smaller orb in the other. A volcanic explosion was in the background, its brilliant, red lava the same color as a ruby in his headpiece and on a heavily jeweled ring that he wore. Silver thread traced his metal breastplate that covered his chest to his shoulders and down to his waist. A white, silken shirt dropped below the breastplate, its sheen glinting off the metal on the man's wristbands. Though the ruler on the white horse appeared strong, this man clearly held more power.

I glanced up to examine his face, but there was none. The area had been threaded, crisscrossed with textured, tan thread. It was at odds with the delicate, conscious work throughout the rest of the tapestry. This figure was meant to be any man. Or any woman.

"We must go," the doctor said, pulling me away.

"Wait," I said, resisting. I moved on to the bottom left corner. Here was another man, smaller still, who looked like he was getting ready for battle.

"No *time!*" Bingwen said, pulling me harder. I waited until the sound of approaching footsteps cautioned me to leave. The doctor kept me walking outside until we entered his own building. The look on his face told me not to ask questions.

Once inside his quarters, he directed me to lay back while he attended to my stomach. "We'll talk later: the body needs silence and harmony to recuperate."

I stared at the silk above me that was draped across the ceiling. It looked like the waves on the ocean, the soft bluish-green providing a calming atmosphere. Incense burned in the background, filling the room with an aroma that cleared out my nose but felt harsh on my lungs. I coughed at the drying effect, wanting to grip my chest.

"It's menthol," the doctor said, pressing a fingertip on my chest. "You feel it here?" I nodded. "Your lungs are weak. This will clear your system, healing you faster than if I were to turn you upside down." He smiled as though he'd made a joke.

I felt the prick of acupuncture needles around my abdomen, in my feet and on my fingertips. When he'd finished, he told me to breathe slowly and open my mouth and lift up my tongue. Drops of a liquid that tasted like licorice were placed under my tongue, "Close your mouth," he directed, suggesting I swirl it around to accelerate the effect. "Now, we wait."

I wasn't sure how long I remained on his table. I dreamt of Bao, the touch of her hands to my cold, wet skin. I saw mother again, accepting my choice to stay with Mia. Then I saw the faceless man, controlling the orb in the tapestry.

The healer shook me awake, carefully removing the needles and allowing me to get dressed.

"How long have I been here?"

"Long enough. Return to your station and see me tomorrow."

I didn't move. I'd promised not to talk before he inserted the needles and I'd done as he'd asked. Now it was his turn to do some explaining.

"When we were walking, you said 'we were expecting an attack.'"

Bingwen shook his head before he rolled the needles in a pot of boiling water. He sighed, turning towards me and offering me a cup of tea. I accepted, sitting up on one elbow to drink it.

"Once a week, the Emperor allows me to give care to prisoners. It was there I learned about the tapestry."

The archivist must have told the doctor that he met me and saw the orb. It made sense that the only person from the outside who would have been let underneath to the prison would be a doctor. Bingwen said Wu had told Bao to look for me, and the man said he and Bao had talked about an attack. Did all three of them know some, or all of the puzzle I was still trying to put together?

"Does Wu—or Bao know what you know?" I asked. I hoped that the orb was still in my chest. Even a person with honor would be curious. And tempted.

The doctor shook his head. "Not about the orb or the tapestry. I told Wu only knew a foreigner was expected and the archivist had made a prediction worthy of imprisonment."

"Wu tried to poison me when I was in the guard's unit because he thought I had something to do with the man being put in jail?"

Bingwen nodded, a look of disappointment on his face. "He misunderstood. When you saved his life, he intended to save yours. Bao knows only that you are special. Not why."

"Did the archivist tell anyone else about me?" Had Qi Tai known about the orb I carried, it would already be in his hands. He was power hungry. So was the General.

The healer shook his head. "I don't think so. Qi Tai doesn't believe a man and two youths are the ones of legend." He had that right. Dad was hardly the stuff of songs and lore. "No one can deny you came out of the ground just at a time when the Emperor was in danger." He stopped, observing me. "Did you know the Emperor was to be attacked? Did you plan to come here at just that time?"

For the first time I realized that I'd already altered history, the second we appeared out of the ground. If we didn't show up, the Emperor would have been dead, killed by one of those arrows. Wi Cheng would have been dead had I not interfered with the arrows coming through the windows. Both men alive because of my presence.

I shook my head no. My head hurt. I had to change the subject. What was done was done, and now I cursed Dad for bringing this on us. There was only one bright spot in this whole bloody mess.

"The girl who helped me. Bao. Is she in danger?" It had been on my mind since the inquisition.

The doctor shook his head though he too, looked anxious. "No. She is protected."

"Bao saved my life," I told him, watching his face take on a bit of pride at the statement. "Was she your student?"

The man's face changed from one of pride to an unexplained sadness, as though the loss of her as his student overpowered his words.

"Yes, she was. She is also my daughter." He ignored the shocked look on my face. Then I recognized what the two of them shared: the touch of the hands and even the words they used. Only she would have been trained to heal, the one person the doctor trusted to send. By doing so, he'd put himself and his daughter in great danger.

"Why?" I wondered aloud. "What do you gain by helping me?" My chest no longer felt tight and restricted with pain, but open and wide. I took in a large gulp of air.

"That's good," he said dryly, noting the expansion of my chest. He moved away from me, as if it was going to discourage me from pursuing him further about what he knows.

"I'll really feel better when you tell me exactly what's going on."

He sighed, an exhale of sadness that seemed to hollow out his cheeks and press on his shoulders, stooping him over, aging him a decade.

"Tell me," I urged. "Maybe I can help."

The doctor's stooped shoulders raised upright. "That is what I am hoping for."

Great. Now we were getting somewhere. "How? What can I do?"

"You can help save my daughter."

A voice outside alerted me our time was over. It was one of the guards, coming to bring me back to the unit.

The doctor motioned me to leave and I heard the door close softly shut behind me.

CHAPTER 18

I left the doctor's building with more questions than answers. Why would I have to save Bao's life? What did the doctor really know about the orb, and the archivist? The Emperor accepted my presence without question. After all, it was my lot in life to die in the line of duty. If I felt that I were well enough to risk my life protecting him, then so be it.

That evening, I searched for Bao among the Empress's entourage. She was attending to the Empress, barely touching her own meal. She had changed her clothes for dinner and was now dressed in olive green silk, with yellow and orange butterflies dancing across her shoulder and chest, and delicate beautiful birds taking flight up her neckline. Her face was painted a perfect gloss of white all the way up to her hairline. Delicate gold earrings dropped along her neck. Bao didn't require an ornate gown or jeweled encrusted headpiece like the Empress to be appreciated as beautiful. She simply was.

I scanned the dining hall for possible suspects. All but the Emperor were possible traitors, including the ministers, and even the Empress. Replaying the day's events prior to the attack, it wasn't hard to determine the source. The General sent me on the mission, not the Emperor. He probably guessed at Wu's directions and made plans with Xing accordingly. With me dead or injured, Xing's return to his previous post was assured. Qi Tai was watching Mia and me, waiting for the right time to hurt us.

And maybe I was wrong about Wu. He had easily stepped into my shoes, guarding the Emperor.

I looked back at Bao and caught her staring at me. She paused, then lowered her lids, though not as quickly as she should have. A slight shade of pink pushing through the white make-up. She turned her head slightly to the Empress, her lips barely moving. I could be flattering myself, but I think she was forcing conversation to keep her from glancing back at me.

Looking around the room, I caught another blank stare from Wu.

Maybe Wu had a thing for Bao, which would give him one more reason to want me out of the way. She clearly didn't feel the same way for him.

Purposefully turning away from thoughts of romance, I spent the long dinner ritual thinking about the tapestry, the orb, along with my family's role. It was an exercise in frustration. Only the function of the round, golden ball was clear. The archivist wanted me to see the tapestry, but what did I really learn from it?

A young male servant walked along the hall carrying a platter of roasted poultry when his toe caught an edge of an oriental carpet. The bird literally flew off the plate and landed on the back of a minister. The minister jumped up, squealing in alarm as the sauce dripped down his hair. I suppressed a smile, and caught Bao's eyes. They glinted with humor. We both turned our attention to the center of the room when we heard a shout.

The servant was being whipped by Qi Tai. He crossed his arms over his head, failing to protect his face from the scarring needles at the end of the leather rope. The boy could not have been more than eleven or twelve, his thin arms no match for Qi Tai's precision.

Blood erupted from the boy's cheek when the tip lashed it, causing a muted cry.

Do something, I mouthed to Wu, but he resolutely looked forward, ignoring me. It was the Emperor's choice to let this continue. I was prevented from intervening, the act of defying Qi Tai in court could result in my own beating or even death.

I looked at Bao, appealing to her, seeing anger in her dark eyes. Though her face remained motionless, a vein in her neck angrily protruded.

Her right arm moved slightly. A touch of her fingers on the Empress's leg must have occurred, for the Empress nodded her head a little then called for a servant. From behind her chair, a runner came to her, listened to her whisper then went to the Emperor.

"Enough," the Emperor said to Qi Tai. The whip was already mid-throw, and the Minister of War cracked it above the boy's head. His face was lacerated with open cuts, the blood trickling down to the ornate carpet. It was messier than the food that caused the problem in the first place.

"Remove this," the Emperor said to no one in particular. Half dozen servants moved forward, quiet ghosts that silently removed the scattered food and rug.

The ministers respectfully waited for the Emperor to give his guidance, eating only after he raised his hand for the meal to continue. With their backs turned to him, and the General hungrily devouring his meal, Qi Tai rolled up his whip, using a napkin to wipe the blood from the leather.

Only I noticed the Emperor look at the Empress across the room. She did nothing other than open her eyes wide, though this somehow sparked him into action. The Emperor called for another servant and told him to take the boy to see the healer. The boy had not moved from his crouched position on the floor. As the servant bent down assisting the boy up, the Empress watched, her eyes soft.

The two must have long since worked out a system for communicating, getting around the stifling restrictions of formality of ruling the country. I imagined that Bao and I would do the same if I stayed here among the elite. We'd create a method for communicating, for meeting. A tilt of our head or expression of eye conveying more than a conversation.

She was now staring at the Minister of War, her expression schooled in a blank face. I guessed she loathed him as much as I did.

When dinner ended, I escorted the Emperor back to his home. Tonight, my station was on the eastern wall, guarding a private doorway to the Emperor's personal zoo. I'd seen glimpses of it from the outer perimeter, but no one save the Emperor and the Imperial Zoo keeper were allowed inside. I had only heard about the exotic animals rumored to be within.

"Cage, come inside," the Emperor called to me.

He stood a few feet away from me, his view to the zoo gate unobstructed. I expected he wanted me to call for the zookeeper.

As usual, I bowed low, rising and waiting to be directed. Tonight, his eyes were bloodshot and dark-rimmed. The thin, scarce hair on his chin appeared more coarse than normal.

CHAMBERS

"You have made an impact on the Palace," he said. His bluntness took me by surprise. He sounded old and tired. Even perplexed, like a principal intending to discipline an unruly student, but not sure of the most effective way. It was definitely not a typical comment from a fourteen year-old.

I bowed again. He hadn't asked me to speak. He stroked the hair on his chin, frowning.

"You saved Wu's life. The Empress tells me you show interest in Bao. The doctor says you will heal but need several days before you are fully well."

He didn't mention how Wu and I nearly burnt the joint down, or me kicking the butt of his other guards.

"Your sister has proved herself adept at tasting food," he continued. "For all that you have done, I am grateful." A pause followed, and I remained silent.

"The Empress believes I should let you go back on your journey soon." He shook his head. "My advisors are unsure. Even Wi Cheng, who is impressed by your knowledge of swords encourages me to let you go. I must wait a while longer. For your loyalty, I can do only one thing for you, within reason. What is it you desire?"

Mia would have me ask to see Dad, determine if he was surviving and update him on what had happened.

"I'd like to visit a great piece of artwork that I've heard about," I said, pushing thoughts of my father far away. "A tapestry that hangs near the Empress's room."

Emperor Jianwen raised an eyebrow. He walked to a sitting chair, and sat, his ornate, heavy robes covering his hands as he clasped them together. I could envision him placing his thumbs on top of one another, deciding my fate with a flick of a fingertip.

"That places you in close proximity to things of great worth," he remarked. I nodded. His wife, Bao, the tapestry, all fit that description.

He abruptly got up from the chair and walked to another window. He motioned me to join him, pointing to lights on a far mountain.

"Qi Tai's spies tell me men are hiding in the mountains, those who would betray me, in league with others not loyal to my reign."

He turned to me, searching my face for signs of truth. "My advisors believe you will use your father and sister to inflict death and evil upon our city. Now you ask to see an important tapestry, but not to speak with your father or sister."

My dad had flicked in and out of my thoughts, only to hope he wasn't being tortured. I expected to be told if that was the case.

"I don't understand your actions," he concluded, stroking the strands of hair on his chin. "Wi Cheng believes you are curious about us and our culture. Is that true?"

Thank you, Wi Cheng. I nodded, telling him I'd heard so much about the tapestry, it would be a magnificent gift. "You saw the embroidery on my own clothes," I reminded him, watching in satisfaction as he pursed his lips as he remembered my hoodie.

He faced me, his eyes dark with concern. "I'll grant you permission to see the tapestry, but first you must attend to a task that will confirm your intent. In a few days you will go to the mountains with me. Bingwen says it will be time enough for you to recuperate. After that, you will go with Admiral Zheng He on his next trip. Xing was to accompany him. Now you shall take his place. Your sister and father will remain here until you return."

I suppressed my disappointment. For a minute, I thought the Emperor had turned the corner, believing I wasn't in the Palace to harm him. He was taking precautions, and my leash was still short. One pull from him and I'd be in the dungeon.

Still, I couldn't fault him for being judicious. Smarter than I'd be if the roles were reversed. If I was providing information about the Palace to outsiders, removing me from the situation would cut off communication. I'd go on a journey to who knows where, return and then see the tapestry. In the meantime, Dad and Mia were prisoners in the Palace.

"Do you question this?" he asked. He'd been waiting my response, taking my quiet as a sign I disagreed.

I bowed. To do otherwise meant I had a reason not to go, or a secret to keep. "A journey sounds interesting," I said. I was speaking truthfully. Providing we didn't drown on the voyage, going somewhere with the Admiral could be cool. A nagging fear of what Qi Tai could do to my sister gave me pause, until I convinced myself I would only be away for a couple of days.

"Tonight, we attend a celebration in the city and in three days, we journey to the Summer Palace. Upon return, we will welcome Zheng He, and afterward, you will leave with him."

I nodded and we turned and began walking towards his room. The days I'd be gone would drag, being away from Bao and far from the tapestry.

"What of your safety?" I asked him, out of turn, yet unconcerned. No one was about to hear my familiar discussion with the supreme ruler.

By then, we'd arrived at his doorway. "I'd be more concerned about your own." He then turned from me, entered his room and shut the door.

CHAPTER 19

Three days later, my team was called to escort the Emperor outside the walls of the Forbidden City. Two ornate carriages were prepared for the journey, along with a half-dozen smaller, less elaborate boxes.

"The entire royal family goes to a Palace high in the mountains," said Wu as we walked towards the procession. That meant Bao was coming. "Two hundred and fifty warriors will walk behind the Emperor until we are outside of the Forbidden City. Even still, we must be ready to protect the Emperor against anyone who could break through the ranks."

"That's ridiculous. The front was completely exposed to the enemy. Half the men should jog in front."

Wu glanced around him before he spoke.

"The Emperor's box would get dirty if the men jogged in front of him," he explained.

The General was at the front of his line of soldiers, behind the last box. Originally, Qi Tai was to have remained behind at the Palace. He was personally orchestrating the grand feast planned for the Admiral, who was expected later that day. At the last minute, he'd changed his mind, telling the Emperor he wanted to meet with his spies who were on the road, nearer to the Summer Palace.

"What about the tasters or soon to be attendants?" I asked Wu, thinking of Mia.

He nodded. "You sister is in one of the carriages," though he didn't identify which one.

"They must really trust her to allow her to leave the Palace walls," I remarked.

"No," said Wu. "She earned the right to come on the trip." That must have made her happy. She was leaving the Palace Grounds, and being carried by a bunch of men. Circumstances had changed for her dramatically while I'd been on my back.

I directed Wu to stand on one side of the Emperor's box as I stood on the side with the door. Two other guards from my unit stood about seven feet away. The last guard was positioned between the Emperor and Empress's box. A second squad of guards manned identical postings around the Empress's carriage.

As I watched the long line of men, I spied a quick movement from the second box. Expecting the Empress, I saw Bao instead. Her eyebrows raised ever so slightly as she saw me, then remained steady for a moment. She pressed her lush lips up and arched eyebrow, almost questioning me with her look. It was the only sign of recognition she gave before she dropped the curtain. It was enough. My heart bounced.

I glanced across the carriage and saw Wu facing forward, not back. He'd missed the interaction. The light hit his hair, giving the black a brown sheen I hadn't noticed before.

The other boxes behind the royal family were sealed, the doors shut. A signal was given and the caravan moved forward. I turned my attention to what lay in front of me.

We passed through the Emperor's inner square, which contained the parks created just for the Emperor, and others for the Empress, special temples for private worship, and the Emperor's favorite, the exotic animal zoo.

We continued until we reached a set of tall, white marble gates which marked the exterior edge of the Emperor's inner domain. The guards here were physically enormous, even by Chinese standards. Thick shouldered, set like square blocks on legs, the men looked capable of breaking a neck with ease.

I recognized the Forbidden City both from my school books and from our first entrance from the tunnel. Instead of the sounds common to a city like Beijing, like bicycles and yelling, all I heard were the soft padding of our feet touching the ground.

We didn't walk on blocks of mud or cement. The roads were covered with hand-painted, multicolored tiles. As I ran, I looked ahead of my pace four or five feet. The tiles told stories. Each row and section unfolded a new chapter in a story line, as hundreds of tiles depicted battles between Chinese warriors and foreign invaders through a stone storybook.

Each Ministry had its own building, each one more ornate than the next. There was beautiful calligraphy on the walls of the Ministry of Writing, the stone steps leading up to massive burgundy-colored doors covered in ornate writings. Next to it stood the Ministry of Food. The smells were so strong my nose itched and stomach grumbled. I envisioned master chefs training hundreds of future cooks, each of whom would one day feed the Emperor's court. I thought of Bao and what it would be like to take her to a dinner picnic, just she and I, in a small, tree-lined park with no one around. Then I realized that was something I could only do back in my old life: custom and culture would never allow that here.

I looked behind, hoping for a glimpse of her in the next carriage. The shades were drawn to prevent outsiders from knowing the occupants. Disappointed, I turned back, eyes focused on every living thing.

In between each building, guards stood at the ready. Each held a spear in his right hand, pointing the tip up when the Emperor's carriage passed. I made eye contact with several. One after another, the men bowed to me, the slight head nod acknowledging my place as the Emperor's lead guard, a visual wave of subservience. I had my mask on, and they had no idea I was a white man taking the place of Xing.

The sound of water caught my attention, and I remembered the scale city in Qi Tai's office. Junks ferrying food and supplies moved along the complex waterways with barely a sound, every person attuned to the presence of the Emperor. Oars dipped silently without a ripple in the emerald green water as they approached the broad, low-lying bank. The procession made its way through parks, up and over bridges and beside an array of temple sanctuaries.

We reached an immense jade bridge, similar to the one I'd run over before being attacked, except much bigger and less ornate. The Emperor's box stopped in the center. One of the servants carrying a small basket ran up to the Emperor's box, waiting for an order. Another servant ran up to the door, placed a rug on the ground and bowed as the Emperor emerged.

The servant then removed a wriggling fish from the basket, dried it off and gave it to the Emperor, who threw it over the side of the bridge. Alligators snapped at one another as they lunged for the unexpected meal. The moat lined the inside of the gate: one more deterrent to would-be invaders. The Emperor continued tossing fish until the basket was empty, then he was presented with a bowl for washing his hands.

Shortly after we started moving again, the Emperor gave the command to go slower. Wu and I slowed from a jog to a walk. Shortly after, the Emperor pulled back his curtain just enough for me to see the side of his chin.

"Cage," he called. "Walk closer. Wu, go to the other side of the carriage."

Wu pursed his lips, unhappy with the dismissal.

"Cage, do you enjoy the quiet?" the Emperor asked from within, his voice barely audible.

"It's very unlike my home," I responded.

"I told you once before to answer my questions." He may be fourteen, but he knew respect.

"I like the quiet, but it's odd. It isn't natural. No shouting means no kids, or those that are around are forced to be quiet. Women should be talking with one another about shopping or cooking. This place is devoid of emotion. I imagine a rule exists to prevent laughing."

As if to prove me wrong, a female voice chuckled from within the confines of the box. I glanced inside and could make out the delicate profile of the Empress. The two were sneakier than I thought. The Emperor stared ahead, no humor present on his face. He found nothing funny about my statement.

"You must learn the areas of importance within the Forbidden City. You saw the model in Qi Tai's office, and covered some of the grounds before you were attacked. Now you will see first-hand the..."

"Alternate routes to take?"

He nodded. "Exactly."

The Emperor began describing the surroundings, beginning with a common area open to the highest-ranking Ministers, special members of the military, and their servants. Seven walls and four parks were within the boundaries, along with two special training grounds.

"This area is for the Imperial Military," the Emperor said, pointing his finger through the silk curtain. Strange, I'd never taken notice of his hands before. They weren't white, but slightly tan. And instead of being thin and boney, normal for a younger person, they were muscular. Hands that strong only came from working out with hand weights, herb bags or proficiency with weapons. My curiosity was piqued. What did he really do during the hours within his Palace rooms? What did he do at night, when we weren't around? What I saw during the day was limited. Perhaps it was all part of a charade to make others think he was weak. It would be easy for Wi Cheng to train the Emperor without others knowing, or would it? It meant putting guards in place that could be trusted...even then...

I followed his finger to the square. Today, large groups of teenage boys were training in hand-to-hand combat and weapons while more advanced guards fought multiple opponents at once.

At the top of another high bridge, a sea of younger boys who looked between ten and twelve stood in a huge, open area. They wore black, high collared shirts, white pants, and white hats.

"That's the intellectual training area. Those boys were chosen from many thousands of applicants to serve the Ming Dynasty Emperors for the rest of their lives." That meant they would be neutered, if they hadn't been already.

"Did they want to do it or was it chosen for them?"

"It is a great privilege to serve the Royal Family," the Emperor said stiffly. The girl riding in the carriage made a quiet comment, one that sounded a lot like teasing, the type Mia gave to me.

The food was good and plentiful, no doubt, and it was certainly an easier and less dangerous life than in the countryside. But to miss the thrill of fighting or a lifetime of friends and family wasn't a superior trade off to serving the court. Then I remembered their strong belief in the Emperor's position as a deity. If serving God was a privilege, the honor of being chosen must give any parent a great deal of pride. No wonder peasants brought forth their children, hoping to give them a better life than the one they had, and gaining bragging rights as well.

"Those who aren't chosen to serve the royal family continue to serve the scholars or in the temples," said the Emperor. "Some become teachers for the thousands of students we train from foreign countries every year."

The Emperor pointed to a huge, golden dragon perched on top of a platform. Its mouth was open, and its tongue split, as if it were breathing fire.

"This area is for executions and punishments."

A short, wooden wall was draped with torture weapons, knives with spikes, chain-link metal whips, and rows of swords and intricate tools perfect for pulling teeth or removing fingers and toes. Next to the wall of weapons were five poles connected by thick, brown, wooden blocks. Each had one hook dotted with a spattering of dark brown spots—dried blood. Others were red. It looked fresh. As we passed it, a rotted piece of finger lay frozen on the ground. I was unnerved that I wasn't more bothered by the evidence of torture. It took a ruthless person to survive in this time.

"That dragon oversees all that happens. It is bound by its spirit to protect me as long as I'm alive."

"How?"

"He stuns my enemies."

"You've witnessed this?" I asked, attempting to keep the skepticism out of my voice.

"Many times."

I nodded, as though this were perfectly reasonable. I guess since I'd traveled through time to become the guardian of a teenage Emperor, I supposed anything was possible.

"You may see for yourself if you are here long enough to witness an execution. Don't your rulers have protectors?" Silently, I nodded. It's called guns and ammo. A lot less expensive and a whole lot more controllable than a fiery, stone demon.

"Your sister is very talented. She caught the taste of ginger in a soup when it should have been nutmeg," he continued, a lilt of satisfaction in his voice. "Gee thought she was going to trick her, but your sister caught it right away. She earned her place on this trip, and it makes the Empress happy to have her around," added the Emperor. I heard more talking from within.

He leaned a little closer to the window. "Serving the Empress isn't an easy task. She will give Bao more…free time," finished the Emperor, who said nothing more as the Empress began to giggle again. Hearing the two, alone, with no pretenses, confirmed they were in love, young and yet wise.

"She will do well as long as she observes the rules," the Emperor said, more to himself than to me. "Will she be loyal?"

I nodded. "Fiercely so. She can be very protective when she believes in a person."

"That is exactly what the Empress needs right now," he said quietly. No laughter accompanied this comment. For a time, the carriage bobbed along as I waited for him to continue the conversation.

"When my Grandfather was dying, he asked Qi Tai to continue to serve me," the Emperor said. "He knew he was dying, and had to name a successor. His son, my own father, had died in battle. The only other person in line for the throne was my uncle. But since I'm the eldest son of the eldest son, the throne passed to me."

No doubt Qi Tai was hoping to be named the ruler, though it never would have happened…unless both uncle and grandson were dead. I could only imagine his reaction to the idea of taking orders from a pimple growing, voice-cracking kid.

"That must have been hard on Qi Tai," I said under my breath.

"His job was easier than growing facial hair," the Emperor retorted. The Empress laughed. "The Ministers are appreciative of your skills and have noticed your loyalty," he remarked, referring to the parrot incident.

"I'll do what I can, as long as they are loyal to you."

"My grandfather chose each one himself when he rose to power. Later, when he began to suspect treason among the Palace staff, he tortured any he suspected, as well as their relatives. Thousands were put to death. The Empress and I—we don't agree with what he did. Some of those killed were our cousins. Our family members. I've tried to change many of those old ways. My people now have more food on their tables, and we have peace in the country."

I said nothing, but kept my focus on the road ahead.

"The Empress wants to know why you never ask about your father."

I continued looking forward. Mia always said my body language was a dead give-away for my feelings.

"The Empress is very perceptive," I said.

"For the third time, you don't answer me. I could imprison you for insolence." This time, the threat sounded hollow. He was genuinely curious, but didn't know how to ask a question without giving a threat of death.

I could have sworn I heard a punch or a nudge from the inside. I was beginning to like the serene, quiet Empress more and more.

"Tell the Empress to stop hitting you," I said, smirking. "Or at least not to hit you anywhere someone can see." This set off a peal of laughter from within.

"She thinks you are mad at your father. Is this true? We both want to know why."

Where should I begin?

"My mother is dead and it's my father's fault," I said bluntly, unable to keep the bitterness out of my voice. It was the first time I'd said the words out loud. "My Dad didn't order her execution, although he might as well have. He could have prevented it, but he chose his selfish pursuits, and her death was the result."

Fury engulfed me, a long bottled up fissure of pain releasing. There was no point in avoiding it any longer.

"One day, when I was about your age, my sister and I were waiting to be…waiting for our parents to come get us from school. At some point, my mother must have given up waiting for my father, and started towards the school. Those who witnessed the accident said that men chased her, causing her to run across the street and be hit by a car." I blinked, pushing past the searing water that threatened my eyes, moving over the emotion of loss to one of hatred for the men who found an easy mark. "When my mother never showed up, I told Mia to go home with a friend while a teacher drove me to where Mom said she would be that afternoon. I found her on the ground, cops around her. Her body was…broken…beyond repair. I pushed everyone aside, and held her in my arms but she was already gone."

Pain, loss, the memory her body heavy in my arms had become my constant companion. It was an experience I never fully shared with Mia. As much as I harbored anger at Dad, keeping the details from Mia was my way of protecting her love for Dad. We were all she had now—well—Dad and me.

All was quiet within the carriage. I ran, pounding down the emotion that filled my entire body.

"Your father? He never came?" I heard the Empress ask from within the carriage.

"He showed up at the hospit—I mean, the medical center, hours later. Told us he was on an assignment and thought Mom would get us herself." My tone conveyed the disgust I'd held onto since that time.

"Of course you don't ask about him," surmised the Emperor, now understanding why Dad wasn't at the top of my list. I heard the low tones of talking from within and a grunt. "The Empress says hate is useless," conveyed the Emperor.

"I know. Mia says as much all the time. It serves no purpose…other than to keep away the pain."

We'd entered another part of the city, an area that was less restricted. Men walked respectfully, though briskly, along the sides of the road. Though the men weren't as well dressed as the ministers, it was clear they weren't peasants. I wondered who they were.

Still, my body tensed in direct relation to the number of people on the road. The armed guards from behind moved to the front, creating a sword-to-sword moving fence around the procession. The guards' reaction was overkill. As we approached, the bodies dropped to their knees with bowed heads in complete submission to their god. We moved faster through this part of the city. The main thoroughfare was wide and clear. Before we left the guard's quarters, Wu told me the Empress liked arriving in the mountains in time for lunch. The morning sun was well above our heads, and the mountains were far in the distance.

Soon we neared the outer wall of the Forbidden City, a massive, four-story red brick structure. As we approached, more armed guards came to the front points, gesturing at the servants to begin the process of opening the doors.

Our speed barely slowed as the three-foot thick doors swung open to allow us through. The noise I'd anticipated finally came with the fetid air outside the thick walls. What smelled like vats of burning soup was mixed with birds screeching, no doubt the last squawk before a butcher's hand. The roaring hum of commerce continued unabated in the background. If hundreds of thousands lived within the walls of the city, millions were outside of it.

The pace of the carriages now increased to a jog. We quickly left the smoky, loud din of the city for the quiet, grass fields and rice paddies that stretched from the valley to the hillside on every direction.

It had been months since I'd been on a long run. The martial arts instructors were vehemently against running. "It's linear," my master had said over and over, pointing out the strain caused the groin to be tight, limiting leg swings, rolls and high kicks. Even so, I'd go out with Mia once in a while to keep her company. Good thing. This jaunt was going to kick my butt.

As we left the grasslands behind and started climbing the hills, my body began to pay the penalty for my choice of extra-curricular activities. My knees ached, my lungs threatened to explode as the altitude carried us up. My thigh muscles felt as though they were going to rip off from my bones, pulling my aching knees with them. I couldn't believe it was only days before that my innards were bursting and I was ready to collapse.

I thought of Mia, riding along in a carriage held up by stocky men much more conditioned than I. Those who carried the boxes on their shoulders weren't even panting. I visualized my body floating out of my skin, hovering above me. It was an exercise we practiced in the dojo to handle pain.

"Physical pain is temporary," read a sign on the wall of the dojo. "The body can endure. It's the mind that must work through the body."

When we reached the top of a plateau, the leader of the caravan called for the group to slow. With gratitude, though no outward reflection of my feelings, I walked again, pushing air in and out of a small gap in my lips to stifle the sound of ragged breathing.

I'd barely enough time to lower my heart rate when the curtain opened again.

"Cage," the Emperor called. "Closer." As much as I wanted to continue deepening the relationship with a discussion, I hoped he wasn't going to ask me many more questions. I was working a whole lot harder now than when were on the flat city streets.

"When I was crowned," said the Emperor without hesitation, as though the conversation wasn't interrupted, "my uncle wanted to come to the ceremony, but I wouldn't let him into the Forbidden City. I was worried he might rally the other princes and start a revolt. Then last month, he asked to visit my grandfather's tomb, and I refused. Qi Tai's spies found evidence that he has been talking to many of the outer kingdoms in an attempt to turn the princes against me. Even though I have promised to leave their territories alone, Qi Tai's spies tell me my uncle has succeeded in gaining the allegiance of half of the princes."

"My uncle controls an army of one hundred and ninety thousand loyal men. He has led the country in many battles with China's enemies and won them all. The other princes see my uncle as a strong man who can maintain China's strength. Now Qi Tai's spies have said that he is mounting his forces in the North Country, near Beijing. We thought the man who came out of the tunnel before you was his spy."

The Emperor pulled back the curtain and looked at me with eyes wide and honest.

"General Li must be prepared to battle my uncle and his minions at any time. He doesn't like defeats. Or surprises."

"Why hasn't he killed me then?" I asked.

The Emperor smirked. "He wanted to. You defeated his son."

The look on the Emperor's face betrayed his feelings about General Li. It was possible that when Xing was kicked out of the Emperor's unit, General Li had one less reason to serve the current Emperor. The Emperor wanted to have the best person to protect him, but at what cost?

"If the people are treated better, won't they stand against your uncle?"

The Emperor motioned to the hills. "The people will support anyone who defends and protects their rice paddies. If my territory were in jeopardy of invading Mongolian forces, I would also give my loyalty to those that protect my family. The people demand a strong Emperor, not someone my age. But I am who my grandfather chose. I have no choice but to rule well for as long as I can."

I dearly wanted to know more about the Prince, the invasion…any fact to help me determine how to best protect the Emperor—at least while I was in his service.

"Is your uncle the strongest prince in the land?"

"Yes. And seven of the fifteen princes have sworn him allegiance. He gains more power by the day." I listened to him with a growing sense of foreboding. "Qi Tai's spies have been informed that my uncle's soldiers took food from the fields to feed his army while blaming my greedy desire for full Imperial storehouses. Teenage girls from the villages were kidnapped, forced to serve the commanders, while their weeping mothers were told their daughters were going to serve at the Palace."

We passed a group of men and women in the field, looking up from their wide-brim hats. The winter sun, still bright and harsh in the high plains, glared down. Recognizing the Emperor's box, the hats went down again, the workers on bended knee, but not before I saw their scowls of hatred. The Emperor's attempts at reforming the tyranny of his grandfather's rule were being negated by his uncle's malicious scheming.

"The very people that should support me turn away when I come," he said, sadness and resignation in his voice. The kid was defeated even before the invasion occurred. Even as he helped one farmer at a time, it was not enough to quell the masses that were being tricked.

"Do you have any ceremonies or events coming up once the Admiral leaves?"

He moved his head so I could see him, his eyes intense. He cocked his head back, a subtle suggestion to keep my voice down should the Empress hear.

"Zheng He has arranged for visitors, European traders who are much interested in our materials. Afterwards the Empress and I move to the Winter Palace, a safe haven high in the mountains where we will be protected." I frowned. Outside the Imperial Palace, without the benefit of the high stonewalls and thousands of guards, he was vulnerable. The roadways like this one was an easy target.

I recalled what Mia has told me about the invasion. The City and Palace burned to the ground; the Emperor and Empress's fate clouded in mystery. I'd assumed they were in the Palace, but they could be anywhere.

"Do you stay away until Spring?"

Emperor Jianwen nodded. "Until the first cherry blossoms bloom. The Empress likes to come down from the mountain when the roads are covered with pink petals."

"How many days until you retire to the Winter Palace for the season?"

"Ten days."

"What...?"

My anxiety skyrocketed as I realized that they never made it to the Winter Palace. The massacre of the Imperial family, the slaughter of thousands, was imminent.

I chose my next words carefully, my eyes darting across the hills on the horizon.

"I've not...seen many other members of the Imperial family around the palace. You said your grandfather killed many."

"Gone," he said simply. I wondered aloud why Bao and her father were spared.

"His father and grandfather before him served the royal family. They have never lived outside the Imperial Palace. When the doctor chose the Emperor over his wife, Grandfather knew his loyalty was complete."

The doctor's sad eyes and his stooped shoulders flashed before me. Bao's words, about her father having to make a choice for the family. He had sacrificed his wife so that his daughter could live.

"But why would any man have to make that choice?" I asked quietly. Poor Bao. To lose her mother and be alive, the guilt of the knowledge, plus her own father's lonely existence. The entire revelation made me want to take Bao aside and hold her in my arms. I'd like to think I'd choose family over living, even if it meant my own death.

As we continued our march, I began looking back to the stomping men so frequently that General Li waved a hand, as though to tell me to stop turning around. I ignored him. The Emperor was my responsibility. I'd inspect his soldiers as much as I saw fit.

General Li rode his horse high, sitting above the large beast with a discomfort that had nothing to do with an inability to ride. He too, was constantly looking around. His lieutenants, also mounted on horses, rode up to him with reports, peeling off to the countryside for random reconnaissance. The next time the General glanced my way, I motioned the other four guards to walk up and down the line of carriages. I waited for a head nod indicating all was well before turning my attention back to the Emperor.

"Now you understand," he said, observing my change in demeanor.

The guards were young because the Emperor wasn't going to risk being killed by a servant or relative with a desire for power. Xing had been the senior guard, having proved himself better than any other fighter in the kingdom, and I knew he was seventeen or eighteen at most. Had he been more seasoned, I'd have surely lost.

"I understand why the Doctor was spared. Why weren't the General and the Minister of War removed or killed?" I'd already known the reason but wondered if the Emperor had worries about either.

The Emperor explained the ruling party was within the same family. "My grandfather also believed they would be loyal to me," he said. "They both made sacrifices to show their loyalty."

Had both men sacrificed their wives? I wondered, disgusted that this was the demand of the former ruler. The Emperor shot down the thought. "The General promised to serve the Emperor until his last day of this life. When his wife died, he gave his complete obedience to the ruling Emperor, promising no other person would be more important. He can never marry again. Qi Tai likes…younger girls."

I thought I was going to vomit.

I clenched my jaw line, grinding the red soles of my feet deeper in to the earth. In less than ten days, my entire family would be dead.

CHAPTER 20

We made it to the summer palace in keeping with the appointed schedule. It could have easily been named the Jade Palace. Green vines snaked over the outer walls made of light olive colored marble. The foliage seemed to blend into the woods around it, the towering maple trees shading the western side, hiding the back part of the fortress. Last year's cherry blossoms were scattered in dried wafers, covering the ground.

The fortress, though large, was tiny compared to the Imperial Palace, though every bit as opulent. Jeweled armory lined the walls, warrior statues silently guarding entrances to the major rooms, and fat, porcelain Buddhas smiled at me from their squat positions on tables, armoires, and from the shelves. Tapestry covered walls were interspersed with murals the length of a basketball court.

The servants who travelled with us from the Forbidden City got right to work, silently moving through the halls, efficiently erasing every particle of dust resting on the floors or walls. They moved among the rooms so swiftly and quietly, I sensed, more than saw, their presence. I followed the Emperor as close as I was allowed, from the entryway through the grand halls of the Palace. Bao walked behind the Empress, her outfit was brightly colored yellow and form fitting. She was no

Alexandria Smith, with her bulging chest and trendy looks, but she was more elegant. Like a jewel, timeless.

We stopped when the hallway ended and rounded a sharp corner. Copper panels served as floor to ceiling doors, each the width of a forearm, joined together. The upper half was covered in stained glass, allowed light from the outside to shine through. Servants at either side slid back the line of doors which opened like an accordion.

"Wow," I said, unable to help myself. The glass and copper pictorial was an identical match to the view outside. The mountain range on the horizon, the crags of the snowcapped peaks, the blue of a valley in the center, its blue waters bright. The orange and yellows of the trees were painted to life, the leaves matching the color and type.

We walked into the crisp air. Instinctively, I looked in all directions, wary of hidden intruders. Wu walked beside me, taking his post on the other side of the doorway. He gestured up the mountain and across, pointing out a narrow path within the trees. A trail for hiking…or trespassers.

The Emperor and Empress looked out on their land. From the corner of my left eye, a slight movement caught my attention. I glanced down, craning to observe the Emperor place his hand over the Empress's fingers. He had indeed touched her, the act eliciting not a single facial movement, blink or breath. Gods weren't supposed to show emotion, or apparently, touch one another, in public or private. I was struck again by the loneliness of the two and their tie to one another.

No wonder they wanted to come here, if only for a night. Few adults were around, except for General Li, who was busy ordering others about. The Ministers were gone, the servants quiet. It was the most peaceful I'd seen the two during my stay. Their interaction in the carriage had been fun and playful. And though the Emperor never fully let down his mantle of ruler, he showed he was still a young man, open to being teased and probably annoyed by the girl who was with him for life.

Over my shoulder, I caught the attention of the Emperor, nodding once. He smiled, thanking me for my perceptivity. I motioned to Wu to give them their privacy, directing him to meet me on the other side of the landing. The Emperor glanced up at the roofline and I saw a sheer roll of silk tied up by embroidered sashes. With a yank, the knots came undone, releasing the transparent curtain of blue silk. It wasn't much more than a token barrier of privacy, but it was enough.

I turned my back just enough to see he was there, but not before I witnessed the two touching hands as the Emperor pressed himself against her, his hand on the small of her back. The whispers in her ear made her smile and lean towards him, her head on his shoulder. I turned then, the image causing a bout of jealousy I was unable to suppress.

Bao chose to walk behind us, the material on her sleeve brushing my shoulder as she made her way towards the hallway. It sent a tingle up my back. I wanted to invite her to stand with myself and Wu, but couldn't think of a way to do it without causing a scene.

He and I stood on the balcony, looking down on the courtyard. I quickly saw Mia, who stood out, not only from her height, but her hair. Though pinned pack, away from her face, it was white blond and yellow, a stark contrast from the black of the others. A man whose back was turned to me gestured her to the front of the line, motioning for an elderly woman to move before her. Mia refused for a moment, pointing to both women. Her obstinacy infuriated the man, for he angrily pointed for her to be first, and she bowed her head in acceptance. Before obeying the orders, Mia bowed in apology to the elderly woman, who I guessed was Gee.

Pride in Mia's countenance and manner was replaced with distaste for a man I suspected of having amorous intentions for my sister, half his age. Who else would it be than Qi Tai, one step closer to Mia?

We observed the interaction in silence until I could take it no more.

"He's not going to leave her alone is he?"

Wu brought his hands together, cracking the knuckles. He shook his head, echoing my thoughts exactly. Without cause, we were unable to take action against someone so powerful.

"Qi Tai is smart," I said, wondering what it would take to abolish a person.

"A marksman could make easy work from that point," Wu said. He was pointing to the hillside path, so close a skilled bowman could easily shoot it inside the walls of the palace, penetrating the chest of the guards. One could mount himself in a tree, feasibly hitting the very spot where we stood. "Xing pointed it out to his father and Qi Tai last year. It needs to be fixed, a barrier put up."

The gaping hole left the Emperor exposed, the obvious target. I was confident I'd hear the sound of the arrow's whoosh before it hit its mark but only if I was standing as nearby as I was now. I stepped closer to the edge of the balcony, looking back at the wall of the Palace. The western face was also exposed to attack, by spear or a force that used pulleys or ladders. Even with the few hundred guards now lining the interior of the Palace, it would be no match for an orchestrated assault on the outer wall.

CHAMBERS

"It's too low," I told him, referring to the outer gate. In reality, I knew I didn't have to worry about it. Mia had said the assault took place within the Forbidden City, not the Jade Palace. We were safe here for the time being, assuming our presence didn't interfere with history.

"Here comes your sister," said Wu. One by one, Qi Tai directed the women to different rooms, leaving only Gee and Mia. Mia walked slowly towards the far side of the Palace, her head high and proud, her gate paced. She wasn't going to speed up for anyone.

I smiled in spite of my worry. That girl had some serious attitude, knowing full well Qi Tai was powerless to do a darn thing about how fast she walked. I glanced at Wu, who was also watching the activity.

Wu flicked his hand, the movement catching Mia's attention from down below. She looked up and winked at me. She schooled her eyes to the back of Qi Tai's head, matching his gate as though in a wedding procession. I'd have to find a way to talk with her during this trip.

A glance to Wu proved he'd been admiring my sister with the same appreciation I'd been giving Bao.

"No," I mouthed, shaking my head. He didn't get to have both Bao and Mia. He smirked back at me, knowing full well we had a friendly challenge on our hands.

Perhaps Wu would be up for giving Bao a letter for Mia, though the task placed Wu a little too close to both women for my comfort. I'd have to think of something before taking off with the Admiral.

The Emperor came back to the curtain and let me know that he was ready to retire. I held the edge of the fabric as the couple walked through and into the security of the building.

The Empress fell behind several paces until we were in the hall. Bao joined her, also several steps back as we all proceeded down another corridor. An intricately carved doorway was on the left, and the other, smaller doorway, again pink, was on the right. As the Emperor turned to enter, he glanced at the Empress before she too moved towards her door. Bao opened it for her, keeping her eyes modestly affixed to the floor, pretending to see none of it. At first, I thought it was so she could be purposefully ignorant of the signals between her mistress, then I wondered if it was to avoid looking at me.

What I wanted was irrelevant. I took my usual position outside the door, giving Wu the entry point to the chamber, twenty feet down the hall. The four other guards were stationed outside the perimeter of the Emperor's quarters, rotating approximately every thirty minutes.

Wu began practicing Tai Chi formations, explaining to me that it was acceptable for the guards to do so during the long hours while the Emperor napped. He moved through Qi Gong breathing, holding air in his lungs for minutes, exhaling when pressing his hands in fluid but firm movements over his head, then down by his feet. The process of lung development took years, a necessity for enduring long battles, or as I had recently experienced, extended time under water.

I chose Bagwa Chung, a modernized form of the traditional movements designed for relaxation and coordination. The year before Mom died I had completed a weeklong training in the hills. Each day at sunset we'd form circles of five or six, walking in a formation according to our rank. Silently, softly, we moved over the ground, stopping at intervals, sliding in, out, jumping up, then turning, then switching directions, walking the circle in the opposite direction. The energy of the group increased with each rotation, a palpable force that grew within. The movement always ended with us moving towards the center, a controlled explosion of force allowing us to jump, hurl, kick or roll far beyond our previous capabilities.

When the masters first told me about it, I wasn't alone in my skepticism. It took one experience to change my naïve cynicism to conviction. I still couldn't explain it, nor did I attempt to try after my Dad paid more attention to his latest Popular Science magazine than me.

Later, when I passed my first and second-degree belts, the force of the group's energy went deeper than purely physical. During one rotation, I felt light headed, feeling the brightness of being my master said was not uncommon when the soul purified itself.

"Like being dead?" I'd asked, intrigued more than skeptical.

"Purification happens throughout this life and after," he explained. "Strive to achieve here what others delay." Older students, ones who'd trained for decades, spoke in reverential terms about the visions they'd experienced during Bagwa Chung, including dreams that had come to pass. I'd wanted to believe it was possible, but I'd never made it past the spots of light.

"You are young yet," my master had said, trying to set my mind at ease. "Control must be let go. Give over your will and your eyes will see what your mind cannot comprehend."

With limited space, I set my feet and hands for a simple Chung pattern. I began the movement, using the five feet in front of the door as my rotating circle. The energy was less concentrated than with a group, though satisfying.

As I paced back and forth, legs bent, silently gliding across the stone floor, arms up, then down and throughout my alternating turns, I focused on my breathing, imagining myself inhaling the essence of life.

I'd reached the point of peace when a screeching sound outside the building cut through the air. It sounded like a hawk going in for the kill. I ignored it until the sound drew near.

I was right, it was a hawk, and the crazy animal circled outside the window nearest me before it came straight through, diving directly for me, its talons stretched out, ready to claw. I ducked left, avoiding a ripped shoulder when it veered right at the last minute. Up it circled, landing quick and soundly on a golden perch outside the Emperor's room.

A few moments later, the Emperor's door opened, and he introduced the animal.

"It's a royal messenger bird," he told me, stroking it with care as he talked in a soothing voice, unfastening the small metal container attached to the bird's leg. "Zheng He and I use it to communicate when he travels." The bird was well trained, holding still as the Emperor read.

As I watched in silence, the Emperor's eyes narrowed, his cheeks bulged as he moved the insides of his jaw, clenching. A flush or red moved through the wisps of hair and he stood straight.

"Summon General Li," he said to the closest guard. He avoided my eyes, looking past me to Wu with a nod. Wu ran forward, bowing, casting a glance to me with a 'what's up?' look. I raised my lashes in response careful to not give offense in front of the Emperor, who by now had turned away.

When the General arrived, the two men walked to another great room with maps along the wall.

"Remain here," the Emperor told me, his voice hard. Wu and I stood together, not daring to talk. Something strange was happening. Though the room was without doors or windows and the Emperor was safe, I felt an uneasy feeling growing.

It wasn't long before the Emperor emerged, strapped a message to the hawk and it departed. An hour after that, the bird returned, this time flying straight to its pad. Once again, the Emperor removed the message, though this time, General Li was standing behind him, ready to read the message for himself.

"Zheng He arrives in one hour," the Emperor announced. His face was red, but not with anger. Noticing me watching him, he explained his concern and disappointment. "I wanted to honor him properly at the City. Now I'll have to make do with what is here." Turning to the servant, he ordered to the man to have one more place set at the table.

The Emperor turned to me. "I will be relieving you of your service to me soon. The Admiral was passing through the territory on his way to the Palace. He does not want to go back to the City at all, as it would extend his voyage. You will accompany him and proceed upon your journey immediately. Protecting the Admiral will be your next task."

Relief turned to major disappointment. I wanted to see the amazing festival planned for the Admiral that was now delayed or cancelled. The change of events also eliminated my ability to speak with Mia, or even to spend more time with Bao.

"Are you sure I'm completely necessary to him?" I asked, keeping my voice so low no one could hear. "I'd be much more valuable protecting you considering we have identified

Xing as the person who has made attempts on both of our lives."

He considered my argument, shaking his head with finality. "My entire country loves and respects the Admiral. If I die, we need the one person I know I can trust. I must guarantee that he will live, and you are the only one I know who can keep the Admiral alive."

CHAPTER 21

Zheng He, Admiral of the Chinese Royal Fleet, was literally a giant, standing an arm's length taller and nearly twice as wide as General Li. He wore a long tunic over his pants and a tent-like cape over his upper body that allowed the air to pass through the billowing sleeves. As he strode toward the Emperor, the Admiral's generously proportioned leggings flapped with each step, whipping the material back and forth, like a flag on a pole. When he was within five feet, he stopped and bowed low.

"Great Emperor," Zheng He's voice boomed. "We bring news."

The Emperor nodded, motioning Zheng He to follow him to the dining hall. Zheng He turned his large body towards me, looking me up and down, obviously noting my position in the Emperor's guard.

"Xing lost to you?" he asked, furrowing his thick, wide eyebrows and then turning his immense back to me. History had glorified this man as the most accomplished Admiral in the world, all by the age of twenty-five. His maps were centuries ahead of Columbus according to *National Geographic*, and his fearlessness in battle was legendary. Perhaps he was the man depicted on the white horse within the tapestry.

During the main meal, General Li and Zheng He were having a heated discussion about the rules of war, the General unable to convince Zheng He about the need for the Imperial forces to occupy foreign lands.

"These are the same countries we trade with," Zheng He said, his booming voice low, but carried to my ears, as well as the Emperor's. The benefit of being near the ruler at all times was the privileged information I overheard. "The value of occupying the territory must outweigh the cost of life."

The Emperor listened, though said nothing.

The massive man turned to me and asked me what I thought.

"You are a foreigner after all," as if the distinction qualified me to offer a valid opinion.

"No need to overrun a country when all the goods can be attained without blood," I answered. "Especially when they want what you have in return, like silk and precious metals. Safe commerce is worth more than gold, but not worth taking a life."

Zheng He nodded his head in approval, returning to the General, who glowered at me. The hair under his lower lip twitched as though he wanted to say something but refrained.

Beyond the men sat the Empress, flanked by her attendants as usual. Our conversation had been overheard if Bao's manners were any indication. This evening, she awarded me a slight smile, leaning in to hear the whisperings of the Empress. In this regard, the mealtime was no different than a high school cafeteria. The boys sat on one side of the room, the girls on the other. We talked about fighting and world domination and they talked about us. Or so I hoped.

The latter appeared to annoy Wu, who shuffled side to side each time he caught me making eye contact with Bao. May the best guard win, I thought to myself, the inevitability of triumph on the horizon.

That evening, a different servant girl brought our evening tea. Mia must have graduated to a full-time food-taster or attendant. I hoped she wasn't under the personal tutelage of Qi Tai, the very thought making my appetite for tea evaporate. Her wink earlier in the day had been so genuine, like this entire adventure was a big charade, a living stage on which she acted out the role of a lifetime. Even though she saw the blood in the square and knew of the death that was to befall the Palace inhabitants, her obvious good spirits must mean she knew something more about the situation than she had told me.

The pretty servant girl handed me the mug, and I felt underneath. Sure enough, it had a thin piece of paper attached to the bottom. After we finished drinking the tea, I retired to my cot. A candle in the corner was lit. I hoped it lasted until I had to use it for my reading.

As I lay next to Wu, I remained silent, though I knew he wasn't asleep. He wasn't snoring, nor was I. The longer we lay in the dark, the more impatient I grew. The letter might have news for me. I turned over, wishing him to snore.

Finally, when I could take it no more, I inquired about the only safe subject—my father.

"He's doing fine in the dungeon," Wu answered, low and quick, telling me he'd heard the other guards talking about the white man in the prison. He didn't want the others to hear him.

Thinking of what Qi Tai had told me, I asked if that was different from the prison.

Wu turned over, a sure signal he didn't want to talk about it. Neither did I really, but I had a feeling Mia's letter included a line about his whereabouts. I couldn't keep saying I didn't know or hadn't tried.

"He's better off. He's in a chamber to himself, chained by his feet to the floor." That was at odds with what Qi Tai intimated.

"Any reason why he was transferred?"

Wu clucked, the sympathetic sound normally used by teachers when I made a mistake in class.

Wu grunted. "I have a cousin who is a guard in the prison."

"What did Dad do?"

"Your father rammed his head directly in to Qi Tai's stomach. Doubled him over." In the dark, with Wu's back to me, I couldn't see him laughing but I heard the satisfaction in his voice.

That surprised me. Dad never stood up for himself or the family. All it took was a prison cell in a foreign country for Dad to finally grow some balls.

"Does the Emperor know?"

"Yes."

Finally, Wu's breathing turned heavy, matching the rise and fall of his chest. It gradually turned to full on snoring, the hiccupping sound of his lips parting the sure sign he was in a deep sleep.

I removed the note from Mia, drawing as near to the candle as possible. The paper was tiny, a fraction the size of her earlier note. She had written in texting style, abbreviating every word, assuming I could decipher her cryptic note.

Cage,

I'm so extd to be here. I passed the final test with Gee, then Qi Tai himself, who promoted me from a full-time taste tester to working more with the Empress. The trip is gr8t and riding in the box was awesome, one of my privileges of being with the Empress. Gee and Bao are showing me how to apply the make-up, do the hair and dress the Empress in her jewels. Picking out the jewels is crazy. She has an entire room full of rubies, emeralds, pearls and diamonds, and I get to help select what she wears with each outfit.

This stopped me short. My sister, the tomboy, suddenly *liking* this stuff? She wore jeans and sweatshirts, her hair invariably back in a ponytail and never touched makeup. As for jewelry, all she chose to wear was a beat-up sports watch given to her by the soccer coach so she wouldn't miss practice. To imagine her handling diamond crowns and ruby earrings the size of golf balls or necklaces with black pearls was inconceivable.

Bao has been very nice, and told me that you are doing well in your role. I think she likes you Cage. She gets quiet when I talk about you, but then asks more questions when no one else is around. Wu has also been awsm, giving me advice about how to deal with Qi Tai.

I hope we can see each other for a few minutes on this trip. I've been thinking more about the 'event' and wonder—if it will be soon. I know we will have to go soon—Cage—we must go soon, no matter what. You know what I'm talking about.

Love you, Mia

That was right. We did have to leave, no matter what. No matter if I wanted to stay with Bao, or Mia enjoyed being with the Empress. As I re-read the note again, I winced with jealousy. 'Awesome?' That was a word she reserved for me. And when did she have the chance to interact with my second in command? He was always working, the same as myself.

I put the note in the half-empty cup of tea, where it would disintegrate by morning. As I lay in the darkness, wondering what Wu could have done to warrant an 'awesome,' I knew asking him was impossible. He'd know we were communicating. For the time being, I'd have to sit back and do exactly what I'd been doing. Nothing.

CHAPTER 22

Screams awoke me from a deep sleep. After the trip to the Palace, on top of the beating it had taken the day before, my body had collapsed, my form an immovable log on the soft mat. I jumped up, awkward from the stiffness of my legs.

"What's going on?" I whispered to Wu. "The Palace isn't being invaded is it?"

"Someone is being taken," he said, a frown on his face, quickly getting dressed, motioning for me to do the same.

"A thief?"

"No," said Wu, "This must involve servants."

We couldn't leave the Emperor, who was still within his chambers.

The sun had barely risen over the mountains when the Emperor came out of his room. He directed us to the inner palace grounds, a tree-lined area designed more for sitting in small groups than the large gathering before us.

Palace guards were standing beside General Li. On the ground, a servant in a grey uniform was on his knees. His long, dark hair covered his face as he bowed low.

"You failed us," said the General, kicking the servant in the ribs. The servant rolled on his side, clutching his ribs. "We have witnesses."

"Please! I would never do what you suggest," groaned the servant. But this was no man. The voice was soft and high-pitched.

Her plea broke from a fit of coughing and I saw blood erupt from her mouth. It spit and trickled in between the cracks of the stones. I still couldn't see her face and for a moment, thought it was Mia. Reason asserted itself. Her hair was the wrong color. That was a relief.

"Wait!" called the Empress, who rushed in to the square, Bao following closely behind. She stood beside the Emperor, one step behind him as rules dictated.

"You cannot do this," she cried. Her hair was back in pins, but her makeup showed signs of imperfection. The black around her eyes were smudged, her lipstick only partially applied, and she was without jewels. She'd gotten dressed in a hurry, just as we all had done.

The General bowed half the distance for her as he had for the Emperor.

"She violated her duty," he said, politely but firmly. "It is the rule." The commotion in the square had obviously awoken Zheng He, who moved his great self between the Empress and the General. He looked at the crumpled figure in the dirt and raised an eyebrow.

"Explain," said the Emperor. His robe was imperfectly bound around his waist, the gilded sword gone, in its place was a short hand-knife pre-attached to this top.

"She missed testing the fish, and the berries were covered in dirt," the General explained. "It could have been poison.

The chef has already been removed and is headed to the quarry pit."

The Empress looked at the Emperor, her eyes glassy. "I tasted no dirt," said the Empress quietly. Bao observantly watched her mistress, her hands halfway up, as though she were prepared to catch her mistress should the Empress faint. She felt my gaze on her and looked up briefly. Her eyes conveyed the concern for the Empress's welfare in equal parts to the girl on the ground. Like me, we could do nothing but observe. "Wei-Lyn was not responsible for this," the Empress contended, her arms gesturing at the meek figure on the ground.

"We have witnesses," said General Li, pointing in the direction of two servants who vigorously nodded their heads. "You know what this means."

The Emperor was in a tough spot. It didn't matter who Wei-Lyn was. He couldn't go against Palace rules, his General and the witnesses, or at least, I didn't think so. The Empress was pale, her lower lip trembled. She knew the rules as well as he did.

The Emperor took a breath, set his chin and spoke authoritatively.

"Wei-Lyn. You are sentenced for lashings and the quarry for five years as Palace regulations dictate. You will remain in the prison until we return to the Forbidden City."

General Li appeared satisfied with the sentence. He did not look at the Empress, who swayed unsteadily into Bao's arms as guards lifted Wei-Lyn from the ground and roughly led her away. The Empress looked like she was going to collapse with distress. Bao held one hand against her mistress's back, the other underneath her arm.

The Empress gave a muffled cry and the Emperor roughly raised his hand in her direction. She choked back her tears, bowing her head in obedience. The servant must have been one of her favorites, though I was surprised by the show of emotion. This had to be a common part of Palace life.

Bao whispered something to the Empress, holding her arm. She looked up at me, her long eyelashes up then aided the Empress out of the area.

When the women were gone, the Emperor went to conduct other business.

"When do you leave?" The Emperor asked the Admiral.

"As we are up, we can go now at your approval."

The Emperor nodded, telling the servants to prepare breakfast.

"You," said the Admiral, turning to me. "What is your name?"

I bowed. "Cage, sir."

He awarded me a look of fire and discipline. "Get your things. We leave." I bowed again to Zheng He then turned to the Emperor for permission to go.

I ran towards the guard's quarters, but instead of heading down the narrow path, I made a direct line for the servant's quarters. I'd discovered the servants lived in an adjoining apartment, attached by an open breezeway, allowing easy access to the Emperor and Empress. Fortunately, it was not far from my own quarters. Since Wu was with the Emperor and the General, no one would notice a few minutes delay.

I ran down the long corridor, hoping to see my sister in one of the adjacent rooms. I slowed, looking in each as I passed by. All were empty, but I heard a muffled crying from behind a carved door. I looked both directions, and cracked it open.

A figure sat at a small table facing a large, oblong mirror, her back turned to me. She was dressed, her hair tied up in the formal bun. I moved a step to her right, just enough to see the female's reflection in the mirror. The sheer, white plaster makeup was streaked with jagged black running down her cheeks. Pink skin emerged between the white and black areas as though a rash had broken out on her face. She looked up in the mirror and saw me.

It was Bao.

I was reluctant to move closer, to upset her more. But she didn't reject me outright, so I moved inside, quickly shutting the door.

"What is wrong?" I asked. "Is it the Empress?" She nodded her head. "Did she hit you? What happened?"

She shook her head, choking back her cries.

"I'm sorry Bao. I must leave with Zheng He in moments. I don't have much time." It wasn't but minutes before that she was the one giving comfort and strength to the Empress. Now she had lost it and who knew where the Empress was hiding out. Mia was nowhere to be seen and I had to go.

I stroked her arm, trying to get her to speak.

She nodded, appearing to understand the urgency. "Last night, the food tasters responsible for preparing the dinner said that two of the eight flavors of the food weren't right," she said, as if that explained her tears. I was mystified. I didn't know much about this rule. Exasperated, the girl continued. "Specific flavors have to be used for the food that the Empress eats. The flavors must be the same ones written in the Imperial cookbook, without substitutions. If the cook doesn't prepare it correctly, the taster is supposed to stop it before it reaches my plate. But last night, your sister was on duty to taste the flavors. She did, and the platters were sent out to the Empress."

I hoped the girl hadn't lost her mind. She was always so calm and in control and this was completely out of character.

"It was Wei-Lyn," I reminded her, my patience on a short rope. "Mia was never mentioned."

Bao vigorously shook her head.

"No! You didn't listen. Your sister would have been put to death had they known it was her. Wei-Lyn knew this. When the Empress didn't eat the food, General Li knew something was wrong. The Empress did taste the dirt and the wrong spices. The General sent for another taster, who verified it. The General couldn't call the Empress a liar, so he went to discover the taster."

She was talking so fast, her words so jumbled I knelt down before her, placing a hand on her leg.

"Slow down, Bao. What happened then? Why wasn't my sister taken away if you what you say is true?" A strand of hair fell in her face. Gently, I curled the hair in my finger, pushing it behind her ear. "Slowly," I said soothingly, summoning all the patience I could muster.

"The General went into the servant's room, demanding to know who was the final taster for the Empress's meal. I knew he was hoping it was your sister. He's been waiting for a chance to imprison you or her, after Xing's disgrace. So did Wei-Lyn. Before your sister had a chance to say a word, Wei-Lyn told the Emperor she was the final taster. At first, he didn't believe her, but two other women confirmed it to the General." Her tears returned, and it was a moment before she could speak again.

"That is all. Nothing happened until this morning, when General Li entered the servant's chambers with guards, dragging Wei-Lyn to the courtyard."

As much as it tore my heart to see Bao so upset, I was incredibly thankful Wei-Lyn took the fall for my sister. Of course, it made no sense. No one wanted to spend five years in a rock quarry.

"Since the Empress had already eaten from the plate, Wei-Lyn will be beaten thirty times on her back with a bamboo stick. She won't be able to move for a month. Then, with her back barely healed and perhaps infected, she'll be forced to work, to carry heavy loads of rocks all day. Most women die within the first months of labor."

"It's my fault I didn't double check your sister's work and let her serve the Empress."

Her words brought me back to Bao's face. The glances we had shared, her smiles, taking care of me, were not unintentional. She had shown me her feelings in the only way she could. We would never go on a date, not in the conventional sense. She and I were bound by the same Palace conventions as the Emperor and Empress, relegated to communicating and passing emotion and little else.

"Can the Emperor pardon her without General Li knowing?" I offered, dropping my hand to her leg. "Or at least stall the beating?" Bao shook her head again, seemingly unaware of the placement of my fingers.

"He can do nothing to alter the punishment for the rules," she said. "They were set by the first Ming Emperors and cannot be changed."

"For no one?"

"No. Not even for the Empress's cousin."

A cousin—alive? Emperor Jianwen made it sound like no family members had been spared in the rush to execute the family members. Somehow she'd escaped, or her identity hidden. No wonder the Empress was desperate, pleading with her husband in her own way.

"I'm sorry, Bao. Was there any way someone could have added the dirt to the meal after Mia tasted the food?"

Boa nodded. "The servers who take it to the Empress are possible enemies. It used to be that the taster was also the server, responsible for the delivery of what was eaten. Qi Tai changed these rules in the last month."

Qi Tai. He was in league with the General. They recognized that they couldn't carry out their plan while Mia and I were in the Palace.

The strand of hair had once again fallen around her face. Once again, I put it behind her ear, my finger lingering on her neck longer than appropriate.

"I promise I'll come back." My hand still in place, I stretched my thumb across her face, the tip under her eye. Gently, I moved it from corner to corner, wiping away her tears.

As we sat, looking at one another, the world stopped and an idea came to me. It was crazy, to be sure. But our entry into the Forbidden City flashed through my mind, and I realized it was fully possible.

I ignored the surprised look and leaned towards her face, so close my cheek brushed hers. She caught her breath as I began whispering. My lips touched her ear as I told her my plan. I wasn't going to take any chances that the walls had secret peepholes for eavesdropping. Her sobs stopped, she leaned her head in a movement so soft but effective, my lips closed. The unintentional kiss stopped the moment it started. I kept talking, this time, my lips staying on her ear. When I was finished, Bao nodded her head. Then, wiping the last of the tears from her face, she rubbed her cheek against mine, stronger than before, then pulled back to look at me.

She touched my hand. "I will watch your sister," she promised.

I said no more, then slipped out of the room and ran down the corridor.

"That was against the rules," said Wu in a soft voice.

Wu stood around the corner, a look of anger on his face. I knew that he would inform the General that I was in the servant's chambers, and I'd be sent to some rock pit and to die of hard labor. Or, I'd silence him permanently on the subject.

He saw my crouch and dismissed it with a wave of his hand. He had no intention of fighting me.

"Follow me," he said. Who knew what or who was around the corner? It could be a trap. "Come," he said, "before it becomes too late for you as well."

He took a shortcut to our quarters and he threw my second set of clothes into a satchel.

Where was his jealousy that I'd spent time with Bao, in her chambers doing who knew what?

"We are even already," I told him. A life for a life. The debt had been fulfilled. "Why then?"

"Because you just took care of my family."

He'd lost me.

Wu nodded. "Bao is my sister," he revealed. "She grew up serving with Wei-Lyn. We are as close to her as she is to the Empress."

The revelation was a great surprise. He wasn't competing with me for Bao's affection. The change in Wu's demeanor, the offering of information. All were tied to his sister's...interest...for me.

"Bao has fallen in love," he said simply. "Her feelings have unintentional consequences that now someone is going to die for." Wei-Lyn knew how she felt for me, and knowing that my sister would be sentenced, she took her place.

"Wei-Lyn had...no one?"

Wu shook his head. "No family or brothers or sisters. No...man."

Knowing that, I felt even better about my plan.

"I have something for you." He reached in the corner of a room, and pulled out my father's backpack.

I had no words for my shock. I'd left it back in the Imperial Palace, within the chest. I almost felt guilty I'd not thought of it for a minute, from the time we ran out of the Forbidden City to standing on the balcony up to the present.

"You must know...the General is replacing those loyal to the Emperor and Empress with his own people," he confided, echoing the words of his father. If General Li was powerful enough to move those in key positions around like pawns on a chessboard, it wasn't just my position that was in jeopardy. Wu's position was threatened as well.

"You've seen the looks Qi Tai has given your sister. The preferential treatment. It won't stop there. I suspect...I'm not sure....but he has something else in mind. I'm watching him, as are the others. You both saved us from losing our positions that day. We haven't forgotten."

He turned. "Put that in the satchel with your clothes," he suggested. When he saw the inquisitive look on my face. "My dad told me to get it for you."

He paused, looked anywhere but me, sighed, then met my eyes, just as he had after I saved his life.

"I can't do anything for your father, but I'll watch Mia," he said, giving me a slight bow. He and Bao and Mia had their hands full, right at the moment I had to leave.

Without another word, we jogged back to Zheng He, who was already waiting, shifting impatiently on his white horse.

"Well?" he said, looking at me. I expected to be running beside him as I had the Emperor.

He pointed a thick, brown finger at a dark horse beside him. "Get on."

I'd never ridden a horse before. The satchel firmly around my shoulders, I slipped my foot in the stirrup, gripped the saddle and launched myself up.

"We go!" Zheng He shouted. A caravan of horses trotted through the courtyard, out the gates and accelerated to a full gallop on the dirt road. I turned for a final look at the Jade Palace, but it was hidden in the dust.

CHAPTER 23

Throughout the ride, I adjusted my bony butt on the thin, leather saddle. The only way to keep my mind off the increasing pain was to figure out exactly what happened with the food tasters and the opulence of food preparation in the Palace. A thousand things could go wrong every meal of every day.

Standing around for hours while the Emperor ate, I'd counted at least one hundred men who came to slice and peel the vegetables, prepare, taste, and serve the meals, and pour the wine. With hundreds of servants who carried food from the kitchen to the dining area, it could have been anyone who changed the flavors served to the Empress.

Wei-Lyn had the qualities of a saint, enough to make her jump in front of the General's death sword for my sister. As I considered the situation, Zheng He told me we were going to make a stop at a sacred place.

"First we stop at the Yungang Grottoes to pay our respects to the spirits."

I'd remembered hearing about the Grottoes when I had lived in China, but couldn't recall why they were important. I imagined some type of underground waterway system, not unlike the Catacombs tunnels.

"When do we reach the boats?"

"Not water grottoes," corrected the Admiral. "These were created for the monks. Are these not famous where you are from?"

I shook my head no. I didn't really want to hear about it, but his talking would serve as a distraction from the pain I was in and my thoughts about Bao.

The Admiral's great chest heaved, a sigh that expressed his disappointment of being burdened with a companion so uninformed as I.

"Over a thousand years ago monks lived in these mountains, quietly and peacefully. Few people outside the area even knew of their existence. The monks cared for the villagers, fed the sick, and tended the crops in the surrounding lands. One day, the Emperor decided he wanted their property. The monks were forced out of their homes and then watched as the Emperor's soldiers burned down their temples. Soon after this, the Emperor fell ill and died. His son believed his death was a direct result of the gods' anger with his father and decided to make restitution for his father's evil deeds. The Emperor's son assigned a labor force of ten thousand men to rebuild homes that could never be burned down, so the homes were carved out of rock. The Emperor also ordered that fifty-three temple grottoes be carved with statues honoring the gods worshiped by the monks. He returned favor to the land by creating the statues, and the spirits allowed him to live many years."

"How many gods are there?"

"Fifty-one thousand."

That was a heckuva lot of guilt, I thought. I asked on the length of time it must have taken to carve the grottoes.

"Five years," replied Zheng He proudly.

I asked the Admiral many questions about the fleet he commanded. When he felt inclined, he answered my questions. With each hour that passed, the land turned darker and drier. The green trees gave way to arid land full of black rock, separated by jagged cracks full of short, tan grasses. It looked like a lava flow I'd seen in northern California that was thirty thousand years old. The glass obsidian jutted at angles, leaning this way and that towards the sun. Heaps of white pumice formed from the ash of the eruption covered an entire ridge.

"Wait. Admiral!" I shouted, trying hard not to sound abrupt. The words were out of my mouth before I considered their impact.

The Admiral reined in his horse, nearly causing a collision with the horse behind him. I drew my horse up short.

"That ridge, over there," I pointed. "Can we get closer? I'd like to get a few rock samples if I may."

He kept his horse trotting. "These are the Datong volcanoes," he said. "Nothing of importance. What's your reason?"

I was so excited, I consciously slowed down and paced myself.

"Maps keep track of underwater currents so you can guide your ships," I began, hoping I was using the right terminology. "Volcanic rocks help identify where and when other eruptions may occur. Some rocks are also valuable for trading."

"Those?" he asked doubtfully. I could see the maps metaphor had got him, but he wasn't sure about my trading comment.

"Not here perhaps, but these are rare where I come from. It won't take much time at all. In fact, you can wait here and I'll ride over myself."

He looked at the sky, as though considering the distance we had yet to travel.

"I'll give the horses a water break. Go."

I quickly took off. Maybe, just maybe, I could find a piece of the obsidian or pumice that matched the hole inside the orb. I was off the horse, picking up three samples from the ridge and back on in seconds. Over on the black run of obsidian, I collected three as well. I'd figure out how to cut or shape the rocks later. I wrapped both in my extra set of clothes in my father's backpack, returning it to my shoulder.

"You were fast. Good," said the Admiral with a hint of pleasure. "Water your horse quickly." I did so, and it wasn't long before we'd resumed our journey.

We accelerated to a gallop, riding hard for another hour, until the sun began to set. The pain was less noticeable, by thoughts inspired by the possibility of placing the rocks in the orb.

To pass the time, I watched the landscape, asking Zheng He more questions about those who occupied the land, the princes who lived close, what he knew about the outlying peasants. In the distance, billows of smoke shot up in plumes, coming from a hidden source in the ground. The regularity of the smoke wasn't natural. It had a rhythm, a cadence that had to be man-made. I asked Zheng He about it.

"Royal armory," he said. "The Minister of Weapons' forgery." When I wondered out loud how often Wi Cheng came to the forgery, the Admiral peered at me from under his bushy eyebrows, a look of surprised skepticism on his face. Not knowing if I'd upset him, I explained I'd met the Minister at the Palace, and spent time with him. Instead of getting the Admiral to talk, my disclosure made Zheng He maintain his silence, curiosity plain on his face.

"Did I do something wrong?" If Zheng He was unhappy with my status as an unwanted visitor being friends with Wi Cheng, he might as well tell me.

Zheng He did the equivalent of raising his massive shoulders. He dropped his head to his left until I heard a crack like a soda can opening up, then rolled it back, stretching his massive neck, skin lengthening and tightening before it jerked back.

"Interesting," he said, electing not to elaborate further. Taking that as a good sign, I told him how Wi Cheng had originally questioned me about weapons and later, had been invited to visit the Minister in his building.

Zheng He moved his hips on the horse as he turned to get a better look at me, causing the poor animal underneath to moan in protest.

"What did you do then?" he asked me, watching my lips as though evaluating whether or not they were capable of lying to him.

"Talked," I answered truthfully. He didn't need to know what about or how I'd gone in with one set of opinions and left with another.

He grunted once, repositioned himself on his beast and changed the subject. Streams ran through open meadows, the trees boasted large, orange leaves that fell in the cool evening breeze. We were heading towards a grey mountain, though as we rode closer, it rose nearly straight up several hundred feet. We were nearly upon it when I saw a rock face carved entirely out of stone.

"We are here," said Zheng He.

The large clearing was already full of other men on horses. Zheng He looked as though he expected the group. He held up his hand, a signal for the others and myself to slow. We did so as the Admiral rode ahead of us. He went directly up to the leader of the group, himself on a large black steed.

He was close enough for me to get a good look at his face. It was hard; two black eyes overshadowed with thick brows, the corners of his mouth drooping. Horns stuck up on either side on his dented, metal helmet, and lining the rim were jagged teeth from an unknown animal. His jacket and pants were dirty from the ride, but gold thread glistened underneath, and an ornate embroidered dragon was stitched on the shoulder.

"Zheng He," said the man.

"Prince of Yan," replied Zheng He. "We have much to discuss."

CHAPTER 24

The two men dismounted, followed by the remainder of the troops, so I went down from my horse as well. Zheng He shot me a look like I'd embarrassed him, raising his eyebrow, though he continued talking with the Prince.

The Admiral's men rapidly set camp, raising tents and preparing for the evening meal. With nothing better to do, I left to inspect the rock building. Zheng He wasn't worried about me running off or he'd have had me watched. Without supervision, I entered the tall edifice.

The entry way resembled a hotel. A group of soldiers had already entered in front of me, carrying torches and reverently proceeded through the entrance. I asked a soldier for one and followed slowly, at the end of the line.

As the others moved quickly, talking about a specific destination deeper within the grottoes, I stopped periodically in front of the statues, pausing to read the inscriptions. I wondered if the statues still existed in my time, sure that they did. Thousands of tombs had been preserved, living testament to the Chinese expertise with rock and carving, just as the terra cotta soldiers and thousand-year-old jade sculptures.

The statues were grouped into different types, but the most frequently encountered statues were those of Buddha. The inscriptions implied that a squat, round, fat man existed for every need. Some warded off evil spirits; others bestowed wisdom, happiness, or love. Three Buddhas offered endless summers and many children.

I quickly walked down a hallway and into a room large enough for dancing. Inside was a two story-tall Buddha with its palm turned out—the symbol for wisdom.

On another wall my torchlight highlighted a sculpture unlike any I'd seen. I bent forward and made out the image of a three-headed man with six arms. It had the upper body of a human and the lower half of a bull. The craftsman had carved large haunches and sharp toes. I gently touched the beast and found it was unlike the other carvings, as it was completely detached from the wall. Only the bull's feet were attached to a stone platform.

I looked around and realized I was alone. I reached into the backpack to check the orb, making sure nothing had broken apart. I felt the sail pointer on the top, pricking one of my fingers in the process. I curled my fingers around the rough object and carefully pulled it out for further examination.

How would I know what to do with the rocks once they were inserted into the orb? I couldn't understand the inscription on the outside, and had no idea whether it needed one rock or five.

"No better time to find out," I muttered.

I cradled the orb between my knees as I pulled out a piece of obsidian. Quickly unscrewing the lid, holding the torchlight low enough to examine the markings within the hollow of the orb.

I felt the lining, feeling one that was smooth, like the black volcanic glass.

"This way," said the voice of a soldier. There was not enough time, I knew, depositing the obsidian in an empty space. I screwed down the lid and returned it to the backpack.

I sat down to wait for the others, resting one hand upon the man-bull's torso. My other hand was at the foot of the statue.

Suddenly, a breeze blew across my face. The torch flickered and dimmed. Startled, I looked around.

"Anyone there?" I asked to the dark. The last time wind had blown past me, in the dark, surrounded by rock, I'd been transported. I absolutely did *not* want to leave this place.

My voice bounced around the room before it went silent. I must be hearing things. To ease the tension, I stretched both legs out straight, put my arms behind me, and gripped each wrist, cracking my back.

Huff.

A breath of warm wind blew across the top of my head, and I swiped my hair with my right hand. A bat, I thought.

Huff. Again, the gust of warm air blew by me. This time, it was accompanied by a foul-smelling odor. I shifted my weight uncomfortably in the dark. I looked around, wondering if a wall was going to open. Yet I wasn't holding the orb in my hands, and a look at my backpack confirmed it wasn't glowing in the dark.

I heard voices ricochet off the inner walls. I squinted down the corridor in the direction of the voices. The echoes carried some distance, just as they did in the catacomb tunnels.

I blinked several times in the dim light to focus on the four hooves before me. The gray stone legs were now covered with rough strings of hair.

Another huff was followed by the sound of a puff of air.

My eyes continued up the body until I saw the man's chest. It heaved, filling with the same air that drained from my lungs. The eyes turned from gray to black to red, and the tip of the nose turned from cold stone to warm and wet skin.

"*AAAHHHHWWW*," yawned one of the three heads. It had awoken from its stone slumber, and the other two heads blinked their eyes and moved their lips. Six arms stretched in all directions, and bones popped and creaked in the darkness.

Complete disbelief and awe collided in the dark. I had brought this statue to life by connecting the orb to rock. Before I could consider all of the possibilities, I heard a click and a smash.

The bull had extricated its hoof from the platform and raised it in the air. The ground shook as it landed with a thud. The man heads snorted in glee, and the three heads began to talk to one another in an animated manner before they broke into jubilant song.

Fast as I was, I'd never outrun the beast, but maybe I could slip away in the commotion. I moved back a few steps, turned, and smacked right into a rock doorway.

The creature heard the noise and turned around, ready for a challenge. In unison, the three heads looked at me while the six arms searched the walls for a weapon. Loud voices carried through the passageway. Two of the heads turned in the direction of the noise then back at the third head, which continued to stare at me. The heads were speaking among themselves, debating whether to stomp me into the stone floor or leave me alone in return for its freedom from eternal bondage.

The voice from the hallway grew loud. Zheng He's men were coming closer. One head gave a loud howl, another battle shout, while the third pointed the way. The beast lowered its shoulders toward the floor and charged into the hallway.

I winced as screams assured me the beast had encountered Zheng He's men. I ran in the opposite direction, crossed one hallway into another, and sprinted out into a small room near the outside of the grotto. The glare of the setting sun momentarily blinded me and I ran full force into Zheng He.

"And where are you going in such a rush?" he demanded.

"I thought you were down there," I panted, standing straight and patting my chest.

"I was," said Zheng He, with a glare. "But a three-headed beast charged, forcing us down a corridor. This hall was a shortcut out of the grotto."

The cool air didn't stop sweat from beading on my forehead.

"A three-headed beast?" I responded, wiping the sweat off my forehead.

Over Zheng He's shoulder, I glimpsed men running in all directions as the beast gave chase like a cat after mice. Zheng He firmly gripped my shoulder, and together we watched as the bull raged over the courtyard. The beast's hands picked men up off their feet and bopped their heads together before throwing them back on the ground. When the men finally fled into the grotto, the heads gave a final howl, and the beast raced off into the distance, leaving a trail of dust and limp bodies behind it.

Zheng He turned to me, his eyes black with fury, his hand a vise, planting me to the ground. I couldn't run if I tried.

"You don't look surprised," he said.

I decided I'd best tell as much truth as long as I could.

"I saw a sculpture of a three-headed part-man, part-bull, yes," I said calmly, as a slow trickle of sweat rolled down the side of my cheek.

"Walk," he said, indicating I go before him. I needed no instruction. I took him to the place where the statue of the bull had stood. Down the passage toward the statues now empty platform.

"The statue of Mohaishou has stood here for nearly a thousand years without interruption, through Imperial changes, floods, and battles," he said. He stepped away, folding his arms as he circled the vacant stand. "Then a young foreigner emerges from the ground within the walls of the Forbidden City, defeats the Emperor's guard, and happens to save the life of Wi Cheng, the Minister of Weapons who has not left his forge more than a handful of times in fifty years." This last bit had more emphasis than defeating the Emperor's guard. "Wi Cheng then invites you to spend time in his inner sanctum, a place so sacred to him that not even I, the Admiral of the Imperial Naval fleet, have been allowed to go. Then, you ask to collect worthless rocks as we are on a journey that you could have known nothing about, and happen to be near a stone statue that comes to life."

I rocked back and forth on my heels, wishing myself on the edge of a volcano. My gut told me he was to be trusted, that he had integrity. He was a person I wanted on my side.

"What is the real reason for the rocks?" he asked. I felt an inner peace about the question. He didn't threaten me with torture or death. He asked and expected me to respond. He would be the judge of my response. "You can tell me now, or wait until we return."

It was my turn. "Are you an outsider to the Palace, or in league with the others?"

The Admiral squinted. His barrel size arms rested on his chest, the massive chin lowered as he considered my actual meaning.

"I serve the Emperor. That's all that matters."

My stomach clenched the moment I considered the possibility. Zheng He is the man I felt right about. I suspected…

"You weren't raised in the Palace were you?" I asked. The Admiral seemed taken aback by the question, pushing his great chin down, nearly hiding it the folds of his neck. I took that as a yes. "What—like on an island or someplace far away, removed from anyone here—any relatives or close friends?" He stared, without nodding, another confirmation of my statement. "Hear me out on this," I said, the potential of telling someone else my secret giving rise to an urgency to get it out.

"You are going to be a great Admiral, greater, better known than you are today. All around the world. In my city, your name is going to be synonymous with traveling the world and creating new routes. I don't want anything to change this, I can't change it. If you want to know everything about what's happened to me, realize that this knowledge might affect the outcome of your life."

"You talk as though you know the past and can change the future."

"I will tell you the reason for the rocks, what I'm doing here and what it means. What I want to know is if you can keep the knowledge to yourself, or use it for good, not to hurt others. Can you do that?"

Once more he studied me, unfolding his arms, the billows of his robe hanging in the dark, the soft flapping sound like bats in the cavern. Torchlight from the hallway flickered, and the Admiral yelled for the men to stay out of the sacred grotto until he emerged.

"I will not keep information from the Emperor if it concerns his safety. But," he continued, seeing my disappointment, "a confidence you entrust to me, that does not need to be shared, will be mine until my death."

I wondered aloud if the man-bull was going to come back any time soon. Zheng He shook his head. "It is running and my men are chasing it. If it leaves to the hills, they may continue until we leave."

I wiped the sweat from my face and nodded. Zheng He motioned me to sit on the stone tablet, and I told him everything I knew: from before we left Washington to seeing the tapestry, to releasing the creature. I withheld the information about the upcoming invasion, though I did imply a battle was going to be forthcoming. I talked until I couldn't speak any longer.

"So you do know the future of the kingdom." It wasn't a question. From my silence, he guessed the truth. "Will the Emperor survive?"

I told him what Mia had related to me. "The historians don't know. Some think they escaped in disguises, and the others argued both Empress and Emperor died in the fire."

He raised a hand, indicating I stop. "Don't tell me more," he asked, and I understood why. To tell more would be to disturb the natural course of history, to cheat life or death. By now, I knew Zheng He didn't cheat anything. He wanted to face his own destiny, without foreknowledge.

Zheng He asked to hold the orb, and I obliged.

My life was in Zheng He's hands now. If Zheng He were to tell the Emperor about the three-headed beast or the rest of it, my quest would end. I adjusted myself uncomfortably on the rock, nervously waiting for Zheng He to stop his examination.

"You have brought evil to this place. The three heads represent wisdom, forgiveness, and love. We felt only pain as it tried to harm all in its path."

I shook my head against such a crazy suggestion. "You think I did this on purpose?"

"No," he said reflectively. "Not by intent, but it happened nonetheless. This orb is an object of great power. A tool to be used for good or a weapon for evil. Every living thing has evil within. Most of us, however, suppress the bad when we embrace good." He turned the orb over again in his hands. As he held it, I waited for him to turn the top and bottom halves, testing it out for himself. His thick fingers held it delicately, as though it were a fragile piece of glass. He took special care to touch and turn it without moving the metal. I could see he didn't want to activate the orb.

Zheng He kicked a piece of wood onto the pile with his mammoth foot. "The Emperor must know." Zheng He's bushy, black brows furrowed so deeply that they hid his brown eyes.

"You can't tell him about the orb," my fear audible in my voice.

"A captain doesn't command the currents of the sea, my young friend. He chooses the best course the sea affords in order to safely arrive at his destination. You may find that you must choose between your own desire and the right choice for your family."

They were one in the same, I thought. I can't leave without my family or the orb. The archivist made me believe that the destiny was already chosen for me.

Zheng He handed the orb back to me and stood resolutely. "I cannot have any more thousand-year-old, three-headed man-bulls running around the countryside."

Zheng He was about to call for his men when the screech of a bird penetrated the air high above. It was the Emperor's hawk.

The bird landed upon Zheng He's cloaked arm. As he carefully unbound the message and read it, his face turned into a grimace. He crushed the message in his massive hand.

"Your sister has disappeared with Wei-Lyn," he said, gesturing for his guards. His countenance grew bleak, the thick jaw hardened.

"That's impossible!" I challenged. That was not the plan I'd outlined to Bao at all. Something had gone very wrong. Mia was not supposed to be involved in our plan.

"No more so than you giving life to a statue," he said, standing. He motioned to a nearby soldier. "Your family has been charged with kidnapping and treason. I'm to return you to the Emperor, where your family awaits trial and execution."

CHAPTER 25

That night, my feet were chained to a post inside a small tent, the pole in the center of the structure. The bed was nearby, with a pot on the floor for going to the bathroom. A soldier had left me with a coarse blanket to keep off the chill.

Zheng He didn't let me hold my backpack, but placed it on the far side of the tent, just out of my reach. He told me it would be placed on my shoulders before my hands were tied in the morning. He muttered about the gods frowning on him, like he was going to get struck down if he remained close to me, or near the objects that had awoken the three headed beast. Even so, he was going to be sure I didn't bring more beasts to life.

When he came to give me the evening meal, I asked him if he had more information about my sister.

"It can't hurt to tell me," I argued. "I can't do anything about it, nor would I even try. I'm sure it was a misunderstanding or someone put Mia up to going against her will."

Zheng He placed a bowl of clear soup before me, bending his legs outward in a standing meditative position.

"A second communication I received told me otherwise. Since you told me all, I will extend the same courtesy to you, even though your sister is likely to be executed anyway."

"The Emperor's caravan returned to the Forbidden City, and Wei-Lyn was brought along so that she would be sent from there to the quarry. After they arrived back at the Imperial Palace, guards noticed that Wei-Lyn was missing, and your sister was gone as well. It is unknown who made this possible. They are nowhere to be found, though the guards locked down the city in a search for the two girls."

I was appalled and impressed at the same time. It was feasible Mia and Wei-Lyn could have disguised themselves as servants, but how would the two have made it past the Imperial Palace walls? Someone else had to be involved.

"Do you know who could have aided their escape?"

I shook my head no. "Mia knew no one," I said, looking him straight in the eye. Since our arrival, her only contact had been with the Empress, Bao, Gee, Wu, and Qi Tai.

"Could she have been set up?" Seeing his confused look, I altered my words. "Was it possible that she was tricked to do something unlawful she thought was appropriate?"

He shrugged. "Qi Tai is in an uncontrollable rage."

I bet. Her disappearance certainly put an end to his ability to make her a concubine.

"Do you really believe she will be executed?"

Zheng He stood, flexing his hands. "Unless Qi Tai wants to spare her." He gave me a knowing look. If the Emperor knew the man's preference for girls, so did the Admiral.

I asked him for paper and a writing utensil.

"What for?" he inquired. "I'm not allowed to have you send her a note."

"I'm going to draw you a map of the world," I said simply. "This will be unlike any map you've ever seen." Several hours later, the flap of the tent opened and his big head poked through.

"Well?"

"Here," I said, offering him my work. I was convinced Zheng He was more interested in the world's oceans than he was in learning how to turn stones into living beings. It seemed that the best way to regain Zheng He's trust was to provide him something of value. "I'm much better with mapping volcanoes than I am with continents and the world."

Zheng He brought the map to his eyes and examined each detail. I knew enough about ancient map-making to mimic a flat format rather than use a modern map layout. I'd drawn the Western and Eastern Hemispheres, outlining Africa, Europe, and the Americas, including as many island chains as I could remember. By including the North and South Poles, I'd noted the trade routes to reach all of the continents. I had no idea when Zheng He was supposed to have discovered all the continents, and didn't want the map to be completely accurate, so I purposely drew California as an island and moved Australia slightly to the right of where it actually sits.

"See here," I said, pointing at North America. "This continent won't be discovered for eighty-one more years by an Italian sent from Spain called Columbus. A man named Magellan won't circle the entire world for a hundred and sixteen years," I continued. "You can do both, claiming the victory for yourself, the Emperor, and all of China. It is up to you to decide if you want to change history by recording the trip or keeping it a secret."

Zheng He carefully rolled the small map and placed it within his billowing shirt. He pulled back the drape of the tent wide enough for me to see the sky.

"I don't know what happened with my sister, but I know she didn't intentionally dishonor the family." Her shame would be mine, in the traditional Chinese philosophy. I feared her impetuous nature had put our lives in jeopardy.

"Storm clouds on the horizon," remarked Zheng He, pointing to the sky. "That one could crush a large ship like a skiff. On land, it throws lightening. We will know soon enough how well our ships do in this weather. I've decided we leave tonight."

***

Zheng He sent the bird off with orders to prepare the fleet, and he told me he requested a partial Armada for the return voyage. He wasn't taking chances I was aligned with an enemy force.

We rode through the night without breaks. My body was ready to collapse, as were the horses by the sounds of it. When we arrived at the port, sailors and soldiers assisted our tired group onto the boats. By the time we had pulled up anchor, the clouds had grown from small, lumpy puffs to large, roiling monsters. The weather had turned bitterly cold. Heavy rain, snow, and hail were falling, and lightning intermittently brightened the sky. I watched the Admiral pace back and forth on the massive deck from his own cabin where I was being held. I was chained to a fixed desk in the center of the room. I had the comfort of sitting for the journey or lying down, and I wanted to do neither. I stood by the door, looking out on the ship's deck. I followed his gaze to a vertical cone of cloud looming in the distance.

"Is it coming toward us?" asked one of the shipmates.

"It is as if we are being hunted. When we were in the mountains, the temperatures dropped and clouds formed. When we moved to the valley, the wind increased its speed. This evening, when we are safely back on my boat, we find ourselves cornered by the storm."

The ship itself was massive. Zheng He said it could carry more than a thousand men. We were now travelling with six hundred sailors and four hundred men-at-arms. From what I could see through the small window, the warriors were skilled archers, their bows tailored for long-range battles, and their short swords and knives showed that these men were also skilled in hand-to-hand combat. I should have been flattered he thought I was so powerful—or at least, those that I was working with could possibly defeat him. I wasn't. The entire situation gave me a sick feeling of anticipation that the fear was misdirected away from the real adversary.

I learned the Admiral was in charge of other ships, including treasure ships, warships, patrol boats, and tankers that carried fresh water or other supplies. This ship held a bit of everything.

The ship's body was curved, like a bowl riding on the water. There were four long, white sails shaped like the fan on a dragon's back. Each sail was made of paper-thin cloth anchored along long bamboo rods. The ease with which the sails flipped and turned without many ropes aided the crew's efficiency. Its flat bottom was built for carrying gifts to trading partners as well as holding the spoils from successful battles.

I moved from the side of the cabin to the front door, trying to catch as much of the deck conversation as I could. What I learned so far was intriguing. We were sailing to meet an Italian ship full of goods Zheng He had asked to trade. A group of Italian merchants were on their way to the Palace at this very moment, and we were to bring back their goods. Zheng He had no option but to carry out this mission, even in the face of the storm.

"Do they want to take some of our women again?" asked a crew member.

Zheng He nodded. "Among other things."

Zheng He yelled an order, and a crewman swiftly collapsed a sail, its weight folding accordion-like down the length of the pole. Winds whipped the Imperial banners attached to the top of each sail. I watched the other ships as they made maneuvers following Zheng He's lead, working in unison like choreographed dancers.

"A storm of this size is unusual for this time of year," Zheng He said to another shipmate outside the window. "I was hoping we'd outrun it."

Zheng He looked intently at the vast sea and roiling clouds. I caught him turning towards the cabin and I ducked below the window. A moment later, the door unlocked.

"I'm not worried about you escaping," he said, unlocking my chains. "For your own good, don't come outside during the storm. Those clouds shower lightning."

"Are you suggesting I might get struck by lightning?"

"No, but if it aims for you, I believe some force will protect you, and the lightning might strike someone else. And I cannot afford to lose any of my men."

I thought the Admiral was making a joke, but Zheng He wasn't smiling.

"You must stay alive no matter what happens," ordered Zheng He. "We have lifeboats ready if this vessel sinks. By the Emperor's orders, you must be in one of them."

CHAPTER 26

A giant wave hit the ship and I was flung against the wall of the hull. The frigid water poured in, quickly rising to my knees.

Another huge wave rolled toward the front of the ship, and Zheng He ran out of the room from me, ordering the skipper to turn the vessel against the cresting arch. The ship skirted beneath the wave and out the other end as it crashed over the aft deck. I locked my hands around two wooden bars until my knuckles turned white.

Lightning flashed in the sky, sending white spikes into the water. A flash burst right outside my window, followed by screams. A man was hit by the bolt and lay unconscious on the deck. The point of touchdown began to burn. In no time, the fire consumed the wood and rope around the man.

I had to save him from being burned alive. Crouching low, I left the safety of the Captain's quarters and ran onto the deck. I grabbed the man by his feet and started to drag him toward a covered area. I slid left and right as the waves pounded the boat, causing the unconscious sailor's body to slither like a snake toward the wall. Grabbing a line off the deck, I tied the man's body to it.

"I told you to stay sheltered!" yelled Zheng He angrily.

"I was saving your man!" I yelled back through the torrential rain, the hail stinging my eyes and pelting my tongue.

"Obstinate foreigner!" growled the Admiral. With a powerful jerk, Zheng He swung the man's body over his shoulders and scrambled toward the canopy. He dumped the man on the deck and stood up just as another lightning bolt cracked.

"Watch out!" I yelled. But the warning came too late. Zheng He was the tallest object around, and the lightning went straight for his big body.

The bolt went directly into Zheng He's broad shoulder. The force blasted him to the opposite side of the deck, where he lay motionless.

I made my way across the slippery deck a second time to help the injured admiral. I couldn't find a pulse. I looked around frantically for someone to help me with Zheng He, but the terrified sailors had deserted their commander, taking shelter below. I was alone.

I tore off Zheng He's tent-like shirt and saw a large burn where the lightning had struck his back. It would heal but would leave a nasty scar to remind Zheng He of his heroic feat.

I placed my hands on Zheng He's chest and pumped. I had only a few minutes to get a small amount of blood to flow from the heart to the brain. I placed an ear to Zheng He's mouth, but with the winds and rain it was impossible to tell whether the big man was breathing. I continued the rhythm of the CPR, alternating between pressing his chest and breathing into his mouth, though I felt dizzy, I was more worried I'd pass out from sheer exhaustion. Suddenly, Zheng He's massive chest heaved violently, unleashing a ragged cough.

"Let's get you inside," I shouted to the Admiral. I slid an arm around Zheng He's wide shoulders, straining to lift him off the deck.

Zheng He looked down at his bare chest and asked me what had happened. "Lightning," I shouted, attempting to get Zheng He to stand.

"Where are my men?" he groaned. The wind was so furious I barely heard his voice.

I pointed below decks.

A lightning burst cracked on the ocean's surface, sending huge plumes of water in all directions.

"Do something with that object of yours," yelled the Admiral, gripping his shoulder.

"I don't know if it will work," shaking my head.

"Just do it!"

I braced for another enormous wave. When it rolled over the other side, we made a dash back to his stateroom.

I heard a *whoosh* from behind as I was able to slam the door shut. The Admiral's room had withstood the brunt of the storm. Though books were on the floor and the chair overturned, the table and bed were both in place, each nailed down firmly with iron clamps. The paintings on the walls were in place, though spattered with water. A small porthole window had been shattered, and shafts of air and water blew in the room.

I took a small pillow from the bed and crammed it into the hole. It wouldn't hold forever, but maybe long enough for me to do something about the storm.

If it can be done, I thought. It wasn't faith in the orb I lacked. It was faith in myself.

I removed the backpack and dropped to the floor. Within seconds I determined that the contents were still safe and undamaged. I took out the orb, wishing for guidance, thinking as intently about changing the direction of the storm as I could. Placing a piece of the obsidian in one cavity had brought a non-living entity to life. The other type of rock I took off the mountain was white pumice that seemed lighter than air. I had no idea what that did, if anything.

Using my thighs as clamps, I held the lower portion of the orb, twisting the top part off. I had barely enough light to see. A jolt knocked me off balance, and I crashed on my right shoulder. By now, my limbs were half-frozen from the extended exposure to the cold. I clenched my right hand in a death grip to maintain my hold on the top of the orb, but the bottom half popped out from my legs, and slid across the ground to the far side of the wall. As I scrambled on all fours and grabbed the orb. I took the two rocks and dropped each one into an open hole. Just as I did, another wave crashed against the hull, knocking the rocks out of the orb and onto the floor. I half slithered to grasp each as the entire lot rolled under the water in to the darkness. I furiously moved my hands, finding a soft rock and another rough. Teetering in the boat, the water crashing all around me, I clenched the orb between my legs again, put the rocks in their right place, and replaced the lid, screwing it down until it seemed as tight as before.

Before I could turn the lid, another wave sent me and the orb flying, and I hit my forehead against its metal side. The point on its top sail broke the skin. Blood trickled down my nose as I picked it up again, concentrating on figuring out exactly what happened when I was in the grottoes. I had put the obsidian in the orb, closed it tight and returned it to my back. I'd not touched it again before the beast awoke, and I couldn't recall thinking anything in particular that would make a statue come alive.

Then I remembered exactly where I was standing. The orb was in my backpack, and I was leaning against the leg of the statue.

"*Turn it,*" came a whisper travelling on the air wafting through the opening in the hull. It sounded like my mother, but I couldn't see her. Whether it was wishful thinking on my part, or my inner voice giving me confidence, I didn't know. I cupped my right hand over the top of the cold metal, and pressed, slowly turning the orb clockwise.

Nothing. Quickly, I turned it the other direction. Again, no action.

Maybe *turning it* meant the other rock, since this one wasn't doing anything. Enforcing calm when I felt none, I opened the orb, noted the location of the pumice and shut it again. I moved the sail to the point right above the pumice.

I started to turn the orb and the bow of the vessel was lurched up, causing my grip to slip, the orb turning counterclockwise. A sudden rock of the boat forced me across the room, and I hit my head again. I heard screams from the men outside, one slowly fading, as though he'd fallen overboard.

"No!" I choked as sea water flooded my mouth, holding on for dear life.

"Turn it again," urged the calm voice. This time it was clear and familiar.

My arm was shaking as I held the top down and turned it clockwise. As I did, the boat's front dropped with the ease of a mother setting down her child. Water splashed against the side of the boat and I waited for another jolt. It didn't happen.

After a few moments, the boat ceased rocking. I rose, still holding the orb. Dripping wet, I replaced the orb into the backpack, waited a few moments to catch my breath, then joined the Admiral.

"It worked," I breathed, placing the pack on my back, my eyes still stinging from the sea salt.

"Look there," Zheng He said. The storm had retreated and the sun was beginning to peak through the clouds.

"Are we even?" I asked.

"Yes, Cage," Zheng He said, letting go the rope. "I was bound by duty to keep you alive. You could have left me for dead. Instead, you saved us all. Thank you."

He gave me a low bow. The others on deck heard the Admiral's booming voice and thanks. Looking alternately ashamed of their cowardice and appreciative they too were saved, they looked at me with a supplication bordering on worship. It was oddly gratifying.

Soon it wouldn't matter. We'd reach the Italian ship, turn around and head back to the Forbidden City. When we reached land, Zheng He would be bound to hand me over to Qi Tai.

CHAPTER 27

The ship had not sustained structural damage to its outer hull, and the crew had removed nearly all the water from below. The captain's servants mopped and dried the floors and even found dry blankets that had been stored in waterproof containers. When the captain's quarters were free of water, Zheng He insisted I return inside.

The next morning, I awoke to a crashing thud coming from a long board connecting our ship to the Italian vessel. I heard Zheng He talking, then another, higher voice, responding in passable Mandarin. I didn't see the Italians, but heard the clanking of ripping sounds of metal, indicating the doors to the lower decks were being opened. The creaking of steps confirmed goods were being transferred between ships.

Afterwards, the ships were unbound and we continued toward our port. Once we docked, I was mounted on a horse, and rode with my hands bound to the saddle. Zheng He neither spoke nor looked at me for the duration of the ride to the Forbidden City. We arrived early the next morning, a few hours before the Italians were scheduled to be presented to the Emperor.

The morning reception had included an extravagant parade, with all the dragons, operatic singers, flower petals on the ground…everything Qi Tai and the ministers had first planned for the illustrious Admiral, save the lit candles on the waterway. The gossiping guards predicted the festivities would continue well into the night, the thousands of commoners eager to trudge up on the hillside to show their respect to the Admiral.

"He should be the Emperor," I overheard one Palace guard say as we rode into the Imperial Palace walls.

"Gah!" replied another, telling him to close his mouth. "The Spirits will strike you down for uttering blasphemy."

"How can it be against the will of the Spirit to have a strong ruler?" retorted the first guard. "We are the strongest people in this world. You wait. The Spirits are not with the Emperor anymore. Change is coming."

"Keep your bad jos to yourself," said the second guard, moving to the furthest part of the wall. His loyalty to the Emperor was unwavering, but I feared it wasn't the overriding sentiment within the ranks. Warriors liked to win. In the end, when it came to a choice of living or dying, they chose the leader who guaranteed life.

I had much more to worry about than the Emperor, who was no longer my responsibility. Saving the life of the Admiral counted for nothing.

***

As I expected, I was immediately brought to a prison cell. I pulled in vain against the rusty, iron chains that bound my wrists and ankles on the cell well. The shackles made it impossible to move more than a few steps in any direction. I should have felt flattered I wasn't with the commoners in the Forbidden City, but within the special confines of the Palace dungeon, deep under the Imperial Palace courtyard. I looked frantically around the room and sunk into the mattress. My backpack was missing.

A slot in the door opened, and a metal plate loaded with gruel was pushed through, spilling onto the floor. I recoiled at the smell. I kicked the bowl with my foot. It was a stupid, childish move. The contents flew across the floor, making the entire room smell worse than it had already.

Hours later, a guard outside my cell announced a visitor.

I hoped it was the Emperor, although I doubted that he had ever been inside the prison. I'd had made several requests to speak with him beginning the moment we returned. He had to hear my side of the story. I'd come clean with him about the orb, tell him everything. What else was I going to do? I couldn't hide and lie, for that would put Zheng He in jeopardy. I would beg him not to take any action that could change the course of history.

"The Minister of War," the guard announced, bowing and closing the door to the cell once Qi Tai entered.

"Leave us," Qi Tai directed the two guards.

"What of your safety Minister?" one of the guards said, looking from me to the Minister, crossing his fingers to ward of unforeseen evil. Word must have gotten out about the incident with the bull, or the ship.

"I am in no danger," Qi Tai said, waiving him away, glaring at me. The guard bowed, departing.

Qi Tai waited until the outer lock clicked before he began talking to me. Today, he was dressed unusually. His normal grey, form fitting outfit was replaced with a looser, more casual robe traditionally worn by a Minister.

He reached inside the robe and withdrew the orb, dangling it a few feet from where I stood.

"Recognize this?" he asked, turning it within his fingers, just as he had the two balls in his office in what seemed to be an eternity ago. The tips of his fingers moved the orb with ease, dropping it from one hand into the other. The effect was mesmerizing.

I nodded my head. The worm didn't deserve an oral response.

"Zheng He told the Emperor you brought a three-headed man-bull statue to life. He also claims you calmed the storms on the sea. An object just like this was first seen thousands of years ago, as you know from the tapestry." His fingers stopped, then started again, rolling, turning at speeds seemingly in line with his words.

"You should not be held in this dank hole," he said, his voice as far from the angry, fighting man as I believed possible. His tone was intelligent, even reasonable. "A young man, on the cusp of adulthood, endowed with such powerful objects." He held the orb up to the dim light, its layer of dirt unable to mute the brilliance, or the inscriptions. Qi Tai's bone-white fingertips turned the orb slightly as he examined it, looking at it thoughtfully before he faced me.

"Your soul, held within your physical shell, is trapped within an artificial cage, just like your name. To think that with a moment's explanation, satisfying my curiosity, you could release yourself, saving your family. To do otherwise…well, that consigns you to death."

"Zheng He has told you all I've told him. Whatever else you want to learn I don't know. Figure it out yourself."

His eyes flicked to mine. A thin curl formed at the side of his lips. Gone was the conciliatory attempt.

"I will," he whispered. He hid the orb within the folds and called for the guard.

His tone worried me. He might very well figure out the secrets the orb held, possibly learning more than I ever could. He wasn't respectfully afraid like the Admiral. He lusted for power. If Zheng He's intimations were right, that a living being's soul could be split in two—one good part and one bad, the bad part from the side that was soulless, it would be far more dangerous than life or death.

Qi Tai continued to stare at me as he waited for the guard. The arrogant man must have a weak spot that I could exploit.

I searched his face, the pale, sickly color more grey than white. Unlike the Emperor, this man wore the experiences of death. A scar crossed an eyebrow, separating the hairs into two sections. His temple had a pronounced bump, his lower cheeks bore evidence of an unkind disease or virus as a youth.

With the speed of a skilled martial artist, he thrust his heel out in an upward kick, hitting my jaw. My head popped back, cracking my neck. I felt blood trickle down, over my Adam's apple, a thin river of warm liquid making its way to my chest.

I was a bobble head, my chest aching and my jaw bruised. I wasn't vain about my looks, but I hoped he didn't crack my nose. It was one part of my body that had been spared during the years of practice sessions.

"As I remember, you heal fast," he said, straightening his shirt. "When I get time with your lovely sister, we'll see if she fares as well."

"You may not find her," I reminded him, steeling myself for more blows.

"All in good time. No one escapes in the Forbidden City for long," the inevitability somehow pleasing him. "Until then, we have you, and your father." The guard came then, unlocking the door and holding it open. "He's stronger than we thought. I'd hoped to spare him additional pain, and now you have guaranteed his life will be very…different…than it is today. His future life, or shall I say, inability to participate in life, will be on your conscience."

A second guard appeared, and this time was accompanied by an older woman.

"What are you doing here?" demanded Qi Tai, pointing at the woman. It was Gee. I'd seen her many times but she always kept her eyes down and her face averted.

"I've been ordered by the doctor to check the prisoner's back, wrists, and ankles. The Emperor wants to make sure the prisoner is in good shape for his execution."

Qi Tai nodded his approval to the guard. Powerful as he was, he wouldn't go against the Emperor's wishes.

"I must have his shackles removed for his back to be inspected," she said, a hint of irritation in her voice.

The guard obeyed the order.

"If he breaks out of his chains and hurts the servant, it won't matter," Qi Tai told the guard coldly. "She is close to death herself." Qi Tai spat on the ground as he left.

The guard moved uncomfortably towards me. Before the chains dropped to the floor, he had bounded back, closing the door of the cell as quickly as possible.

The old woman looked me up and down, running her brittle fingers across my body.

"You must eat more," she said in a tone loud enough for anyone listening to hear. "The doctor wants you in good condition before the execution. I must check your back."

She gestured for me to take off my shirt. As I did so, she took from her pocket a black sack and withdrew a sheer, white shirt.

"Quickly," she whispered, changing her manner to that of a kind, but stern grandmother. "Slip this on. It is from your sister. She said it is a gift."

"What?" I whispered.

Gee shushed me and nodded, looking behind her. "She slipped back in the Palace and gave this to me before she was taken into custody. Qi Tai will know soon enough. Quickly now."

I struggled to lift my arms. Qi Tai's heel had hit its mark. He knew precisely where to land his foot in order to crack ribs but not puncture my lung. A slight twist and his assault would have shattered the entire rib cage. He wanted me in pain, but not debilitated. I saved my thoughts of Qi Tai for later, telling the woman what he had done.

"I'll need the doctor," I said. She nodded, deftly lifting the shirt over my arms.

"He did say to keep you healthy," she replied, winking at me.

Once I put the shirt on, I looked down at my chest.

"Where'd it go?" I asked in surprise. The shirt was no longer visible. The old woman put her fingers to her mouth to silence me. She then withdrew a piece of paper from her pocket and slipped it under the mattress. She mimed that I was to read the paper and eat it when done.

"If you aren't dead by tomorrow, I'll visit you in the morning," she said loudly. "Bao sends you her heart," she whispered, then winked at me, calling the guard.

Once my hands were bound again and the door was shut, I carefully lowered myself to the bed and opened the paper. This time, Mia had written in English, not abbreviated but in longhand.

Cage,

I have so much to tell you. Gee is taking care of me. The General ordered my feet broken so I can't run away. The doctor was ordered to do it, but he has not. Don't worry when you see me. I just pretend my foot was broken and shout in pain all the time, but I am fine. Qi Tai will be furious when he sees what has happened, since I know he wants me healthy in order to serve the Empress. I think he likes me too, but don't worry about that either. I'm kissing up to him to help us out. As long as you and Dad are safe, I'd do whatever I need to do.

Please don't be mad at me for taking Wei-Lyn out of the city. Your idea wouldn't have worked. It was too dangerous for Bao, so I took her place. I'm so sorry I made Bao break her promise, but Qi Tai and the General were watching. Wei-Lyn is now with a holy man who healed her back. He will return her to her home village.

The shirt you are wearing will protect you from harm. It cannot be seen as long as it is next to your skin. The holy man gave me the most amazing gift. I'll tell you about it later.

Don't worry about me. I'll be fine. Love, Mia

CHAMBERS

The constriction around my chest intensified. Mia had no idea what she was doing, or what she had done. Impetuous, obstinate girl. She had this perfect view of the world, that she could handle any situation. Why couldn't she have just listened to me, for once? I tore up the paper, pressing it against the moist earth with my shoe until it evaporated. She was wrong. The situation wasn't going to be all right. It was worse than ever.

My plan had been simple. Wei-Lyn would fake a sickness and be taken to the doctor for examination. I was sure Qi Tai wanted a healthy prisoner, and would insist she was well cared for right up to the time he threw her in the rock quarry. Bao's father was to arrange for Bao to take her out for a walk, preferably disguised as kitchen servants traveling home. I knew the gates to the Forbidden City were raised twice a day to allow Palace servants to return home. If they walked with others leaving the palace, they would be able to pass through the tree-lined streets and out the City gates without anyone noticing. With Mia taking Bao's place, she didn't stop to think about the consequences. Her actions put me in prison. And now we were all doomed. Overcome with exhaustion, I closed my eyes, waiting for the comfort of a dreamless sleep.

Even that was denied me. My unconscious tortured me with blurry images, the ones from my mother's accident. It was a recurring scene—she looked around the room, packing a box, her abstract patterned scarf tied fashionably around her neck. She looked out the window and saw two men running up the street, and she picked up the box and hurried to her car. She'd just made it, opening the door when the men saw she was getting away. One called on a phone, alerting an invisible conspirator. Instead of attacking the car, the two men watched from the street corner as another vehicle sped around the corner and t-boned her on the driver's side of the car. Her head shattered the windshield, ripping her forehead, the force throwing her back, cracking her neck. The two men rushed forward, but a bystander beat them to it, calling for help. Citizens ripped open the car door and attacked the driver of the other vehicle who fought off the strange hands. He made off, pummeling those who would stop him. The two men who would have hurt my mother further watched in anger as they were rendered helpless. I saw myself, running towards my mother, screaming at the others, who let me through.

Her eyes closed, and mine opened. The vision had given me details I hadn't seen before.

***

When Gee returned the following morning, she talked about my sister.

"Your sister returned with another gift, something so great, Qi Tai will want it forever if he learns of it."

I stretched out my hands, thinking it was something else for me to wear.

Gee shook her head. "No, no. It is not physical. It is the ability to see what men want."

"Say that again?" Gee repeated the words. It had to be something more than the obvious. Before I could ask, she continued.

"Mia learned that Qi Tai was stealing the Empress's jewels. The Empress suspected it has been going on for some time, and Mia found evidence Qi Tai is behind the thefts. She and the Empress believe Qi Tai intends to place the blame on Bao in order to insert a servant loyal to him next to the Empress. Once that is done, only Mia and myself are left to be removed. The Empress will be completely vulnerable. When that happens, it won't be long before she is given poison, another Empress chosen, and Qi Tai will be all that much closer to the throne."

The scenario was all too clear, and easy to pull off. The amateurs running this place, myself included, were no match for two powerful, conniving rulers. "She gave me this to give to you." Gee pulled a slip of paper from her inside pocket. "It may be useful to you."

Instead of another letter from Mia, it was a list of all the missing jewelry from the Empress's room.

"Does the Empress know Qi Tai has been in her room?"

"Yes, she is angry, and afraid to stand against the Emperor's trusted Minister."

He's the one that should be scared. It was instant death for a male, who wasn't a eunuch, to be within the Empress's personal quarters. She spoke loudly, talking about the need to return tomorrow, and called for the guards.

***

Before long, I had another visitor—the last person I expected to see.

"You were not so lucky this time."

It was Xing, who had come to gloat over the fact that I was imprisoned. My ribs hurt, I was hungry. He was irritating.

The torch flickered, casting shadows behind my visitor. He had dark circles under his eyes and the entirety of his cheek was brown, a small laceration healing. The wound hadn't been inflicted by my hand.

"What happened to your ugly face?" I asked.

Xing touched his cheek then turned. Something in his manner told me it wasn't a question he was going to answer. Suddenly, it dawned on me. His father. An uncomfortable rush of emotion passed through me, bordering on compassion. I despised my father for his weakness. I *hated* Xing's for beating up his son. People gave what they got, and Xing was no different. Even in my misery I felt pity for Xing.

"You'll get your old job back soon enough."

The comment was not what he expected, for he started to speak, reconsidered, and then stopped.

"Soon now," he agreed. "I came to make sure you are still alive."

"I won't offer you much of a fight," I said. My chains had been reattached, stretching out my arms like a scarecrow. "Make yourself an asset to the Emperor. He needs your protection."

Out of nowhere, Xing's palm firmly slapped my lower back. It was a smack to the vital organs, intended to bash the kidney or liver.

I bent over, expecting a blast of air to escape my mouth. But it didn't. I felt the pressure of a punch without the pain.

When I didn't react, Xing hit me again with a one-two punch. I remained unfazed, and Xing was furious. He stared at his hands as if he questioned their own strength. "What spirit protects you against my fists?"

Had my ribs not already been in agony, I would have smiled with my sense of superiority. Instead, I turned slowly, showing none of the tremors associated with such a pounding.

CHAMBERS

"Even in prison I serve the Emperor. Since I have good intentions, the spirits protect me. Check my shirt if you don't believe me."

Xing practically ripped it off my chest. He staggered back, pointing, gaping.

"You will discover for yourself that the traitor in the palace isn't me, my sister, or my father. It may be someone close to you. A person in a position to overthrow the Emperor and kill us all."

Xing touched his cheek. The bruise was large. Xing had either been defenseless, which I doubted, or he'd chosen not to defend himself.

"I'm sorry he hit you. I'm not here to create problems. I'm still not exactly sure why I was sent here at all. But I can tell you what has happened since I've come."

Xing immediately dropped his hand. The dark of the night didn't hide the flush on his face. I'd been right. His father had been the one.

He glanced one more time at my stomach. "If I find out that you are lying, I will kill you. And no spirits will be able to stop it."

CHAPTER 28

An hour later, Xing stood immobile, coldly staring at me, his arms folded as he listened to my story, including the part about Mia and how she helped the Empress's cousin. Despite my display of strength, Xing smirked as I talked.

"Your sister was apprehended inside the Palace after she'd snuck in. She was attempting to go back to her room. Qi Tai has taken over torturing her, believing my father wasn't being harsh enough. Soon, she will tell us who she met with outside the gates and return Wei-Lyn. You'd save her a lot of pain if you told my father and Qi Tai the names of your conspirators."

"I can't tell you what doesn't exist."

"They've already broken her feet, and I was told she passed out from the pain."

That's my Mia. She was always a ham, and probably relished putting on an act that was so eagerly accepted.

"Qi Tai has put your father out on a rack in the square, hoping he can tell him when we will be attacked," he continued.

That was news. While I didn't want to give him the only information I had about the situation, Xing left me no choice.

"I suppose you'd choose to follow an emperor who was a liar and a thief over someone who wants what is best for the people," I said, sitting on my bench. "I'm not talking about your father either."

Xing stopped short. He walked a step away from me, telling me to be cautious about making false accusations.

"I have proof. Inside my pants is a list of jewels the Empress is missing," I said. I told him to remove the piece of paper from inside the drawstring of my pants. He looked at me like I'd lost my mind. "If you want to prove me wrong, do it!"

Xing tentatively looked aside as he placed his fingers along the edge of my pants, feeling for the paper. He removed the rumpled document and read it.

"Is this a joke?" he asked.

"I believe that Qi Tai has been stealing from the Empress' chambers. You know that even getting near her room means imprisonment or worse."

He stopped short, reviewing the paper again. "This is ridiculous," he said, crunching it with his hand.

I shrugged. "I know why you are loyal to your father, Xing. I don't have a mother either…"

"Shut your mouth," he said harshly, gripping his fingers so tightly they had turned pasty white.

"No, you must listen. My mother died too and my Dad—he could have prevented it but he didn't. It was an accident, and I hate him for it. But at least I have a Dad that is still alive, that's still trying. Your dad is being used, Xing, used by someone who will eventually betray him and the Emperor."

Xing raised his fist high, preparing to strike. I lifted myself higher, ready to take it.

"Hit me all you want, Xing, but you can't ignore the truth. Set aside your pride and think about the very thing you say you cherish, which is honor and loyalty. You have sworn to protect the Emperor and Empress, and you are bound to this promise whether or not you are the lead guard. I'm telling you, listen to me with a clear head, not one full of shame and anger."

Xing was still, my verbal lashing far more painful than any beating.

"I've been with Zheng He for days, and as you can see from the sparseness of my cell, I have no writing utensils. I could not have written that list if I wanted to. Do some good by finding the true traitor instead of harboring anger that I beat you in a fight."

Xing called the guard, so angry his voice was shaking. He wasn't buying any of it. I'd failed.

With Xing gone, I realized that the temperature inside the small, underground cell was beginning to drop. From my tiny window I could see low clouds bringing with them the first signs of frost and snow. Shivering, I'd moved against the inner wall. I wondered how my dad was faring outside, his arms shackled. I doubted he was doing well.

When darkness descended and the prison grew quiet, I heard the sounds of running feet, slamming doors, and the shouts of men. Moments later my cell door swung open, the guard stepped inside and unlocked the chains on my feet, but left those around my wrists. Without a word, he led me to the main entryway.

"You have been requested," he said formally. The guard gave the keys to Xing, who motioned for me to follow him.

CHAMBERS

Xing opened a metal door, leading me through a passage that was lined with pebbles and rock. He lifted a torch from the side of the wall.

"Put out your hands." His voice echoed off the square walls, an eerie, hollow noise bouncing down through the dark.

I extended my wrists, and Xing inserted a key into the lock. With a click, the chains around my wrists dropped to the floor.

"Put this on quickly." It was a black guard's fighting outfit with a hood; identical to the one Xing wore. The hood covered my head and face, except for a rectangular opening for his eyes. Xing motioned for me to following him through the winding corridors, cutting off my questions. "Be quiet. Our voices echo," he said, breaking in to a run. "Faster," Xing hissed.

"I can't," I said, slowing to a gait.

"We must free your sister," Xing said, as though this would encourage me to quicken my pace.

I told him how Qi Tai had injured my chest.

"Are you lying to me?" he demanded. The question caught me off guard until I remembered he'd lifted up my shirt and it bore no evidence of the Minister's kick.

"Do you think I'd delay helping my own sister?"

Finally, we stopped at a nondescript wall and Xing handed me the torch. Then, Xing dug his fingers into the low ceiling to pull down a recessed set of wooden stairs. He climbed up into the darkness and unlatched a panel. Xing craned his neck, looking.

"She's not here," his tone irritated and worried.

"Who?"

"Gee. She was supposed to meet us here with your sister."

I looked down the tunnel in both directions.

"Xing, what is going on? Why are you helping me?"

He looked forward, shielding his eyes as he spoke. "I was disgraced in the courtyard and stripped of my post. It was my plan to expose you as a liar and make certain you remained in jail for the rest of your life. But now things are different."

"Why? What happened?" I pressed, holding my aching side.

Xing turned to me then, his eyes were dark with anger and shame. "Qi Tai's a liar and a thief, but he's not a traitor. It's my own father."

That made no sense.

"I followed Qi Tai," Xing continued grimly. "Those items, the ones you said are missing. It's true. All gone. Qi Tai stole the jewels to bribe my father to stay loyal to the Emperor."

I was incredulous. "Qi Tai was trying to *help* the Emperor?"

"Yes."

"Then why are you releasing me?"

Xing hit the wall with his hand. "It was me who tried to kill you at the Jade bridge. That is my shame alone. But my father has shamed the Empire. He has accepted stolen property for his loyalty and has brought disgrace upon himself and our family. It is against the honor code. And if you were right about Qi Tai's misdeeds, I now believe you might be right about other things as well." He shook his head then. "I don't know who threw the spear at Wi Cheng. That was not me. I've been trying to track down that person but whoever it is, he has eluded me."

As surprised as I was about the General, I also knew that Qi Tai was also guilty. Qi Tai had no intention of handing over the orb or the jewels to anyone, even the Emperor. The General was nothing more than a pawn in Qi Tai's grand plan.

"Do you think the General—wants to become the Emperor?"

"I don't know. That's what we must learn. This generation of ministers cannot be trusted."

Xing led us farther down the tunnel and stopped when we reached a heavy, metal gate.

"We are under the main hall now, under my father's quarters," he said softly. "It is how I followed Qi Tai without his knowledge."

He crawled up a wooden ladder attached to the wall.

"He's giving orders to his lieutenants," whispered Xing.

"Move over, so I can fit," I said.

I crawled up the ladder next to Xing, our ears close to the lid as we tried to hear the conversation. Three small cracks in the floor allowed us to see General Li standing next to his large desk, and his military guard stood near the doorway.

"When will the advancing army arrive?" we heard Xing's father ask.

"Within the day, General."

"I must consult the Minister of War one last time. Go now," he said to a runner.

Xing turned to me. "Why didn't you kill me when you had the chance?"

I knew he was referring to their fight in the courtyard. "You'd done nothing wrong."

"I tried to kill you."

I shifted uncomfortably on the ladder. "You'd been ordered to fight, just as I had."

Any response Xing might have given was cut short by the sound of a door opening and a flutter of hurried footsteps crossing above our heads. Qi Tai had arrived.

"Yesterday you weren't prepared to join me," the General said to Qi Tai. "You were still loyal to the unfit Emperor. In the face of the invading army, do you still stand by his side?"

Qi Tai laughed. "Much has changed since yesterday, General. We have a new power within our reach, unlike any other in this world. I will help you defeat the Emperor. But that is only one small step in what is now my much larger plan."

"You are merely a Minister of War," he said roughly. "But at least you are a better fit to be Emperor than the boy."

"Be careful what you say, General. Think of the armies I can produce and the people I can kill."

Silence fell on the room.

"Your ambition has indeed grown. But what of the Prince?"

"Let him come as planned. He will capture the royal family and be placed on the throne. Together, you and I will control his armies. Then, when the time is right, I will kill the Prince, and we will rule China."

The General murmured his agreement. "What about the foreign family?"

Qi Tai waved his hand. "Let Xing get Cage to talk. But until we find out how to use the orb, we need to keep the girl and father alive. Once the boy reveals what he knows, he and his father will burn in a mysterious palace fire that will also consume the lives of the Emperor and Empress, leaving no trace of their existence."

"And the girl?"

I waited for his response, but heard none. The only sound was Qi Tai's chilling laughter.

CHAPTER 29

Xing and I hurried back through the tunnel to see if Gee had arrived at the meeting place. Xing pulled down the ladder again and lifted the hidden door an inch and whispered Gee's name.

"I'm here." The old woman was crouched low to the ground, as if she were looking for a lost trinket.

"Where's Mia?"

"She's being kept with the doctor. Qi Tai assigned another guard to her door who won't allow me to see her." Xing thanked her, telling her to hurry back as we took off in the opposite direction.

"Then we must create a distraction. But Xing, we can't let the royal family be killed. We've got to save the Emperor and the Empress."

"We can't do both at once. There are only two of us."

"Where is Bao?" I asked.

Xing kept running. "They are getting her ready."

I skidded to a halt. "What—what are you talking about?"

"She's fine," he said, not understanding my concern. "She's going to be given away as a gift in marriage."

"To the Italians?" I asked.

CHAMBERS

"Yes. The leader of the Italian group told my father they want to forge an alliance that can't be broken. Since Wei-Lyn is gone, my father offered Bao and Mia, and the Emperor agreed. The Empress is so angry with his decision that she has confined herself to her room and won't leave. The Emperor is furious."

"When do the Italians depart?" I was hoping that we had a few days.

"Tomorrow."

***

Xing rapidly led me through the back hallways of the Imperial Palace, staying on the lesser traveled paths as we crossed the parks and headed towards the execution area. Gee had told him that Mia was headed there. As we ran, Xing said we would be relatively safe, because all of the guards were focusing on the dinner festivities. Zheng He had been hosting the five Italians within the Forbidden City. They weren't to enter the Imperial Palace at all, unless the discussions went well, which they had, and the Emperor invited the men for a dinner at the Palace dining hall.

"Xing, if someone finds us, we have to pretend that you've heard I've escaped the walls of the Palace, which will confuse your father and Qi Tai. If they think I've escaped, they'll go crazy trying to find me." That would only make it harder to get out.

We found the Emperor's protective dragon, and hid behind it until we saw a procession of guards leading my sister down the path, toward a waiting group in the execution area.

Tears streamed down Mia's pink face and she cried out with every step she took. She walked towards the far side of the square. Her shouts bordered on the hysterical, which was strange considering that she had once broken two toes during the state soccer finals and she had completed the game without so much as a whimper.

As she got closer, I could see that she was covered with purple and black bruises on her cheek and arms. Those were real. From my vantage point I could also see my father for the first time in weeks. He was bound by iron shackles that hung on the wooden poles. Mia was placed beside Dad, though her chains hung looser, allowing her arms to rest by her sides instead of shoulder height.

Dad looked gaunt and pale. His hair, thick and dark like mine, had turned completely gray. His eye sockets were sallow, as though the moisture had been sucked out, leaving the skin below in bags above his cheekbones. His torn clothes hung like an old pair of farmer's pants on a field scarecrow.

Qi Tai spoke to an audience that included the Emperor, his ministers, the Imperial guards, and Zheng He, who all listened intently as Qi Tai explained how the family of foreigners had arrived under suspicious circumstances and had gained favor in the Emperor's eyes.

Qi Tai turned and pointed an accusing finger at Mia and my dad. "While we extended this family our trust, it was abused by this girl, who took a prisoner out of the city, leading her to escape punishment."

The court officials mumbled among themselves.

"Can we be sure the palace is now safe?" asked a man in a tan robe.

"Nothing is certain," replied Qi Tai. "She had no reason to help Wei-Lyn escape."

"She was wrongfully accused," Mia yelled stubbornly.

Immediately a guard pulled out a short stick and whacked Mia across the face. The purple turned a shade of red, and Mia clenched her jaw in anger, pain-produced water at the corner of her eyes. Stubborn girl. I could practically feel her desire to take him down.

When Dad saw the blood dripping from the corner of Mia's mouth, he surged forward, the chains preventing his movement. He received a vicious jab in the stomach from one of the guards for his effort.

"Higher and tighter," Qi Tai ordered. A tall guard moved to my father, removing his wrist chains, one at a time, raising them high above his head. When it was up, he drew the harness tight, his arms wide in a V-shape.

At that moment, I felt worse for Dad than I had in a long while. Blood seeped out of the cuts on his wrists, running down his arms to his body. My father's heart, surely already pumping hard in the cold, wasn't in the best of shape since he never worked out. I didn't know how much longer he could survive this ordeal.

"The son has also been imprisoned. He went to the Sacred Grottoes with Zheng He, where he opened the door to the spirit world and called upon evil itself. With this!"

He held the orb high for all to see. The murmuring in the courtyard stopped as those assembled crossed their hands in front of their faces to ward off the presence of evil spirits.

"And what did he intend to do with this evil? Bring it into the Imperial Palace and destroy us all."

Qi Tai raised a clenched fist that had turned white from the pressure. He spoke as though he were protecting the orb's evil from seeping into the assembled crowd and appeared like a man possessed as he paced back and forth.

"Is it true a sacred statue was brought to life?" asked an old man.

"Zheng He said it was Mohaishou," interjected the Emperor, speaking for the first time. He looked at the Admiral for confirmation. The great man bowed, his creased eyes showing his disapproval, which wasn't directed at Dad nor Mia. Instead, his gaze was fixed upon the Minister of War, who was now standing near my sister. Zheng He's enormous hand was on his great sword. He watched and waited.

"The sacred three-headed man-bull honored for its kindness in life, rode out of the grotto trampling your men in its path, did it not?" asked Qi Tai.

Zheng He nodded once. He wasn't going to help the man's mission.

"This family will bring destruction to us all by raising thousands of creatures to do their bidding," said a blue-robed courtier, pointing at Dad.

"Kill him!" shouted another.

"Destroy them all!" shouted a third.

"Yes, yes," said Qi Tai, his voice at once agreeable and deceptive, waving his hand in the air. "We cannot afford to keep them alive, for our own fates may rest in their hands. But why turn their power away?"

"We must take the power for ourselves!" cried a man I could not see.

Qi Tai nodded with a disturbing smile on his face as he turned to my father. He had orchestrated the meeting with the prowess of a politician. The Emperor was going to be pushed into a decision without Qi Tai's direct request. Qi Tai rubbed his hands together. "Tell us what you know so we can make the Emperor invincible, and we will spare your life."

Cheers went up in the courtyard, and the Emperor nodded. Qi Tai now had the support of the Imperial Family to raise an army of ancient idols to do his bidding. There was no telling how many others were scattered around the rest of China—or the world for that matter.

"Wait," interjected the Emperor. "First, I want to see a demonstration for myself."

"Agreed," Qi Tai said diplomatically, his voice carrying a hint of condescending satisfaction. It was what he wanted.

"Who shall we test it on?" Qi Tai politely asked the crowd.

The group debated the merits of the statues in the courtyard until General Li suggested a statue of an Imperial Dragon.

"Zheng He, please, you can't allow that to happen," my father said. For once, Dad was right. It would kill everyone in the area.

Zheng He shook his massive head in agreement. "It's too big," he said. "We have nothing here that cannot harm the Emperor."

Qi Tai frowned at the comment. "No, but we do have an object we can contain."

He pointed to a white marble statue of a unicorn that stood to the right of the dragon. The Minister looked at the Emperor for approval.

"For the Emperor's safety, I suggest you circle the statue with armed men," Zheng He said to Qi Tai.

Qi Tai and the General concurred. One group of guards fell into position to flank the Emperor, while another group circled the statue. My father and Mia were left vulnerable, bound and shackled.

"Show us how this is done," asked Qi Tai of Zheng He.

"The rock didn't work for anyone other than Cage at the Grottoes, but I will try."

Zheng He walked up to the unicorn, placed the rock on the statue's leg, and stepped back. The stone had no effect. Instead of returning the orb to Qi Tai, he set it at the base of the unicorn.

"You!" commanded Qi Tai, pointing to my father. He gestured for a guard to release my father.

When the guard approached, Dad kicked the man full on in the crotch. He doubled over, another guard moving forward, double punching him in the stomach. Dad gasped and heaved, barely able to breathe. His face turned grey, then a gurgle of blood made its way forward.

The guard strapped his legs together from behind, leaving him unable to walk more than a few steps unaided. He then unlocked the shackles that bound Dad's wrists. His gasping made me feel bad for him, but also a bit ashamed. Once again, I wished he could be half the athlete Mia or I were.

The guards brought him over to the unicorn, and one picked up the orb. Dad closed his fists, punching the orb out of the man's hands. For this he was awarded another hit to his kidneys. The thudding sound of compression was deep. Dad's shoulders arched up, his back curling.

"Don't break his back," said Zheng He. "You will not get what you want from a paralyzed man."

Qi Tai pursed his lips, considering the advice.

The guard looked at the Minister, then the Emperor, for more direction.

"Force him," commanded Qi Tai.

"Without pain," the Emperor added, hands on his waist.

The two guards gripped Dad's hands, forcefully unclenching his fingers, one at a time. Qi Tai walked over, picked up the orb and placed it in Dad's hand. The guard placed Dad's other hand on top, holding the two tighter over the orb. Qi Tai directed the men to make Dad press the orb against the unicorn's body.

My father tried to move away from the unicorn, but the guards at his side prevented him from budging. It didn't matter. Nothing happened.

Qi Tai was infuriated; my father relieved, the Emperor was doubtful. He turned to Zheng He.

"Get Cage," he said to the General.

"Uh-oh," I said to Xing.

"I thought this would happen," he said. "Come with me."

We ran back the way we came, this time, stepping out in the open. He told me to strip off the black clothing. I had just thrown the garments behind a bush when a runner turned the corner.

"Xing!" he said, confused. "How did—?"

Xing said cut him off. "I'm bringing him at the Emperor's earlier request."

The runner bowed low. It was not his place to question the son of General Li, regardless of his earlier disgrace. "He's injured, and cannot run fast. Go ahead to the Emperor and tell him we come."

Once they were out of sight, I spoke. "You know what will happen if they learn the truth."

At first, Xing didn't respond. When he did, his voice was flat. "Blood will be spilt no matter what."

All movement stopped when Xing and I stepped onto the execution grounds. Dad had been placed back up in the paddock. Xing walked me up to the Emperor, and I bowed low as he eyed me warily. I wondered if Zheng He had told him I'd saved his life, in addition to raising the sacred statue.

"Give him the orb," the Emperor said, his eyes not leaving mine. "Show us what you did at the Grotto."

Bowing, I walked toward my father. The soldiers immediately dropped their swords to stop me, but a single bark from Zheng He lifted their tips. As I went past Mia, I touched her arm briefly, removing my hand before the guard could push me away.

"Don't worry," I said in English. Her lips were purple, a cheek was swollen. She winked back, her spirit strong.

In front of dad, I asked him in English, "Why can we both operate the orb for time travel, yet you can't make it bring something to life?"

"I don't know how you did it, Cage," he said, giving me a proud look. "I've been trying to figure it out for years. And that stupid prick thought he could kick and punch it out of me."

I smiled at him. The man had attitude after all.

I went right up to Qi Tai and held out my hands. The fury he showed at handing over the object made me feel momentarily superior. I walked toward the unicorn, asking for guidance. From whom, I had no idea. The great orb God in the sky. My mother. Anyone. In the absence of a voice or wind blowing in the air, I turned to the Emperor.

"I will do as you request," I said, bowing. My comments brought immediate gasps of horror. I'd spoken out of turn. Qi Tai looked ready to call for my immediate execution, but was torn. Dead, I was no use, and we all knew it.

"So, I require you promise me two things in return."

"You dare—," said the incensed Minister of War.

I ignored the maggot and continued. "First, that my sister and father are released, unharmed. They have done no wrong, nor have I. The second is that Bao remains with the Empress as her servant."

The Emperor raised both eyes at this request. Raising a hand to silence Qi Tai's objections, he nodded his head once, lifting his hand to indicate that I should proceed.

As leisurely as I could, I placed a foot on the pedestal of the unicorn. I hoped it would be enough to draw the power of the orb.

It was only seconds when I saw a purple tinge of blood flowing through the white marble of the statue. Qi Tai exhaled a satisfied sigh as the hair lifted from its dormant marble state to stand up on the unicorn's mane and cover its body. The tail bushed out in a single fluff. The unicorn stomped its feet like a caged racehorse ready to charge, thrusting its powerful nose in the air as it broke the ancient stone beneath its feet. From my peripheral vision, I noticed the soldiers involuntarily stepping back, away from the animal when its long, bony horn shimmered, and the pink nose glistened.

"You see, Emperor?" slurred Qi Tai victoriously. "This is the key to raising an invincible army!"

The unicorn snapped its head in Qi Tai's direction and charged. Qi Tai had the wits to jump behind the guard standing on the right side of my father. The unicorn plowed its horn directly into his chest; its long, spiral, horn impaling the unsuspecting man. With a tremendous thrust of its long, white neck, the unicorn tossed the guard's body from its horn and hurled it into the air. The body landed on the cobblestone courtyard, broken and crumpled. The unicorn looked around for Qi Tai and galloped forward once it located the Minister of War.

"Kill it before it harms Qi Tai or the Emperor!" screamed General Li.

"You are instructing it to kill me," accused Qi Tai as he pointed his bony finger towards me.

I stood with the orb, somehow protected by its very presence. The guards nearest me had heard the direct order, but were unwilling to take the chance until the Emperor seconded the opinion.

"Cage!" Zheng He said, drawing his thumb across his throat.

"I can't!" I shouted back to him, then at the Emperor.

"Protect Mia," my father yelled. He was useless, his chains were fixed.

"Do not let them escape!" Qi Tai cried as he ran behind another statue. The coward. I would never leave without my family. Any idiot knew that.

CHAMBERS

It wasn't until that moment I realized Wu and his team were nowhere to be seen. That was strange: they would have been the assigned day unit. I guessed that either Qi Tai or the General had changed out the duty roster, knowing what would take place. Neither wanted the five best warriors to stand beside me, defending the Emperor. I suspected the Emperor's death was the intended outcome, all at my hands. I'd be executed, Mia given away and Dad left to die, hanging in chains.

I stepped in front of Mia, the orb still in my hands.

Zheng He grabbed the fallen guard's spear and lifted it expertly over his shoulder to hurl it at the unicorn's heavy, white torso. The silver arrow penetrated the muscle-bound chest and ripped it wide open, but it didn't stop the unicorn's progress. With a shake of its mane, it whinnied in pain and lowered its head as it tried to dislodge the spear with its teeth. When that failed, the unicorn lifted its forelegs and kicked the spear back and forth until the staff end broke off. Without the spear encumbering its momentum, the unicorn focused on the Admiral instead of Qi Tai and charged forward, impervious to the spear tip still embedded in its chest. The unicorn's horn dripped blood from the first impaled guard as it lowered to meet Zheng He head on.

Zheng He stood on the left side of Mia, his short sword gripped in both hands, ready for a second assault. The unicorn snorted at the challenge as it charged. The amazing animal was going to run right beside me on its way to its target.

As it passed in front, I let the orb fall, catching it with the tip of my foot, depositing it softly on the ground then thrust out my hands, palms up, extending a double-chung punch to its side. The full force of my shoulders, back, and hips surged through my arms and out my hands as I dropped into a crouch for an additional source of power. The contact moved the spear deeper into the unicorn's massive chest, and the unicorn whinnied again in pain. The unicorn turned its beautiful head around and focused its unearthly red eyes upon me as its forelegs ground to a stop. It was just enough time for the Admiral to take his knife and plunge it into the base of the animal's neck. Still, the animal moved, the new assault barely affecting its motion.

"Get down, you fool," cried Zheng He, pushing me backward, into Mia, causing us to hit her like a ball crashing down bowling pins. Mia's chains held us up, and she groaned with the weight of the Admiral and myself pulling the chains against her wrists.

I dropped to retrieve the orb as Zheng He reached over my back, grappling with the unicorn's tail, pulling with all his strength. Had it been any other man trying to stop the steed, the unicorn would have trampled my father and sister. Only a massive figure like the Admiral could attempt to contain the monster. Even with the Admiral's might, the unicorn maintained speed, on a direct path towards the Emperor.

"Xing—the spear!" I yelled.

He picked up the spear and sent it flying towards me.

"Let him go, Zheng He. Now!" I yelled.

Suddenly freed, the beast rushed towards the closest victim, the Emperor.

Though a line of guards stood valiantly in its way, the incredible beast leapt in the air, its legs extended, ready to pulverize him with its hooves.

With all my remaining strength, I threw the spear into the beast's broad chest. The beast turned, breaking the shaft and rolling to the right. The wounded animal teetered off balance and fell to the ground, its chest plunging onto the weapon through its core, jutting out of its spine. Zheng He came from behind and thrust another spear into the animal's back. The beast whinnied one last agonizing cry and arched its head back in a final posture of death.

The crisis over, guards immediately surrounded me as Zheng He poked the beast.

Qi Tai's eyes burned with excitement as he strutted like a peacock in front of the group. Slowly, the men from the audience formed a loose circle around the dead animal, and the Minister raised his voice to capture their attention, requesting they draw closer to him.

Blood seeped between the cobblestone, outlining the bricks with dark red goo. It crystallized and hardened, a morbid testament to the life I'd raised and then ended. The men stepped between the red, carefully avoiding staining their silken shoes.

When the men moved, I gazed upon the muscular beast. It had been beautiful, a majestic creature with a will to live. Killing was what it did to survive. Unlike the three headed creature from the grotto, it didn't have a choice to escape, nor an outlet to do so.

"Leave it," said the Emperor. "Finish this quickly," he ordered Qi Tai.

I observed the group. The Emperor's face was red, the Empress appeared fearful and Mia looked mad. Dad hung limply, his pale skin was beginning to look a translucent green. He was fading.

"You see, my Emperor," Qi Tai said smoothly, continuing his speech as if he'd already forgotten man and beast had been killed and he had nearly lost his life. "These creatures are mortal. They cannot live forever, but with this, I believe we can create an army to be raised again and again."

"Are you proposing we bring the unicorn back to life for a second time?" asked the oldest man in the group.

"What better way to know if we can continue to bring our soldiers to life after they've been killed?" reasoned General Li, motioning his head to the dead man impaled by the unicorn.

I dusted myself off, the orb still within my hands. The circle of men stood several paces around me. No one dared go near me.

The ministers shook their heads, looking at one another squeamishly. The next person on the ground could be any one of them. Seeing a lack of support, Qi Tai changed tactics.

"What about using a man who is not one of us?" Qi Tai asked quietly. "Not a heroic soldier. A foreigner."

For a moment, I wondered if he was going to kill my father for his experiment. Qi Tai motioned for someone I could not see. Soon enough, I smelled the foulest stench ever to reach my nose.

Draben's corpse was brought forward on a stretcher and dumped unceremoniously on the ground.

"You have proven that this metal object has the ability to give life to stone. Don't endanger others in further pursuit of this experiment," suggested Zheng He.

Qi Tai waved a hand in the air, dismissing the comment. He looked at the Emperor, who struck me as equally curious and repulsed as I was.

Two guards gripped me from behind, dragging me over to Draben's corpse.

CHAMBERS

I gagged at the odor of Draben's rotting flesh. Maggots oozed in and out of the hole left by the sword, and a worm slithered down a withered ear. I told myself it was just like health class, and that I wasn't going to puke.

"Don't make me do this," I asked the Emperor. "It's not safe." Although I had just saved his life, he rejected my request and motioned me to proceed. For once, the Empress's non-verbal request of her husband was ignored. Appalled, the Empress turned away and left the area, unwilling to watch the procedure.

"Cage," Mia said quietly. "Don't."

It was the first time she'd spoken in the courtyard. Her eyes were bloodshot, and I noticed her one wrist was the size of a grapefruit. It must have been crushed or broken when the Admiral slammed against her.

I shook my head, ever so slightly. I had no choice.

The Minister of War smirked and nodded to the guards, who removed my right hand and shoved it on Draben's arm. Unlike the unicorn or Mohaishu, I was touching flesh, not stone. I didn't think it would make a difference, grateful I wasn't forced to touch a gaping wound.

Instantly, a current of energy moved from my left hand holding the orb, up and through my arm, across my chest and down into my right. The sensation electrified my body, seemingly lifting me up, giving me a heightened awareness and intensity I'd never before experienced. It was thrilling and scary at the same time. It was a surge of Power. This time, I didn't have to look. I knew what was to come.

Qi Tai and General Li edged closer to Draben as his body started to come to life. They peered in horrified wonder as Draben's chest heaved, and his fingers moved as he breathed the air. Dirt and worms spilled out of Draben's eyes when he blinked. His eye sockets were bone white and soulless, though he had the remnants of rotting eyes.

This was no man. This was a zombie. Zheng He had been right again. The soul and the body had separated; the good and the evil had become undone. My stomach churned as the body moved. The glassy eyes looked at me, waiting.

"Get up," Qi Tai said to the zombie.

It remained motionless. Qi Tai became angry and frustrated that once again, I had all the power.

"How do you feel?" asked Qi Tai without a hint of decency.

"I said, *'How do you feel?'*" Qi Tai repeated, testy and irritated.

The others moved, shuffling in discomfort.

"He won't respond to you," surmised Zheng He.

"Tell it to stand," Qi Tai said to me.

"This is going to be a short discussion, Qi Tai, since you can't make me talk."

Qi Tai gestured to a guard who then kicked me in the stomach. I remained standing, unshaken. The guard repositioned himself, a look of dread on his face, his abilities now in question. He jumped up high, landing his foot on my chest, directly on my heart.

"Anything else?" I asked Qi Tai, knowing that only a hit to my legs or head would be deadly.

The Emperor has walked forward, now intrigued with what he was witnessing.

"Do it again," he ordered. I was now a science experiment to him, like Draben. Using two fingers, he pointed to another guard. "Both of you," he directed.

I set down the orb and stood, fervently wishing both to hit above the waist. In true martial arts fashion, they did. As the furthest guard ran at me, he crouched, then lifted himself up in the air, kicking is right foot out, keeping his other close to his groin. I didn't bother defend myself, but instinctively braced against the impact. I fell forward, then righted myself, dusting the dirt of his shoe off my shoulder. The kick to my back should have shattered my shoulder blade.

"No!" cried my sister.

As I looked behind me, I felt another punch and kick to my left front. The same area Qi Tai had damaged.

My body moved back from the one-two pummel, and I fell to the ground. With Qi Tai watching in shock, I once again stood, erect, completely unharmed.

The Admiral coughed, breaking the awkward silence.

"Enough," said the Emperor.

At that, Qi Tai walked over to Mia, took the sword from the soldier next to her, and placed it on her neck.

"Tell him to do what I say. Make him stand up."

Mia pursed her lips. Perhaps she guessed what was to come, or knew of her impending fate. She shook her head, once again, telling me no.

"Stand," I said to Draben.

Draben slowly rose to a standing position and looked at his surroundings. He placed his fingers into the center of his chest and withdrew a handful of wriggling, slimy creatures. He dispassionately tore off a piece of his filthy shirt to plug the hole in his chest. Qi Tai stroked his chin as he considered this new development.

"Now ask the man how he feels."

A new swell of hatred flowed through me where power had moments before. I can give life. I can give death. Everything I'd learned in martial arts was at my disposal, plus the greatest power I'd ever known. I hated giving any of it away, especially to Qi Tai. *When I have the chance*, I thought, *I'm going to make you feel every ounce of the pain you have inflicted.* I unclenched my teeth long enough to ask the question.

"Like a dead man," responded Draben in perfect Mandarin, spitting out a tablespoon of green slime. A week among the dead had not dulled Draben's arrogance or his hostile attitude one bit.

"Are you immortal, or can you die again?" asked Qi Tai.

When I hesitated in repeating the question Qi Tai pressed the steel edge harder against Mia's flesh, causing her to cry out. I asked Draben the question, cursing Qi Tai under my breath.

"How would I know?" Draben retorted, picking a large bug out of his stomach.

"We can test that." Qi Tai left Mia to slide the blade straight through Draben's stomach until the tip came out his back. Draben's eyes rolled back in his head, and my father winced.

"Draben?" I asked. No one should die twice, but a breathing, talking, walking zombie could only worsen my family's predicament.

"I'm still here," Draben replied, his eyes rolling back in their sockets.

"Can you ever die?" asked Qi Tai, moving the sword near Mia's side.

"Wait!" I screamed at Qi Tai. I didn't want to see the maggot-covered sword against Mia's neck. Qi Tai smiled as I repeated his question.

"Yes, I will die if my body is completely torn apart," Draben said.

"How is it that you *live* again now?" asked Qi Tai. By now, I knew where the disgusting man was going. I could ask the questions myself and save us all a lot of time.

"I am not really living. You brought my physical body to life. But I don't feel complete. I need my soul."

"How can they be reunited?" I asked.

Draben scraped a mound of dirt off his face with peeling fingernails and said, "The orb."

Qi Tai peered at Draben closely, leaning forward to watch his lips as they moved.

"What do you know about the orb and the rocks?" I asked Draben in English. "And answer in English."

"It has been around for centuries, used by high priests here in China and in many other cultures around the world. There were once many orbs, but this is the last one that I know of. And it's mine," he answered.

Qi Tan raised a suspicious eyebrow. "Speak in our language. Repeat your question."

"Did you know what my father wanted when he came here with you?" I asked in Mandarin.

"He wanted to raise your mother from the dead because he knew it was his fault that she died. The naïve sap told me the entire sordid story."

"Can you hurt me?" I asked in English.

"I would try, but I'm hindered by the fact that I can't do anything until you command me: as you are holding the orb. But once I get it back, I guess I could do anything I want." Draben gave Qi Tai a look of interest, as though the man needed the suggestion.

Qi Tai's face had turned dark red at being left out of the conversation.

"What was he going to do with the orb?" Qi Tai asked in his high-pitched voice. He roughly grabbed Mia's arm, pressing four fingertips deep into her flesh. She involuntarily gasped and bit her lip.

I repeated his wording quickly before Qi Tai could inflict additional pain.

"Rule the world," Draben said in his detached monotone.

It appeared that Draben was incapable of lying when the person holding the orb asked a question. It dawned on me he said nothing about the rocks within the orb. Dad couldn't tell Draben what he himself didn't know. Now I was the one with the knowledge and power.

I was the only one who knew four powers: bring someone or something to life, get the new life to do my bidding, change the elements, or at least water, and time travel.

Qi Tai continued to ask me questions.

"How did you come to our land? What was in the hole in the ground where we found nothing?"

I didn't answer. My father weakly lifted his head, then dropped it again, his energy gone. Seeing our resolve, Qi Tai removed the knife and slapped Mia's face with the back of his closed hand, his ruby ring impacting her cheekbone resounding through the courtyard.

I winced, then knew. Qi Tai's ring. I'd seen it before: it was an identical match to the ring worn by the giant in the tapestry. That ring must have belonged to Zheng He, if he was indeed the man depicted in the artwork. But why didn't he notice it?

"How did you follow your father through the tunnel?"

Qi Tai raised his hand to strike Mia again, but the Emperor yelled for him to stop.

"Emperor, this girl took a prisoner out of the Forbidden City," Qi Tai reminded his leader. "I'm sure she is the one responsible for stealing many of the Empress's most precious jewels. Surely, she is no loss to us, should she die for refusing to tell us how she and her family came to our city."

"A thief?" I broke in, trying to deflect Qi Tai's attention from my sister. "Who are you to be calling anyone a thief? You are the one who has been stealing from the Empress's chambers. Why don't you tell everyone why you are blaming her?"

Qi Tai grabbed Mia by her hair, jerking it to the side. "Be careful what you say, boy," his voice was low and deadly. "It could result in a preventable death." He then did something that utterly repulsed me. He pressed his cheek to my sister's, breathing so heavily the steam drifted up in the air. Slowly, he extended his tongue and licked up from her chin to her ear. Mia was unable to move.

My body surged with hate-fueled adrenaline.

"You are the one who should be afraid," I said loudly. "The penalty for theft is the removal of the hands that have taken the bounty. Tell the Emperor where you've been taking the Empress's jewels, Qi Tai."

Qi Tai stopped, then gazed at my sister with hardened eyes.

"Well?" asked the Emperor. "How do you respond?"

A controlled Qi Tai turned from my sister, his answer laced with irritation, the thinly veiled contempt ripening his response.

"Emperor, it is a fabricated charge. This girl stole the items. Let us not continue this conversation," he finished, waving his hand.

Zheng He seemed to be the only person unaware of the bantering. He walked straight up to Draben, inspecting him from head to toe. He took his finger, and poked different parts of Draben's body, evidently testing for the strength of the muscle.

Draben stood immobile. He could neither speak nor respond unless I commanded him to do so.

Mia found her voice, and told the Emperor about the list, and what was on it, including the jade necklace that was his wedding present to his young bride.

"Bring the Empress back. Now," the Emperor commanded. The minutes ticked by as the entire group waited for the one person who could condemn Qi Tai and free Mia.

When the Empress was presented, she took her place near the Emperor, fear in her eyes. The Emperor had Qi Tai summarize the events, watching his wife intently.

"Is this true?" the Emperor asked.

The Empress nodded, looking at her husband, not at Qi Tai. It was clear she feared the Minister of War, ruler's wife though she was. "It was missing weeks before this family arrived," she said quietly, swallowing.

The Emperor looked at her with a flash of concern before he steeled his countenance to face the Minister.

"What have you to say to this?" he asked Qi Tai.

"Emperor, even if I did have a desire to do so, it is impossible to get near the Empress," he waved his hands in the air dramatically. "Guards are posted at all entrances, and only eunuchs and women are allowed inside her personal chambers. Had I been even a building away, an alarm would have sounded, and I would have been apprehended."

It was true. The guards and the eunuchs were everywhere, and though castrated, many of them were large and well capable of taking on the Minister, or calling others who would. How then did Qi Tai slip in and out of the Empress's chambers so many times without being caught?

Qi Tai took advantage of the silence. "No more distractions, these questions are simply a diversion. Tell us how you arrived here or I hit the other cheek." Or lick it. Qi Tai raised his hand, almost daring the Empress to yell again. He was pushing it now, his arrogance leading him to the edge of insubordination.

"If I stole the jewelry, then why don't you tell everyone what you are doing with the Empress' diamond and sapphire bracelet that is in your pocket?" Mia said impetuously. The corner of my lips instinctively curled in pride. That girl could raise the temper of any male, no matter the age.

Qi Tai pulled her hair, jerking her head and drawing her shoulders back. Her face was as white as bones and her inner resolve just as tough. She held her mouth tight. She'd go through more pain before she was going to show emotion in front of this man.

"Minister!" said the Emperor loudly. "Control yourself."

Qi Tai glared at Mia then dropped the hair from his hands. "This pocket?" asked Qi Tai as he turned it inside out for all to see it was empty.

"No, idiot. The other one."

I had to hand it to my sister. She'd lost none of her attitude, bruised and beaten up as she was. Qi Tai wasn't about to follow the order from a teenage female. He looked at the Emperor, who nodded.

Qi Tai opened his pocket, and pulled out the bracelet, lifting it for the hushed crowd.

"I found it hidden in your room of course. The guard said you offered it to him to let you escape. I've kept it safe."

The man handed the Empress the bracelet, and she confirmed it was hers.

"When would I have had the chance to take it?" Mia asked. "I've been in the medical facility since I was captured."

"How long has this bracelet been missing?" asked the Emperor.

Coward. He could have called the Minister a liar and jailed him right then. Instead, he took the easy way out, asking him a soft question, hoping for the Minister to incriminate himself.

"I don't know," answered the Empress, her eyes uncertain, still avoiding Qi Tai.

Qi Tai raised his voice again. "Emperor, we cannot waste any more time. For your safety, we must use the orb and start building our troops."

The Emperor gestured for Qi Tai, General Li and the Admiral all to come forward. While they talked, I spoke with Draben.

"What were you planning to do with the orb?"

The dead man choked up blood and black bile that made me convulse but I asked the question again.

"I told you. Use it to live. Rule the world."

I prepared to ask him a series of questions when Dad interrupted.

"Ask him if he's a descendant of the Serpent King," he said weakly, in English.

"A *what?*" I asked him.

"Not A. *The.* Just do it!" he implored, glancing at Qi Tai.

I wasn't interested in anything other than learning how far the powers of the rock and orb extended, but asked the question anyway.

"Yes," Draben responded. No elaboration. No commentary.

"Take out your left eye," I said.

Draben turned to me with a look of pure hatred, echoing what was in my mind.

"Cage, that's disgusting!" exclaimed Mia, repulsion on her face.

"Listen," I said to Mia and Dad, "what if we find what we need and he's still around, do you want to risk me being forced to give him his soul back, making him a dangerous living enemy instead of a gut-churning zombie?"

Mia was uncertain, Dad rolled his head from one side to the other.

"He can't see as well with one eye," I explained. "And he can't follow us if his legs don't work."

Draben lifted a rotting hand and pushed his fingers into one of the hollowed-out sockets without so much as a flicker of pain. The eye made a popping sound as the fingers plucked it out.

"Now, tell me what the Serpent King does," I commanded him, "and do it in English."

The zombie spoke in a monotone, the words flat, devoid of any emotions save pride.

"The Serpent King is the creator of evil. The essence of Power. A force that can change lives, civilizations. He comes at will every fifty two years, when the door to this world is open. He is waiting now, to come, to find and gain what he needs to rule this world."

My fingers felt cold, my stomach burned acid. "How does he get here?"

"Through the orb. When it's used, he can enter this world."

I didn't have time to ask more, as Zheng He was arguing in the background.

"If Cage can raise an army of zombies and control their movements, we cannot kill him," I overheard Zheng He argue. "He could turn them against us."

Qi Tai turned abruptly. "Ask him if anyone else can control the orb, now! Or I kill your sister with one thrust."

I asked the question, and Draben asked, still holding his eye in his fingers.

"No. According to legend, the one who found it, controls it."

Qi Tai considered this, and Mia noticeably shivered in the cold. The weather was cold and dry, the fluffy, low clouds sure to drop snow.

"If you are going to use his sister or father as tools to get him to cooperate, we cannot have them freeze to death," said Zheng He somberly.

Qi Tai grunted agreement and ordered that Mia be returned to the infirmary, and my father brought back to jail.

"Snow won't bother a dead man," Qi Tai said, gesturing the soldiers to tie Draben to the post. "Leave Cage outside as well," Qi Tai ordered. "The cold will increase his willingness to talk."

As my sister was led out of the execution grounds, the guards unshackled my father and put me in his place, next to Draben. I watched Dad vainly attempt to struggle against the hands that were pulling his arms high above his head. The hours in the cold appeared to have taken their toll. Bluish veins protruded on his neck, a lighter color on the rim of his lips.

When the soldiers lifted up his arms, a rip was heard. It sounded like his shirt, but I saw no blood. His body hit the ground like ice shattering on pavement.

"Get up," ordered a guard, kicking him in the ribs. Dad rolled on his arms, growling. His torn arms were useless as levers to push him off the ground. A guard on the opposite side kicked his toe under Dad's stomach, rolling him the other direction.

"Lift him," said Zheng He. The soldier did so after a slight pause. I liked to think Zheng He was showing compassion on my father rather than a selfish desire to get out of the cold. Zheng He at least realized Dad wasn't going anywhere.

CHAPTER 30

Anger kept my body warmer for the better part of several hours, but as the temperature outside plummeted, it wasn't enough to stop my skin from itching, then cracking. My lips split, the blood freezing before it hit my chin.

The sky had long since gone full black, the outer darkness interrupted by lights from atop the Emperor's Palace. Guards stood around the execution grounds, as though the zombie Draben and I had a chance of breaking the chains that bound us.

Spastic shivering wracked my body; the first stage of hypothermia. My shakes soon gave way to dizziness. I struggled to keep my head up. My neck felt heavy, a lead block of frozen connective tissue gradually eroding in the cold.

I concentrated on the guards, forcing my eyes to focus on the details; a set of eyes, a pair of lips, a sword. My body could be warmed from a frigid state, my mind could not. When my eyes ceased to see the men who were just a few feet away, I went inward. At first, I tried to think of Qi Tai, the hate a means to keeping my mind alive. But his angry face gave way to the lovelier Bao. She walked towards me, words from her delicate mouth encouraging me to be strong. I tried to recall her scent, the warmth of her hands and the compress she applied to my stomach, as though the memory could now help prevent the welcoming promise of death.

Then she too, blurred. My neck folded and I snapped my head back up. Some other part of me knew what felt as a quick jerk probably resembled slow motion. I struggled to turn my head, squinting to see my wrist in shackles. They looked off white, the color of a whale's underbelly. Purple veins struggled to pulse blood to my fingers, and I saw the threaded movement as it ebbed and flowed.

I'd begun hallucinating. Pressing my eyes as hard as possible, I then opened the lids wide, feeling the cold air sear my pupils. If I could keep my senses functioning, I knew I'd be able to live through the night.

So tired, I thought, the weight of my lids dropping down.

"Cage, hear me."

Mother's voice was an inspiring sound on the wind. Soon I'd be with her, as would Mia and my father. We'd be together. No more thoughts of the tapestry, the orb, or zombies.

"Feel my hand against your heart." The imaginary pressure of heat from her palm covered my chest. It beat again, a jagged, uncomfortable thumping inside my chest. I struggled to maintain the heartbeat knowing sleep was much easier.

"It is not your time to be with me," she said kindly. "You must fight against the one who has killed us all."

She disappeared as quickly as she came. It started snowing, the grounds turning into a white sheet. Then I heard more hallucinations.

"Get him down," said a familiar voice.

"On whose orders?"

"The Emperor's command. Do it," the voice was firm and urgent. It was male. My eyes refused to open again, my arms unresponsive. I couldn't have resisted if I tried.

The clanking of chains opening and my body dropped to the ground, a muffled thud the signal I'd been released, for I felt nothing.

"Hurry. His heart beat is slow and faint."

I tried to open my eyes, but couldn't. Time passed as I faded in and out of consciousness.

"Here," said the voice. "Lay him flat. Go now," the voice ordered, cautious and worried. The cold stone iced my back, my chest lifted instinctively to get away from the feeling.

"Bao, the compresses. *Hurry.*" I heard the fear in his voice. As I slipped further from consciousness, his worry for me surpassed my own. I'd leave this world, and no ball was going to bring me back. My friend…my…sister? She'd come too. Then we'd be together, those that loved me, the people I could love back. Then a darkness clouded, me, a sadness of sorts. I'd be leaving someone behind. Someone who was kind…someone I liked…who I wanted….and who wanted me, but in a different way. The one who had saved me, the one who smelled so nice… It made me desire to stay, for a just a little longer…

"Bao," I tried to say, but it came out as a whisper of air.

"Father, did you hear that?" I was sure it was the voice of an angel. It was the person I needed to talk to most…

"Lilies." I was now speaking to someone in a field of flowers, who's warm hands and light touch told me to lay down, to be quite and conserve my energy. She told me to let my arms relax, to close my eyes and not to speak. The angel laughed when I told her I wanted to see her beautiful brown eyes one more time, and then stopped when the man spoke.

"Put a warm compress on his head."

I cried out, telling him to give me back my angel. He laughed at my anger, but held down the compress to my eyes. "Your skin will burn in excruciating pain as we bring it back. Bite your lip. Do not make a sound."

The visions of two angels above me stayed, talking to one another in words only angels understood. They sounded distant, a part of heaven I'd not seen and wasn't allowed in. I must be trapped inside a waiting station, a place where spirits resided when the body was dead, but didn't have a destination. Finally, the voices left, and darkness crowded in. This was it. The decision was made and I was being sent somewhere else, where the angels weren't.

"The first one is very cool," she said softly. "I will gradually place warmer towels on you as the skin warms." Inside the confines of my useless body, I lay trapped, wanting to talk yet disabled. My voice was gone, lips frozen, hands immobile. There were no angels in my mind any longer. Only voices I recognized.

***

"Father is very skilled," she said. "No skin is lifting." My heart surged with relief. It was Bao, telling me what her father was doing. He was cutting off my clothes that had been frozen to my body. "Much of your body is still frozen. Father tells me the condition will change as you heal."

An image of the outer layer of an onion came to mind, and I imagined my skin bleeding a clear, translucent color. The vision was appropriate. I was as useless as a vegetable, being undressed by a man and his lovely daughter. This was not the way I'd envisioned presenting my nakedness to Bao: on a table, unable to move.

"Try to drink this," Bao said, as a warm broth flowed down my throat. I choked, unable to swallow. I assumed she lifted my head, encouraging a bit more down. My vise-like lips made drinking impossible, the liquid pouring down my cheek in a sloppy mess.

She chuckled. "Thought that might happen," she said. "You cannot swallow yet by yourself. At least you tried," she said, lifting a cloth to my mouth.

"This will help you sleep," she said, placing her thumb on my bottom lip. The touch sent a shiver through my shoulders, and a giggle escaped her lips. She pressed it down, her fingers under my chin, then they were at my throat, massaging my neck. The sensation was odd and sensual at the same time. Lifting the cup back to my mouth, she carefully watched the liquid move down my throat. I choked again.

Up and down her fingers went, until I felt myself swallow. "You did it," she said, removing her hands.

Sleep came quickly. The weight of my body lifted as I was transported to the inside of the catacombs, the world where it all began.

Within my dream, my mother appeared again, this time standing over me, resting her hand on my head as she did whenever I was sick with a fever. She lifted a compress from my forehead, dabbing away the moisture.

"I'm sorry I didn't tell you before," she began, her deep blue eyes full of regret and pain. "It's so complicated. Your mind will tell you this is a dream, your imagination. It's not. It's our life. You must remember it when you wake, and never forget.

"We—the other families and I--thought the Serpent King had been killed in another part of the world. He did not show up for many cycles; hundreds of years. We kept coming to different people, in different times. He was nowhere. Now we see that we were wrong. He became smarter, inhabiting rulers that used their power to destroy cultures and civilizations, many losing their souls in the most unfathomable way. Over the centuries, the other guardian families sworn to protect their assigned areas have not been so fortunate. We are now the only family left."

"Cage," she said, her voice full of fear. "It is worse now than before. We must cover the entire planet, not just our area. He will continue to return until all of the artifacts are brought together and the return ritual is performed by his priests. If he were to collect all of the rocks and artifacts, the world as we know it would end."

"Why don't I remember? And why doesn't dad know? Wasn't he a part of this?"

"A veil has dropped over your knowledge of past lives. It is the way of our eternal fight. You will travel across time and gain this knowledge again, on your own. Your father…he has been blinded by his own desires, his focus to bring me back. It has blocked him from remembering and unlocking what he once knew."

"So he could control it if he wanted?"

"Not now. His time has passed. It is now yours to control." She started to fade.

"Mom, wait! If…someone dies, can I get their soul back? Can I make them whole?"

Mom touched my hand, stroking it as she so often did when I was frustrated or confused...or got ahead of myself. Then she gestured to a scene behind her, animals roaming the Serengeti, mother lions with cubs, giraffes and their offspring, living together in peace.

"Nature is two parts, one mortal, born from physical parents, animal or man. For man, what we know is learned by what we see or touch or hear. The immortal side of us, the spirit, what we have been taught to call the *soul*, lives beyond, forever. It must be fed, more than the physical mind can comprehend."

"That's what Dad has been doing isn't it? Trying to bring you back and make you whole?"

Mom nodded, then changed the scene in front of me.

I could see myself standing beside Mia, a golden wave of heat emanating from our bodies. I could almost see our minds enlightened with a vision, and my heart, giving me a confirmation of feeling, her hand, touching a benign object.

"What cannot be explained can be felt. Ask for the power to have a clear mind and heart, to see that which is not visible. You will be led to do what is needed. You have the gift. You just haven't yet used it."

She raised her hand, and a tapestry appeared, the one from the Palace. "Stand firm in what you have been called to do," she finished, placing her hand on my head, as though bestowing a gift. "The day will come when you will be tested, and unless you choose free will over power, kindness over hate, your soul will be lost. We will lose."

My heart burned, a body-filling experience that caused my skin to tingle, then itch. My mother was gone. Her soul—was it still with her? Had it been taken? The thought terrified me and I opened my eyes, screaming a cry of pain.

"Hold him!" the doctor said, clamping his hand over my mouth before inserting a rag. "I told you to be soft," he admonished Bao, his worried voice low and urgent.

My back arched uncontrollably, though I had enough wits to fight back a desire to lash out my arms and legs in all directions. The pain was unendurable.

"How is he?" asked a male voice, one I recognized, but could not name. It was the voice of a friend.

I clenched my teeth. "Not good," I answered.

A chuckle followed my words. "He's going to be fine," said the visitor. "That black nose stands out though."

Bao told him to hush. "You have no black nose," she said, removing the compress from my eyes. "Open your eyes slowly now. Can you see yet?"

I blinked in the dim light, shutting both eyes tight again as another wave of pain traveled up my legs and across my chest. Xing was standing beside Bao, holding my arms.

"Hold him down again," requested the doctor.

Bao and Xing placed their hands on my chest and arms. This time, I could feel their hands.

"You have all your toes and fingers, legs and arms," Bao told me quickly, casting a glare at Xing. I ran my tongue across my lips, feeling the jagged skin. "Father says your skin will heal. You will have no lasting damage."

"Cage," said Xing, shaking his head at the doctor who was gesturing for him not to speak. "You heard what Qi Tai intends. He is ready."

I blinked, willing myself to concentrate on listening to Xing instead of the words my mother had spoken to me. I'd fought against the visions I'd had, the dreams and the inspiration. It was no use. She didn't need to tell me once again this was real. My role here was vital. And it was not up for debate.

"The Minister of War can't get the orb to work," continued Xing. "Cage, he broke both of your father's legs trying to make him talk." Before my mother's visit, this would have slightly pleased me. Now I was pissed.

I craned my head, arousing a scolding from Bao as I looked at the doctor for confirmation. He nodded his head.

"Good for Dad," I croaked. It took him forty years, but the guy was coming around.

"His legs will need to be re-broken for the bones to properly heal," interjected the doctor. "Qi Tai stopped only when Zheng He intervened."

I attempted to lift myself up on my elbows but failed. I'd kill Qi Tai. One moment without his guards was all I would need. Remorse, regret, fear, were not my reality. He was as good as dead.

Bao placed her hand on my arm. Had she known my plan, she might not have touched me.

"There is something else." She hesitated, looking at her father for permission to speak. He nodded and she continued. "I'm to be given to a stranger and we will leave the country—"

Even though I already knew that, the heat of awareness colored my face. "Qi Tai has talked about taking your sister for his wife as well, though I think she would do her best to physically harm him. If he can't tame her, I think he will give Mia to the Italians."

CHAMBERS

I searched the ceiling, working back the timeline from when we arrived, counting the number of days before I knew the Palace would be stormed. The battle of two armies was imminent. One of zombies, one of murderous invaders.

I looked at the doctor and Xing. "Heal me. I don't care how painful it is."

CHAPTER 31

The doctor shook his head. "I'm sorry Cage. Right now, we cannot do anything more for you. It will take two weeks for you to fully heal and regain your strength." That wasn't acceptable. By that time, Bao and Mia would be gone.

"Where is the orb?" I asked Xing. The General's son shook his head. He didn't know.

Bao had stayed close to my side when she wasn't attending the Empress, who had remained in her room since being summoned to the torture area.

"I think I know," she said. The Empress had been summoned by the Emperor to his Palace late the evening before, and returned with an embroidered sheet, hiding something heavy. "She wouldn't let me see it," Bao said, "but I heard her open the chest in her room. It's by the side of her bed."

Xing shook his head thoughtfully. "Why would the Emperor give the Empress the orb?"

I knew. The Emperor didn't trust Qi Tai with the object, nor did he trust the General. He couldn't afford to place his life in their hands. The one person the Emperor could trust was his wife. But this was a dangerous gamble: Qi Tai had proven his ability to move in and out of her chambers without detection.

"What does Wu think?" I asked Xing.

"I haven't had a chance to talk with him. He's guarding the Emperor around the clock, unwilling to leave even when the other guards come on duty."

The doctor and Bao also shook their heads with worry. Wu had to be told some of what was to happen. He and his men had to prepare if I wasn't around. Screw historical consequences. History didn't anticipate me.

"Get the orb out of the Empress's room. It's not safe," I told the three. "Mia proved Qi Tai has had access to her jewels. Bao, can you talk with the Empress and hide the orb where it won't be found without getting in trouble?"

She frowned in thought. "I'll try."

I had to get the orb, take Xing and return to the grottoes. I had an idea that might work, but it all depended on timing.

"The tapestry," I said, looking at Bao's father. "Can I see it again?"

He shook his head no. "It's dangerous and you can't move for at least another day. Bao can draw a picture."

"Look, I feel like my body is literally healing itself. I can feel the muscles becoming tighter, stronger. The pain is lessening with every moment that passes. But it will still be days and we don't have days. I don't know what is happening, so I won't question it. But you can see it…" then I lifted up my shirt for him to inspect my chest. Some of the bruising and most of the swelling had disappeared.

The doctor's eyes grew wide.

I dropped my shirt down, convinced the visual effect had done the job. Mom had given me a mission to fulfill, and sure, she said I had free will. I could get back home. But it wasn't in my nature to run. Besides, Qi Tai had a whole lot coming to him, and it wasn't the easy road to becoming the Emperor.

"I need to see the bottom half of the tapestry, the lower left corner. I want to know more about the man with the orb on the right as well." Bao would do what she could, starting tonight.

Xing informed us he had to leave. The way to protect the Emperor best was to stay close to his father.

"Bao, can you also bring me the orb tonight? I won't need it long, and you can return it to its hiding place when I'm done. You don't even need to tell me where it was hidden if it will make you feel better."

She remained silent, though she placed her hand on mine. The slightest touch yielded a ripple of excitement up my arm, and for a moment I didn't feel the pain. Bao felt it as well. Slowly, she caressed my skin, carefully avoiding the sorest spots. Her father removed himself to the side room, leaving us alone. I felt an honest appreciation for a culture that made unions of the young possible. Bao and I weren't two hot-headed kids in lust. We were adults, living and dying, saving one another, falling in love.

The conflict was plain on her face. Her life was changing in so many ways: she was being sent to another land, without her family, and her fate would be under the control of a complete stranger. She also knew how much I desired her, and that my future was less than certain. No matter what happened to either of us, we were destined to be apart.

"It's not my intention to leave, not yet. I must use the orb to stop the… destruction of the palace."

She cautiously intertwined her fingers in mine. "And after that, you will leave."

"Would you come with me if I asked?"

Her thumb stroked mine, though she lowered her eyes in sadness. She bent over, placing her lips in my palm, brushing it up and down, the caress sending shivers up my spine, tingling my inner thighs.

"I have no choice but to leave with the Italian merchants. If I were to leave with you, I'd disgrace my father and my family." I got it. Until I was vindicated, I was the enemy. By then, it would be too late, yet, I'd still made her father a promise.

"Then before I leave I will make sure that you and your family will be safe."

"You cannot make such a promise," she said softly.

I curled my fingertips around her chin, drawing her face down to my own. She didn't resist, her lips touched mine, the soft skin pressing harder, her passion intense. My other hand touched the small of her back, drawing her to my chest until I had an involuntary spasm of pain. Her lips lifted in a knowing smile, and she gently withdrew. I held her hand, unwilling to release it.

"Bring me the orb so I can heal myself."

***

The warmth of Bao's fingers remained after she'd left the room. Her father returned, and we waited anxiously for her to bring us the orb and the drawing of the tapestry. In the meantime, he began another round of acupuncture treatments.

"How much do you know about the tapestry and its secret message?" I asked him.

His hands worked quickly. He was placing tiny needles up and down my arms and legs, working around my stomach and chest.

"Enough to recognize that you are wearing the same shirt that was depicted in the ancient tapestry we sent Bao to sketch."

I'd completely forgotten the garment was against my chest. My hands felt my chest and sure enough, when I slipped a finger on my stomach, pressing it under the shirt, it appeared on top of my hands.

That he knew didn't bother or surprise me. He'd known my role long before I had.

"Be still," he commanded when I wanted to move. "The needles must remain in place."

He worked and spoke quietly. "What I don't know, I guess. The archivist had told me that strangers had come from a different place, and there you were in the Emperor's court. You knew about the tapestry before I brought you to it, and you certainly recognized the orb right away. And this time when you were brought to me, I found the shirt." He paused then, holding my eyes. "While we worked your wounds, you were talking to someone, asking questions. Repeating things that I thought were only superstitions."

"I saw my mother in my dreams. She told me about our lineage. Chosen families."

He hummed. "Everything that has happened since you arrived, the death threats on the Emperor, bringing the statues to life, matches what the archivist had told Qi Tai. For that, he was placed in prison: he knew too much."

I bit my lip, a decision that I immediately regretted, for blood poured forth, streaming down my chin.

"Do you have more to tell me?" he inquired, placing a cloth against my chin and beginning to remove the tiny needles from my skin.

I'd promised Bao to keep the family safe before I left. Maybe the doctor could help me save his family if he knew everything.

"I am learning much the same way you are, piecing my story together. I am from a different place, but I'm also from a different time. Before I came through the tunnel, I was living 600 years from now. I know what will happen next in your world, but I don't know what to do about it."

Then I told him of the impending invasion. I told him how the history books mention Qi Tai, but not the Emperor's doctor. He could figure out an escape before the next ruler came to power.

"Qi Tai is right about one thing," he said, his fingertips tapping the top of the needles. "The orb is worthless without you. You are the key."

By the time he was finished removing the acupuncture tools, Bao slipped through the door, coming to my side with a small package in her hands.

"We must be quick. The Empress is terrified Qi Tai will ask the Emperor for the orb while it is gone." She handed the sack to me, unwilling to open it herself. I told them to stand back. I carefully removed the orb, making a note of the direction of the spindle on the top. When I unscrewed the lid, I lifted the top directly up.

I guessed that the sail had been over the obsidian when I was able to animate the bull statue, the unicorn, and even Draben. It brought things back to life. If it could do that, and my theory was correct, perhaps it could be used for healing the living.

Bao and her father watched me as I replaced the top half and rotated the spindle. This time, I had enough light to notice the engravings on the metal case.

"Look at my chest again," I asked Bao, indicating she lift up my shirt. As she and her father looking on, I placed my hand on the lid, pressed down, and turned it clockwise.

Suddenly, my skin loosened up, all over my body. It changed from feeling stretched, like ice on the surface of a frozen lake, to a more normal state that was subtle and pliable. My lips stopped hurting, and a quick run of my tongue across the surface confirmed the cracks had healed. Bao's eyes lit up, and her father opened his right hand, his forefinger and thumb touching, an ancient signal of being in great company, as my arms changed colors, from the hypothermic burned brown to the pink-tan color of healthy skin.

The external transformation was nothing compared to what was happening inside. I felt a rush of energy, alive and aware in a way I'd never before experienced. The martial arts masters had reverentially talked about an altered state of consciousness, where the mind was electrified with inspiration, controlling the body with a force bordering on supernatural, where instinct took over before the brain had the chance to give a command. Now I truly understood what that meant.

I looked outside the room, seeing through the darkness, into the courtyard, identifying a guard breathing in the harsh night. I heard each of his exhalations as though I were standing next to him. I turned to Bao, and felt the pulse of her heartbeat in my own body, and the satisfaction of meeting her eyes and hearing her heart speed up. A rush of desire moved through her, mixed with strong emotion. She was in love with me. The greedy part of me wanted to turn the top slightly more, but my heightened awareness alerted me to heavy footsteps. It broke the moment.

"Hurry," I said, pushing the orb into the sack and giving it to Bao. "Leave immediately. People are coming."

She looked shocked and frightened, but did as I said. She was gone in an instant, and I lay down, closed my eyes, pretending I was asleep. The doctor calmly went about his business, moving slowly back and forth to the washing bin against the wall.

Moments later, Qi Tai and the General were at my side.

"Well?" said General Li to the doctor. "What is his condition now?"

"He's sleeping," said the doctor, his back turned from the sounds of it. In a louder voice, he said: "He's over the worst part."

I could feel the pace of the Doctor's heart, beating steady and calm. He didn't fear Qi Tai nor the General. I could recognize that he disliked Qi Tai intensely, but strangely, he felt a compassion for the General I didn't understand.

"Will he be useful tomorrow morning?" Qi Tai asked, talking over the General.

"I drugged him when he came in order to fix his wounds. He will be back to normal when he wakes and has tea."

The General poked my arm. "He has very few welts from the freezing," as though the doctor were being untruthful.

"The mind can freeze, General, causing permanent damage. Let us hope this hasn't happened."

Qi Tai exploded at the General, as though it were his fault I'd been nearly killed. My fingers were so close to the man's neck. I could feel the adrenaline course through my brain as I controlled myself from reaching up and placing my thumb against his Adam's apple. I could crush his vocal chords in an instant, silencing him forever. An elbow jab to his groin would turn him into a eunuch, as efficiently as the operations the thousands of others in the Palace had to endure.

"Bring him to the gates tomorrow. Seeing his father will encourage him to talk again."

"If he's alive," said the General.

I focused on the force coming from Xing's father. He was clearly a man who had no problem killing when it was justified. His spirit had waves of lust and power like Qi Tai, but tempered with the pride of a father who still stung from the defeat of his son. I saw a color emanate from him, a yellow and orange, reminding me of spring. There was a wife and a daughter: he had lost one, but retained the other. Xing had never mentioned a sister. I could see in his mind's eye his daughter, far away in some village, hidden under a hat, working in the field, disguised as a boy. The General worried for her, wanted to protect her. His lust for power was driven by his need to protect his family. The doctor bowed deferentially.

"Ministers, I'm afraid that seeing his father might infuriate him. Imagine what he could unleash once he realizes his father has two broken legs. You would be giving him the orb to raise the dead, and instead, he turns it against you."

Qi Tai dismissed the thought. "Have no fear. Should he attempt to hurt us, I'll take care of him. Bring him to me before the afternoon meal. Bao will be presented to the visitors and depart tomorrow evening."

A wave of anger and loss swept over me. It came from the doctor. He projected an overwhelming shadow of grey, the color of sadness and grief. He was consumed by the guilt of choosing the Emperor over his wife, though consoled by the knowledge it was the only way to save his two children. His wife had gone willingly, knowing it was her destiny. Now the doctor once again faced certain loss. He could not prevent Bao's arranged marriage. She was given away as a tool to ensure Chinese trading dominance in the region. The Emperor had compassion for the doctor, and did not relish taking away the Empress's attendant, or depriving the doctor of his child. Wu would remain with his father, in close proximity. It was a gift many others within the Palace would not receive, and the doctor knew this.

I searched the doctor's aura for revenge. There was none. He was void of hatred or malice, full of forgiveness and kindness. The doctor had his children to preserve the memory of his wife. A son, a father, a daughter. His family had become my family.

CHAPTER 32

When the ministers left, the doctor squinted his eyes, a habit I associated with repulsion. "We will wait until Bao returns so we can look at her drawing of the tapestry. Then we will talk."

His response baffled me. I had thought it better for Bao not to hear some of the conversation. He must have another reason for the delay.

"Qi Tai's power comes from his ring. Do you remember the ring from the tapestry? It can freeze things, turning them into statues."

I remembered the Emperor telling me that the dragon protects him and that it 'stuns' his enemies. Even Zheng He had acknowledged he'd witnessed this event.

The doctor acknowledged the power of the dragon, but he believed that it was really the ring on Qi Tai's hand that made it possible.

"The Emperor doesn't know about the ring. He believes the dragon protects the deity on Earth."

Qi Tai couldn't have been the first to wear the ring. It had to have been given to him by his father or another Minister. Did it belong to the Serpent King? My mother had told me our spirits were immortal, that I'd lived and fought before. Was the same true for Qi Tai? Was he a chosen one, a member of some priesthood, and emissary of evil?

Bao came back to the room. Her love for her father was incredibly powerful, her unity with Wu as complete as mine with Mia. Yet her familial bonds were being overwhelmed with her growing love for me. I could tell that she wanted to be impulsive, to leave behind her world at the Palace for the unknown, but not with the Italian to whom she was promised. The idea of the adventures she knew she'd have with me thrilled her. It also scared her. Her sadness was more for the life she could have experienced were it not for her obligations to the Empress and her loyalty to her family. The knowledge of her emotions gratified me, almost as much as if she were crushing her body against mine.

"Stay on the table," the doctor said, telling me we needed to take precautions lest Qi Tai or the General return unannounced.

Bao extended her hand, showing me the drawing she had made. I slid my legs over the bedside, sitting upright. She sat down beside me, so close our hips and legs touched. Sitting next to Bao, my body felt electric. Good thing I was the only one to have the sensitivity to auras or her father would have put a metal wall between the two of us.

We looked at the drawing together, her father peering over her shoulder. As directed, Bao had concentrated on the lower part of the tapestry. The page contained two separate images. On the right was the giant, faceless man. Bao had used red ink to identify the ring. It had intricate symbols around the edges of the setting and on the shaft that held the oval ruby in place. I'd not been close enough to Qi Tai's hand to determine if it was the same or not.

"I didn't have time to copy the inscriptions," said Bao apologetically, pointing to another drawing of the jewelry that was worn by the man fighting in the tapestry. "The writing looked the same on each one," she said, pointing to the surfaces. "I don't recognize any of the characters or pictograms." Surrounding the mighty, faceless man were many individuals wearing ornate robes of varied colors and styles. The master weaver had spent many hours threading the embroidered outfits.

"Have you ever seen any of the other items depicted in this tapestry besides the ring, the shirt, and the orb?" I asked both Bao and her father, wondering if the Emperor had a staff or one of the other items. They shook their heads.

"Nor is the archivist aware of any such objects within the Empire," said Bingwen.

Too bad. The archivist had the benefit of records dating back thousands of years.

"What do you think my father meant when he asked about the Serpent King?" I leaned away from Bao, instantly missing our physical connection, and glanced over my shoulder at her father, who shook his head.

"Qi Tai must be a priest," I said, knowing the statement was true the moment it was out of my lips. The doctor pursed his lips, mulling over the question as though he didn't want Bao to hear his reply. His eyes focused downward, and I took the hint, staring at the paper. It was there, he was telling me. Look for myself.

Then I understood. The man without a face. Those that stood below and around were people of power who served him.

CHAMBERS

I started to ask another question when the doctor tapped the left hand side of the page. I'd been so consumed with the ring and anonymous figure I'd ignored the final quadrant.

Unlike the other sections, this one bore the look of a professional cartographer. True, it was only Bao's interpretation of the tapestry. If I never saw the actual work again, I'd know her replication was accurate.

"I copied things I don't understand," she offered, apologizing for not adding more details. She directed my gaze to a line at the bottom. There was a scale and a legend of sorts, and a compass, although the symbols weren't directional. Instead it had dots, diagonal lines and zeros, evenly spaced. Could it be a calendar or some type of clock?

"Is this drawing identical to the tapestry?" I asked her. It was hard to imagine she'd counted the number of dots, slashes and zeros.

She nodded. "I took my time," she said, her look somewhere between taking offense at my statement and being humored. "There are fifty-two," she said, pointing to the dots on the outer circle. Fifty-two weeks? Years?

"Every fifty-two years," Wi Cheng had said, "the window of evil opens." I searched the drawing for other symbols, finding an oversized head that seemed out of place. It looked like the kind of image carved of stone by the ancient people of South America.

"Keep searching, Cage. Time is short," Bao's father said, looking outside the window.

The phrase annoyed me. I hadn't had a moment of peace since we arrived. I'd have none until this was over.

The quadrant contained five scenes. The first, in the upper left, was a near-perfect replica of the Forbidden City, complete with the walls, main gates, inner buildings, and the Imperial Palace. To the right of the Forbidden City were two parallel black, jagged lines, which looked like a river. Opposite the city, there was an image of burnt mountains, destroyed homes, trees hewn down, and death. It could be a picture of anywhere: North America, Africa, maybe even Europe or Russia. Directly below was another small city full of pillars and columns.

"Those were white in the tapestry," Bao said thoughtfully, seeing my inspection. The tops were domed, and she'd drawn a statue resembling a Greek or Roman god. Further below this were pointed, teardrop shaped roofs atop golden buildings. India or Russia I guessed. To the left, Bao had drawn the final location, a metropolis greater than the Forbidden City, if the scale was accurate. It had a pyramid unlike those in Egypt: the sides were squat and wide, the tops flat. The avenues leading up the edifices were wide, with square entryways leading to and from.

"Gravesites with headstones were everywhere," Bao said. "Tall and wide. The faces on them were mean. Fierce looking."

These could also have been from Central or South America. I cursed myself for not paying more attention in history as well as geology. Had I remembered more, I'd have this part of the tapestry nailed. The best I could do now was hope to describe the images to Mia or show her the drawing.

My mother said my family was destined to fight against evil, living through time. That implied we'd lived not once, but many times, for centuries, fighting the battle against the Serpent King. Perhaps we held our same bodies, race and origins, or maybe we'd changed generationally, in each fifty-two year cycle. And if we could change, I wondered if the

Serpent King also had the power to transform his likeness to the state best suited to win the battle.

"Concentrate," said Bao's father, who had observed my inattentiveness.

"The adversary must have been helped or supported by priests," I mused out loud. It was the only way someone like Qi Tai would know to find the items in the tapestry. "Though he seems stupid to have locked up the archivist when he is the only person around to help."

Bao gripped her father's arm, her eyes wide, worried with fear.

"What?" I asked.

The doctor scanned his daughter's eyes with one of regret. He nodded, placing his hand on hers.

"What you say is true," Bao began, speaking when her father was unable to do so. "The archivist only told one other person about this. And that was my mother."

Her father then began talking, his voice hesitant and quiet.

"My wife, Bao's mother, was the scribe to the archivist," he began. "She had the most exquisite handwriting in the Empire. Once Emperor Jianwen's grandfather saw her writing, he had to have her in the Palace. It was so beautiful that he asked her to train the scholars, the only female in all the kingdom to have such an honor. Even for a foreigner. It was why she was given to me as my wife."

He choked, gripping Bao's hand tight. The emotional upheaval of the memory apparent on his pained face.

"She also had the gift of interpretation. She could see things within that others could not. The archivist knew the legends, but the secrets had been lost. She helped the archivist interpret the tapestry."

"One night, not long after their work had begun, she came to me, agonized with the burden of her knowledge. She told me everything." He fought his torment, his eyes now fixed on his my face, as though he were willing himself through the pain retelling caused.

"Please, tell me," I urged.

"The archivist was bound by duty and honor to tell the Minister of War. In confidence, he admitted my wife had assisted him, and that she knew more than he. Qi Tai had her arrested, and threatened her with torture if she didn't share what she knew about his ring. Qi Tai promised to release her once he had the knowledge. She did not believe him and asked for one last visit. She wasn't allowed to see the children, only me. She insisted I lie, for the sake of the children, and not tell Qi Tai I knew what she learned. She said..." The doctor stopped, struggling with the memory as he looked at Bao. "She was destined to die so I could live for the children. She said it was her fate."

It took another touch from Bao to her father's arm for him to continue. "Believing Qi Tai was to kill her no matter what she said, she didn't tell him everything. Somehow, he knew. When Qi Tai told the Emperor what she had done, the man gave her a chance to change her story and live. She chose to die."

His chest caved in with the words, his spine a mere hanger for his bony shoulders.

Bao stroked her father's arm. The doctor coughed and regained his composure. He stood erect, chest out, briefly placing his hand on Bao's cheek.

"Qi Tai fears the archivist knows more than he has shared. It's why he's keeping him alive. One day, he will be executed. Any remaining knowledge he has, gone with him."

His wife told him more than the map displayed. He'd admitted the secrets had not been hers alone when she died.

"What is it that you aren't telling me?" I stared at the man hard.

The doctor's lips moved slightly, a signal he wanted to speak, but was bound by some unspoken rule he wouldn't, or couldn't, explain.

"What is stopping you?" I asked.

The man stepped back from me, searching not only my face, but my entire being. I could see his internal struggle in his body language. Does he risk exposing the very information his wife died for, or hold back to protect his son and daughter?

Bao's hand was still on her father's arm. I appealed to her for support. She had to persuade him to give up the information he held so dear. It was the only way.

"After all you have done to help me, the pain I've gone through, the death of your wife," I said. "It can't be in vain. You must trust me if I'm to help both our families."

Bao lowered her eyelashes in agreement. "For me, father," she said, her voice pleading, full of the adoration she clearly felt.

At that moment, it hit me how hard my heart had been broken when my mother was killed. I'd had no opportunity to save her. No choice in her destiny. This man had a chance to do something, to save others. His dithering would guarantee death, an outcome I wasn't going to allow.

"Look at me," I said fiercely. "Do not consign your children to the fate of being parentless, which is what you will guarantee by not helping me." My words were as good as slapping him, for a red tinge colored his cheeks.

Then I waited, severely watching his eyes as each heartbeat that passed took us another step away from success.

"Father," nudged Bao, shaking him, "please."

He blinked. Tapping her hand, nodding his head, he said she was right.

"Do you have the translator?"

The what? I had no idea what he was talking about. If this were some sort of test, I'd failed.

"Can you describe what it looks like?"

The doctor squinted. He removed his hand from Bao's, lifting it up, waste high.

"It's about this big," he said, placing his other hand out, the distance of perhaps a book-size. I had no idea what he was talking about.

I shook my head, disappointed. I envisioned an ancient looking glass with metal rods or a contraption out of the Masonic days with secret codes and special tools. All I had that size was a metal binder with empty pages.

"My Dad had a metal notebook in his pack. But it was empty. I can tell you everything that was in the pack, but they seem meaningless," I said, not bothering to hide the frustration and disgust at the memory. The doctor's facial expression transformed from skepticism to confidence. "Sometimes, the most precious items are not what they seem," he said. He asked me to describe the items we found with the orb.

One by one, I told him all I remembered from that one time, when I'd dumped the contents on the floor of the catacombs, seeking a flashlight and finding inoperable items.

The doctor listened in silence, revealing nothing. As he contemplated my words, I realized that there might be a way for me to help Dad. With the power of the orb, I could heal his legs in seconds.

"Where are they keeping my father?"

Bao and her father exchanged uncomfortable looks.

"Father and I attended to his wounds," Bao said, grimacing at the recollection.

"He's within the prison. They are keeping him on the highest floor," the doctor answered.

"I could take you to him," she offered. For the moment, her father's reticence to confide in me was set aside. She and I, making the trek down to the prison, afforded us precious time alone.

"Bao, it is too dangerous. Soon you will have to return to your duties with the Empress," her father said, placing a restraining hand on her shoulder. The orb was vital, but not if she were going to be physically harmed.

Bao looked up at her father, unwavering. "He can't do it alone."

As much as I wanted to be with her, it wouldn't be possible. She was obligated to be with the Empress during the one time when the entire Palace would be engaged. Dinnertime. Her absence would surely cause the Minister and the Italians to raise alarms. I had a better idea.

"Gee could take me," I told them.

During the evening meal, we could sneak down to the prison, I'd use the orb to make him whole and return to my present location, all before the orb was discovered missing from the Empress's room, or I from the doctor's bed. As the entire ministry would be at dinner, very few members would be walking around the grounds.

This particular dinner was special, I reminded them. The entertainment planned was sure to be spectacular and longer than normal.

"Your plan is fraught with risk," Bingwen said. "Guards will be posted along the way. You are meant to be in this room, not with an elderly woman."

I nearly smiled when I answered. "How do you think I'll look in women's makeup?"

For the first time in a long while, Bao smiled. "Beautiful."

***

General and Qi Tai paid one last visit to my bed before the evening meal. Believing me to be asleep, they left for dinner, smug with the knowledge of their plan. Gee brought with her a small makeup kit as well as clothes big enough to fit my stature.

She stifled her laughter as she helped Bao transform my appearance.

"Mia was much better at this than you," the old woman chided me.

Gee matted my hair with thick fish oil, pressing a large wig on top, then shaved my face with a razor.

"Stand up and take your clothes off," she said, her hands already unfastening my top. Bao sat back, separating the link between us as she moved her legs.

In seconds, I was stripped to my boxers, the women unblinking and without awe or emotion. The neutrality eliminated the discomfort I might have otherwise felt in the presence of an attractive, compelling female like Bao. The two placed a skirt around my waist, fastening the strap tight.

"I can't breathe," I wheezed in an exaggerated fashion.

Gee gave me a brittle smile.

"We are trying to give you a waist."

The top was on, the outer bun affixed and pulled as close as my lungs allowed. It was worse than a padded sparring jacket.

"Uh-oh," I said, holding out the arms. The sleeves were short, above my wrists. My hairy, black arms looked anything but female.

"I'll return," Gee said, hustling from the room.

Bao sat and worked on fixing the back of my hair. "You are too big!" Bao complained, unsuccessfully attempting to move my legs. "Help me!" Despite the urgency of the situation, she laughed as she pushed my body one way, then the other. Her knees touched my legs, the current of energy sweeping up and into my groin. She applied the white base with a soft brush, telling me to close my eyes, look up, look down, to the right, and then to the left.

"Keep still," she commanded, unable to stifle another giggle. Bao held a thin, black paintbrush in her hands. "Close your eyes," she commanded. I felt her draw eyebrows over my own, and imagined a wide, arching curve.

"Now open your eyes and look directly at me," she said, her voice firm.

Unmoving, I watched as she applied the soft ends of a make-up brush under my eyelashes.

"Look up," she directed.

Caught up in my own thoughts, I hadn't noticed Bao had stopped. She was staring at me. Or rather, my eyes.

"What?" I asked, my lips barely moving, the rest of my face as set as a mask.

"I've never seen light green eyes," she said, looking at my left eye. "Brown around the rims, and a bit of blue on this one. Your other eye—it's, unique."

"Thicker," advised Gee, coming from around the back, critiquing Bao's handiwork. Bao blinked a few times, and re-applied the black, then writing a line atop my eyelashes that made me want to blink time and again.

I requested a look, but Gee clucked.

"Not until the lips are done."

That was the hardest part of all. Bao leaned closer than ever as she used the tips of three fingers to dab a sweet smelling substance on my lips before stroking it back and forth along the lip line.

"Open," she said softly. She concentrated on applying the lacquer to the inside rim of my lip. I'd never had a female touch my lips. To now have one stroke the outside, then the inside, was driving me over the edge.

I adjusted my position on the seat, causing her finger to jab the top of my tongue.

"Sorry," I muttered.

The corner of her mouth curled up, though she said nothing. She moved to the top lip, running her finger down each side of my top lip. The stimulating experience was more than I thought I could handle. Only Gee's pulling and pushing long needles through my hair bun kept me in check. "I'll apply the rest after you put your top on." She didn't want to stop any more than I did. Gee's presence was the deterrent.

"Done," Gee announced, walking to the window, checking the breezeway outside the room. Gee knelt, rapidly unstitching the thread on the sleeves. Bao assisted, threading the material just as quickly. In minutes, I had sleeves long enough to cover my hands to the knuckles. Bao then applied a skin-colored crème to my hands and cut my nails.

Bao directed me to sit again.

"How?" I asked rhetorically. The straight jacket was like having a pole jammed up my backside, extending from pelvic bone to the back of my head. I could barely turn one direction or another.

"How do you move in this thing?" I asked, the wonder and awe in my voice coloring her face.

"Hold very still," Bao answered with a slight smile, the compliment received. She wiped the white cream from her fingers and selected a bright red brush and a jar of red paint. She told me to close my lips, not in a hard press, but lightly. "No frowns," she suggested.

Bao placed her left fingers under my chin, holding me steady. She was inches away from my face, her breath floating out and up as I inhaled. It was as intoxicating as much as the power of the orb was stimulating. She dipped the tip of the brush in the red, filling in the lip lines she had previous drawn.

"I said close your lips," Bao whispered, gently pushing up my chin. I flushed. It wasn't conscious. My lips naturally parted with her touch. My hands ached from restraint, the intense pulse of desire coursed through me as I felt her breath from her mouth on mine.

"Almost done," she said, brushing the outer lips inward. Up and down, the stroking of the brush itself a sensual experience.

"There," she said, her finger at the corner of my mouth. She raised her eyes to mine, aware of my intense yearning.

Bao picked up a small mirror, and turned it to me, redirecting my attentions. I supposed another girl, in another time, would have been less reserved. In light of her shyness, I lifted the mirror. The face was not mine. It was definitely a woman and not entirely ugly. I wasn't sure how I felt about that.

The final step was fixing the shoes on my feet. I stood, fell over and stood again.

"Crouch over," Gee advised. "Like an old woman." When that didn't work, she handed me another pair of shoes with shorter platforms. It was better, but not perfect. My respect for women multiplied in minutes. What an ordeal.

The doctor entered a few moments later. "It's time," he said solemnly.

He asked Gee to retrieve the items from the Empress's room. She gave a last, disappointed tug on my shoe, grumbled about my inability to accomplish a task so easily done by a six-year-old girl.

The doctor inspected my ensemble with a scientific eye. "Too tall," was all he said, crossly. It wasn't what bothered him.

"It's possible she won't go with the Italian," I said somberly. "Give me what I need and I'll do more than anyone else to keep her safe."

He nodded once. "My wife didn't know how to operate the translator; it was a vision she saw in the tapestry. She said "it came alive." Does that mean anything to you?"

My dreams, the visions of my mother, but no translators.

"She said languages, symbols, the interpreter was capable of all."

My body tingled with the thrill of the knowledge. It was a different power than the orb, in some ways, more potent. The orb controlled the physical body, but one had to speak and talk with the leader of a people to persuade and command. Without a means for communication, the orb was less effective, killing or healing with one rock, commanding the elements with the other.

We both eagerly awaited Gee's return. She gave me my father's backpack, and I spread the contents on the table. She excused herself, telling the doctor to call for her when we were ready to depart.

The translator must be the notebook; that much was obvious. How it worked was the mystery.

The doctor lifted it up, glancing at me for permission. He proceeded to uncoil the leather strap, flipping the page just as I had done. He inspected the front and back.

As he did, I reviewed the other objects, hoping for a glimmer of inspiration. If I was a resurrected being, one that had lived before, I'd experience insights or impressions, the kind felt by those that claimed to have out-of-body experiences.

More than ever, I purposefully tried to slow down the adrenaline, focusing on the objects. The cracked mirror and broken compass I didn't bother picking up. The metal brush holder caught my eye. For a notebook needed a writing utensil. They had to be connected.

"May I use that?" I asked the doctor.

He handed me the tablet, watching as I laid it on the table, turning the page. It was empty, just as I'd remembered. I held the metal pen and wrote my name on the page in English.

My heart beat heavy as I waited for my hypothesis to be proven. It wasn't long. A light on the adjacent metal plate appeared. It was the curvature and symbol for the Cage, which would be my character in Mandarin. Without hesitating, I wrote 'Mia' next to my own name. Once again, the tracing outline appeared, the golden characters shining through as though a flashlight were behind the metal, or within.

The translator could recognize the time and place of its location, adapting the language to the requirement of the writer. With it, I had no boundaries of time, of location, or language. I had the device for perfect knowledge.

To be sure, I wrote out the symbols for *Beautiful Treasure* in Mandarin. The metal plate responded.

Bao. The thrill of the translator gave way to fact.

"It is time for you to go," the doctor said quietly. All that he had suspected was now confirmed. We were reaching the end of our time here. The jowls on his face drooped, the weight of his future without his daughter pulling at him.

"Did your wife say anything else?" I asked him softly.

He shook his head. "Nothing that pertained to what you have there," gesturing to the translator. "She struggled to convey a feeling, a darkness, a presence that didn't allow for words. 'It comes in and out, like a mist.' She was sure of whatever that presence, a thing or being was, perhaps a spirit. She said to me, 'it lays in wait.' Does that mean anything to you?"

Every fifty-two years, the Serpent King waits for the chance to enter this world. He has to come in somehow...and in some form.

"Did she know how it comes?" I asked.

He didn't. My disappointment was evident.

"What does a mist do?" he asked rhetorically, trying to help me, even if it was in a small way. "It appears, invisible to the naked eye, falling, covering all."

"A mist also seeps into the body," I added thoughtfully. A life form that rides upon the wind, like the elements. Had she meant to tell us the spirit of evil was all around, unbridled? No, that was different from what Mom had said. The window of evil opens, allowing evil through. It must first open.

With a horrible, sinking feeling, the light of revelation burned within.

"It lays in wait until we open the door," I whispered to myself. The orb. It was the only possible explanation. It was the door through which we moved through time. That was what it laid in wait *for*. It had been dormant, waiting for us to use it to do our job.

An unconscious tremor went up my back. The orb had been activated to bring us exactly to this place, at this time.

"Your face has gone pale," the doctor observed, his eyes squinting in concern.

I was speechless. Who knew how many times Dad had been back and forth to different places and times. Had the evil presence come through then? Was it here, around us, drawn to the power of the orb?

"Something I can't do a thing about," I said, pursing my lips. I had to get out of here. Now.

The doctor called for Gee and gestured for me to wrap up the notebook and pen.

"I expect you will have approximately one hour to get down to your father and back. Do not take that long."

CHAPTER 33

The doctor had told Qi Tai my father might die of shock and blood loss if he were not checked throughout the evening. Qi Tai relented, allowing him to send Gee and a female assistant. The doctor himself looked in on him after the dinner. It was going to take me at least half that time just to get to and from the prison; the high heel thongs were murder on my feet.

"You have to do better than that," whispered the old woman.

I towered above her, a giant in stilts. I bent my back to appear older than I was, a deformation of the spine, I told her, the only plausible excuse I could come up with should someone ask. I scooted along the pathways as quickly as I could.

The sounds of music emanating from the grand dining hall faded as we moved toward the prison. Gee carried with her a small jar of ointment, a bowl of water, and towels atop the orb.

Gee greeted the guard, who scoped me up and down. I stood taller than him, even bent over. It was, I hoped, the only time I'd be cross-dressing. Getting looked over by another male wasn't as interesting as having make-up put on my face by Bao.

As soon as we passed the guards, the overwhelming scent of vomit hit my heightened olfactory senses. Gee appeared not to notice. We made our way past two empty cells. The third held my father, lying on his back, an arm draped across his face. He was lying in a pool of his previous meal. As we waited for the guard to unlock the door, it was evident why he'd not moved. He couldn't. A bone jutted from the middle of one thigh, the white tip had droplets of red blood. The other leg was black from hip to knee, and swollen so large it was double the size the other.

I hoped Dad had passed out from the pain. With such wounds, it was a miracle he was even alive.

Sweat emerged from between my shoulder blades, the heat and moisture stretching down my spine.

Gee sensed my shift in emotion. "Stay calm," she counseled.

I dropped my shoulders and exhaled trying to appear old and stooped, not tall and aggressive. The guard let us in, relocked the gate and immediately departed, the assault to his senses every bit as repulsive as to our own.

Dad remained motionless as we neared. I bent over, removing his hand from his face and gasped involuntarily. His nose was pushed nearly to his cheekbone, grossly disfigured. The mouth barely visible. The lips were hanging, as though each had been nearly ripped off. I leaned forward to his mouth to feel for the exhalation of air. It was there.

Gee removed the bandages, bowl of water and left the orb in its place until I nodded my head, confirming I'd seen the guard move to the outer station. She held out the opened box to me. She wasn't inclined to handle the orb any more than Zheng He.

I removed the orb out of the box and placed it on my lap. All I could think about was the damage I was going to inflict on Qi Tai, and the pain he'd feel for what he'd done. As much as I disliked my father, even at that moment, I was still his son, and he my father. I still wanted him alive, no matter what.

"What are you waiting for?" Gee prodded.

My fingers couldn't get the spindle over the obsidian fast enough. I pressed down, turned and held.

Nothing.

Frustrated, I checked the orb. Perhaps the bottom half had moved when I gave it a turn. This time, I squeezed the lower portion firmly and turned it again.

There was no change.

Gee was quiet, adding to the pressure. Sweat now dripped to my pants.

Fury boiled over. This would work, and when it did, I'd rip the lips off Qi Tai with a razor blade if necessary. He'd make his own pool of crud.

"Your eyes are angry," she whispered in my ear. "Nothing good comes from anger."

The advice irritated me as much as the power of the orb and translator had thrilled my body. Why check anger when I my skills were expanding, along with the tools I had at my disposal? Now was not the time to intone about the downside of hate.

I checked the spindle, opened it up again, and screwed it back on. Everything was in place, and time was wasting.

A cold, withered hand landed on my arm.

"Your mind is blocked," she said. "The spirits cannot aid you when you close your heart. Open it."

I took a deep breath through my mouth, willing myself to listen to Gee instead of redirecting my rage. Dad's grey and discolored face was lifeless. The room reeked. I did my best to shut out the revolting scene and leaned forward.

"I'm here to heal you," I said. "I'm going to make you whole."

As I breathed in the rancid air, I closed my eyes. Upon the exhale, I did my best to release the built up emotions. Eventually, my muscles relaxed, followed by a burning in my chest. It was the first indication the promise behind the words would be kept.

My left hand felt strong as I held the orb. The warm flow of power began to surge through my bones even before I placed my right hand on its top. The old woman had been right.

The exhilarating power surged through me as I turned the metal object. I wanted to touch my dad's leg, but could not hold and turn the object and touch him at the same time. I doubted the mechanism worked by looking at a certain point of the body, rather, the contact of the skin. I extended my leg, touching his.

Gee's saggy face lit up with amazement at the miraculous transformation of Dad's legs. First the protrusion of the bone disappeared as it slid back underneath the skin, closing itself over the wound with newly healed flesh. The other leg reduced in size, the black, purple and red dissipating to his normal coloring. His face was next, the lacerations gone, his nose which was pushed to one side was now straight again. The lips lifted up from the chin, the underlying muscle reattaching to the epidural layer.

His outer self was perfect now, though his eyes were closed. I wondered if his brain had been damaged, but was reluctant to turn the orb any further.

"Dad," I whispered. "Can you hear me?"

He stayed still, his eyelids twitching, as though he were dreaming. A flood of images appeared in my mind, as clear as though they were playing out in front of me. Dad's face had been whipped with metal tipped balls, accounting for the jagged gashes and torn skin, the displacement of his mouth and nose. His legs had been placed on an angled box, then cracked in splinters when a heavy wood weight was dropped on them. Whips had continuously snapped at his skin until Zheng He had appeared and put a stop to the madness. Dad's mental state had held until the end, when delirium took over his consciousness. He'd thought of nothing but Mia and me, his will to keep the family secret outlasting his flesh. My throat constricted, and I blinked against the emotion. He was more of a father than I ever gave him credit.

I managed to return the orb to the box without spilling a tear, swallowing several times as Gee covered it with the towels.

"I must cover his wounds," she said softly. She applied the bandages to mask the healing that had taken place. Nothing could be done about the visible difference in his face. Qi Tai would berate the doctor for doing his job too well.

"Dad, you are well. Wake up," I said. I shook him gently, but to no avail.

Gee told me we had to leave. She called for the guard, who opened the cell door, and admired our handiwork from afar.

"He's going to die in his own vomit," the guard said dispassionately. "It will make the Minister happy. He has something special in mind for tomorrow."

A zombie, I thought. It would make him happy to force me to raise my own father from the dead. He would be disappointed.

The festivities were still in force as we passed the dining hall. Through the windows I saw elegantly dressed men on the far side of the room. The dark-haired, olive skin contingent was eating quietly, observing the spectacular feast before them. I was sure it made the Italian court pale by comparison, with the hundreds of servants, the swinging, flexible acrobats that blew flames and twirled silken ropes between bodies that lifted up, around and through one another. No magicians this time, no parrots.

As we walked by each window, I noticed one of the Italians, the oldest of the group, staring at the main table. His forehead was long, extending past the normal hairline, giving him an odd, equine look. Dark, bushy eyebrows nearly touched in the middle of his forehead, the arching ends indicating his interest. High cheekbones accentuated his age, as did the grey in his hair and pointy chin, which he'd shaved into a spear-like goatee.

He was fixated on something or someone, ignoring the entertainers, barely touching his food. Periodically, his eyes darted back and forth, observing a moving entity.

It wasn't obvious what had captured his attention until we came upon the final window.

"Keep moving," urged Gee, tugging my arm sleeve.

Unconcerned with the time, I slowed to a standstill. Mia stood behind Bao and the Empress, moving and talking to each as needed. Every so often, she gave a wince, like her feet were hurting her. Why in the world was she here, serving the Empress and then Bao?

The Italians. Qi Tai had ordered her here so the Italians could feast on Mia's beauty, and decide which one would have her. It appeared both Bao and Mia were completely unaware of their future husband's interests.

Gee pulled at my elbow again. Before I moved on, I saw the man's table partner respectfully tap his arm, talking into his ear. This second was younger looking, perhaps in his twenties. His face was unlined, toned, his arms muscular underneath his tight-fitting jacket.

The elderly woman didn't have to pull me away a third time. I knew we had to return. In the time I'd been watching, the performers had ended their routine, making way for new servers who brought forth tea.

Gee accompanied me to the doctor's building where she left me. She had to return the orb and the satchel to its hiding place.

***

Inside the doctor's quarters, I exhaled a short sigh of relief. It wasn't occupied by guards. I was safe, for now.

I rapidly discarded my clothes, scrubbed off the makeup and threw the wig in the corner of the room, under a pile of old rags. I lay down on the bed, revisiting the thrill and power of the orb, temporarily putting aside my lingering worry about my father's refusal to wake.

Unexpectedly, the door opened and my heart jumped with it. It might be the doctor, but I hoped it was Bao. Caution took over, and I closed my eyes.

"He might be asleep even when they leave," the doctor commented, sounding as though he were in the middle of a conversation.

"And to think they wanted both," the General remarked. He sounded surprised and pleased, I thought. I had never heard him talk with either emotion.

"I'm going to give the foreign girl one last opportunity to change her mind," Qi Tai said, his lilt of arrogance present.

"Wake up," General Li yelled at me.

He pushed my shoulder and I opened my eyes, affecting grogginess. A sharp point was at my throat before I had the chance to respond.

"Don't move," Qi Tai said, holding the weapon. The doctor stood behind both men. Worry was on his face, his eyes were red. The stress of the deception was showing.

"We have a gift for you," Qi Tai began, leaning toward me. "You should thank us for being merciful to your family."

A flash of red caught my eye, and I looked at the knife. It was made of plain metal, no ornamental designs or jewels. The flash had come from the ring on his finger. It was inches from my face, the inscriptions on the either side of the enormous ruby stone clear.

"The Italian count has taken a liking to your sister, though she is much younger than he," said the General, a knowing look on his face. "We have agreed to give her to him as a present in return for goods important to the kingdom. Unless…"

"Unless she can be persuaded to stay with me," finished Qi Tai. "I would keep her here, with you and your father. Safe, under one roof. I'd treat her... *very* well." I felt what Qi Tai was going to do to my sister. I didn't want to hear it or see it.

My fingers curled. The insinuation behind the statement disgusted and appalled me. The instinct to hurt had never been so strong.

The doctor saw my reaction and shook his head almost imperceptibly. Bao's father knew what I wanted to do. I'd no doubt he felt the same about his daughter. His cautionary signal was meant to save both girls and us. Now was not the time. Be patient.

"Of course, we can't guarantee how she would be treated once she's out of the Palace," the General said, turning to Qi Tai.

"Nor what they'd make her do when she's in their possession," the Minister agreed.

"You are fortunate to have the knife at my throat then," I said evenly.

"It is only hours now until they will be gone. If you want her to live until then, you will listen and obey."

Qi Tai lifted my shirt, his frigid hands cold through the invisible shield I wore.

"You are well enough to be transferred to the prison," he said. The General ordered the guards in from outside, waiting until two were on either side before he put away his knife.

"No more visitors," Qi Tai ordered the doctor. Bao's father nodded, picked up my shirt and handed it to me.

"He must stay warm to live," the doctor reminded my captors. Qi Tai looked dubious, but nodded once.

Minutes later, I was thrust into the cell next to my father. He had not moved. Something was terribly wrong.

CHAPTER 34

The night was long and cold but my wits were as bright and clear as the moment the orb healed me, my hearing and sense of smell acute. The sole benefit of the chill was the reduction in stench of the puke near my father. He was quiet, except for a random exhalation of air.

I could not force myself to sleep so I didn't try. Instead, I positioned my body in a classic meditation pose, legs crossed, the tips and thumbs and fingers touching in a triangular pose. I inhaled through my nose, exhaling through a thin gap between my tongue and roof of mouth. I visualized pure, clean air flowing through my system and pushing out and away the dark, rank poisons of my surroundings. Emotions of hate kept resurfacing. In and out, the battle was joined between what I knew to be the right frame of mind and my actual desires. The two could not coexist.

I finally turned from the view of my father. Separating my fingers, I patted a thin slip of cloth from the lining in my pants below the waistline. It was where I placed the drawing of the tapestry folded flat, unobtrusive and invisible to the casual observer.

In addition to the paper, a hard object was within. I pulled it out, finding a small, black chip of coal.

What on earth was this for? I wondered, rubbing it between my hands. The act made its purpose clear. The black made tracks on my skin.

I wondered…removing the piece of paper, I found it was two, not one. The first sheet was Bao's map, the other, a smaller piece, absent of writing.

For a return message.

The torch in the hallway flickered, throwing light in between the iron rods. I spread the paper on my right leg, hunching over to write out the words in the smallest possible size. The doctor required one more check before I went before the Emperor. It was all I needed to save Bao and my sister.

Satisfied with the note, I read it once more, folding it as small as possible, placing it back within the fold of my pants. Little was left of the coal. I found a corner in the cell, wedging it between the wall and the floor.

My master had told me deep meditation was known to bring forth visions from the subconscious. "The mind protects what the body cannot handle," he'd intoned in his wise, knowing manner. "When you are ready, knowledge will present itself."

I took a breath. That was theory. This was reality.

No student I'd known had experienced an out of body event, though I believed my master. If he said it was possible and he'd done it, he had. Hypnosis unlocked a relaxed mind, why not attempt to do the same while coherent? My wits were sharper and better functioning than ever. Assuming Mom was correct, that the veil of secrecy was all that stood between my subconscious and knowledge, I'd give an out of body experience a try.

CHAMBERS

I let my mind go, freeing myself of sentences, structure and thought. With each inhale, I visualized a clearing, full of nothing but white space, the symbol of enlightenment. On the exhale, I pushed the same white matter out, cleansing and purifying my mind, over and over, untainted particles of light expanding my consciousness.

The flow of intellect differed from the power surge of the orb. This had to do with the mind, my very inner self raising higher, up and out of my body.

In that instant, the tapestry came alive in my mind. It was what I imagined Bao's mother experienced. I was back in the Empress's cubicle, standing in front of the full-length wall hanging, every image moving in three dimensions.

The time was not accelerated. A cart moving along the roadway in the Forbidden City moved just as slowly as it did in real life. I could have watched for hours, spending my life in front of the tapestry instead of within my own existence.

Some part of me knew I was in a vision, for I forced myself to seek out that which I still didn't understand.

I was drawn to the figure in the lower right. The anonymous leader who held the spear, wore the glistening jewelry and basked in the light of the orb. His bracelet was an item I hadn't seen before. I could not identify its value, or that of his ring or headpiece, by looking at it or attempting to touch it. I could tell that I needed to hold them; that they were key elements of my journey. As I watched, the faceless man turned towards me, a move so fluid and deadly, I felt a stab of fear. Instinctively I turned from him to stop his action. I wasn't going to risk a sword thrown at my face, even if it were a vision. If I died in my dream, I wasn't sure I'd wake.

I understood that the cities shown on the tapestry were the realms I'd have to travel to find the other stones for the orb, and the jeweled objects of my enemy. The Serpent King had entrusted these to his priests, though I was sure their roles and titles were to be different in each location.

Looking more closely, I noticed that these places existed in different times. In one the dress was ancient, and in another it was much later, closer in style to my own, but not exactly. A third was somewhere in between. My conscious felt the increase in my heartbeat. The journey had been dangerous so far, and nearly deadly. It was also going to be thrilling, if I made it through alive.

The orb, located near the base of the tapestry, shone bright. Streams of gold light came out and through me as though I were not present. The feelings of unbridled power shot in all directions. I didn't have to verbalize the orb's significance. I felt it in every part of my being, as though my very blood were going to explode in a transcendent, glorified existence.

It was what the Serpent King desired. Unparalleled power to control all.

I looked back at the tapestry and the image of the faceless ruler had come alive. This was the Serpent King. As though he knew I was watching, he turned to me and lifted his right hand, the one with the ruby ring. He focused it on me, and though I couldn't see a face, I felt him smiling, a grimace of hate. A burst of light shone forth from the ring, a laser to my heart.

It stopped.

I snapped my eyes shut, closing the vision down. I was back in my body, my fingers still touching, though sweat dropped out every pore.

CHAPTER 35

My mind barely had time to process the unearthly experience when I sensed a presence behind me, watching me. The eerie feeling made my skin crawl.

I looked over my shoulder and jumped. My father was standing, as close to the bars as possible, each hand gripping the rusted, dark rods. His body was visibly different than I'd remembered. His scrawny shoulders now filled out the shirt, and taut, white skin exposed through the torn cloth. His neck was still covered with half-frozen vomit, reminding me more of a dirty football player after a long night than an academic with a half-grown beard. Even his hips and legs appeared to have widened. The ripped, loose fitting khaki pants covering his stick legs were now tight over his brawny thigh muscles.

Uncomfortably, I scanned his face. It was my dad, but at the same time it wasn't. A hard jaw, angular and strong, replaced his middle age flab. Had I created a zombie?

I searched for a feeling of gratitude from him, expecting one to come easily.

Nothing. A dull heartbeat broke the emptiness I felt. His mind wasn't available, and neither were his emotions. It was as though his physical shell were empty of the life within.

I unwillingly met his gaze. His pupils were intense and darker then I'd remembered. He was taking me in as though he'd never seen me before. I wondered if I'd talked out loud during the vision, waking him from a dreaming state.

Why had the orb's healing manifested such a change in him, and not me?

"Are you ok?" I asked him. His eyes darted to mine but he said nothing.

Shouts from the guards caught my attention. Commotion was happening in the front of the prison, and I heard Wu's voice giving a command. The gates unlocked, a door swung open, and Wu was walking down the hallway, the doctor by his side, led by the prison guard.

"You and your father are requested," Wu said. His manner was formal and stiff, what I expected towards a prisoner with dubious intentions.

I felt for his emotions, the act now second nature. His heart was closed towards not just me, but everyone. He carried the wariness of self-preservation, the fear of loneliness, the anger of betrayal. Now he was acting, hiding his thinking behind the mission he was instructed to carry out.

I looked at Dad, who still gripped the bars, his eyes fixated upon my own.

The doctor entered, asking me to raise my arms for an examination. I did so, lifting my shirt, turning from side to side. When I appeared to be finished, the guard told me to follow him.

"Wait," the doctor said, interrupting the guard's efforts to move us along. "I need one moment to assess his health as the Emperor requested."

The guard nodded curtly.

The doctor requested I turn around so that he could examine my back.

Smart. His back and mine were to the cell door. As he leaned in, he lifted my shirt, touched my skin, asking all the while if I felt pain here or there. It gave me the cover necessary to lift out the note.

"My stomach hurts," I told him.

His fingers crossed in front. "Here?" he asked, pressing the flesh. With a subtle movement of my finger, I slid the paper under his fingertips.

"Higher," I said. "There."

The doctor pretended to press, noting my lack of pain. "You are well enough to go," the doctor concluded, pulling down my shirt.

The door opened, and when I turned, I saw Wu avert his eyes away from me. He was staring at my father's new physical appearance. He did nothing to mask his surprise. He'd noticed not only that the wounds were healed, but that overall my father looked dramatically different than before. If he knew about the orb from his father or Bao, he gave no signal. He motioned for Dad to follow him, again, receiving no response.

Once the other guards were in place, they waited for Wu's command.

"Drop your arms," Wu commanded Dad, his voice aggressive. Of all the times for Dad to gain a sense of confidence, now was not one of them.

"Dad!" I yelled, breaking his trance-like state, gesturing for him to follow Wu.

He opened his grip and dropped his hands, stepping between Wu and the guards. Once he was chained and the guards were prepared, I was let out, and told to fall in line after my father. I'd been taller than him since I was fourteen. Now he matched my height and was a physical brick. Had his transformation included fighting skills and coordination as well? A tinge of jealousy made me lose my focus.

Doesn't matter. As long as he was well enough to travel. Besides, when we returned home, *if* we returned home, he'd find our relationship was going to be very different than the way it had been before.

We made our way out of the dank cavern in silence. I knew better than to ask Wu where we were going. Mia and Bao were to be given to the foreign visitors this morning. Then I'd be required to use my powers for Qi Tai's purpose. Again I wondered if the orb drew the faceless man forward, closer to us, ready to strike. And kill.

Qi Tai was an idiot, thinking his leverage was my father.

We entered the academic training complex, and I supposed we were on our way to the execution grounds. Gongs, in rapid succession, pounded from every direction.

The sound startled Wu and the others, who exchanged anxious looks.

"Do we leave him for the Emperor?" the second in command asked Wu.

Wu studied me and his men, unsure.

"The City is being invaded," shouted another guard to Wu. "We must go!"

The pounding of hundreds of feet lifted to the air, rapid slices of air denoting the raise of swords. The clanging of metal meant weapons were being removed from the armory was matched by the stampede of horses, the noise bouncing off the walls throughout the city. The Imperial soldiers were preparing to fight the invaders. I wanted to be one of them.

I grabbed Wu's arm.

"Release me! I can help you. I can help the Emperor escape," I said in a rush. "We have time to get the Emperor and the Empress and their family out. Maybe others," I emphasized, implying his own sister and father, my eyes begging him to understand what I was not going to say in front of the others. "First the outer fortress of the city will be stormed, then the inner Imperial Palace. We have time!"

Wu shrugged off my arm, anger filling his eyes. He didn't *want* to believe me. Something had happened, and it prevented his logical side from trusting me as he had done before. "Why would I save your life before to end it now?" I yelled. He stood still, precious moments passing as he delayed answering my question.

I couldn't take it anymore. I lurched forward, grabbing his right shoulder.

"Listen to me!" I yelled. He gripped the top hand with his left, curled it up, flipping my right elbow at a ninety-degree angle. He meant to break my wrist, then land me on my back. I knew it instinctively; it was what I'd have done.

Since my hands were still connected by a twelve-inch chain, his attempt to break and throw me failed. I dropped and executed a reverse spin, throwing off his hand while wrapping both of mine around his forearm. The move ripped him down, throwing him on his back as my leg kicked out his legs from under him. I pressed my elbow to his throat, prepared to sever his larynx.

"*Wei shen me?*" I whispered. "Why, for what reason?" I had done nothing to provoke the attack, other than to try to save the Emperor.

"Bao," he said, croaking out the word. He wasn't obliged to say more. The other guards pounced on me, swords to my neck and back, I was lifted to a standing position. Dad remained silent.

"What have I done to Bao?" I whispered to him. He stomped ahead of me, his glide off centered and angry. He wasn't thinking clearly. Had he been afflicted by the greed and power of the General and Qi Tai? It was possible, but not probable. He cared about Bao as much as I did. Impossibly, he'd come to believe I was somehow going to harm her. Though in fact, the truth might bother him just as much.

In a moment, I saw the cause of Wu's ire. Bao was standing between Imperial Guards, as was my sister. Bao wore a pale, pink dress, the high collar buttoned with jewels that took in the little light in the square. The long sleeves dropped to her delicate wrists, the silver and gold threading intertwined, weaving a pattern of doves on her chest. Diamonds hung from long, pearl-strand earrings, matching pearl combs in her hair.

Mia wore a form fitting white dress, the silk accented with red and blue lilies. She looked innocent and elegant, her blond hair held back, bound in twists and combs. Her face was heavily made up, the black eyeliner and blue eye shadow matching her outfit, and her wide, full lips popping from the red stain.

Alongside the women, a group of five men stood, hands on their swords. Each wore voluminous, ground-length sleeves, the rich, velvet material jeweled at the neckline and the wrists. Two men wore large hats with feathers, another hood.

Beneath the coats, the men wore doublets and hose, shiny, elegant riding boots and each one had a jeweled sword at his waist. The men stood at the ready, each had his hand on his sword, prepared for an attack.

None was required.

Beyond the two teen girls and five noblemen stood the Emperor, the Empress, Gee, the Minister of War, Zheng He, and General Li. Instead of the Emperor's Imperial army, several hundred uniformed soldiers in unfamiliar clothing stood in their place. Coming up fast was a man riding a white horse.

No wonder Wu didn't answer his men. He knew about the invasion, and that the Emperor had already been captured. He was in on it.

The man on the white horse drew near, and I recognized him. He was the same man who had met Zheng He outside the Grottoes. The Prince of Yan. He had invaded the City and captured the Palace.

CHAPTER 36

The Prince expertly dismounted, striding to the Emperor in a few, long paces. His solid body moved in fluid motion, a cat ready to pounce on its prey.

"You knew this day would come," he said to the Emperor, without courtesy or formality. His men continued to stream through the courtyard, the shouts of fighting continued unabated, punctuated with cries of terror and death.

"Your men are dying. Do you feel pity?" he asked Emperor Jianwen.

"For you," answered the teenager, with all the calm of a person still in charge. "A man with no conscience deserves pity."

In a single movement, the Prince leapt and gripped the Emperor by his throat. The Prince towered above the teen, his mass double that of his nephew. Effortlessly, he lifted the Emperor up, off the ground.

With just one flex of his hand, the Prince could snap his neck or crush his throat, leaving him dead or mute. The Emperor's feet held still, dangling loosely.

"He is nothing to you now," said Zheng He, diplomatically interrupting, motioning for the Prince of Yan to place the Emperor on the ground. "The others are awaiting your direction."

I refused to believe Zheng He could be a part of a treasonous plot. His actions had always been honorable and true, his word kept, up to informing the Emperor about my deeds with the orb. Had he lusted for power himself, he would have kept it a secret. He also helped save my family from the unicorn. His loyalty was to the Emperor, beyond a doubt. Now the situation had changed. He would surely change with it. Survival dictated adaptation, but didn't eliminate compassion.

"Yes, indeed," the Prince said, releasing the Emperor unceremoniously, turning to the Italians. "What to do with them?" The Emperor landed on his feet, his stance ready for a fight.

The Admiral stepped forward. He told the Prince about the vast trading network that had been established with the Europeans. The wealth had come from the Italians, along with the goods the Empire desired. "Even her," Zheng He said, referring to Bao. "Her mother was Italian, revered for her exquisite handwriting and ability to interpret ancient texts. They have been valuable in the past and will aid us in the future. Cultivate this trade, do not extinguish it," he advised.

The Prince considered his statement and agreed. "Wise counsel," he said, inquiring if they spoke Mandarin.

The Admiral shook his head no.

"Do they bring valuable goods on this trip?"

"They have brought much already, gold and silver, as well as clothing for the Imperial family. It has not yet been touched."

The Prince liked the notion of unspoiled products. Then he squinted warily, touching his sword.

"What do they receive in return?"

"Silk and trading access." Zheng He had purposefully left out one key part of the deal.

"That is not much," the Prince responded, skeptical of the perceived imbalance.

"And those two girls," chimed in Qi Tai, directing the Prince's attention to Bao and Mia.

Loathing for the man permeated my entire being. He could have kept his mouth shut, alleviating the Prince's requirement to give the girls away.

The Prince's eyes moved to Bao, his look of disinterest plain. My sister affected an entirely different reaction. She stood tall, nearly his height. Her green eyes sparkled against her blonde hair, the bruise on her face masked with makeup. Her rebellious spirit seemed to nearly burst from within as she jutted out her chin, daring him to defy her.

"And you?" he said to her, with more than a passing interest. "Do you go willingly?"

Qi Tai shuffled, though the Prince didn't award the Minister a reaction. He wouldn't know this was intruding on the Minister's plans.

I watched Mia push out her lips, a pucker that was both insinuating and insulting. I doubted the Prince of Yan knew the difference. She was a seventeen year-old bombshell going toe to toe with a thirty-year old conqueror destined to be the greatest Ming Emperor of all time.

It was the impression she gave to others, and especially to me. She knew she was desired by more than one man. She practically glimmered inside with the knowledge of her feminine power. They didn't stand a chance.

"I go where I want, when I want," she replied calmly. It wasn't my imagination; she licked her ruby red lips at precisely the right moment. She was actually challenging him.

With a swift movement, his hand gripped her chin, and he crushed his lips to hers. My eyes widened in shock, a look not mirrored on Mia's face. To my amazement, she wrapped an arm around his neck, pressing her lips back to him in a kiss that would have made a movie director blush. I'd never even seen her kiss any guy before.

At precisely the right moment she put her hands on his chest and withdrew her lips. The experience left the Prince pulsating with desire. He responded by gripping both of her hands in his, holding them tight. He kissed her again, then broke it himself, smiling at her. She'd met her match.

"We shall see," he promised.

The Prince turned to the Admiral and Qi Tai. "Let them take her," he said, gesturing to Bao. "This one stays."

"But we have agreed— " refuted Qi Tai. The Prince silenced him with a glance. He was willing to use his sword on anyone countering his demands, and Qi Tai knew it. Qi Tai bowed low, glowering, his own loathing for the Prince increasing by the moment. I could see what he was thinking. All along Qi Tai had wanted Mia for himself, but not out of sexual attraction. Qi Tai desired Mia in order to break her, make her serve him, feed him. I knew he saw her as a whipping post, a horse to be broken, and ultimately discarded, then killed.

"Offer another woman, or two women. Or more jade in trade. She stays. Take her and leave," he said, dismissing the men.

Qi Tai moved to the group of five, bringing with him the Minister of Languages. I listened to the interpretation, not understanding Italian, but not needing to. The oldest man expressed fury, loudly shouting words I expected were curses. Finally, he was mollified when Qi Tai explained that there was a new Emperor. He suggested the visitors take what was being offered, for their lives depended on the grace and good attitude of the new ruler.

This sufficed. The leader asked for more than double the amount of jade, and Qi Tai agreed. He wanted the Italians gone as soon as possible. When the negotiations were complete, the Minister of Languages gestured for Bao to follow him. She stood behind the man, a handful of the Prince's guards nearby. She walked resolutely, her face emotionless and beautiful.

One Italian man stepped forward, his hand extended. He looked younger than the others, probably in his mid-twenties. His dark, wavy hair rested on his shoulders, partially covering the fluffy gold pads that extended down to his elbows. His dark eyes weren't greedy, like the Prince's. He bowed to Bao, rising, respectfully opening his palm.

She slowly walked to the waiting men, bowing her head modestly, stretching out her hand. Opening the palm, it contained a seashell. The gift of long life with one family, she said. As the interpreter translated her words, the men murmured with pleasure.

I watched Bao search his face, then in a moment, it was as if she made her decision. She placed the seashell in his hand. He smiled, giving her a kind look, extending his other hand. My heart pulsed as she placed hers within it. I saw the pressure of his fingers against hers. Bao's aura was acceptance and her demeanor respect. She would not cause trouble.

She knew her duty to her family and to the Imperial family. Her role was not to disgrace, but to please.

As she moved out of the courtyard, I sensed her loss, tied to me and her father and brother. Like her dad, she didn't harbor anger and resentment for those guiding her fate. She turned back briefly, a glance to the courtyard, her eyes finding mine. I felt her heart. A pain, like a knife hit me, her strength finally breaking as she left the square. I'd been in lust plenty of times, but never in love. Her swell of feeling encompassed my mind, my heart, warming my chest…my soul.

The next moment, she turned the corner and was gone, severing the connection. My loss was instant, as was my attention to survival.

Qi Tai observed me with black eyes, giving me a knowing glance. The first part of his agenda was complete. We were both losing something we wanted, for very different reasons. The fight now was going to be between me and him. I welcomed it.

The Prince lifted a hand to Mia's cheek, running his forefinger down her jaw. Instead of leaning away, she leaned towards it. Was she playing now, or did she actually like his touch? Watching it gave rise to mixed emotions, jealousy that I hadn't experienced more with Bao, and confusion that Mia seemed to want his attention.

"A surprise gift," he said, his voice low and serious, his lips pulsating once again with the fire to continue where he'd left off.

Abruptly, he turned from her. "She will bear tall children, good warriors," he remarked, the comment drawing a flat smile from the General. He didn't approve of the Prince's choice, welcoming to a foreigner in the royal household. But he would do his duty and obey the Prince. It was for the good of the country, the General firmly believed. Good for the people to have a strong man in charge to help fend off the invading neighbors to the north and south.

"Where is this thing they call the orb?" the Prince of Yan asked the Empress, taking my attention from Mia. "Qi Tai said you were the last to have it."

"It was in my room, where the Emperor asked me to keep it," the Empress responded. "Between my closet and my gowns, in a chest that only I could unlock. Yet it is not there. It has been taken."

The Prince slapped her across the face. Jianwen lurched towards him, stopping when a sword was placed on his stomach. The Prince leaned close to the former Emperor, his towering figure looming over the younger man.

"You may request mercy for the Empress after I get what I want," he said. "Who did you give it to?"

The Empress shook her head. "No one! No one knew where it was."

"The punishment for lying is death," Qi Tai intoned. He'd already taken sides. My hate for Qi Tai increased every time he opened his mouth. It would be a shame if the Prince found him out and killed him before I had a chance to get in some physical punishment.

"Bao moved it," cried Gee, astonishing all present. I turned to Wu, searching his face. He did not seem surprised.

In that instant, Bao's calm acceptance and courage became clear. She had risked herself for me, and Wu knew it. He hadn't been in on the invasion. This was why he hated me now. He must have known the Empress was going to be captured and accused of moving the orb, but that Bao would take the blame. Her actions were done for one reason: to save me. At least she was gone, and Wu would remain the Emperor's personal guard.

Maybe that was why he allowed me to be brought to the square, even with the Prince present. My death would now be payback for her removal from the Palace.

"She was only following orders," Gee said calmly, talking directly to the Prince of Yan. "General Li's son, Xing, informed her that Qi Tai demanded the orb, she gave it to Xing without question. Had she known he was a traitor, she never would have given it to him."

Her words drew gasps from the immediate crowd. General Li drew his sword as though to cut out her tongue. Before he took two steps forward, the Prince slashed it down, cutting it in half.

"Get back," he said to the General. "You were the one who opened the secret door to the outside and let us in. Don't believe I'm foolish enough to trust you yet."

"We need a new Emperor," General Li said, acknowledging his role in the capture of the Palace. "But my son is no traitor," said General Li.

"Where is Xing?" snapped Qi Tai.

"Xing did not tell me where he was taking it, only that you ordered it to raise your army of zombies from the dead." Gee boldly thrust out her chin, the old face full of belligerence. "Kill me if you must. The truth will stand on its own after I die."

The Prince of Yan paused, then turned to Qi Tai and said, "If you are double-crossing me, your head is the first one I will stick on a post."

I suspected Gee had another motive for claiming Xing was a traitor. The longer she distracted the Prince, the less time he had to torture anyone else, or kill the Emperor.

The sounds of death, fire and a city submitting to the hands of new rulers carried on around us. My father remained still, beside me now, silently watching the scene in front of him. I said nothing either, knowing my turn to speak would come soon enough. It was only a matter of time before the possessor of the orb was asked to wield its power. First, it had to be found.

"What do you know of this?" the Prince asked Mia.

"I have been serving the Empress since I came to this land," she said, shivering in the cold. In a moment, he stripped off his coat and draped it around her.

"She lies," said Qi Tai. "She, her brother and father came to our city with the orb. She knows of it as well."

The Prince adjusted the sash around her neck, holding it tight. He slid a finger down the center of her chest, resting the forefinger halfway. With a flick of his finger, a piece of her dress was torn open.

"I don't want to harm something that will be with me many years." He produced the tip of a metal blade to her chest, pressing it in just enough to indent the material. Mia tilted her chin coyly, as though she were being asked out on a date instead of threatened with her life.

"I haven't seen it since," she replied evenly. "I've hardly done a thing lately. I've been hindered by two broken feet."

"So you say…" The Prince dropped his sword, lifting her dress. Both ankles were heavily bandaged, the skin underneath hidden. He sliced off the wrappers, revealing finely figured ankles. "Which one was supposed to be broken?" he asked.

"You said both were broken," growled the General, pointing an accusatory finger at his Qi Tai.

"The doctor…" Qi Tai whispered, the anger real. He genuinely wanted my sister's feet destroyed to give him an advantage over her mentally as well as physically. "The consequence for protecting this girl will be death," Qi Tai vowed, directing a nearby guard to retrieve Bao and also find her father.

The Prince stayed the order. "She is not worthy of disrupting a valuable trading partner and ally. We need the orb. If Bao gave it to Xing, we must find him. Now."

The Prince sent off two soldiers to track Xing down. "The doctor served my grandfather, and has already proved his loyalty with the loss of his wife," the Prince continued, nodding approvingly at the recollection. "His daughter now gone, he has no reason to be disloyal."

"Besides," he turned to Mia again, "I will need him when my new concubine bears my sons."

At this, Mia raised up her lip, another invitation. I couldn't believe what I was seeing. But her shrewd handling of the man had already saved Bao.

The Admiral gestured the Prince aside and the two talked in low voices. I heard the Prince ask about Wi Cheng, and was told he'd returned to the forge in the mountains. No wonder I'd not seen him. I hoped he was safe, hiding far away from here for the time being. The Prince was unlikely to touch him, or his craftsman. Their knowledge was vast and invaluable.

As the men talked, the Prince ignored Draben, but his insistent hacking, wheezing, and spitting up of black and green slime was distracting.

"What is this man doing here?" the Prince finally asked Zheng He.

"This man is the one Cage brought back to life using the rock and the orb. He cannot be killed, and he responds only to the commands from the person who gave him life."

"You will harness this power for my army…" the Prince said to Qi Tai, processing the notion. Qi Tai rubbed his temple and nodded. The ruby ring flashed. The Prince of Yan turned to me, acknowledging my presence for the first time.

He was sizing me up as a potential adversary. "It was you who defeated Xing and brought the statue to life. Is it true that this once dead man tried to kill your father?" he asked, awarding my father a glance. The two were equal height, and dad was now nearly as wide as the Prince. My father didn't have an ounce of fighting skill, but the Prince wouldn't know it.

I acknowledged the Prince's statement with a curt nod of my head.

"Where did you say you first saw this dead man, Qi Tai?" asked the Prince, turning from me.

"Outside the palace within the Forbidden City, when he and the family came out of the tunnels."

General Li immediately offered to send his men to the hole, but the Prince objected.

"Neither of you leaves my sight," said the Prince.

"Dad?" asked Mia. My father looked at her, and said nothing.

The Prince walked over to the weapons wall and selected a long whip.

"He is trying to protect you by not talking. However, I know that you both can hear me quite well. Xing is likely in league with your brother. You, being the sister, know what he plans on doing." The Prince snapped the whip against the ground.

"We have no plan," I said firmly, "nor do I know where Xing is hiding. I've been in prison, as multiple guards can witness."

"So I've heard," the Prince responded smoothly, cracking the whip in the air. He swirled it again, several times above his head then drew it quickly to him near Mia's head.

She was unshaken, her evident faith in her ability to manage the Prince well exceeding my own. I wasn't going to give her the chance to prove it out.

"I can trap Xing," I offered, "but it must be a surprise. You need me and the orb. Not just one or the other. You and I know my sister is not a part of it." He had no choice. He must accept my proposal and take the chance, or he would be without the object of power he desired.

The whip stopped moving overhead. I desperately hoped Xing was underground, hiding, listening to all that was going on. The Prince gestured, and two soldiers came forward. "Go with him," he ordered.

"I need my hands," I said logically.

The Prince laughed. "I'm not a fool."

I bowed, ever so slightly. "Even a fool knows that to fight a warrior, I must be capable to do so. Xing is a warrior, who I defeated once before with only my hands."

"You will run," he said, gesturing to the soldiers on either side of me.

"You have my sister and my father," I said, looking him dead in the eye. "But that is not why I will return. An honorable man does not run." I intended to fight the Prince when I got back, and he knew it.

"I accept," he said, dropping his own head slightly, acknowledging of the challenge. He ordered that my hands be released, and I was on my way to find Xing.

CHAPTER 37

I ran back through the Palace with the Prince's armed guards, my own companions yelling for their peers to step aside. The Palace was not yet completely overrun with the Prince's men, but the elite units had been dismantled, and bodies were piled up on either side of the halls. I pushed out the sadness and horror of the guards, many younger than me, who had been needlessly killed in the onslaught. They were boys compared to the seasoned warriors that stood in their place. Why had the Prince ordered the men to be killed, not taken?

Qi Tai. That murderous, traitorous sack of evil. He wanted the boys dead. They were going to be his army, his men to control. He had truly manipulated the Prince of Yan to do his own dirty work, slaughtering those in order to make his eternal warriors of death.

The repulsive thought of the Prince slaying tens of thousands who remained in the City made me run faster. I had to control a potential massacre.

The Ministers were quiet, as usual, standing respectfully aside as they assessed the direction the new Emperor was going to take. They were harmless. I remembered Mia's comment about the third Ming Emperor. The Prince of Yan would be China's greatest rulers of the Ming Dynasty. It had been destined to start out with death.

"This way," I yelled as we zigzagged through the avenues and down to the prison cell. I was betting Xing had been underground, listening to the conversation the entire time. By now, I had no doubt Bao had indeed given the orb to Xing. He had likely explained the betrayal to the doctor. If his daughter could aid in helping the royal family to escape, the decision to support Xing's plan was easy.

The moment we opened the underground prison gate, I saw more bodies on the floor.

I was ready. I lashed out at the guard on my left, cutting into his abdomen with my left side thrust, collapsing his body. I kicked up my right leg, landing my heel on the jaw of the other guard. Both dropped to the ground. A black figure moved from my left, gagging and binding the men.

"You ran fast," Xing said, handing me a cord to bind the guard's feet. Once both were strapped to the bars, he gave me my backpack.

"I met with Gee and she gave me the pack she was supposed to return to the Empress's room. It's all there. Nothing was moved." I was stunned. Xing had gone to the trouble of placing the orb within the pack itself, and I quickly felt through the objects, each one accounted for, and seemingly, undamaged.

"I'm hoping you have a plan," Xing said, looking at me with anxious eyes.

I grimaced in anticipation. It was time for retribution.

***

CHAMBERS

"We are going down into the catacombs," I told him. "Chambers underneath the ground created by volcanoes." I told him about the grate, and he made a detour that took us up and out from below.

"I don't believe that area is connected," he said, directing us through back alleys. Keeping to the shadows of the tiled roofs, we darted between the buildings. Soon Xing found the grate that I'd opened to arrive in the Forbidden City.

We sprinted for the top, he lifted it, dropping in and I plunged down after, pulling it shut tight.

"No light," he said, standing in the dark.

"That's temporary," I told him, pulling out the orb.

The use of the object was still a mystery, and though I wasn't sure what made the light appear, I mentally directed it to aid us. The ball started to shine, highlighting the fear and anticipation on Xing's face.

"This way," I urged, guiding Xing deeper into the catacombs, keeping an eye out for a tall pillar in the center of the tunnel, one with long strings hanging from top to the bottom. As we searched, I prepared Xing for what we were about to encounter.

"We are going to go to the Sacred grottoes."

"How will we create a distraction?" he asked.

"You will see."

"We don't have much time, Cage. Bao is far away by now, and your sister—if she's not dead, she's—well…" He left the comment hanging. We both knew what the Prince intended to do with her.

I couldn't think about that now. "We have to talk."

He shrugged my hand off with force. "Are you crazy? We have no time!"

"I'm making time. Listen to me," I began, struggling with the words. No matter how I phrased it, I was going to sound crazy and he might be insulted. "When I was with your dad, after I was healed…I saw…I felt things…things that were in his mind and his heart. He's not the bad person you think he is."

I didn't need to witness the change of surprise to anger on his face. "What are you saying?" He demanded. Feelings of jealously and insult colored his manner, rightfully so. Who was I to be presuming I knew his father?

"Look, I know it sounds absurd, but you have to believe me when I tell you this. His intentions were not to overthrow the Emperor for the sake of killing him. He's trying to protect you…and your sister…"

"What…did you say?" he whispered harshly.

"I saw your sister in a…vision…or something. She was disguised as a boy, working in a field, far away where no one can take her and make her do what she doesn't want to do—like become some man's slave. Your father did that to protect her. It's what he's doing now for you. He believes the only way to keep you alive, and reunite the family is to have a strong ruler who will govern the country under a firm hand. It's bloody now, but he is acting in your best interest."

Xing was stymied with shock. He told me he'd not known his sister's whereabouts. He thought she'd been abandoned by his father, who had turned from someone he admired to a person of Qi Tai's ilk. His heart lifted as my words sunk in, the respect and admiration growing moment to moment.

"The only way to ensure this was to align himself with Qi Tai—for the time being. He doesn't trust him though." I touched Xing's arm again, and this time, he didn't brush me off. "Give him another chance."

Xing acknowledged my comment, focusing on what we were about to encounter.

"Get ready."

I cupped the orb in my palms. I visualized what I needed to find and why, along with every detail of my desired outcome.

After a few moments of anticipation, a warm breeze signaled my request had been granted. A bright light within the orb shone more brilliant, illuminating the entire cavern. The sail turned itself, pointing to the location I'd use as a portal. The light continued to grow until the cavern was bright as daylight. At that moment, crackling sounds filled the room, and the wall disintegrated.

"Follow me, Xing. Stay close."

As soon as the opening was large enough, I entered and Xing followed. He understood the implications of lagging behind when the rock wall closed.

Once we were on the other side, I instructed Xing to look for a way out.

"The exit will be on the roof or on the side of a cave," I said, searching all around me.

"There it is!" pointed Xing.

The hole was in the upper right corner of the ceiling, at the far end of a long, flat stretch of rock. It was covered with stringy, gray and green moss. Xing climbed up and out of the hole. I followed, still holding the orb in one hand.

"This is it," I said, my faith in the orb complete. We were back at the Datong grottoes.

"Are you going to tell me what we are doing now, or surprise me?"

"I'll tell you while we run. It might take some time to find it."

"Find what?" asked Xing, exasperated.

"A thousand-year-old man-bull creature with three human heads. It was what I brought to life when I was here with Zheng He. We are going to trap it and take it back with us."

"How do you know it will come with us?" Xing contended, eyes displaying fear and skepticism.

"I don't. But it will either choose to come with us, or die."

CHAPTER 38

I explained to Xing how the beast must be trapped within the cave as it rested. As we entered, we both heard the sounds of breathing, and laid ropes around the exits. When I gave the signal, Xing shouted.

The breathing stopped, the pushing and lifting of its body from the ground gave way to a gallop.

This time, I yelled. A rumbling grew louder and louder, the very stone vibrating. My arms tensed and I crouched, ready for the encounter.

The three heads yelled their war cry in unison, the red eyes glowing in the darkness. The heads jeered, raising its arms to pick me up and pull me apart. When the beast was a few strides away, it stepped into the ropes. The snare tripped, causing the beast's front knees to collapse. The back legs kicked and fought, as the arms reached and grabbed for the coils Xing and I attempted to throw around the neck.

We realized too late the futility of the strategy. It would fight us until we killed it. I had zero desire to kill another animal I'd raised from its resting place.

I pulled out the orb. All three heads howled in rage as Xing held the front legs tight and I walked to its heads.

With no time to spare, I gave the beast a choice.

"Follow me and fight," I offered. "To refuse is death."

"We get to fight whomever we meet?" asked the first head.

I nodded. "But you can only defend yourself until you reach the center of the Imperial courtyard. You can fight anyone but the Emperor and Empress, two women wearing white, and my father—"

"Or *my father*," added Xing.

"That leaves you hundreds of soldiers," I said, responding to the looks of disappointment. "And the Prince, who has killed hundreds already. You can't miss him."

"What then?" asked the second head.

"After we reach the courtyard, it's up to you to do what you want. Stay and fight as many people as you'd like, or escape the palace. But you have to promise one thing. No killing anyone unless they try to kill you."

The heads discussed my proposal.

"No fun," remarked the third head.

"I love to fight," said head number one.

"Better to die now than wait another thousand years to have the chance to fight again," said head number three.

"And we can do whatever we want as long as we don't kill those named," affirmed head number two. I added Bingwen, describing him in detail.

They came to a silent agreement, as all three heads responded in unison. "We accept."

***

CHAMBERS

We waited behind a thick grove near the Imperial Zoo. Hidden within dense evergreen bushes, we could hear the proceedings.

"Let's charge," said one of the heads.

"Not yet," I said. "We must wait." My sister was speaking. She was using her gift to instill a fight among the remaining leaders.

"She's good," said Xing, a touch of admiration in his voice. Not another one. The girl had skills.

Although we were yards away, I saw her tilt her head and raise an eyebrow. "I'll answer your question, Prince," I heard Mia say. "If you first tell me why you have the Empress's jade necklace that was her wedding gift and is now hidden in your coat pocket. I'd like to be with a man of your—power—but won't consider a man with no honor. How did you get it?"

I heard the shuffling of feet, and Xing told me he saw a few guards look at their leader.

"You think you know what is in my pocket?" the Prince asked my sister, more intrigued with her than before. His look was one of open desire for the challenge she presented a man of his position.

"I'll make you a deal Prince," Mia offered. "If it's not the Jade necklace, then I'll willingly be your bride. If it is, then you grant me my freedom."

The Prince considered her request, then laughed. "You are a strong one," he said, unwilling to go with her plan. "It so happens this was a gift from the General." He lifted the jade necklace out of his pocket. The Empress bit her lip when she saw the piece in his hand. "Where he got it is not of my concern. And you are mine regardless of the answer."

Mia clucked her tongue, tilting her head in the other direction.

"She's more beguiling than the jade," observed Xing appreciatively.

"And where do you *think* the General got it?" Mia pressed the Prince.

"It is unimportant," interrupted Qi Tai.

"Qi Tai stole it from the Empress and gave it to the General. Just like the bracelet in your shirt pocket. That was also stolen from the Empress."

"Even the look of dishonor detracts from a man's ability to rule," Mia continued, her voice reasonable and soothing. "You will be the greatest Ming Emperor to live. Don't bring shame on *our* rule."

The Prince gazed at my sister. I held my breath, wondering what would happen next. Even the beast seemed to understand the precariousness of the situation, the mouths of each head were breathing shallow and low.

"Your words have wisdom," the Prince said appreciatively, his eyes still dark. He was a brutal man, bound by honor, not conventional rules of kindness. "I know the code as well as you do," the Prince replied. "Victory bounty is mine. It is not stealing."

Mia rose up, her eyes now bright.

"Then you must agree Qi Tai and the General are the ones who should be hanging here."

"Get ready," I said. The beasts craned their heads and their hoofs churned the ground.

"Qi Tai is getting a weapon from the wall," Xing said, readying himself to move.

"The truth will spill from your blood," Qi Tai said, ignoring the Prince's command to stop.

"No!" cried the Empress.

The crack of a whip and a single scream were the sounds I needed to hear in order to move. We sprung into the courtyard, the beast charging ahead of us, hurling bodies on the ground left and right.

I'd seen pictures of the famous bull chases through the streets of Pamplona, Spain, but had never experienced anything like it until now. Even though the three heads had promised not to kill me or anyone else I wished to protect, I didn't entirely trust the beast not to knock me down or tear me apart if I accidentally got in the way.

"Follow me!" I shouted to Xing.

I crashed through the ring of guards and gaped at the scene in front of me. My father and Draben had been behind a line of guards, strung to a different set of pulleys.

"The square!" I shouted to the man-bull. "Bludgeon everyone but them," pointing to my family, the Empress and General Li. The Emperor had turned his back and I hoped they could discern his ornate clothing from the others.

One of the heads carefully studied each of the protected individuals I'd identified as the other two heads turned intently upon the sea of soldiers in the courtyard. Using its six arms to slice razor-sharp swords through the air in preparation for attack, the beast started its rampage.

Qi Tai shouted orders to capture Xing and me and was abruptly countered by General Li, who quickly changed the order to seize me and kill the beast. As they raced out of the bull's line, they began countermanding one another.

"Kill the bull!" commanded the Prince of Yan, assessing the beast presented a far greater danger than either Xing or myself. The guards in the courtyard drew their weapons, preparing for battle.

Screaming an eerie battle cry, the man-bull raced forward, waging an assault upon the advancing guards. Though many in number, the Prince's men were no match for the swift movement, strength, and fighting ability of the beast. The six eyes of the beast's three heads locked on Qi Tai and a group of guards closest to him and the General.

Meanwhile, Qi Tai maneuvered himself behind the furthest row of guards. The bull parted his line of protection with the ease of a ship passing through calm waters. As bodies fell lifelessly at the hands of the beast, Qi Tai stood and raised his fist, his ruby ring glinting.

With a loud victory scream, the beast reached over its shoulder with one of its six hands and plucked an arrow from its back quiver and shot it at Qi Tai. The arrow went straight through the center of Qi Tai's palm and out the other side.

Shrieking in pain and fear, the Minister of War held his damaged hand and ran, panicked and directionless. But Qi Tai wasn't fast enough to dodge or outrun the bull. One of the beast's hands slapped Qi Tai's head, like a cat playing with a mouse, while another flicked away his black cap and pulled his ponytail. One of the heads laughed with glee as a hoof connected with Qi Tai's backside, causing him to lurch forward. Before Qi Tai could fall to the ground, another hand grabbed his flailing body, lifting him off his feet.

Swinging Qi Tai by his hair, the man-bull made several laps around the square, bashing his shoulder against statues and wooden posts. Qi Tai tried to fight free, but four of the arms held his legs and arms, making it impossible. As the beast raced around the courtyard, the frantic attempts by the Prince's men to release Qi Tai were unsuccessful.

When Qi Tai's bludgeoned body appeared as though it could take no more damage, the heads grew bored and raised one hand with a sword for the final kill. The moment was going to be great. For the pain he gave my father, for the lies, the death he was about to cause through his complicity with the General and the Prince, he deserved it.

Mercy. The thought, a voice, was soft.

A man came to me, ready to kill. I lifted my sword, fended off a soldier, kicked his hip, breaking it, dropping him to the ground. That was my version of mercy.

I turned back to Qi Tai. The beast was arguing with itself as to who got to remove Qi Tai's head from his neck.

I hated Qi Tai. I wanted him to be run through with a sword. I wanted to do it myself, to rip the metal blade from his innards, drenched with his streaming blood.

Qi Tai's life will end soon enough. Don't stain your hands with his blood.

Mother, of course. It was the way she would have worded the phrase.

I rebelled against the request for a moment, mentally raging just as the bull had done, then gave over to the higher command. I ran to the weapons wall and grabbed a five-pronged metal star. I positioned the star and prepared to throw, carefully anticipating the direction and forward momentum of the bull. If it were to run to the left, an errant toss would cause the star to strike one of the heads, and if it were to run to the right, the throw might hit someone behind the beast. Patiently, I watched the bull straighten its course.

Part of the deal I'd made with the beast was that neither Xing nor I would attempt to hurt it in any way, and I wasn't going to violate this pact. Focusing, I aimed for the only target that would release Qi Tai from the beast's grip. Taking great care not to aim for the beast's hand carrying Qi Tai, I flung the star directly at the space above Qi Tai's head.

The razor-sharp star sliced through Qi Tai's ponytail like a hot knife through butter, separating him from the beast's grip. He tumbled to the ground, rolling several times before stopping in a crumpled heap.

The bull reared a head, leaving Qi Tai on the ground, fixating on its next target—Zheng He. The bull didn't recognize the Admiral from the description I had given.

Dodging left, Zheng He speared the bull's hind end with his sword. It barely entered the tough hide, causing no more than a yelp before the beast turned around on its hind legs.

"No," I cried. "That's the Admiral!"

I shouted to the man-bull to stop its pursuit. The beast snorted, and the heads yelled in frustration before it turned to face the group of soldiers around the Emperor.

With all the screams and commotion in the courtyard, none of the six ears heard my command. I feared the beast would not know the Emperor, who could easily be impaled by a sword from any one of the six arms or be trampled by the stomping hooves.

One of the three heads yelled a battle cry as it raced by the weapons wall, selecting a *kama*, a metal weapon that resembled a sickle that is also used for cutting down cornstalks and tall grass. With a quick grip of the wooden handle, the beast swung the blade through the air. It would lop off anything in its path.

I knew that even if the Emperor were skilled enough to use the metal weapon in his hands, he couldn't withstand an attack with a kama. I couldn't be responsible for the Emperor's death, and I surely would be if I didn't try to stop the being I brought to life.

I grabbed a curved *naginata* sword, a good defensive weapon with its thick, metal blade.

"Emperor!" I yelled, flinging the sword to the teen, hoping he had the skill to catch it without slicing off a finger. To my surprise, the Emperor caught the flying sword with a smooth downward catch, slicing the blade through the air. He threw off his silk robe, showing a lean, well-muscled torso.

"Ayeeee!" cried head one, answering the challenge.

My yell intended for the beast was cut short by a push from behind. A kick knocked the wind out of me, dropping me forward. I released the weapon in my hand, rolling on my elbow then shoulder, springing forward in my legs. Ducking a round kick aimed for my face, I pivoted, kicked the attacker in the lungs with the force to split the sternum. Dropping that leg, I popped out the other behind me, making my invisible attacker pay for the punch to my back. He groaned, collapsing. His bowels wouldn't function properly for a month.

Within the time I was preoccupied, the Emperor contended with the bull's arms with the skill of a black belt, blocking an attack, thrusting the beast off balance, even connecting with the beast's hind tissue several times.

With one of its free hands, the beast lifted a leather rope from a nearby pole while another hand quickly created a slipknot. The third hand threw the rope on the ground. As the Emperor continued to defend himself from the three arms bearing weapons, he stepped backwards into the center of the loop in the rope. The second the Emperor's foot was inside the loop, the middle head yelled, and the beast surged forward, allowing the rope to tighten around a foot. The hand with the rope held it tightly and with a jerk lifted the Emperor off the ground. When the Emperor hung upside down, the beast grabbed one of his arms while another arm grabbed the Emperor's free leg. The three hands held the Emperor while the rope was wrapped around him by yet another hand. Then a hand raised a knife high in the air.

"Stop!" I cried at the top of my lungs. "He is the Emperor. Don't kill him!"

The three heads roared in displeasure, as their second quarry in a row was about to get away. But the beast honored its pact.

With the Emperor completely wrapped, the beast ran to the far side of the courtyard and dropped him unceremoniously on the ground and finishing it off with its version of a calf roping.

While the Emperor worked feverishly to untangle himself, I tried to take my father down from his shackled position. Behind me, the Prince gave a mighty yell, and I turned in time to see him raise his sword as he challenged the three heads. Three pairs of lips smiled in anticipation as the beast stopped, dug its heels into the snow, and lunged forward, now completely focused on the Prince standing in the middle of the execution grounds.

The beast charged straight at the Prince, as though to run him over. Without flinching, the great warrior gripped a long broadsword with both hands and circled it above his head. He blocked a downward attack from one of the arms before turning the blade to slip it easily into the shoulder of the beast.

Screams of rage escaped the beast's mouths, and two swords sliced downward for the Prince. Evasively, he spun around like a top, uncoiling with his hands above his head. A hiss signaled the blade's path through the air. The precision of the movement allowed the blade to cut through two wrists.

One head howled in misery as its hands dangled by thin strips of skin and muscle. One of the remaining arms lifted a sword and hurled it end over end at the Prince. Instinctively, the Prince blocked the sword with the flat side of his own steel blade, knocking it to the ground. In the same motion, he flipped the toe of his boot upward, and the sword flew into the air. He caught it with his left hand, and in one jab the beast was impaled. Shrieks filled the air, and blood spilled across the snow-covered ground. The Prince picked up the sword, plunging it deep into the body of the creature. It spit forth an awful howl before it reared back, removing itself from the end of the sword. The beast raised its hooves in one final act of defiance, slamming the Prince on the head and knocking him to the ground. The bull then painfully galloped out of the courtyard, leaving a trail of blood on the snow.

By this time, all the men in the square had scattered. The Prince saw me and gripped his sword in his hands.

"You help the Emperor and the Empress, and I'll get my family," I said to Xing, who had come to his aid, his eye still on the Prince. Wu was now beside me, and I asked him to release Mia and my father.

"Why?" he said, belligerent and hurt. His sister was gone. Never to be seen again, by either of us.

"I vowed to keep her safe. I will keep my word. Please help me."

Wu nodded crisply. He knew my intent was pure, even if he didn't forgive me for his sister's choice.

"Now you die," said the Prince, striding toward me.

A sudden blast from behind him was strong enough to send the Prince flying and knock the sword from his hand. His body hit the unforgiving, snow-covered cobblestones with a thud, going limp. The armory housing the fireworks had exploded. It was on fire, and glittering reds, blues, and yellows lit up the gray skies and falling snowflakes. I wanted to fight him, to have a real challenge. But this was the break we needed.

Wu stepped was within the cloud of rolling smoke, still aiding my sister.

"Thank you," I said, gripping his shoulder.

"I'm still the Emperor's guard," he said, shrugging off my grip. "If you help him and my sister escape, I'll help you."

The three of us, Xing, Wu and myself were momentarily left standing without opponents to fight. "I'll get the Emperor," said Xing, "and meet you where we planned."

Xing sliced the Emperor's ropes while I released Dad from the iron chains. Wu was helping Mia down from the wooden pole.

"What do we do about Draben?" she asked. I'd completely forgotten about him. The dead man still hung from the metal hook, a faraway look in his remaining eye as he watched the mayhem in the courtyard. Fireworks continued to explode, and screams mixed with angry shouts filled the air.

I hesitated. "Cut him down," I muttered.

"Are you crazy?" asked Mia, incredulous.

"He can't go anywhere without my command. That means he won't ever have the opportunity to get the orb or hurt us."

The dead man heard me, and responded with a hollow, withered look. Wu sliced Draben's bonds, and he dropped to the ground with a splat, a part of his guts spreading out from his stomach.

I bent over Mia, checking for broken bones.

"I'm fine. Let's get out of here!" she argued, pushing me away. Still my sister. In control and ordering me around.

Turning, I placed Dad's shoulder under my armpit. His deadweight bulk was at odds with his healthy appearance.

"What happened to him while we were gone?" I asked Mia. His head still lolled one side to the other, as though he'd been hanging for hours, leaving his neck weakened or his head lacking blood.

Before she answered, I saw a figure step out from behind a statue.

"Give me the orb or die."

Qi Tai held his injured, bleeding hand close to his chest. He was no threat to me.

"You're crazy if you think the Prince is going to let you keep it," I said, adjusting Dad, beginning to walk away. He was no match for me, his soldiers had fled. Let him talk all he wanted.

"Mia, help me," I told her, as though Qi Tai didn't exist.

"The Prince will be dead from my sword before he recovers from the blast that has knocked him unconscious. Then I'll have the orb and the power to rule China."

I looked at Mia, rolling my eyes. She winked back, and at once, we lifted my father. We'd moved him no more than a few feet when my legs stopped working. I put my right foot in front of my left, and the left stayed in place. I started to fall forward, unable to catch myself.

"Cage!" Mia cried. My weight drove the three of us to the ground hard. I was unable to break the fall since my arms were now frozen.

Qi Tai came towards me, jamming his boot on the side of my head. It crunched, the sound of bone grinding in the ground.

"You thought it would be that easy?" he hissed pressing harder. I felt the pain of his boot ripping my cheek, the warmth of the blood flowing down on my neck. "I'm the one person who knows how to use the orb. I already have one of the sacred artifacts and, shortly, I will have another."

Qi Tai rolled me on my side as he greedily scrambled to get the orb from my hands.

It was not as easy as he thought. My fingers were as good as molded steel, locked around the orb. No amount of pulling was going to unhinge the grasp. He'd have to cut my fingers off.

In his zeal, he forgot about Mia, who jumped on his back, scratching and clawing his face.

"It won't work for you," she hissed, ripping his collar.

Qi Tai twisted from side to side, trying to throw Mia off his back, but she held on like a cat. Finally, he rolled on the ground, breaking her grip. He scrambled to his feet and raised his wounded hand. I lay helpless on the ground, watching the sideways view as Mia jumped up and ran towards him again, her right foot out and ready for a goal winning kick to his groin. She was within several foot lengths when Qi Tai pointed his hand at her.

When he did so, Mia froze, her actions stuck mid kick. She fell over then, her face a look of fury, her hands still extended toward Qi Tai, fingers bent in an attack position.

"Where was I?" said Qi Tai, kicking my sister in the shoulder for good measure.

"Stop him, Draben!" I commanded the zombie. "Break his ribs so that he can't move!"

Qi Tai didn't have a chance to escape before Draben leapt behind Qi Tai, encircling the little man with his decrepit arms. He lifted him up, off the ground, squeezing, until the sound of cracks began.

Qi Tai shrieked in pain, grasping and raking Draben's arms to break his grip.

"Stop!" Qi Tai commanded the zombie. The ruby ring wasn't pointed at Draben, and therefore had no effect. It needed a line of sight to work. Or did it? Maybe it didn't work on zombies at all.

Qi Tai's struggles became weaker as Draben's vise-like hands produced a series of cracks. Blood sprang from Qi Tai's mouth as the crushed bones penetrated his internal organs. I'd half expected to hear my mother's voice ask for mercy once again. This time, the only sound on the wind was an exhale of life from Qi Tai's mouth. He'd been given another chance at life and decided to pursue death. The time for mercy had passed.

I was still immobile as Qi Tai's body turned as gray as the sky. When Draben's task was complete, he dropped Qi Tai's body to the ground and stood awaiting his next command.

With Qi Tai dead, my arms and legs surged with energy. The spell of the ring had been lifted. I walked around Draben and knelt beside Qi Tai. I removed the ring and placed it on my middle finger.

It fit.

The scare of the three-headed man-bull and fireworks was wearing off, and guards were returning to the courtyard to support the Prince.

"That's mine now…"

I whirled to see the Prince standing above me, his hand outstretched.

"They are *both* mine."

He pointed to the orb.

I gathered myself up, standing in front of him. We were the same height. His shoulders broader by half, his chest and legs, thick and wide compared to my own, leaner body. We appraised each other's stance, our hands, the odds of winning.

"Qi Tai wasn't smart enough to command both ring and orb," I said. "If he weren't dead, I would have had to kill him."

The Prince awarded my confidence with a smile. "Or I would have done so. Treachery doesn't equal dishonor, as your sister said."

"Something else you'll have to learn to live without," I responded, pulling back the hand with the orb, purposefully moving my finger so he could see the ring.

"But if you want it…" I bounced the ball up in my hand, "catch!"

I threw the orb to the Prince's left. As the Prince jumped to catch the orb, I flung myself to the right and ran as fast as I could, hurled myself through the air and landed at the feet of the dragon statue. I touched its claws with my hand, extending my foot to touch the prince's leg.

I didn't wait to see the reaction. Guards swept in from both sides grabbing my arms to pull me away from the dragon.

"You are mine," he said.

The Prince wasted no time. He raised his sword and sliced it into my chest.

Mia screamed.

The Prince withdrew his blade and yelled in defiance. The blade was clean. He thrust the sword again, this time into my abdomen. The Prince twisted the sword back and forth several times. Again, nothing happened.

I smiled.

The Prince threw down his sword and shrieked in rage. In that moment, Mia snuck from behind and kicked the orb straight out of its holding place in the crook of his elbow. It shot toward me, a bullet aimed for my stomach. I caught it, the force of the motion stopped by my arm whipping around, up and under my chest.

I gripped it like a football, prepared to tackle the Prince if necessary. I had to get through or around him.

"Cage, behind you!" Mia cried.

An explosion of fiery heat spread across my back. The heat wasn't from the fireworks. It was a blast of fire shooting from the mouth of the golden dragon.

I flattened myself against the cobblestone, rolling to the left, towards my father. I'd touched the great beast while holding the rock of life, and now the dragon was alive. It was another beast without a soul.

The next blast of heat blew the Prince backwards. His arms flew out as he landed full on this back. Screaming for his guards to attack me and kill the dragon, he used his hands as a shield for his face.

The deadly monster marched forward spouting flames, incinerating everything in its path. Despite the snowfall, the wooden buildings surrounding the courtyard lit like dry kindling in the middle of summer. The fire jumped from building to building as a circle of heat and death closed in on them.

I wasn't going to hang around to find out whether the dragon would obey me. I had to get Mia and Dad out before the dragon crushed them and our escape path through the buildings closed.

"Mia!" I yelled from the ground, motioning her towards dad. Together we placed our arms around Dad. "Okay, Mia. Lift!"

As we made our way out of the courtyard, the Prince removed the cloak from a dead warrior to use a shield. He focused his attention upon the larger threat lumbering toward him.

"Destroy my kingdom, and I destroy you!" shouted the Prince at the dragon.

I looked about for Wu and the Emperor and Empress, but they were gone. I had no idea where he'd taken them. Mia had said folklore of their fate wavered between burning in the Imperial Palace during the invasion and escaping by boat. I hoped it was the latter.

I led Mia across the courtyard while dragging my incapacitated father. As we moved directly in front of Qi Tai's body, I couldn't tell whether he was alive or dead. His skin was nearly as pale as the muddy snow on the ground.

"Cage, wait a minute," Mia said, and dropped down beside Qi Tai and removed the Empress's diamond bracelet from his pocket. "I wish I could have taken the jade necklace from the Prince," she said.

Just then, the dragon bellowed in pain. The Prince's broadsword struck the leg of the dragon, and it extended its long claws, scraping the pole where Dad's body had hung. The Prince's sword dove into the dragon's claw once more, and it screamed as it lifted its other leg. This time, the tip of one claw missed the pole and tore through the side of Draben's immobile body where it stood, slicing it down the side, splitting him in two.

"I didn't command him to move," I said, feeling odd. It shouldn't have bothered me, but it did. He'd wanted to kill Dad, and showed no remorse. Yet he'd helped me save Dad as well, though at my command.

The dragon was still breathing fire. Soon, it would be upon me and my family.

"Dad, are you all right?" I asked him as we moved.

His eyes opened and focused for the first time.

"Thanks for saving me, son," he said, awkwardly. Twice in fact, but I'd point that out later.

Chaos controlled the entire area as I looked for the wall Xing had mentioned.

"Cage! This way!" Xing called to me the far side of the courtyard. Xing ran over to help shoulder the weight of my father as we headed toward the back gate.

With the Prince fighting the dragon, no one was left to bother the four of us, and we made our way across the courtyard.

"Stop!"

Not again! I thought without turning around. How could the Prince have already killed the dragon and come after us?

But the command came from Zheng He, standing in the shadows. I separated myself from Dad, prepared for another fight. It wasn't one I wanted. I genuinely liked Zheng He. He was honorable. Zheng He put up his hand.

"We will not fight, young man. I want to help you escape."

CHAPTER 39

Zheng He led us through the alley to a dock on the river, where the Emperor, Empress, Gee and Wu waited.

"Where is your father?" I asked him. Wu bowed his head, his eyes full of anger, and to his dismay, tears.

"Qi Tai had him executed for not following his orders to harm your sister," the Emperor told us.

"I'm sorry," I said.

From the look on Mia's face, she too was terribly upset.

"I never would have asked him to put his life in jeopardy for mine," she said. "You have to believe that."

Wu nodded. "Our father wanted it this way. He sacrificed his life so we could live. Just like my mother."

Though the crushing loss was plain on his face, he held his head high, his shoulders back and arched. He was proud, as he should be. His father was a great man, a good person. I wondered if it was his fate, his destiny written before he was born, and if he chose it in this, mortal life, or it was chosen for him. Where did the line between fate and free will stop?

"He would be proud of you," I told Wu. "Thank you," I added, wanting to tell him 'for everything,' but I stopped short. Words weren't necessary.

We gave each other a bow, and before he could move an inch, Mia bounded in front of me, giving him a hug. When she released him, he gave her a sad smile, then straightened his face. He was now the Emperor's personal guard, waiting to escort the true Imperial family on their escape.

"Let us go," Zheng He said, gesturing for the Emperor and Empress to proceed down the dock.

The Emperor gripped Zheng He's arm in an uncommon display of admiration. "You must stay, or you will be hunted in every corner of the country. I cannot have that."

Zheng He's massive body bowed low. "My loyalty is to the Imperial Family."

"Enough people have died. I will not have you lose your life as well. Loyalty must be with my uncle now."

As the Admiral stood motionless, I noticed the Emperor look past him at his wife. Her face flushed red, her eyes steady, uncaring if others noticed. The love and strength she exuded matched the fear that he would die as well. He nodded, almost imperceptibly before taking her by the hand. He was going to protect her, and together, they were to face the rest of their life as one, a couple against the world.

"If you don't stay, Zheng He," I broke in, tilting my head to the Emperor and Empress, "all our efforts will have been pointless."

He turned his great head towards me, perplexed. I imagined what the man was thinking. He was the greatest Admiral on the planet, although a humble one, reduced to receiving advice from kids. But then, I didn't feel much like a kid anymore.

I gave Mia a look, imploring her to say something. She caught it.

"Zheng He, you must stay here with the Prince of Yan, or the future will be drastically different," said Mia, voicing the ever present concern of time travel. "The world would not be circumnavigated, Magellan claiming the prize for the feat, the preeminent position of the Chinese naval fleet forever altered all because we had aided in the escape of the rulers."

Still, the Admiral remained, unmoved.

"Zheng He," I said, touching the center of my chest. "This is your *destiny*."

A moment later, his mind was made up. "Agreed," he said, putting up a hand before I completed a relieved exhalation. "*After* I ensure the safety of my Emperor, I will return to serve the Prince of Yan."

The Admiral gave Wu a look and a nod, whereupon Wu extended his hand to the Emperor. The boy walked down the short plank and stopped in front of the wooden plank. The Empress followed after, aided by the Admiral, then Gee.

Zheng He then turned to me, chest out and chin arched. "How do I say thank you in your culture...with respect," he added.

I extended my hand, fingers straight, thumb up. He regarded the gesture, replicating the movement and I clasped his hand, squeezing. When I smiled and pressed, he gripped hard, until I winced. "Thank you," he said, unable to stop a head nod.

Once in the boat, Zheng He gave Gee a small pile of coarsely woven clothing. Gee helped the Empress first, then the Emperor, transforming the two from recognizable figures to anonymous holy men. It was a smart disguise, because the monks of the court took vows of silence.

"Let me help the Empress get this makeup off," Mia said, swiftly moving down the plank, kneeling down alongside Gee, helping her place a soft padding on the seat.

I watched as the Mia carefully wiped the white powder off the Empress's cheeks and removed her jewelry. Then Mia lifted the hood up and over the Empress's face, placing the jewels back in her hand.

"I have something else for you," Mia said, reaching into her pocket. It was the bracelet. The Empress's eyes swelled with tears, though she was silent as Mia fastened it around the girl's thin wrist. "I'm sorry I couldn't get back your necklace." Gee clucked, patting Mia's shoulder like a grandmother, and from the look on her face, just as proud.

The Empress wavered a moment, vacillating, the emotions on her face as confused as her body, on the edge of giving a bow though her arms tentatively raised then dropped.

Mia took control. She smiled, lightly placing her hands on the Empress's back and hugged. The girl's eyes widened in shock from a foreigner's hands touching her so informally, her body stiffening. It was clear Mia didn't care. She hugged her harder, her affection for the girl coming through her squeeze.

"You'll be okay," I heard Mia whisper. The Empress's body relaxed, her eyes softened. The girl was leaving her way of life behind. "You'll make friends, maybe even see Wei-Lyn again," said Mia with confidence.

"Do you think so?" asked the Empress with a faint glint of hope in her eyes as she looked to me. Mia nodded. I was proud of my sister as she gripped the Empress one last time, just as she did with her teammates on the soccer team before a big play. Releasing her, Mia adjusted the brown hood a little lower to shade the girl's eyes.

"Meeyah," said Gee, stepping forward. The old woman had been silent during the goodbyes. Until that moment, I'd not given her situation a thought. She was destined to live out her life in the service of the Empress, she too, leaving her family behind as well. Children, grandchildren, extended relations who lived in the Forbidden City. I wondered if she had gotten word to her family, or if her disappearance would be an unanswered page in the history books as well. No. Mia had said the servants were executed. Her family would assume she died.

The old woman lifted up the outer layer of her garments, revealing a black fanny pack. She cracked a smile on her wintery face at Mia's exclamation of surprise.

"It took me a long time to understand how this works," she said, pinching the sides of the buckle, a contraption any five-year-old in our time could operate. "I thought you might want it back," she said, motioning for Mia to lift her jacket. With a snap, it was on, and Mia doled out another hug.

Ready to go, Emperor Jianwen turned to me and, in front of everyone, bowed low.

"I owe you an apology, Cage. You have protected us, just as you promised. I am sorry."

He looked into the distance. His life would never be the same.

I gave him a bow of forgiveness.

"Here, let me help you into the boat," I offered, putting my arm out.

"I'll take them through the waterways and to a private ship," Zheng He told me. "From there, they can decide where they want to go in China, or perhaps to the New World you talk about." He sat down and began covering his face. *Now* we are even," Zheng He said to me.

On impulse, I jumped forward.

"Wait—Admiral," I said.

"You have something—*else?*" he asked, his voice teasing.

I bent over, whispering so the others could not overhear. He thought for a moment, his great head looking up, consulting the sky.

"The east exit," he said, giving a wink.

I bowed one last time and turned away.

"We must hurry," Xing said. He'd waited, anxious, looking back and forth along the dock throughout the farewell process.

"You go ahead with Mia and my dad," I directed. "I want to make sure the Emperor gets off okay." A few more minutes and the group would be gone, downstream, under Zheng He's care and Wu's protective hands.

Mia and Xing were out of sight, leaving me to watch the shallow boat full of brown-cloaked monks float under a white marble bridge.

"Ayyaa!!"

I snapped my head around. Standing on the arch above the water, on the very bridge the group had just passed under, was the Prince. His face was bloodied and his cape torn from his fight with the dragon. The majestic creature must be dead. The notion disheartened me. Nothing seemed to stop this warrior. The Prince raised his broadsword high in the air and pointed it at me.

"Seize him!" he yelled to his guards around him, who raced down the overpass and on to the lane. I ran in the opposite direction of my sister and Xing. I had no choice but to lose the pursuers in the maze of the Palace and meet up with Mia and Dad at the entrance to the catacombs.

"Good luck!" I yelled back, mocking the Prince.

The Prince screamed again, and the chase began.

CHAPTER 40

I had to distract as many soldiers as I could to give Xing and Mia the chance to make it to the tunnels beneath the Palace. It was how Qi Tai had gotten in and out of the Empress's room without getting caught, and how the Emperor and Empress made their afternoon rendezvous. I should have known. The Emperor didn't just get sick during the middle of the day. He was having a moment—just as I wanted to have with Bao— with his wife. The tunnels were helpful for one more thing. They were how I intended to save Bao, *if* the doctor had done his part before he was killed.

I heard the thud of backs falling flat on the hard ground as I raced toward a cargo ship being unloaded, jumped down and teetered to get my balance as I danced across the goods and bounded back on land. Two guards chased me onto the small boat, causing the vessel to wobble precariously. One lost his balance and fell into the frigid water, while the other ran by, ignoring his comrade's desperate pleas for help.

I made it inside a canal storehouse, seeking an alternative for a quick escape. I ran into the back room and located a door beyond a large pile of sacks. One quick test of the sacks, and I knew they were too heavy to move. In desperation, I looked up at the ceiling and found another small trap door. Grabbing a ladder I leaned it against a wall and scrambled up. I found myself on what looked like a garden with a sitting area, complete with a bench and statuary.

A crashing sound below told me the guards had followed me into the storehouse. I jerked up the ladder, just as a guard jumped up to grab it. I slammed the door and placed a bench on top so they couldn't follow. The distance between buildings prevented me from jumping from rooftop to rooftop, and the ground below now swarmed with more of the Prince's men.

I spied a large tree adjacent to the far side of the building. It was located behind a tall wall surrounding one of the Emperor's royal parks. I guessed this park was the one known as the Garden of Delight and was the only one that backed up against the cargo office and storeroom. No one except the Emperor and the Empress were allowed within its walls—even the Emperor's personal guards were forbidden. The park contained rare plants and exotic animals from the Imperial Zoo. I didn't care about any of those things then and certainly didn't now, but it could provide the escape route I needed. I couldn't remember the size of the park, but was pretty sure it would take me near one of the gates leading to the Forbidden City.

I climbed down the tree and lost my grip on a branch. I started to fall but then landed on the back of a large animal. Like a cowboy on a bucking bronco, I instinctively grasped a handful of hair, which was attached to a very long neck. I was perched on the back of a giraffe.

The animal took off the moment it sensed a foreign presence, and I was nearly thrown as it loped forward with huge elongated strides. I leaned to one side, trying in vain to get it to turn around. The giraffe was headed in the opposite direction of the outside gate at high speed.

I kicked in my heels as hard as I could, moving my full weight to the other side, hoping to change the direction of the speeding animal, but the giraffe continued undeterred. A high wall loomed ahead and the giraffe skidded to a stop, throwing me into the air and against the ground, hard.

Stunned, I dusted myself off and looked around. I was now behind a fence of high bars with spikes on top.

Before I had time to figure out where I was, a claw ripped into my back. I closed my eyes and held my breath. A paw pressed on the left side of my face, and snow forced its way into my ears and eyes. Warm, smelly breath covered my face. The nose of something was right next to me.

"Jai Sing! Stop!"

I remained motionless as the paw lifted off my face. Another command called the animal to retreat. With his eyes closed, I couldn't see the animal leave, but I heard the steps of someone coming closer.

"Who are you? What are you doing here?" a man's voice asked.

I cautiously opened my eyes. The voice belonged to an old man wearing thick gardener's clothing and a wide-brimmed hat, which shielded his face from the snow.

"Who are *you*?" I asked.

"Don't talk. You are hurt badly....But wait...you aren't even scratched!" The man examined my back and said solemnly, "That was Jai Sing who clawed you, the Imperial Bear. You should be dead."

"I'm lucky, that's all," thinking about Xing's obsession with luck.

The old man removed his hat. He then knelt on the ground, holding the hat in both hands.

"You are a Great Spirit." The man bowed low before me. I awkwardly told him to stand up.

"I'm not a spirit of any kind. I'm just trying to escape."

"Then by what powers were you protected from the bear's claws?"

"Someone gave me a gift," I replied. I might as well tell the truth, since it sounded as unbelievable as anything I could make up.

"I understand. Great Spirits do not reveal all," said the man, barely looking up from the ground. "What is happening outside these walls?"

I told him of the invasion, the Emperor's disappearance, and his own pursuit by the Prince.

"I must get to the Forbidden City. Not all great spirits can disappear when they want to. Some of us have to run and walk."

"Ah yes," said the old man. "Keep up the appearance of a human. I understand."

"I really have to be going now," I said, moving in the opposite direction of the bear.

"You can't escape that way," said the gardener, motioning to the gate in the fence. "You can go through it, and through the park, but on the other side is a gate lined with guards. If what you say is true, the bridge will be raised."

"I can go in the water. Swim below the metal poles and out the other side."

The man chuckled softly. "The teeth of alligators won't hurt you, but the cold water is uncomfortable."

I hoped the alligators would be dormant or very slow in the cold weather, but had no idea whether that was true.

"Come, Great Spirit. I have a better idea."

We walked past the sitting bear, which still eyed me warily.

"Why doesn't the bear attack you?" I asked the man.

"I raised him from a cub. I have fed and cared for these animals since the first Emperor brought me here years ago." He reached into a metal bin and threw a fish at the bear's foot, where it flopped around for only a couple seconds. With a dainty stomp, the bear crushed it and lifted the body to its mouth, eating only the tail. "Since I remain in the zoo, I was spared when others were killed when the Emperor's reign changed."

I followed the man out of the bear's compound and into a covered building.

"I don't believe this!" I whispered in awe. The room was filled with water slides.

The man chuckled again. "The Emperor's summer palace is in the northern area, outside Beijing. Near the grounds are many rock formations; natural slides that run into pools and lakes. Emperor Jianwen wanted to have rock slides all times of the year, so he had these made for his personal use."

As warm water filled the room, I imagined how much fun a slide park in the dead of winter would be. Unfortunately, I had to remain focused upon reuniting with dad and Mia.

"Where do these go?"

"The pool drains out past the moat into the Forbidden City. The Emperor wanted one escape that only he and I knew about."

"Can you open the gate for me?" I asked, looking up at the water slide.

"In one moment." The man left and came back smiling. "It is now open, Great Spirit. Climb to the top of this long slide, and I will turn on the water. Go straight in, swim under the raised metal gate, and straight through to the other side."

I started to climb a ladder, but a shout from the man stopped him.

"Wait a moment," said the man, disappearing into a small building. "I have something for you," he said when he returned, handing me a waterproof sack. "Here are dry clothes. Even great spirits can catch a cold in the snow. Remember to swim hard, or you will run out of air."

"May blessings come upon you," I said uncomfortably. I wasn't quite sure how a Great Spirit would say thank you.

I gripped the sack and sat down on the top of the rockslide. A gush of water from some unseen corner propelled me forward and downward at great speed. I yelped and held on to the sack tightly as I twisted down around a bend, which turned me backwards.

My speed accelerated down a long slide that flipped me on my stomach and then dropped me face-first into a deep pool of warm water. Remembering the man's advice, I took in just enough air to reach the surface, I swam hard toward the gate and under the fence. I pulled myself out of the water and onto the bank, barely resting to catch my breath. When I opened the sack, I found clothes of a field worker.

The tower to the Forbidden City was behind me; I'd gone right under the moat, just as the zookeeper said I would. I ran beyond the trees and heard a cry from above.

"Martial law is in force. Who is there?" I ran faster, ducking beneath the dark cover of trees. The sound of stomping feet and shouts grew loud as other men saw me.

"Tell the Prince! Open the gates and seize him!"

The Prince was nearby? How could he have known I'd be going through the gates? Qi Tai! He must have mentioned where we had first emerged out of the ground. That meant only one thing. The Prince could already have his forces waiting for Dad and Mia.

CHAPTER 41

Thanks to the renewed energy of the orb, I had speed I'd never had before. I put block lengths between me and my pursuers, running through the streets of the Forbidden City. It had been deserted, the occupants ordered to their homes, locked down under martial law. I used the mental map the Emperor had provided as I made my way past shops, ministries and homes closed at the Prince's orders.

A man yelled at me from a crack in the door, telling me to get inside or be arrested. "Anyone caught outdoors will be given ten lashings," he hollered before shutting his door tight.

I found the square where we arrived empty of people, while looking urgently for my sister, father and Xing and the grate at the same time. I checked several metal plates, lifting each one and peering inside until I found what I thought was the right one.

"Mia! Xing?" I whispered, concerned about being caught out in the open.

No response. I heard a moan that sounded like a wounded cow, and voices arguing and pleading.

I looked both ways before darting into the brush, moving slowly toward the bull-men. The beast screamed in pain as it tried to raise itself but fell back down. Its panting was heavy and ragged, each breath pulling on its chest cavity. Two of the six hands tried to stop the flow of blood that poured from a large gash in its front and side where the Prince's sword had entered its body. The upper torso and the three heads were fine except for a few cuts on their arms and faces. I then saw the two hands that had almost been sheared off. I looked straight ahead and took a deep breath.

One of the arms raised a sword to warn me off, but I persisted, determined to help.

"I'll kill you," said one head, its mouth drooping in pain.

"And if he doesn't, I will," said another. The third was too weak to do more than grimace and frown menacingly.

"No you won't," I said. I'd raised it from its perfectly eternal existence. I wasn't going to let it die an ignominious death in the underbrush. "I'm so sorry you got hurt," I said, genuinely, extending my hand, palm up, a sign of peace. I told it I thought its victory in the fight was possible, not grotesque injuries.

All six eyes watched warily as I held the orb within my hands. They remained silent, watching the me and the orb.

Holding it in front of me, I checked the placement of the sail. By now, I knew where the needle had to be positioned along the inscriptions. For a moment, I considered the magnificent blessings of the orb, the superior strength and awareness of senses. Father's experience had been different, though it healed him physically.

I turned the orb, excited with the anticipation of the healing to come. "You will enjoy this," I promised.

As the blood from its chest and side stopped gushing, and the wounds started to close, the heads exclaimed in excitement. I turned the orb even further, smiling with satisfaction as the tendons of the two severely injured hands reconnected and all of the internal tissue and skin pulled back together. Soon the wrists were as good as new.

One more notch for good measure, turning the orb a tiny bit more. I might as well make the beast feel better than it had before the fight.

When I finished, the beast, still covered red from the fresh blood, rose dramatically on its haunches and thrust up its three necks. All eyes turned to inspect the now-healed body parts while, patting, twisting, and wriggling its arms and wrists.

Three voices shouted in harmonious joy at being healed. My heart jumped. I started to walk backwards, holding the orb against my chest, but the heads turned to me at once, gesturing for me to come back.

"We won't hurt you," said one head.

"Come back, warrior. You have healed us," said another, extending his brand-new hands.

"You can't have this," I said, thinking it wanted the orb.

"It's yours," said the third. "We don't want it."

I still didn't quite trust their words. The beast seemed nice enough, though the actions of the unicorn in the square were mean and horrible. I'd turned the dragon from stone to a living creature, and it proceeded to torch everyone in the square.

The man-bull then bent down on its knees, and one of the six arms reached for me and shook my hand. The next thing I knew, all six arms were patting me on the back, bowing and placing their hands together in thanks.

"You're welcome," I said. I was relieved the animal was healed. "I've got to go. I think I can send you back to where you came from, or you can stay here. What do you want to do?"

The heads looked at one another and smiled, then motioned to the ground with its six hands.

"Stay," said one.

"Live," and "Play," said the other two at the same time, with four hands pointing to the hills.

"Be careful. That Prince is nasty."

I looked out at the square and saw my father limping out with Mia and Xing. They were dressed in brown clothes, baggy and worn looking, except for Xing, who was dressed like a merchant.

"Where have you been?" I asked, exasperated.

"Xing found us new clothes," Mia said. "We were drenched."

"How are you feeling, Dad?"

"Bad," he said, blinking his eyes. It was hard to imagine the bulking, block of man was the skinny man with a paunch just days before. I still had the orb in my hand.

"Hold on," I urged. A bit of snow had gotten on the orb, and my hand slipped as I turned it. Instead of clockwise, it went counterclockwise.

My father groaned, clutching his stomach. He involuntarily vomited, groping my sister who uttered a yelp of pain.

"Cage!" Xing said, gripping my arm.

I muttered an apology, immediately turning it the other way. As soon as the cry of agony started, it stopped, followed by a sigh of relief. The color returned to Dad's face, his eyes regaining their color while his skin tone changed yet again. I wanted to continue with the turn as I had with the beast, but stopped short. The last time I healed Dad, he seemed to go catatonic for some reason.

"You good?" I asked him, concerned. He nodded, rubbing a hand against his bicep.

"Now?" he asked me, looking for my direction.

I heard men beyond the square coming before I saw them.

"In the tunnel—go!"

Without hesitation, Xing opened the grate and pushed Dad down. He shouted for Mia and she dropped into the darkness with Xing following right after.

The Prince ran through the square. He would be on me in seconds. The Prince let out a cry of impending victory, raising his sword high into the air.

Even if I got down in the tunnel, the Prince would pursue us. He'd already stabbed me twice, killed the dragon and nearly killed the bull. This man was unstoppable. I didn't have enough time to activate the orb to get through the portal before the Prince could drop down and follow us through. And what about Xing? The Prince would surely kill him and take Mia.

I waited until the Prince was nearly upon me when I held up the ring, making a fist with my fingers until they went white. I visualized him stopping, but wasn't sure it was required. The instant the ring pointed in his direction, he froze mid-stride, his sword still high in the air, his eyes wide with rage.

When the soldiers saw their leader frozen, some dropped their swords and ran, while others screamed in fury and continued to pursue me. I had a split second to consider my options. Use the ring and freeze the attackers one by one or try to use the orb. If it caused pain with Dad, perhaps it could stop everyone at once. I had no choice.

I turned it counter clockwise with a push, much harder than the soft accident with my father.

An invisible blast swept through the entire courtyard, felling warriors like trees after a volcanic explosion. Men on the ground writhed in agony, gripping their stomachs and rolling over. Others fainted, eyes rolling back from the pain. The Prince, already motionless, dropped over, his sword beside him.

The area was oddly quiet, a smattering of explosions in the background, the crackling of burning buildings. Heat and smoke blew across the courtyard, over the metal grate covering my family and Xing.

The metal grate moved and Xing appeared. He saw the ground, raised his eyes in awe and approached the Prince.

"Did you mean to kill him?" Xing asked me, nudging the immobile man on the ground.

I shook my head. "Just stopped him."

"Once again, you are lucky," Xing responded. With his toe, Xing rolled the Prince over. His chest was moving.

My hand was at my side, the ring no longer pointed at the Prince. I twisted it on my finger. It would do me no good to freeze myself.

"Do you think he'll remember anything?" asked Xing.

"I don't know. What will become of you?"

"Don't worry. I make an excellent Emperor's guard, especially since I'll tell him I saved him from death." For the first time, he gave me a smile.

"And your father?" Xing gave me a pat on the back.

"He has done nothing to warrant the Prince's retaliation,

but his actions stand alone," he said, resolutely. It was the warrior way. "Nonetheless, I will be here for him." Xing would be alright. He'd find his place with the new Emperor and likely live a long, full life in the Palace. He deserved it.

I recalled the history books had written General Li as being executed, but I hoped not. The man had a daughter who loved him, and a son who forgave him.

"Thank you for helping us," I said, bowing low, pressing the fist of my left hand to the palm of my right.

"No, Cage," replied Xing. "You have done our family a great honor, and the kingdom. If you ever return, we will have to fight one more time."

I smiled, accepting the challenge.

"Someone is waiting for you," Xing said, his smile wide.

My heart jumped. The doctor had pulled it off.

I dropped down in the catacomb, nearly running into Mia and Bao. They were hugging and crying. Dad was silently observing the young Italian man who had escorted Bao from the square.

"Thank you for coming," I said, bowing, then extending my hand.

"You have it?" he asked me, his wary eyes darting from me to my father.

"Give me a moment." I searched the dark tunnel, seeing a glint at the base of the long, floor to ceiling pillar of rock. I retrieved the pack, left by the doctor. From within, I pulled out a small, jade egg. It was elaborate, carved with dragons and the phoenix, a priceless object, taken from the Emperor's Palace.

I reverently handed it to the Italian, who held the heavy piece in his hand.

"It's magnificent," he said softly. He bowed to me. "Our business is concluded, then."

"In a moment. I need to say goodbye." Turning to Dad and Mia, I told them I needed a minute.

Taking Bao away from the others, in the dark of the corner, I put my arms around her. I held her tight, stroking her slim back, up and down, then pressing her body against mine. Her lips searched for mine, and we found one another, conveying the pent up longing that would never be released.

"She's coming with us?" I heard Dad ask Mia, disbelief in his voice.

Bao's fingers pressed against mine when she recognized the satchel. When I released her to put it on, she lovingly helped adjust the front straps on my shoulders. It was unnecessary yet I adored it. Bao straightened the leather, pulling it off my top, patting down the woven cloth underneath.

"You are going alone," she said, her voice weak, her lower lip trembling. She was trying to be strong, holding back the tears I felt. I kissed her a moment more, knowing the end had come. I'd release her now from me to another, forever. She laid her head on my chest, softly weeping. Her arms encircled my ribs, and we held one another. I kissed her forehead, brushing my cheek against her skin. Feeling moisture on my chest, I wiped the tear from her face with the back of my finger, kissing the corner of her eye. Maybe not forever. I dropped my hand and took hers, holding on with the excitement of a first date.

"Where I must go—it's not safe," I murmured. She, more than anyone save her own father, knew the danger of our journey. It was to continue, the blood, the death. Her own life, thrown to the unknown. Protecting Dad and Mia was hard enough. I couldn't—didn't want—to be responsible for her safety. It was better she stay and live, than go and face a terrible death.

She pressed her cheek against mine, moving closer.

"Look at me," I said, moving my hands from her back. I gently placed my hands on either side of her face, drawing her up to me, her lips close to mine.

"I would stay here with you. In this time, forever. You—you are perfect for me. You are strong. Intellectual. Fearless." I punctuated my last comment with a smile, and a shake of my head.

I drew her close, dropping my lips to hers. She responded, pressing her body against mine, her hand tight on my back. My head spun in a way external power could never replicate. She was the woman I wanted. The one I couldn't have. At least not yet.

Bao tentatively withdrew from me. Her will stronger than my own.

"We have no more time," she said, regret heavy in her voice. I nodded, placing my lips on her forehead. The Prince, still above, would wake from the blast, disoriented, angry. Her life depended on her leaving. Now.

"You will always be my beautiful treasure," I said, kissing her again. I hoped the red stain of her lips were on mine, the last memory I'd have.

"We are ready," I said to the Italian, who looked eager to leave.

He followed me and Bao up, out of the hole.

The men and Prince were still on the ground, motionless,

with Xing watching over.

I introduced the Italian, explaining the situation.

"The East exit," I told Bao. She nodded, confident.

Bao motioned the Italian to follow her. Giving me a final glance, she turned and hurried from the area, leaving her heart behind her, moving towards her freedom.

A moan behind Xing shortened the good-byes.

"Go in safety, wherever you travel," he said.

I looked around one last time, gazing at the empty space where Bao had been standing, before I jumped down the tunnel.

"Where am I?" I heard the Prince ask as I slid the cover over the hole. "What happened?"

"I saved you from an attack," Xing answered. Those were the last words I heard before I ran to join my Dad and sister.

The two were standing in the dark hallway, the red glow unmoved.

Mia had thrown her arms around Dad, who left his arms at his side.

"Are you hurt?" I asked, worried I'd not turned the ball far enough.

"Hug me back," Mia demanded, teasing Dad.

Something was different in him. He possessed an unidentifiable characteristic that had developed since the first healing. I wasn't going to bring it up now, and not at all if Mia didn't notice the change. I'd get blamed for changing his personality though I'd only meant to heal. I searched for a feeling from him, and received none. I hoped the sensitivity to the auras I'd been feeling wasn't going to remain in China.

Dad returned her hug, squeezing her so hard she exhaled.

"Be careful," Mia coughed, giggling. "Cage made you too strong!"

"Are you ready to go home?" Dad asked.

Mia was busy untying her hair, doing her best to put it back in a ponytail, using a piece of the long, blond strand as a loop to hold it in place. Mia caught my appreciative look, giving me a coy smile.

I sighed. I'd sensed battling her potential suitors was going to be one more challenge for me as we journeyed through time.

"We're not going home," said my sister. "And I don't think you're getting your pack back," she said with a twinkle in her eye.

Dad looked at my back, hesitating. It was his after all.

"I'll continue my search while you two are in…school." He extended his hand for the pack.

Right or wrong, Dad wasn't going to lead us. Mom had come to me, not him. I had discovered the immense powers of the orb, not him. He hadn't saved us, I had.

"This isn't about mom, her soul, or bringing her back," I told him. "At least, not yet. We have a few things do to first. Follow me," I said, ignoring Dad's outstretched hand.

I walked down the hall, picked up a lantern, gesturing Mia to come. Dad could stay or he go with us. My anger towards him had gone during the course of events, but it didn't eliminate the memory of what we had. Or lost. I was focused on winning now, of taking this battle to the next level. It could be done, and we were going to do it. It *was* possible to come back when this was over. I knew the timetable of a year was fixed. We would be the same age. I could find her, Zheng He and Xing would help me.

I led the way down through the catacombs. Each step moving further away from Bao. I nearly missed a step and refocused. Romantic notions and possibilities were on hold until I got out of here.

"Here it is," I announced, more to myself than the others. It was the wall with the long, rough lines of hardened lava streaming from ceiling to floor. I lifted the orb in my hand and nodded at Mia and Dad.

We'd entered China at the beginning of the year of evil. Now we had approximately eleven months to find the missing rocks and artifacts before the Serpent King could gather them, build and army and defeat us—or destroy millions.

I took a breath, and silently asked the orb to send us where we needed to go. After a moment, the ball started to glow bright, and the wall opened, bit by bit, until it was a huge, gaping hole.

Mia's eyes were bright with anticipation. She touched my back, just as she had when coming to this time.

"Let's go," I said, having no idea where we'd would emerge on the other side…or who would be waiting for us.

Chambers 2: The Spirit Warrior

A new warrior, not bound by a physical body, now hunts Cage and Mia. Separated then reunited, Mia's new abilities give her a reckless confidence, putting her family in jeopardy. To regain the advantage, Cage must face the dark warrior in a realm where neither of them are fighting in their own bodies. The question will be; if you die when in another form, is it forever?

HISTORICAL NOTES

Emperor Jianwen was the second Emperor of the Ming Dynasty, appointed by his grandfather. He ruled from the time he was twelve to age fourteen or fifteen.

Historians dispute the fate of Emperor Jianwen and the Empress. Some books claim they burned in a fire and that their bodies were never found. Other historians believe the two escaped from the palace disguised as monks.

General Li served Emperor Jianwen, and history books identify that it was he who opened the door to let in the Emperor's uncle, the Prince of Yan.

The Imperial Palace burned down due to fires that started during the invasion by the Prince of Yan. It is not known who started the fires.

The Prince of Yan, Emperor Jianwen's uncle, became the third Ming Dynasty Emperor and moved the Imperial Palace from Nanjing to Beijing. There he built a new Forbidden City and Imperial Palace, which exist today.

Qi Tai was the Minister of War under Emperor Jianwen. Historians believe the Prince of Yan executed Qi Tai, along with every other person serving under Emperor Jianwen. It is estimated that thousands died.

Zheng He's naval career started under Emperor Jianwen, but he was made an admiral under the Prince of Yan. Zheng He is revered as China's greatest admiral. China's navy was considered the best fleet in the world for many hundreds of years after Zheng He. Historians debate whether Zheng He was the first to circumnavigate the globe and find North America, preceding the discoveries by Magellan and Columbus by decades. In 2006, a Chinese map of the world dating back to the early 1500's was found, and historians think it was written by Zheng He. This research continues.

Mohaishou is a statue located in the Yungang Grottoes near the Datong volcanoes. It is located in Cave 8 and has three heads and eight arms (not the six the author chose for the book) and is half-bull. Over fifty thousand statues reside in the Grottoes, and the story about why they were created, and by whom, is recorded by historians.

Wi Cheng, Bingwen, Bao, Xing, Wu, Gee and Wu are fictional characters (who I love).

ACKNOWLEDGMENTS

Lucas Foster, who gave me the harshest, most constructive criticism on that fateful Sunday night, and has been the voice of honesty throughout. I couldn't have paid for better motivation to improve my writing. Thank you for giving me a chance to fulfill my dream.

My brilliant, wonderful sister Ann, who is really my backroom publicity and marketing guru, for making me look much better than I deserve.

David Majors, for providing an amazing illustration of "my" version of the Forbidden City and the Emperor's Palace. Lyuben Valevski for the cover art, capturing so beautifully what I couldn't put in to words.

Roger, who had supported my "habit" for seven years, keeping the lights on and bills paid, taking care of the girls and being okay with missed golf dates and fishing outings. I hope to get you that bamboo pole soon.

Finally, my dear son Conor. It was you who gave me the idea for the book, when you were twelve, as we climbed the mounds of obsidian outside the volcanic crater in Medicine Lake

ABOUT THE AUTHOR

Before she began writing novels, Sarah was an internationally recognized management consulting expert. Her two dozen books have been translated into four languages and are sold in over 100 countries.

OTHER BOOKS BY SARAH GERDES

<u>Suspense/Thriller</u>

Above Ground

Global Deadline

Incarnation Series

    Incarnation (book 1)

    Incarnation 2: The Cube Master (book 2)

    Incarnation 3: Immunity (book 3, fall 2022)

<u>Romantic Suspense</u>

A Convenient Date

Danielle Grant Series

    Made for Me (book 1)

    Destined for You (book 2)

    Meant to Be (book 3)

In a Moment

OTHER BOOKS BY SARAH GERDES

<u>Historical Fiction/Action Adventure</u>

Chambers Series

    Chambers (book 1)

    Chambers: The Spirit Warrior (book 2)

<u>**Non-Fiction and Business**</u>

Sue Kim: The Authorized Biography

Author Straight Talk

Navigating the Partnership Maze: Creating Alliances that Work

The Overlooked Expert: turning your skills into a profitable consulting business

REFERENCES & RESOURCES

Web site: www.sarahgerdes.com

Instagram: sarahgerdes_author